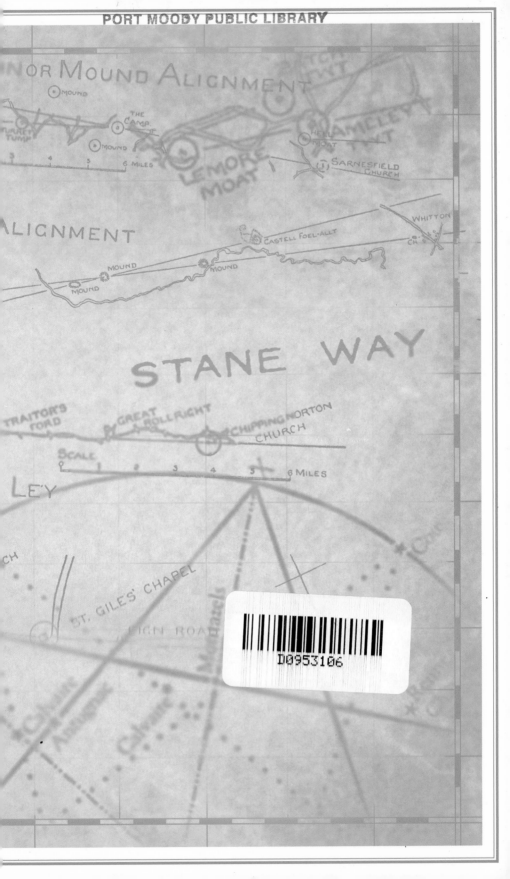

THE
FATAL TREE

Other Books by Stephen R. Lawhead

A BRIGHT EMPIRES NOVEL

QUEST THE LAST:

THE
FATAL TREE

STEPHEN R.
LAWHEAD

THOMAS NELSON
Since 1798

NASHVILLE   MEXICO CITY   RIO DE JANEIRO

Published in Nashville, Tennessee, by Thomas Nelson. Thomas Nelson is a registered trademark of HarperCollins Christian Publishing, Inc.

Page design by Mandi Cofer

Thomas Nelson, Inc., titles may be purchased in bulk for educational, business, fund-raising, or sales promotional use. For information, please e-mail SpecialMarkets@ThomasNelson.com.

Scripture quotations are taken from the King James Version of the Bible.

Publisher's Note: This novel is a work of fiction. Names, characters, places, and incidents are either products of the author's imagination or used fictitiously. All characters are fictional, and any similarity to people living or dead is purely coincidental.

Library of Congress Cataloging-in-Publication Data

Lawhead, Steve.
   The fatal tree / Stephen R. Lawhead.
      pages cm -- (Bright empires series ; 5)
   ISBN 978-1-59554-808-5 (hardback)
   I. Title.
   PS3562.A865F38 2014
   813'.54--dc23

                              2014020114

14 15 16 17 18 19 RRD 6 5 4 3 2 1

For my mother, Lois
It all started with those Little Golden Books

Oh, Thou! That dwellest wide diffus'd around,

Where all creative energies abound;

Omniscient Power! Eternal, Undefin'd,

Productive Essence, and Mysterious Mind:

What shall we call Thee?

How Thy powers express?

Or, how Thine awful majesty address?

O'er earth we see Thee, and Thy footsteps trace

Through the Bright Empires of unbounded space . . .

—FROM *THE ACHILLEAD* BY WILLIAM JOHN THOMAS, 1830

Contents

Important People

Anen—Friend of *Arthur Flinders-Petrie*, high priest of the temple of Amun in Egypt, Eighteenth Dynasty.

Archelaeus Burleigh, Earl of Sutherland—Nemesis of *Flinders-Petrie, Cosimo, Kit*, and all right-thinking people.

Arthur Flinders-Petrie—Also known as *The Man Who Is Map*, patriarch of his line. Begat *Benedict*, who begat *Charles*, who begat *Douglas*.

Balthazar Bazalgette—The Lord High Alchemist at the court of *Emperor Rudolf II* in Prague, friend and confidant of *Wilhelmina*.

Benedict Flinders-Petrie—The son of *Arthur* and *Xian-Li* and father of *Charles*.

Brendan Hanno—Attached to the Zetetic Society in Damascus, an advisor to ley travellers.

Burley Men—*Con, Dex, Mal*, and *Tav*. *Lord Burleigh's* henchmen. They keep a Stone Age cat called *Baby*.

Cassandra Clarke—A post-graduate paleontologist who accidently gets caught up in the quest for the Skin Map.

Charles Flinders-Petrie—Son of *Benedict* and father of *Douglas*, he is grandson of *Arthur*.

Cosimo Christopher Livingstone, the Elder, aka Cosimo—A Victorian gentleman and founding member of the Zetetic Society, which seeks to reunite the Skin Map and learn its secrets.

Cosimo Christopher Livingstone, the Younger, aka Kit—*Cosimo's* great-grandson.

Douglas Flinders-Petrie—Son of *Charles* and great-grandson of *Arthur*; he is quietly pursuing his own search for the Skin Map, one piece of which is in his possession.

Emperor Rudolf II—King of Bohemia and Hungary, Archduke of Austria, and King of the Romans, he is also known as the Holy Roman Emperor and is quite mad.

Engelbert Stiffelbeam—A baker from Rosenheim in Germany, affectionately known as *Etzel*.

En-Ul—Elder statesman of River City Clan.

Giambattista Becarria, Fra Becarria, aka Brother Lazarus—A priest astronomer at the abbey observatory on Montserrat, and *Mina's* mentor.

Gianni—See *Giambattista Becarria*, above.

Giles Standfast—*Sir Henry Fayth's* coachman, *Kit's* ally, and erstwhile servant of *Lady Fayth*.

Gustavus Rosenkreuz—Chief assistant to the Lord High Alchemist and *Wilhelmina's* ally.

Lady Haven Fayth—*Sir Henry's* headstrong and mercurial niece.

Sir Henry Fayth, Lord Castlemain—Member of the Royal Society, staunch friend and ally of *Cosimo*, and *Haven's* uncle.

Jakub Arnostovi—*Wilhelmina's* wealthy and influential landlord and business partner.

J. Anthony Clarke III, aka Tony—Renowned astrophysicist and Nobel nominee, he is *Cassandra's* concerned and protective father.

Rosemary Peelstick—Zetetic Society host, colleague of *Brendan Hanno*.

Snipe—Feral child and malignant aide to *Douglas Flinders-Petrie*.

Turms—A king of Etruria, one of the Immortals, and a friend of *Arthur's*; he oversees the birth of *Benedict Flinders-Petrie* when *Xian-Li's* pregnancy becomes problematic.

Wilhelmina Klug, aka Mina—Formerly a London baker and *Kit's* girlfriend, she owns Prague's Grand Imperial Kaffeehaus with *Etzel*.

Xian-Li—Wife of *Arthur Flinders-Petrie* and mother of *Benedict*. Daughter of the tattooist Wu Chen Hu of Macao.

Dr. Thomas Young—Physician, scientist, and certified polymath with a keen interest in ancient Egypt, he is also referred to as *The Last Man in the World to Know Everything*.

Previously

It appears that we left our questors in a bit of a cliff-hanger in Damascus, circa 1930, where they were gathered at the Zetetic Society headquarters on Hanania Street in the Old City. It should be recalled that the society and its offices function as the nexus point for all those of goodwill who seek to understand the phenomenon of ley travel and what can be learned from it. For example, we learned that certain cosmic events have been set in motion that now threaten to bring about the apocalypse of annihilation known as the End of Everything. This discovery impelled a conclave of questors to discuss the impending cataclysm—discussions that went precisely nowhere . . . until several small but significant events occurred in quick succession and changed everything.

It began when Kit Livingstone innocently and inadvertently revealed that he had once, whilst "dreaming time" with the venerable En-Ul in the prehistoric Bone House, encountered the late, great Arthur Flinders-Petrie at the mythical location known as the Spirit Well. How did he know it was Flinders-Petrie? There could be no mistaking the man's identity, because his torso was tattooed with the symbols representing his many and various journeys throughout time and space. When Kit saw him, Arthur was wading into the Well of Souls—another name for the Spirit Well—carrying the lifeless body of his beloved wife, Xian-Li. When he emerged from the well, Xian-Li had been miraculously restored to the land of the living.

This disclosure was overheard by Mrs. Rosemary Peelstick, formerly a ley traveller herself but latterly hostess-in-residence at the Zetetic Society headquarters. The venerable Mrs. P immediately grasped the significance of Arthur's action, and, indeed, the shock of hearing it was such that she lost control of her tea tray and sent the entire assemblage crashing to the flagstone floor. No great catastrophe in itself, you might think; such messes are easily dealt with. Cassandra Clarke was present at the scene and, in an effort to be helpful, reached into her pocket and drew out her handkerchief with the aim of mopping up the spilt tea.

Careful readers will remember that, whilst this particular handkerchief was nothing more than an ordinary square of white cotton cloth and one that Cass used in all sorts of ways, it had most recently been employed as a work surface in her attempt to reverse-engineer one of the Shadow Lamps. Those clever devices had been helping guide our questors through the maze of portals and pathways constituting the illimitable network of ley lines.

During her investigations, some of the rare earth contained within the Shadow Lamp spilled onto the surface of the handkerchief and caught in the fibres. Before Cass could deploy the handkerchief as a mop, Kit perceived a faint yet unmistakeable image on the cloth: a spiral whorl with a straight line directly through the centre and three separate circular dots spaced evenly along the outer edge of the spiral curve. Kit intervened and, upon closer examination of the cloth, both he and Cass realised that all things are interconnected and there is neither chance nor coincidence: the cloth bore one of the designs that Kit had seen on Arthur Flinders-Petrie's chest in the form of a blue tattoo.

Meanwhile, others who had been somewhat sidelined in the pursuit of the Skin Map were advancing their own quests. Lady Haven Fayth and her faithful retainer, Giles Standfast, had made an unfortunate ley leap that landed them on the empty, windswept steppes in the time of Emperor Leo the Wise. Their attempts to locate a ley or portal that might take them out of their circumstances failed and, unable to orient or protect themselves, they were taken into the custody of the Bulgars, who were making their way through what we might now call Central Asia on their way to the great city of Constantinople. It began very much to look as if Lady Fayth and Giles' ley-travelling days were over.

And so we pick up the story of Wilhelmina Klug, Kit's former girlfriend and now co-owner of the Grand Imperial Kaffeehaus in Old Prague—and also of Fra Gianni Becarria and his new friend, the renowned astrophysicist Dr. Tony Clarke, aka Cass' father, who tends to take a scientific view of all these events. And, last but not least, of the degenerate criminal Archelaeus Burleigh and his nefarious Burley Men who are, at present, languishing in gaol below the Rathaus in Prague owing to their assault on the baker Engelbert Stiffelbeam, Wilhelmina's business partner.

As we proceed, the certainties on which our questors have come to rely seem to be very much in flux and, with them, we now enter a world in which everything we know is wrong.

PART ONE

The Dissolution

CHAPTER 1

In Which the World Takes a Turn for the Weird

G ordon Seiferts looked out the window of the operations module of Skybase Alpha. He blinked and looked again because he saw something that should not have been there: the moon.

Captain Seiferts was undertaking his daily background radiation reading and thermal image of Earth, but the blue planet was nowhere to be seen in his field of vision. He swivelled the camera 230 degrees and was able to bring Earth into view, but the metrics were all skewed. Fearing that the space station had somehow drifted out of orbit, he hurried down to the command module, where the mystery was compounded.

Instead of his colleagues and fellow scientists—men who had been working and sharing living space for the last three months—he found a crew of extremely astonished Russian cosmonauts. Seiferts did not speak Russian, and the cosmonauts did not speak English, so

it took some time to work out that Seiferts was not aboard Skybase
Alpha as he supposed, but on Mir 2, which was on a survey expedition to map the moon. Following this revelation, Seiferts grew so
agitated and incoherent he had to be sedated and bound to a ham-
mock for the duration of the mission.

Near Tacoma, Washington, fourteen vehicles plunged into Puget
Sound when the highway bridge on which they were travelling disappeared beneath them. In all, thirty-two people were killed. However,
local fishermen passing through the sound on their way out to sea
were able to pull three extremely confused survivors from the water—
none of whom could give a credible account of what had happened.

Able Seaman Mike Taylor of the *Orca IV* expressed utter incom-
prehension of the event. He was quoted in the *Tacoma Times*: "It was the
craziest thing I've ever seen. I mean, those cars came from nowhere—it
was like they just fell out of the sky. I still can't figure what happened.
Those poor people . . ." The accident occurred in the area of the
newly proposed Tacoma Narrows Bridge—a fact that was not lost on
the Puget Port Authority, whose public relations office commented,
"Obviously, a disaster like this is tragic for those involved. But whatever
the explanation turns out to be, it does raise serious questions about
whether that is the best place for a bridge at all."

The incident was put down to a severe weather inversion result-
ing in a freak tornado. Such extreme weather conditions, although
rare, are not unknown. In the Midwest, tornados have been known to
pluck objects from the ground and transport them over many miles
before depositing them in unlikely places.

Howard Smith went to sleep in his bed in Carol Stream, Illinois, and woke up on a floating agricultural island on the edge of Lake Texacoco in Mexico.

After kissing Julie—his wife of thirty-five years—good night, he closed his eyes in the bedroom of his suburban Chicago home, slept soundly, and awoke the next morning to find himself surrounded by wary Aztec farmers discussing the baffling presence of this pale-skinned alien who had appeared in their midst. They decided he was a sky god and, despite his strong protests—uttered in a language they could not understand—the farmers took him to the priest, who gave him a collar of gold and established him in the temple at Tenochtitlan.

In the Laxmi Nagar district of Mumbai, India, Sireena Shah prepared breakfast for her three children who were getting ready for school. She fed them and sent them out the door with their lunch pails—only to return to the kitchen to find them still dawdling over their food. She assumed they were playing a trick on her and was giving them a good scolding when her husband appeared on the scene, wanting *his* breakfast. She would have gladly given him something to eat, except for the fact that he had eaten and departed for the office forty minutes previously; his dirty dishes were still in the sink.

The entire R&D team of Arcosoft Games of Cupertino, California, disappeared while on a conference call with executives at Gyrotek, a marketing firm in San Francisco. When repeated attempts to reestablish contact failed, a secretary sent to the boardroom reported that the team had apparently staged a walkout as some kind of protest and left the building.

From the team members' point of view, however, the boardroom simply vanished—to be instantly replaced by a battlefield occupied by two opposing forces during what would later be called the Battle of Balaclava in the second month of the Crimean War. All eight men and five women of the Arcosoft team were slaughtered during a cavalry charge when British troops failed to identify them as noncombatants.

In Damascus, Rosemary Peelstick stood in front of a greengrocer with a sack of oranges in her hand. *What am I doing here?* she wondered. She looked down at the net bag, but had no memory of purchasing the oranges. The grocer smiled and offered his familiar greeting; she gave him an embarrassed wave, then walked home. It was, she decided, a sign of age, what was called a senior moment. She had another such moment later that day when, on the way to the genizah to join the discussion there, she turned into the hallway and found herself in the front room, again wondering why she was there.

Later, when talking to Tess Tildy, she suddenly heard herself saying the same words in the same conversation they had exchanged not an hour before. When she mentioned this to Tess, the elder woman confessed to having similar memory lapses. "It happens when you get older, dear," she said. "I don't think there's anything worth worrying about."

But when Mrs. Peelstick saw Gianni Becarria in the courtyard talking to Brendan Hanno and then, not three seconds later, turned around and saw him sitting in the front room reading a book, she knew there was something very much worth worrying about. The sight of the Italian priest nonchalantly thumbing the pages of the *History of the Ottoman Empire* sent her running back to the courtyard to find another Gianni and Brendan still immersed in conversation. She grabbed Cassandra Clarke, who happened to be passing by, and instructed her to look in the courtyard. "What did you see?"

"Well, Gianni and Brendan are talking physics, from what I can gather. Why?"

"That's what I thought. Now," said Mrs. Peelstick, "go and look in the front room and meet me in the kitchen. But don't say anything to anyone before you speak to me."

Cass regarded her curiously. "You're white as a sheet, Mrs. P. What's up?"

"Just do as I ask, please. There's a good girl."

Cass moved through the hallway and put her head through the door into the front reception room. There she saw Gianni reading his book; she did a double take and ran back to where Mrs. Peelstick was waiting in the kitchen. "Okay, what's going on?" she demanded.

"Shh! Keep your voice down," warned Mrs. Peelstick. "You saw them too?"

"I saw two Giannis, yes," Cass confirmed in a harsh whisper. "Why? What's happening?"

"I think we have a problem," she said.

"I'll say. This is deeply weird." Cass turned her wide-eyed stare toward the hallway as if fearing what would come through the door next. "We've got to tell somebody."

A hasty kitchen summit was convened—to which neither Gianni was invited—where Mrs. Peelstick informed certain key members of the Zetetics of her alarming observations. "I don't want to start a panic," she told them, "but we have a situation." It quickly transpired that she was not alone in noticing a range of small but significant anomalies: "odd little wrinkles in reality" was how Tess put it. When those wrinkles began to proliferate, the company knew that the dimensional reality they presently inhabited was growing increasingly unstable. The instability, Tony Clarke informed them, would only increase as the underlying structure of reality grew ever more volatile.

"Worst case?" said Tony. "When the anomalies accumulate to a level that can no longer be sustained, the dimension will collapse."

"Collapse," mouthed Brendan. "By that you mean be destroyed."

"Not destroyed, per se—more like *extinguished*. It would be as if this reality had never existed."

"What would happen to us?" asked Wilhelmina Klug.

"You, me, and everyone else who happened to inhabit this dimensional reality would simply cease to exist too."

The temperature in the room seemed to plummet. Kit Livingstone gazed around at his fellow questors. "Is this it?" he wondered. "Is this the End of Everything?"

"Merely the first wave, I would say," replied Tony. "Toward the end, the destruction will be far more devastating."

His words were still hanging in the air when the first of three explosions rocked the building, breaking glass in the windows, rattling the furniture, and sending stucco from the ceiling crashing to the floor. Kit was struck by a chunk of falling plaster. "What the—" he sputtered, shaking white rubble out of his hair. He jumped up and ran down the hall.

"Kit!" shouted Cass as the second explosion sent dishes from the cupboards crashing to the floor.

"Stay back!" cried Kit. "I'm going to check it out."

He raced to the reception room. Gianni was gone. Pausing at the front door, Kit pressed his ear to the wood and listened, then opened the door a crack and peered out. He saw nothing unusual, so he stepped out onto the threshold and looked down the smoke-filled street, where he saw something that had not been seen in Syria in two hundred years: a horse-drawn caisson pulling a cannon into position. Soldiers in tall, black square-topped hats, blue coats, and white trousers accompanied the cannon; they wore black boots and carried muskets fitted with bayonets. An officer with a red cockade and white ostrich plume on his bicorne hat observed the operation from the saddle of a brown horse. The officer carried a naked sabre and shouted orders in French to a company of soldiers who appeared to be moving house-to-house and pulling out residents. The air reverberated with the screams and cries of frightened citizens and the shouts of the soldiers.

Kit had seen enough. He darted back inside, almost colliding with Cass as he turned around. "Don't go out there!" he shouted. Grabbing her arm, he slammed the door.

"What is it? What's out there?"

"I think Napoleon has invaded Syria."

She gave him a blank look, shook off his hand, opened the door, and looked cautiously outside. "You must be—"

"Back to the kitchen," Kit told her, pulling her away with him.

They rushed back to the dust-filled room, where more Zetetics had crowded in—Richard, Robert, and Muriel among them. Tess was sitting in a chair and Mrs. Peelstick was dabbing at a cut to the old woman's head. Wilhelmina was picking up broken crockery; Tony and Brendan were assessing the damage.

"What did you find out?" asked Richard as Kit and Cass hurried back into the room. "Are we under attack?"

"Shh!" said Mrs. Peelstick. "Let him speak."

"We *are* under attack," Kit told them. "But"—he hesitated—"this is the weird part—"

"Yes?" said Mina. "Tell us already."

"It's the French. Napoleon, I think." He flung a hand in the direction of the street. "There are foot soldiers and men on horseback, and there's a cannon at the end of the street. They're going door-to-door and rounding up the locals."

"Napoleon?" said Robert. "Is this some kind of joke?"

"Do I look like I'm joking?" demanded Kit.

"It's true," said Cass. "I saw them too."

"How do you know they're French?" asked Mina.

"The bloody uniforms!" cried Kit. "That's not the point. Whoever they are, they'll be here any minute."

"Right," said Brendan. "We cannot stay here. We've got to get out while we can."

"What about the mission?" said Tony. "We cannot abandon the mission."

"It will have to continue elsewhere," said Brendan.

They quickly hashed out a plan. Tasks were assigned, times and meeting places agreed upon.

"I will inform the rest of the Zetetics," said Mrs. Peelstick. "We will migrate to safer places and continue to provide support for those of you in the field. Leave that to me. I'll see everyone safely away."

"Don't worry about us," said Tess. "We can take care of ourselves."

"That's it, then," said Brendan. "Use the ley line in the alley. That's the closest." He gazed around at the tight circle of anxious faces. "Just do your best and pray we are not too late."

"Tch! Listen to you," scolded Tess. She rose shakily from her chair, steadied herself, and said, "Too late? I don't believe it for a moment." She glanced defiantly around at her fellow Zetetics and threw out a challenge. "Does anyone here doubt that mitigating this catastrophe is the reason we have been brought to this place and time?"

When no one made bold to reply, she continued, "For this purpose we were formed, and to this place our steps have been directed. This is the battle to which we have been called, and we must trust in Him who has led us here to lead us on."

With those words still ringing in their ears, the questors fled Damascus.

CHAPTER 2

In Which a Lesson Is Learned the Hard Way

*K*it Livingstone and Cassandra Clarke stared at one another over the breakfast table. "She should have been here by now—we both know it. I'm afraid something bad has happened to her. Something really bad."

"You don't know that," Cass told him.

"You don't know that it hasn't."

"Listen, you said yourself that Mina's the most accomplished ley leaper among us. Whatever's happened, she can handle it."

They were sitting in a corner of the Grand Imperial Kaffeehaus eating *krapfen* and drinking coffee as the place filled up with its early clientele. "The question is, should we go on without her?" said Cass, taking a sip of coffee.

Kit stuffed the last of a doughnut into his mouth and chewed for a moment. The three of them were to have journeyed to Prague and met up before going on to Big Valley to see if they could discover a way to get back to the Spirit Well. The problem was that on their last visit to the portal, they found it guarded by an enormous yew tree that had grown up and blocked the way. Whatever else happened, they were going to have to find a way around that. "I hate to say it," Kit said at last, "but I think we have to go without her. We're sure not doing anything by cooling our heels here."

"Then we'll go." Cass set down her cup. "We'll write Mina a note and leave it with Etzel. She can come on and join us at the tree when she gets here."

"*If* she gets here," added Kit gloomily.

"Just stop it, okay?" Cass gave him a stern look. "We've got to stay positive or we might as well give up right now. And you know what? We can't give up."

"You're right," sighed Kit. "All this sitting around waiting has got to me. We'll leave this evening when the ley becomes active." He pushed back his chair and stood up. "I'll get our gear together. We'll need a few bits and bobs to take with us because we might be there a few days."

"Not so fast, Speedy. We're not going anywhere until we finish this plate of lovely pastry and have at least one more cup of coffee. Sit down and eat—it's the most important meal of the day."

After breakfast, they assembled some basic items that Kit reckoned they would need to make life in camp a little less spartan: a flint and steel, two hand axes, water flasks, fishing line and a handful of hooks, a hank of hemp rope, an assortment of knives, a pound of almonds, and four rolls of fruit leather. They divided these items and a few others into two sturdy canvas rucksacks. The idea was to travel light, and anyway, Kit reasoned, this was a fact-finding mission and they did not plan to stay very long.

They napped in the afternoon, and as the shadows began to stretch across the Old Town Square, Kit thanked Etzel for taking care of them and, handing him the note to give to Mina, wished him farewell. Then he and Cass left the city and made their way at a leisurely pace along the river road to the shaded path containing the ley line that led to Big Valley. The leap went off without incident, but they landed hard—buffeted by a fierce wind and stinging sleet. Cass threw up and Kit, for the first time in a long time, felt queasy and disoriented. It took them both a few minutes to pull themselves together; when they did, they saw that it was late afternoon and the sun was already sinking below the rim of the great limestone canyon to the west.

The Big Valley Ley deposited the two travellers on the path leading down to the river at the bottom of the gorge and, at first glance, everything seemed to be just as Kit remembered it, with no sign of the dimensional instability that had infected Damascus. Cass watched him for a moment, then asked, "Well? What do you think?"

"So far so good," Kit replied. "All appears to be in order, but time will tell. I think we call it safe until we find out otherwise." He glanced around. "I want to go to the tree, but we'll have to hurry if we hope to get back to the gorge before dark."

He led them back up the path to the canyon rim, where he paused a moment to get his bearings and take another reading of the sky before heading off across a plain of waist-high grass toward the woods in the near distance. "It's this way. Stay close and keep an eye peeled for predators, okay?"

"What kind of predators?" asked Cass.

"All of them," replied Kit. "Lions, bears, wolves, hyenas, tigers— you name it. They're all here in abundance."

An hour's trek through dense woodland brought them to a copse of close-grown elder all spindly and sun-starved. "We're almost there," Kit announced. They pushed through the elder and came to what appeared to be a hedge of young beech trees. "The clearing is through here," he said and pushed through the saplings. Cass followed on his heels and stepped into a clearing created by the outflung branches of the most massive, majestic yew tree she had ever seen.

The colossal trunk rose from an overlapping tangle of roots to form a veritable fortress, a round tower of wood as dense and heavy as iron from which hung the broad, spreading limbs that supported innumerable branches of dense, dark foliage—the soft-needled, green-black leaves spiked with blood-red poisonous berries characteristic of the species. The great heavy boughs rose rank on intertwining rank to a truly astonishing height before tapering off in a gently rounded crown that, viewed from below, seemed more like the domed crest of a looming mountain peak than a treetop. In amongst the thickly layered branches, the shadows deepened and multiplied. Whatever mysteries those dusky limbs concealed remained unseen and unknown, for no light penetrated the substantial foliage beyond the first few inches. Nor was light allowed to infiltrate the area directly beneath the circle of those branches; that and the continual rain of spent needles kept the ground all around the tree devoid of any competing vegetation whatsoever. Thus, the titanic tree stood proud of its surroundings, dominating its place in the forest, suffering no rivals: an absolute monarch, a tyrant king without peer.

"Incredible!" gasped Cass as she tried to take in the towering bulk before her. "It is . . . humongous."

"I think it's even bigger now than the last time I saw it," observed Kit. "Which means we're probably a few hundred years adrift, more or less. It's had more time to grow, that's for sure." He gazed up into the rising branches, dark against the pale blue sky, and it seemed as if he were looking into the shadowed obscurity of a mystery deep and impenetrable as time itself.

The sky turned golden with the coming sunset as they stood marvelling at the mighty tree. The forest around them filled with an auditory tapestry of birdsong; every bush and branch sang with a feathered chorister, each staking a claim on its night territory and noisily telling the world to stay well away.

As they were standing there, a blackbird alighted on a branch of one of the young saplings ringing the clearing; its sudden movement attracted the eye, and both Kit and Cass saw the bird appear. It looked around curiously, then flitted to a nearby branch of the yew tree where it perched for a moment. The bird cocked its head from one side to the other, then stretched its neck up as if to utter a call. But before the first note could sound, the creature shivered all over as if in the grip of a violent seizure. The bird stretched out its wings and, beak gaping, toppled from the branch—dead before it hit the ground.

"Wow!" said Cass. "Did you see that?"

"Come on, let's check it out."

They proceeded around the clearing to where the bird fell—taking extreme care not to so much as brush up against a yew twig—and knelt to examine the feathered corpse. There was nothing to indicate the cause of death, and if they had not witnessed the creature's demise with their own eyes, they would not have given the dead thing a second thought.

"Death by contact," observed Cass, bending over the tiny body. "Did you know that would happen?"

"I knew the tree was powerful," Kit told her. "It melted our ley lamps last time we were here." Indicating the dead bird, he said, "So that's one thing we've learned. Let's see if we can find out anything else."

They moved cautiously around the base of the tree, viewing it from every angle, then spent some time just sitting and observing. Aside from the birds flocking to their roosts for the night, the forest round about was silent—which Kit thought indicated an absence of wildlife in the nearby wood. Beyond that, nothing else happened, or seemed likely to, so he decided to conclude their first observation session. He climbed to his feet and found that his right leg had gone all numb and tingly. He took a step and stumbled back onto his hands and knees. "Ah! Ow!" he gasped.

Cass bent down beside him. "What's wrong?"

"My leg has gone to sleep." He tried to stand and grimaced. "Oh!"

"Here, let me help you," offered Cass. She stooped slightly to take Kit's hand and, unbalanced, raised her other arm. Kit reached for her hand, and at the instant of contact, a sizzling crack and a blinding flash—like the dazzling radiance of a photographer's flashgun— illuminated the entire clearing with a sudden, searing scintillation of bright blue light. Kit felt a jolt tear through him, and he was lifted off the ground and hurled onto his back. He felt this as a force, as if he had been knocked off his feet in a hard-charging rugby tackle—not like touching a live wire or being electrocuted; it was more like being slammed with a giant fist. Other than that first blinding flash, there was no spark, no zap, no smoke.

Dazed, Kit glanced around, trying to perceive what had happened. One instant he had been reaching for Cass' hand, and the next he was lying on his back, staring up at the sky and wondering why he could not breathe. Shaken in every bone of his body, he rolled onto his side and looked across to Cass, who was lying in a heap ten feet or so away. On hands and knees he crawled to her side. "Cass? Are you okay?" He reached out to her.

"Don't touch me!" Her eyes rolled in her head and she pushed herself up on her elbows.

"Any broken bones or burns or anything?"

She sat up and patted herself here and there. "Nothing broken," she reported. "But I've got a terrific buzzing in my head. I think I'm deaf in one ear. What about you?"

"No buzzing, but I feel like a bug slammed into a windscreen. Ohhh . . . *man!*" He collapsed beside her. "That was extreme."

"What *was* that?"

Kit thought for a moment. "The tree stands on a portal," he explained. "Like a ley line, but more of a—"

"I *know* what a ley portal is, Einstein," she told him, her tone sharp, almost accusing. "Did you know that was going to happen?"

"Obviously not," Kit replied. "The only other portal I know is at Black Mixen Tump back in England. That one is activated by raising your arm in the air." He turned his gaze to the tree and the place they had been standing only moments ago. "Apparently so is this one."

"Apparently," Cass echoed. "You should have warned me." She brushed herself off as if shedding a bad memory and gave a derisive sniff. "Smell that?"

Kit lifted his head and drew in a tentative whiff. "Yeah—it smells like electricity."

"Ozone," replied Cass. "Formed when high-energy electromagnetic radiation breaks the atomic structure of oxygen in the air. Electrical discharges make it—which is why you can often smell it in elevators, or after lightning storms." She pushed herself upright. "I think we should move along—in case the charge or whatever builds up again."

"Good plan," Kit agreed. He levered himself up off the ground, and after shaking his arms and legs and rolling his head from side to side, he shouldered his pack. "Okay, important safety tip. Waving your arms around is not a good idea."

"Seriously," agreed Cass.

"Let's go," Kit said. "We don't want to be caught in the forest after dark. We can come back tomorrow. With any luck, Mina will turn up." He turned and pushed through the ring of saplings forming a hedge wall around the tree. "We need to get down to shelter before the bears come out."

CHAPTER 3

In Which Rage Leads to Reverie

The slops bucket was full to overflowing and the stink was thick in the fetid, clammy air of the underground keep. More worrying was the fact that Burleigh no longer minded. He seemed to be getting used to it, a circumstance he looked upon with loathing. Also disturbing, his men had ceased complaining about their sorry lot and had quit badgering him about doing something to enact their release. Nor were they picking at one another nearly as much as during the first weeks of their confinement.

Instead, they sat slumped and dejected in their respective corners, or occasionally paced along the back wall of their communal cell. None of them spoke much, as none of them had anything new or useful to suggest. There was nothing any of them could do or say that would turn the unhurried wheels of justice.

The only event that altered their existence—and another thing that Burleigh despised with an unreasoning passion—was a visit from Engelbert the baker. It galled Burleigh that the sole person in the orld who cared whether they lived or died was the reason for thei imprisonment in the first place.

In a less grudging mood, he might have been moved to acknowledge that his assessment of the situation was not strictly accurate—but admissions of guilt were as foreign to Burleigh as feathers to a fish. Nevertheless, as day gave way to unforgiving day, Archelaeus Burleigh was forced to confront the prickly fact that savaging Engelbert in order to obtain information regarding the movements of his rivals in the quest for the Skin Map had been a grave error of judgement.

The self-made earl had never been one to wallow in either shame or regret for any length of time. The demands of his obsession to possess the secret of the Skin Map forced him always to forge ahead. The quest was a merciless taskmaster, whipping him on in relentless pursuit of the elusive prize—even when he encountered evidence that seemed to suggest that the much-decorated parchment might be something other than a road map to the cosmos. Burleigh never looked back, never questioned his defining philosophy that his end more than justified his means.

Thus, this period of enforced quiescence in a dreary dungeon cell weighed more heavily on him than anyone—even Burleigh himself—might have imagined. When given the leisure to reflect, to contemplate, he found he did not care for either the mood or the results. All his reflections and contemplations tended toward the singular conclusion that his fate was in the hands of a faceless bureaucrat of some stripe, and he was utterly powerless to alter or sway the outcome. For a man long accustomed to having his own way in absolutely everything, this was a novel development, as rare as it was deplorable.

A thin, scrabbling sound roused him from his meditations. He glanced up to see a rat making off with a large crumb of something between its sharp yellow teeth. Burleigh picked up his empty wooden drinking bowl and flung it at the thieving creature as it disappeared into a crack in the damp, mouldering wall.

"Filthy rats," he muttered.

"Boss?"

Burleigh looked around to see Tav's haggard face looming above him.

"He's comin' back." Tav glanced toward the cell door. Footsteps could be heard on the flagstones in the corridor. "You wanted me to wake you when he came back."

Burleigh pushed up on an elbow. "I wasn't asleep."

Presently, there came the now-familiar rattle of the key in the lock and the rusty squeak as the mechanism clicked open. The jailer entered first and gave the cell a cursory inspection, saw the overfull slops bucket and retrieved it. He motioned their visitor into the cell, then closed the door and locked it again. Engelbert, a simple smile on his bland face, cried, "*Guten Tag, meine Herren. Guten Tag! Ich habe Essen für Sie.*"

The Burley Men levered themselves to their feet as their jovial visitor moved into the centre of the room and unslung a large cloth bag; he untied it and rolled down the edges. "*Hier ist Brot,*" he said, lifting out a large round loaf of dark brown bread. "*Gut und Frisch.*"

The baker passed the bread to Con, who was first and closest. The others received their loaves in turn, and then the baker delved into his sack and brought out chunks of sausage and lumps of fresh cheese. Burleigh, holding himself somewhat aloof from the others, watched as if from a great distance. The way his men bowed and scraped to the lumbering dolt of a German—all smiles and grovelling appreciation, so absurdly, pitifully grateful—was pathetic.

"*Für Sie*," said Etzel, holding out a perfect loaf of fragrant, wholesome bread.

Burleigh gazed at it, and then at the hand offering it, and then into the baker's round, friendly face. The marks of the vicious beating were fading, the traces of his injury at Burleigh's hands beginning to heal.

Curiously, the big baker seemed to bear no ill feeling toward his tormentors, a thing that Burleigh could not understand. Stiffelbeam brought them food and drink enough to keep them alive—fortuitously, too, since Burleigh's own resources had run out weeks ago. The first delivery had caught him off guard. But when Engelbert returned a few days later, Burleigh suspected revenge: the food would be tainted, poisoned even, and would make them all sick. Though Burleigh cautioned his men against eating anything offered by the baker, one by one his men succumbed to hunger and ate. No one got sick or died, and they soon grew to trust the handouts as wholesome and genuine offerings of concern.

"*Warum?*" he asked in his rudimentary Deutsch. "Why?"

"*Bitte?*" said Etzel.

"Why do you do this?" the earl growled, forcing his tongue around the awkward German language. "Every week you bring us food. Why?"

Etzel regarded him thoughtfully for a moment, then shrugged. "Who else will bring it if I do not?"

"No," countered the earl. "I mean *why*—what is the . . ." He struggled to find the German word. "*Zweck*—what is the purpose?"

"To eat," replied a mildly bewildered Engelbert. "If I do not bring this food, you will starve."

Burleigh glared at his unlikely nemesis and his mouth dropped into a bewildered frown. This was getting him nowhere. Perhaps his German, basic as it was, could not cope with the rigours of abstract argument. He backed up and tried another tack. "*Why?* Why do you care? What is it to you if we starve?"

The baker gazed at him and shook his head. "I do not understand."

Losing his patience at last, Burleigh shouted, "You do this for us! You give us food. I want to know why you are doing this!"

Finally, Engelbert seemed to comprehend what was being asked. A wide grin broke across his bruised countenance. "It is what my Lord Jesus would do," he said cheerfully. "How can I do less?"

CHAPTER 4

In Which a Problem
Is Laid to Rest

Turms the Immortal opened his eyes on the 9,265th day of his reign. He rose from his gilded bed to face a blood-red dawn the like of which he had never known. Though the long history of his race recorded periods of war and turmoil, during his time on the throne Etruria had known only peace and tranquillity. The brutal attack of the Latins and their invasion of his kingdom had unleashed a day of slaughter and bloodshed unprecedented in living memory.

The raid was brief—begun at dawn and ended before midday—but the damage and injury would persist for years to come. Mounted raiders from the greedy North had sacked and burned two villages. They drove nearly three hundred people from their homes and holdings, and took eighty Etruscans into slavery before fleeing for the safety of their borders once more. The trail of destruction was a wide swath of ashes and death.

Numbered among those injured and wounded in the raid was the man known as Duglos, the great-grandson of his old friend Arturos and a guest of the royal household. A great pity that, and so unnecessary. For if Duglos had only stayed in his house, he would have escaped harm. Etruscan soldiers arrived shortly after the enemy reached the outskirts of the royal precinct and successfully repelled the attack. At the arrival of the soldiers, the raiders simply scattered and made a swift retreat.

Duglos was found on the road bleeding from a vicious spear wound. He had been carried back to the guesthouse and placed on the table in the main room, where the royal physician and healers set to work. They cleaned the wound, which continued to bleed profusely. Unable to stanch the blood flow, they resorted to the extremity of heating iron probes and cauterising the wound with red-hot metal; acrid smoke and the stench of burning meat filled the room, but at last the issue of blood stopped.

They had just set about a final cleaning of the gash when there arose a commotion outside; voices raised and a door slammed. An instant later Duglos' companion—the pale, wraithlike youth with the large head and empty eyes—burst into the room. He halted on his heels when he saw the body of his benefactor naked upon the table, blood pooling on the floor. The boy gaped, opened his mouth, and uttered a sound none of those in the room had ever heard from a human being—an animal shriek of rage and triumph. Then, as swiftly as he had entered, he darted away again. The door slammed once more and the boy was gone.

Somewhat relieved, Laris, the chief physician, returned to his work. He ordered an unguent of olive oil, nard, and garlic to be applied liberally, and the wound was bandaged with clean linen strips dipped in a mixture of honey and wine. As the last bandage was secured, the king arrived. Laris dismissed his helpers and beckoned the king to join him. "Most Excellent One, all that can be done has been done for your guest," he said. "Whether he lives or dies is now in the hands of the god who made him."

"Such is the fate of all who walk this world," Turms observed.

"I will sit with him and await the outcome," offered Laris.

Turms thanked his physician and said, "You have more pressing work elsewhere. There are many injured—go and see to them."

The physician bowed and hurried away to tend others wounded in the attack. Turms stood by the table regarding the body—so still and white, the chest barely moving. He watched for a time and, assuring himself that the injured man was in no distress, summoned a servant to keep watch, then left the villa and rode out with his bodyguard to assess the damage to his kingdom. Turms hastened first to the devastated villages and heard reports of the attack from the victims; pledging his support to aid in the rebuilding, the Priest King of the Velathri continued on to survey the ruined fields and woodland burned by the Latins in their senseless attack. Through all this, the single question jangled in the king's mind: *Why?*

The Latins were a restless, war-loving race; that much had been understood for generations. But the two realms had been at peace for many years, and the attack was completely unprovoked. This development augured ill for the immediate future. Something would have to be done to forestall further incursions and strife. To that end, the king would consult his advisors and make the appropriate sacrifices, hold council, and, only then, determine what to do.

After a long, wretched day touring the destruction and offering what solace he could to his people, Turms returned to his palace to find that the wounded man had succumbed to his injuries. "He died a little before your return, my lord," the servant informed him.

Turms nodded thoughtfully. "Was there pain in the end?"

"No, sire. He entered the life eternal in peace."

"What of the strange boy? The youth who stayed with Duglos?"

The servant shook his head. "I cannot say, my lord king. I saw the youth but once and only briefly when he bolted into the room. He looked upon the body, screamed, and then ran away. I cannot say where he has gone. Perhaps he will return."

"Perhaps not. Either way, I am content."

Turms discharged the servant and, drawing up a stool, sat down with the body to contemplate the unknowable twists and turns the path of a life could take. Despite his best intentions, it seemed that destiny had decreed a different outcome for this sad, broken soul. Although as king he was convinced that in keeping Duglos and the feral youth here, he had chosen the wise and proper path, the priestly part of him wondered whether he had done enough. Had he failed his duty to his friend? More importantly, had he failed his duty to the future and the well-being of the world?

"I am sorry, Arturos," he murmured after a while. "I should have observed better care for your kinsman. The debt is mine, and I will find a way to repay." After a moment's thought, he rose from the stool, shouting, "Pacha! Pacha, come here. Attend your master!"

He heard the slap of the royal housekeeper's feet on the stone floor outside, and Pacha put his round, shaved head into the room. "Your servant attends you, my lord."

"I have decided what is to be done."

"That is well, sire."

"Out of respect for my dear friend Arturos, I will bury his

kinsman in my tomb. In that way I will honour the memory of my friend and also redress any offence I may have committed in this unfortunate matter."

"Your personal tomb?" Concern ruffled Pacha's usually placid features. "Sire?"

Turms heard the note of caution in his servant's voice. "You think me too hasty?"

"Never, sire. And yet . . . ." He put out a hand to the dead man. "To be buried in a royal tomb . . . To my knowledge he was not born of nobility."

The king paused to consider the situation, then declared, "I am noble, and the tomb will be my place of rest. Let Duglos have the sarcophagus that is ready. I will have a new and greater one carved for myself." Turms smiled, happy with this gesture. "Let it be as I have decreed."

Pacha summoned the embalmers to collect the corpse and begin their work. When they were finished, the prepared body was laid on a bier at the foot of the royal hill. Together with a number of priests, a handful of soldiers, and a small gathering of curious onlookers, the king in his scarlet robe and golden sash, his high-crowned ceremonial hat on his head, descended the pathway barefoot. In one hand he held an olive branch and in the other a curved knife with a blade of gold and a handle of black onyx.

A yellow-robed priest brought a silver bowl containing water mixed with resinated wine and took his place beside the bier. Turms bowed to him and, dipping the olive branch into the bowl, sprinkled water and wine over the body; he did this three times and then placed the olive branch on the corpse's chest. Two more priests joined the first, and the three wound the body in its shroud, bowing to the king when they finished.

The ritual of Last Ablution thus concluded, Turms put on his sandals and took his place at the head of the hastily convened procession. The body was taken up by the priests and carried to the Sacred Road—the narrow corridor carved deep into the tufa below ground level—and borne to the tomb the king had constructed for himself. The king stepped to the door and, taking the golden knife, scraped the blade along the doorframe, down either side and across the top and bottom, breaking the thin screed of red mortar that sealed the door to the tomb.

Using a special tool, the hidden latch of the door was lifted from the inside and the heavy stone covering was slowly pulled open to reveal a dark cavity room, empty save for a large sarcophagus made of amber-coloured alabaster and carved with the familial symbols—swans, dolphins, and lions—of the royal resident-to-be. Turms dipped his ceremonial knife in the silver bowl and sprinkled holy water on the doorposts and lintel, then stepped into the tomb and repeated the procedure, shaking water into every corner of the square-cut chamber. He did the same to the sarcophagus and then directed three of the soldiers in attendance to open the alabaster casket.

The enshrouded corpse was placed in the large stone box and the lid secured once more. Raising his hands to shoulder height, Turms intoned a brief prayer for the soul of the deceased, saying:

"O Great of Heaven, Creator of Life, Your children come forth at the dawn of life; the wise among them worship You and give thanks. O God of the Creation, You shower high and low alike with the blessings of life; those who are deserving of favour rejoice in Your presence. You alone, O Lord, give light and warmth to those who dwell in the House of Life.

"We come forth today, justified in Your presence, for we have conquered our enemy who invaded our lands. His chariot is broken, his spear blunted, his dagger sheathed. His army is destroyed, and those who run with him have fled into the wilderness.

"Hail, Great of Might, Guardian of the People, grant us divine protection, for we are Your followers and provide sustenance in Your temples.

"Hail, All Wise, Architect of the Universe, who creates life by dreaming it. Hail, Supreme and Eternal One, Creator of Time, Ruler of all that is and is yet to be. We bow in homage to You and receive the blessing of Your mercy, and ask that You receive into Your company the soul of Duglos who stands before You now.

"King of Truth, Creator of Eternity, Prince of Everlasting Glory, and Sovereign of All Gods, You give life and receive it. Blessed be Your name forever. So says Turms the Immortal, justified and eternal, by Your will King of these Velathri and Chief Priest of the People."

The ceremony concluded, the king and his entourage exited the tomb but did not close the door. The lintel and doorposts of the tomb were painted blue and garlands were hung to festoon the entrance to the burial chamber. In accordance with tradition, the tomb would remain open for three days to allow mourners and well-wishers to leave gifts of food and wine for the deceased and his family.

Then, his obligations fulfilled, Turms and the group of priests, courtiers, and hired mourners departed, leaving two young soldiers behind to guard the grave site. As soon as the funeral party had climbed up from the Sacred Road and was once more on the trail leading to the palace, the king sent the others on ahead so that he could have a little time and space apart. His thoughts turned to his long friendship with Arturos and the strange events surrounding the arrival and death of his great-grandson. There was a mystery here, a deeply unsettling secret he had yet to penetrate. He turned his eyes inward and sought a sign or a word that might illuminate the darkness that was Duglos.

Arturos, the friend of his callow younger self, had a son, Benedict, whom Turms knew well—he had aided the birth of that child when other physicians had despaired of saving either mother or infant. Both Arturos and his son had been good and upright men; Duglos, however, was far from either good or upright. A venal and degenerate soul, the man possessed none of his forefathers' virtues. What Turms had done, he had done out of respect for his old friend and to honour the memory of that friendship—not, he confessed, out of any obligation owed to the dead man himself.

Burdened by these thoughts, Turms the Immortal arrived at the path leading up to his hilltop palace. He turned and placed his foot on the road, but had not yet taken his first step when his eye fell upon a small splotch of dark and light gleaming dully in the shadow of a cypress tree at the very bottom of the path. Ever alert to omens, and with the keen sight of a true seer, Turms glimpsed the object and halted in midstep.

Resting his hands on his knees, the king bent down for a closer look. It was a tiny hatchling bird—bald, covered in black pinfeathers, still damp—fallen from the nest somewhere in the branches above. The poor little dead thing was newly born; there were fragments of eggshell still clinging to the wet, translucent skin with larger pieces of broken shell around the miniature corpse. Turms regarded this unfortunate tableau for a moment, then raised his eyes to heaven and breathed a sigh of gratitude for being granted the sign he sought. Then he bowed his head to contemplate the meaning.

The bird had hatched out of season; it was late summer, long after all the other birds had fledged and flown. The little thing had begun the process of birth, but that progression had been interrupted and the bird consigned to death. Indeed, it was doubtful the creature had even lived long enough to take its first breath. Before it could open its beak to drink of life, Nature had decreed that it should not live. This happened sometimes, as Turms knew only too well. When the parents have been unlucky in raising a brood, they will try for a second one, but the hatchlings are most always born too late in the year and cannot grow strong enough to survive the coming winter. In such cases, death is a mercy. Fallen from the nest, the poor, doomed creature had landed at the very first step of the royal road—Turms' road, leading to Turms' house. Therefore, the king himself was implicated in some way. This was yet another death he must own.

Accepting this judgement, the king knelt in the dust of the path and scooped up the little corpse, carried it to the side of the road, and, using the edge of a stone, scraped a shallow grave in the dirt. He placed the baby bird in the hole and covered it with soil and put the stone atop the tiny mound. Then he gave thanks for its life, and as he rose to continue up the road to his palace, the full meaning of this sign broke upon him.

It was a portent given in response to the mystery posed by Arturos and Duglos. Here was the answer that had so long eluded him. He saw it all so clearly now—all the figures present, himself included—spread out on a shining path that represented time. He saw again the arrival of Arturos and the heavily pregnant Xian-Li, and remembered how he had helped save the life of the mother and her son when all the other physicians had given up hope; he saw the infant Benedict and heard him draw his first breath and cry.

Oh, but like the tiny nestling bird fallen from the nest, that was a birth that never should have been!

Turms saw that now. While it is never wrong to intervene in saving a life, his action had allowed a train of events to continue that never should have occurred. Heaven in its infinite wisdom had decreed that individual life—and all the events and interactions that would flow from it—should not be. Turms the Priest King of the Velathri, in his feeble, limited wisdom, had determined otherwise.

Now, behold: Heaven had stepped in to restore order once more. With Duglos' death, the matter was at last concluded. That the end had taken place in the very room where the misadventure had first begun was not lost on Turms. It was a chastisement and one he humbly accepted. It had happened this way so that he would learn from it and be reminded, yet again, how mysterious were the ways of God and how just.

Turms shook his head in wonder at the intricate design of Heaven. It was beyond human comprehension. All he could grasp was a single thread or two of a patch of tapestry being woven on a scale to span the entire cosmos.

There were yet more lessons to be learned from this, and Turms would learn a few of them in the days to come. But there were other lessons he could not know that were yet equally important. What other events had arisen from Arturos' meddling that should not have come to fruition?

That was a question for others to answer. For Turms, just now, there were more pressing commitments and protocols, more funerals to conduct, more burials to attend. The season of sorrow and mourning and deep contemplation throughout Etruria had begun.

CHAPTER 5

In Which a Final Destination Is Reached

L ady Haven Fayth had heard of Constantinople, of course. No student of either Latin or history could travel very far into their books without arriving in the fabled metropolis spread upon the shores of the Bosphorus. Her education, while fairly patchy in most respects, had at least included a mention or two of the place where so much of Western history had been wrought. In her wildest flights of fancy, she had never so much as imagined visiting the city, much less seeing the great domes of the Hagia Sophia gleaming gold in the early-morning light. Yet life is stranger than anyone can imagine, and there it was: the great church of Emperor Justinian, a poem in painted stone, a towering psalm of praise to last the ages, rising proud on its hill overlooking the silver-sparked expanse of the blue Marmara Sea.

Haven filled her eyes with the sight, luxuriating in waves of relief and gratitude. At last, the long travail was over. "Oh, Giles," she said a little breathlessly, "have you ever seen anything so beautiful?"

"Never," agreed Giles from his customary place beside her. "Nor as big. It must be the size of three Londons together."

"It would be wonderful at half the size."

For Haven, the journey out of the steppes had been an awkward blend of fascination, fatigue, and mind-numbing tedium—ingredients impossible to combine with any degree of satisfaction. The day-to-day toil of travel was so drearily monotonous that most days it was all she could do to put one foot in front of another without screaming. Lightening the weariness, like black currants in a stodgy pudding, were occasional insights into the largely alien culture in which she was submerged and that flowed all around her.

Caught between warring armies, she and Giles had been captured on the battlefield and brought to the attention of the ruler of the marauding invaders: the Bulgars, as they called themselves. He had determined that the two foreigners were to accompany him—as slaves? envoys? pets? Who knew? While being kept as royal accoutrements was not ideal, Haven comforted herself with the thought that at least the *khan*, or king—an educated and enlightened fellow named Simeon—was a cultivated Christian and not a brutish, godless lout.

The Bulgars themselves seemed a contradictory race in almost every way. Capable of heroic acts of kindness and largess, they could be bloody-minded and brutal, even to their own. While professing a fierce devotion to honour, they could be savagely treacherous and wildly unreliable in even the smallest undertakings. A warrior might pledge blood and bone to the protection and defence of his comrades, and yet abandon the field at first whiff of a losing battle.

Conversely, they might fight to the last breath though all hope of winning had long since fled.

Taken as a whole, they were clever without being boastful; cheerful when hardship rained down upon them; simple in their appetites and pleasures and vainglorious in appearance; undemanding and content in whatever circumstance Fortune's Wheel sent their way, but fascinated by wealth and tales of riches; modest in person, yet proud in tribal unity; small of stature, yet mighty as giants in the strength of their limbs; humble in demeanour, yet haughty in attitude, assuming they knew best in any circumstance they might meet. A more contrary people Haven was certain she had never seen.

But as she got to know them better, Haven discovered that in one area, at least, they seemed to be completely without guile or duplicity: their deep and abiding reverence for religion. Christians all, they were docile, worshipful, obedient sons and daughters of Mother Church and, from infant to elder, along with the baptismal waters they were soaked head to toe in a kind of rough chivalry, holding faith and honour above petty personal interest. They also exhibited unstinting affection for their khan. As an individual, Khan Simeon shared many of the characteristics of his people, but tempered with a greater grace and sophistication, as demonstrated by his treatment of his guests. The king himself had made thoughtful provision for them: he had given them a place in the royal entourage and assigned his chamberlain to shepherd them along; he presented them with new clothes—long, belted robes similar to his own and soft leather boots; he arranged for a family to look after them so that food and basic necessities could be provided and so that they might learn something of the culture and language of the people.

In these things and others, the khan took an interest in their welfare. In manner, word, and deed, Simeon was a true nobleman. He was also, Haven quickly came to appreciate, a leader steering a very tricky course through treacherous waters. He was a king at war with a more powerful and numerous enemy. Yet, owing to greater intelligence, skill, and determination, he had prevailed against the greatest empire the ancient world had ever known. Simeon had fought his way to the very gates of Constantinople to issue terms of peace to the emperor himself.

All this and much more she had gleaned during the long trek from the empty plains of the Istros Valley to Constantinople. Like a wool picker gathering bits of fluff from the brambles and thickets where sheep had passed, Haven collected whatever intelligence came her way, adding it to her store. Her primary source of stray information was the khan's chamberlain, Gyorgi, a busy fellow with a weakness for camp gossip. But the most reliable source was the king's chief advisor, a bald-headed barrel of a man named Petar, who spoke Latin and Greek, as well as Bulgar and, apparently, several other languages. Khan Simeon's travelling company also included several priests, dour fellows with long black beards and heavy black robes. For all she knew they might have been willing to share in her education, though as they only spoke Greek, they were of little use to Haven, who possessed only a basic, workmanlike Latin.

But where Gyorgi was a fountain, Petar was a pump. Every drop had to be extracted with an effort. Gyorgi would prattle on endlessly about this and that whether anyone was listening or not; Petar had a maddening tendency to part with his words as if he were parting with his money. Each tiny scrap of information was weighed and assayed like a gold coin before being dispensed—so much and no more—and Haven soon learned she had to be happy with whatever she was given.

Always, she relayed what she learned to Giles. As they followed the sprawling army over the seemingly endless hills, they discussed what they learned and gleaned from the life they observed around them, and gradually a picture of the world and their place in it emerged. Gradually, too, Haven began to sense in Giles a ready mind to go with his steady temperament. She undertook to teach him the rudiments of Latin—at least, as much as she knew—and they practiced together over endless miles beneath a burning sun. In return, to better protect her from the merciless rays, Giles made her a wide-brimmed hat from the dried leaves of rushes that grew along the river. He also obtained a waterskin for her and filled it every morning so that she would not forget to drink.

Thus, as the days passed, so too did the rigid class division between them; the brittle artifice of nobility and servility could not stand up to the rigours of their current circumstance and bit by bit simply crumbled away.

Making sense of their curious position consumed them. Endlessly, they circled around the question of how they would find their way home, or at least to a ley line that might start them on their journey back. In this, however, they were frustrated; lacking a map or guide of any sort, there was nothing they could do to advance the cause, and neither had so far discerned any of the subtle visceral signs—the slight tingling on the skin, the quiver in the gut—that often signalled a nearby ley line or portal. But in other areas their efforts at discovery were well rewarded. They learned that the Bulgars were at war with the people called Rhomaioi who, as Haven eventually deduced, were known to her as the Byzantines. The conflict between the two peoples had been simmering for a generation or more, flaring up from time to time in ferocious but largely indecisive and costly conflicts. Apparently, the emperor, or *basileus*, had unwisely prompted the rapacious Huns to raid into Bulgar lands. Enticed by promises of grants and trade routes, the Huns—who needed very little prompting—embarked on a reckless invasion, which Khan Simeon had not only decisively crushed but carried to the very walls of Constantinople before which his central force now stood.

Such were the upheaval and turmoil caused by this disastrous campaign—Haven and Giles had witnessed some of this firsthand— that Emperor Leo had capitulated while Simeon was still some distance away. To minimise looting, pillaging, and the displacement of his subjects, Leo had sent an escort to conduct Simeon to the capital. Thus, the fighting had ceased, the elephants had been sent home along with a large portion of the mounted bowmen, and the last hundred miles had been in the company of Byzantine soldiers. And now, as they stood outside the sprawling Bulgar encampment on a hilltop to the north of the city, they were waiting to be met by the emperor's personal troops, the palace guard.

"Do you think they will let us go down there?" wondered Giles.

"I dearly hope they do," Haven replied without taking her eyes off the splendid display before her. There was something about the place that enticed; the mere sight of it aroused something in her she had never felt before—a longing, or a sense that before her lay the answer to a question she had never known to ask. If the first glimpse of an unknown place could awaken a desire, then this glittering city had done that. She felt it as keenly as a desert thirst, and Haven knew she would not be able to rest until she had drunk her fill.

"Here they come," said Giles. Haven stirred herself and glanced around to where he was pointing. Down on the stone-paved road, a body of men was moving toward them, spears and helmets gleaming in the morning light. Soon they could hear the rhythmic thump of their marching feet. Two men on horseback accompanied the troops, and as the greeting party drew nearer, the riders sped on ahead to announce their arrival.

The troops had been sent to conduct Khan Simeon to the place where Emperor Leo would meet with him and his advisors to hear terms and negotiate a peace settlement. "What will happen then?" Haven asked Petar as they stood watching the khan's bodyguard form around Simeon for the final approach to the imperial palace.

"The emperor will agree to our blessed khan's conditions," replied the chief advisor.

"You are certain of this?"

"The sun will rise tomorrow. Of this, I am certain." He looked at her, then turned his face to the sun newly risen in the east, and walked away.

Giles had followed this exchange. "What did he say?" he asked after Petar had passed beyond earshot.

"He said he expects the emperor to accept Simeon's conditions."

"And then?"

"The sun will rise tomorrow."

Giles frowned. "What did he mean by that?"

"I suppose we shall have to wait and see."

Waiting was just what they did. Three days and nights the Bulgar war host remained camped within sight of the city walls. At first Haven was glad for a chance to rest; to remain in one place two days together seemed a luxury. She and Giles spent time relaxing in their little skin tent or wandering around the camp and pitching in to help with some of the domestic chores, which always attracted a bevy of Bulgar children, drawn as if by magic to Haven's russet hair and pale skin and Giles' imposing stature and booming laugh. Eventually these simple pleasures began to pall. Boredom set in—and frustration at being so close to that glittering, majestic city and yet not allowed any nearer. Occasionally a rider would appear with a message from the king, and rumours would race through the camp only to die for lack of information. On the fourth day around midday, the gates opened and a procession emerged in which the khan, surrounded by priests and musicians, was seen riding in a chair carried by Nubian slaves. The soldiers accompanying him were those of the emperor; his own were not among the entourage.

People came running to greet their khan and hear what he had to say. There was much pushing and shoving for prime places near the front. The soldiers enforced a rough order, and as soon as everyone had quieted sufficiently, Simeon climbed onto the seat of his chair. Raising his hands, he shouted, "It has pleased God and the Blessed Saints to grant us the victory we have so ardently pursued. The emperor of the Byzantines has recognised our sovereignty and the right of our peoples to live in peace on their own lands."

The khan paused to allow his words to be translated into the tribal dialects of his people, for unlike himself, few of his subjects spoke Latin. Haven also interpreted for Giles, who nodded appreciatively. "Petar was right, then," he observed. "The king got everything he wanted."

Khan Simeon was speaking again. "Tomorrow, in celebration of the treaty that has been agreed to, a feast has been declared. Today will be spent in prayer and preparation for tomorrow's festivities." He paused and, allowing himself a broad grin, declared, "This is a great day in the history of our people. I invite you all to enter into the triumph your blood and sacrifice have made possible."

There was more after that—about the arrangements for the celebration—but Giles was anxious to know what had been said. "There's going to be a feast to celebrate the victory," Haven told him. "We are to spend the day getting ready."

"I believe I am ready now," Giles said. He puffed out his cheeks and blurted, "Solemn truth, my lady, I fairly ache to see that city. To have stood here and watched it from afar these four days has chafed me raw."

"Patience, Mr. Standfast," Haven cooed, patting him on the arm. "Your ordeal is soon at an end."

A few hours later the first wagons began arriving from the city—a long line of mule-driven carts and wains, each piled high with goods and supplies: bulky bundles of firewood and baskets of charcoal, enormous cauldrons, iron tripods, spits, and other cooking paraphernalia; sacks of flour and baskets, bags, and hampers of raw foodstuffs for the feast, as well as teams of cooks, bakers, and kitchen helpers. A space was cleared in the centre of the camp for a great canopy to serve as a makeshift kitchen, and numerous fire rings were established. Carts loaded with beer in wooden barrels and wine in enormous amphorae were next; other wagons trundled in with long, trough-like containers and jars of fresh water. These were distributed around the camp—not for drinking, but for bathing—so that every-one could wash and make themselves presentable for the celebration. Lastly, a mixed herd of oxen, goats, and sheep were driven up to hastily erected pens on the outskirts of the encampment; the animals would soon be slaughtered to provide meat for the feast.

The imperial cooks and bakers set to work at once. Under the captivated gaze of the Bulgar children, they built ovens, dug fire pits, and erected tripods and spits for roasting. Meanwhile, the khan's priests drifted through the camp ringing bells to call the people to a special mass of thanksgiving and deliverance. Haven and Giles, along with most everyone else, made their way to the field just outside the last rank of tents where an altar had been erected.

These outdoor church services were much the normal routine for an army pursuing a nomadic campaign, and Haven had taken to them almost immediately. Although she could not understand much of what was said or sung—the liturgy and readings were all in Greek—she found the chanting utterly compelling. The way the voices of the priests rose and fell in cadence, intertwining and blending, lifted her heart, sometimes leaving her breathless with a sort of yearning for something that she could almost touch. At these times, she could feel herself straining toward it, but, ever elusive, transcendence remained just beyond her grasp. Although she did not catch the thing she pursued, the effort always left her content and strangely comforted—as if attainment, though denied, had nevertheless been rewarded.

This day, however, with the sun bearing down and the smoke from the cooking fires wafting across the field into their faces, the service remained stubbornly earthbound, and so too her soul. When at last it finished, she and Giles made their way back to the centre of the camp where they paused to observe the cooks and bakers and their helpers toiling away. "All very well they work so," Giles said. "But the feast is to be here tomorrow, not in the city."

"So it would appear," agreed Haven, taking in the almost-frenzied activity of the cooks. "Poor Giles, I would pray otherwise for your sake."

"It is of no matter," he muttered, disappointment darkening his tone. "I have seen cities before."

They started back to their tents and were met on the way by

one of the khan's yellow-robed body servants. "Come with me," he ordered.

Haven knew better than to ask why, so she and Giles merely fell into step behind the man as he led them to the king's tent. "Wait here," he said, disappearing behind the door flap, only to reappear a moment later bearing two cloth bundles: one white, one red. "Your festive garments," he said, passing the white bundle to Giles. The red one he handed to Haven, saying, "You will wear them for the celebration."

Haven thanked him and asked, "Are we to join the khan?"

"You are to be included in the khan's retinue." The servant looked them up and down, then said, "Clean yourselves and return here when you are properly dressed."

The servant retreated into the tent once more, and Giles, eyebrows raised, looked a question at Haven. "He says we are to dress for the celebration in these clothes," she explained, indicating the bundles. "For some reason we are expected to put them on now."

They retired to their respective tents where they stripped, washed, and dressed themselves in their festive clothes. Giles' robe was fine linen, much better quality than the wool one he wore most days; Haven's was silk and also finely made. Both garments had wide, richly embroidered belts of contrasting colour, and both came with new shoes made of felt embroidered with tiny beads. Arrayed in their festive robes, they returned to the khan's tent to see what was expected of them.

By the time they reached the tent, the chief advisor was waiting for them with a sour look on his face. He made quick work of examining them, adjusted their belts, and then pronounced them ready.

"For what purpose are we ready, Petar?"

"You are ready to proceed to the feast," he replied. "Wait here."

"But the feast is not until tomorrow," Haven pointed out, keeping her tone light. "Do you mean for us to stand here all day?"

"Tomorrow for the people," he told her. Just then, the tent flap opened and out stepped the khan's hulking bodyguard, now encased in newly burnished mail and carrying a long pike tied with streaming pennants. The warrior greeted Petar with a grunt and moved aside as Khan Simeon emerged from the tent behind him.

The khan, resplendent in silk and satin, fairly glittered in the noonday sun. He wore a simple tunic and trousers—the clothing favoured by Bulgar horsemen—but of spotless purple, belted with a wide, handsome sash made of cloth of gold. Over his tunic he wore a sleeveless coat woven with so many golden threads that he glistened like water as he moved. On his head he wore a circlet embellished with rubies and pearls, and on his feet were boots of soft black leather studded with black pearls and tiny beads of gold. In his hand he carried a slender rod topped by a wrought-iron eagle with spread wings. Behind him came his body servants, dressed in bright orange tunics with tall-crowned rimless hats of red felt. Taking up positions around the khan, the servants raised a canopy of blue silk, the poles of which were long spears decorated with pennants.

As soon as the canopy was stretched above his head, Khan Simeon struck the ground with the end of the iron rod and the procession started off. At a gesture from Petar, Haven and Giles fell into step behind the chief advisor. They moved through the camp; people came running to watch their triumphant king pass by, cheering him on his way. At the camp's edge, a division of warriors on horseback fell into line, bringing up the rear, and drummers joined the train. The great thumping beat of their drums stifled all other sound, so that it seemed as if their king came striding into the city on peals of thunder.

"I believe we are to see the city after all," surmised Giles, leaning close to make himself heard over the rolling boom of the drums.

Haven took his hand and gave it a squeeze. "I should not be surprised if we see the emperor himself!"

CHAPTER 6

In Which the Wheels of Justice Grind

Rudolf, King of Bohemia and Hungary, Archduke of Austria and King of the Romans, tapped his long fingers impatiently on the arms of his favourite throne and waited for the battle to commence. The first of the multitude of irritations he would combat that day was just now coming his way over the polished floor of his audience chamber. This particular annoyance took the form of his Minister for Domestic Affairs, an effete, bloodless noodle of a man with a manner so self-effacing as to render him all but invisible.

"Well? What have we today, Knoblauch? Eh? What is that paper you have in your hand?" Rudolf frowned a truly regal frown of displeasure. He had been kept waiting for nearly five minutes! At this rate, he could not hope to finish his appointments until midafternoon. "Speak, man! We beg you."

"Sire," replied Herr Knoblauch, pausing to offer a low, courtly bow, "it has come to the attention of the ministry that there is a man in gaol claiming to be a friend of this court."

"Is that so?" demanded the emperor. "If we had our way, half the court should be locked up without delay!"

"Indeed, my great king," intoned the minister smoothly. "This man is demanding to be released in your name."

"The infernal impudence!" snapped Rudolf. "Who is this bold fellow?"

The minister glanced at the scrap of paper in his hand. "He appears to be a foreigner, sire—an English gentleman by the name of Burleigh, Lord Archelaeus Burleigh, entitled as the Earl of Sutherland, or some such place."

"A nobleman?"

"So it would appear. Do you know him, Majesty?"

"Burleigh? Burleigh?" Rudolf rummaged around in his memory. "We cannot place the scoundrel."

The diffident courtier consulted his brief once more and said, "Lord High Alchemist Bazalgette's name was mentioned in some regard, I believe."

"Bazalgette!" cried Rudolf. "Why are you standing there? Summon Bazalgette at once, and let us get to the bottom of this affair before it devours the whole day!"

"At once, Majesty." Knoblauch bowed and beat a rapid retreat.

The emperor endured another interval of waiting while the chief alchemist was summoned from his sanctum and brought to the audience chamber. In a rush of dark green velvet, Balthazar Bazalgette swept into the room, his tall blue hat askew and his golden sash half knotted in his hurry to obey the summons. At the foot of the throne, he stopped and bowed, then stood blinking and breathless. "I am sorry if I have kept you waiting, my great king."

"Yes, yes." Rudolf waved aside the apology. "See here! What do you know of a man named Burleigh—a foreigner, by all accounts, who has got himself locked up by the magistrate?"

"This is the first I have heard of the matter, sire," replied Bazalgette. "But the man himself is known to me, yes. May I learn the nature of your inquiry?"

The emperor flicked a finger at his minister, who had followed the alchemist into the room. "Tell him, Knoblauch."

"This man Burleigh has been arrested and imprisoned in the Rathaus gaol," answered the minister. "He is demanding release in the name of the emperor."

Bazalgette's notoriously bushy eyebrows bristled and bunched with concern. "And the substance of his crime, Herr Knoblauch?" he asked.

"Affray, I believe, and causing grievous bodily harm." The minister examined his paper, adding, "Through assault and battery."

"Upon my word," gasped the alchemist. "That is most upsetting."

"This villain is known to you?" said the emperor.

"He is, yes, Highness. By your leave, sire, I might venture to suggest that he is known to Your Majesty as well. You met him once or twice when he came to court on business."

Rudolf's eyes narrowed suspiciously. "What business?"

Bazalgette blinked innocently at his unhappy patron and friend. "Why, the little devices, sire." He held up his ink-stained fingers to describe a roughly oval shape. "Made of brass . . . the size of a swan's egg . . ." At the emperor's deepening frown, his voice trailed off. ". . . for use in astral travel?"

"Astral travel?" roared the King of the Romans. "We know nothing of this astral travel." He turned his gaze on his minister. "Do we, Knoblauch?"

"No, sire," the minister assured him smugly. "We do not know a thing about it whatsoever."

"B-but, sire," sputtered Bazalgette. "It was with your express approval that we made the devices for Lord Burleigh's experiments. Shadow Lamps, I believe they are called—or so I am informed."

"Shadow Lamps," huffed Rudolf. "Ridiculous name."

"To be sure, Majesty. At all events, we were positively assured that this project had Your Majesty's highest endorsement and unbridled enthusiasm."

"Ah! Who assured you of this?"

"Well, *he* did," confessed Bazalgette meekly, beginning to see the error of his ways. "The earl told me in no uncertain terms that Your Highness wished to keep the venture a strict and confidential secret, lest others steal a march on us, so to speak." He thrust out his hands imploringly. "We were confident of your full and unreserved support in this . . . as in so many other things."

"He lied to you, Bazalgette. Lied!" shouted the emperor, his voice ringing through the hall and down the corridor. "The rascal lied!"

The Lord High Alchemist hung his head. "I see it now. We were most callously used and betrayed by a base villain." He brightened again almost at once. "Locked up, you say?" he asked, turning to the minister. "For assault and battery?"

"And affray," added Knoblauch. "Do not forget affray."

"To be sure. May I enquire whom Burleigh has assaulted and battered?"

The minister consulted his paper for a moment, his lips moving silently. "A cruel and vicious attack was made upon a worthy citizen by the name of Engelbert Stiffelbeam."

"We do not believe we know the man, do we?" wondered Rudolf.

"I fear I must beg Your Majesty's pardon once again," said Bazalgette, "but I rather believe this man *is* known to you—very well known indeed. He is the baker who owns the Grand Imperial Kaffeehaus in the Old Square. You granted him a royal warrant for the supply of strudel to the royal table."

"The baker with the divine pastries!" cried Rudolf. "Why must everyone speak in riddles? Of course! We know Stiffelbeam and his strudel, and set great store by his kaffee. Why, the man is a very angel of the oven."

"Oh, he is, sire. He is, indeed," agreed Bazalgette warmly.

"Herr Knoblauch, we must have some of Stiffelbeam's Grand Imperial strudel at the soonest opportunity. See to it."

The minister bowed low. "It shall be done, sire."

"Was he hurt, Majesty? The baker, I mean—was he badly hurt in the assault?" asked Bazalgette. "It would be a very great shame if injury prevented him from fulfilling his baking duties."

Rudolf II looked to his minister, who, in anticipation of the question, was already referring to his brief. "The extent of Stiffelbeam's injuries is not specified, sire." He read a little more. "Still, I can tell you that Herr Arnostovi—a Jew of some prominence and good repute in the city—caught Burleigh in the act and raised the alarum." He read a little more, then added, "The earl and his men were caught at the lower gate trying to flee the city in order to escape their crimes."

"Men?" wondered the emperor. "There were men involved?"

"Yes, sire. It appears Lord Burleigh had four men with him."

"A gang of cutthroats, no doubt," muttered the emperor.

Indignant now, he drew himself up in his throne. "See here! We will not tolerate this outrage! We have been lied to, and the sovereignty of our court has been violated, our goodwill traduced—"

"Our trust betrayed," offered Bazalgette helpfully.

"—and our imperial trust betrayed by a malicious and deceitful criminal," continued Rudolf, his voice booming as he hit his stride. "A heinous offence has been committed against a valued and worshipful member of our community and a friend of this court. This barbarous act will not stand." He thrust a long finger into the air. "This crime will be punished."

"A very wise decision, if I may say," affirmed Bazalgette, happy to have any residual blame deflected.

Satisfied, his imperial majesty slumped back in his throne. All in all, it had been a good morning's work. He would suspend his court duties for the rest of the day. Seeing that the matter was settled, the Lord High Alchemist begged leave to return to his experiments.

"Yes, you may go with our thanks," Rudolf told him, then looked around at his minister. "Well? What is it, Knoblauch?"

The minister held up the much-consulted paper. "What is Your Majesty's pleasure?"

"We are not pleased in the least, Knoblauch," replied Rudolf, rising from his throne. "We are not pleased at all." Rudolf took two thoughtful steps down to the floor and started for the door.

"Magistrate Richter requires an answer, Your Highness. What shall I tell him?"

"You may tell Magistrate Richter that the rogue Burleigh can stay in prison until he rots."

CHAPTER 7

In Which the Tump Is Not to Be Trusted

Wilhelmina stepped quickly off the rutted lane and into the shadows. She had marked the place where the road dipped below the crest of a long, gradual rise and was momentarily lost from view. When she reached the low spot, she made her move, jumping across the water-filled ditch, worming her way through a bramble-and-hawthorn hedge and into the barley field on the other side.

The feeling that she was being followed had been growing with every passing mile since leaving the Fox and Geese Inn that morning; and now, almost within sight of Black Mixen Tump, the impression had grown too strong to ignore. Once inside the sheltering hedgerow, she found a place where she could watch the road without being seen and settled back to see whether her fears would be confirmed.

The day was fresh and dry, if a bit blustery, and she had time to kill—unfortunately, the ley portal atop the tump would not be active until sunset, and that was a few hours away. If she could just stay out of sight until then, Wilhelmina figured she had an even chance of getting back to where she should be. With that goal in mind, she found a place to hunker down and think. What she thought, chiefly, was that dimensional volatility was a real nightmare. Not only was it making everyday reality unpredictable and untrustworthy, it also made tried-and-true ley lines undependable. With every failed attempt, hope for a quick reunion with Kit and Cass dwindled that much more.

Since leaving Damascus, what should have been a straightforward hop-skip-and-jump to Prague had become a series of wildly random translocations. Each leap had become a leap into the unknown. Even though she did not seem to be getting any closer to Prague, at least her latest destination was a place she knew. At the moment, that was the only thing between her and despair.

All this would be so-o-o much easier with a Shadow Lamp, she thought. *This is just like the bad old days.* Funny how one became so quickly dependent on that clever little device. Navigating ley lines and times without it was a real chore; it was like trying to hit a bull's-eye on a moving target hidden among a multitude of near-identical targets . . . blindfolded.

She was still lamenting the demise of the gizmo when she heard voices out on the track. Staying low, she crept to the edge of her leafy bower and looked out. Three figures had just come over the rise and begun their ascent. One glance told her all she needed to know: the long black coats and threatening aspect were a dead giveaway; and if any doubt remained, the presence of the preternaturally large slope-shouldered cat swept it clean away. *Burley Men!* muttered Wilhelmina to herself. *Well, that's just bloody fantastic.*

Now what? Avoiding her pursuers on the road would be child's play next to evading them on the hilltop, where they would be watching for her and waiting to pounce. The top of Black Mixen was flat as a table and almost as bare. Save for three great oak trees, there was no cover, no place to hide. As soon as she showed herself, she was dead meat—literally, if they let Baby off the chain.

Carefully, she withdrew into the shadows once more and found a place in a clump of bracken to lie low until the trio of thugs had passed. Whatever she did, she reckoned it would be more easily done if she kept the Burley Men in front of her; if nothing else, she would not have to be always looking over her shoulder. At least there seemed to be only three of them. Minutes passed, and she heard the voices grow louder by degrees. She flattened herself to the ground, and when they stopped dead even with her position, she froze entirely, hardly daring to breathe. Had the cave cat caught her scent? Straining her ears, she could hear them disputing among themselves but could not make out anything they said. After a tense interval, the trio and their attack lion moved on. The voices diminished slowly, and when Mina could hear them no more, she eased up and stole back to the edge of the road.

She saw only two Burley Men with the young lion . . . What had become of the third? Making an about-face, she scanned the road behind her and caught a glimpse of black coat just as the fellow disappeared from view over the top of the hill—most likely to prevent her doubling back and returning to the town.

This just gets better and better, Mina huffed. *As if I didn't have enough to worry about . . .* She let the thought go and moved back into the barley field, then set off along the hedgerow, pursuing a roughly circular course she hoped would bring her to the tump from the back door, so to speak. The country lane passed by the southern side of the great earthwork; she would approach from the northwest and hope to evade detection.

Working along the hedgerows, she made good progress and, despite her circuitous route, arrived at the ancient mound as the sun touched the tree line to the west. She paused at one of the little clear-running brooks that seamed the Cotswold valleys, unslung her rucksack, and ate a handful of nuts and a bit of dried beef and drank her fill from the stream. Then, removing her boots and socks, she dangled her feet in the water and sat back to keep an eye on the dark hill looming before her.

Black Mixen Tump breathed an air as old as the woods themselves. Certainly, it was an intrusive, almost alien presence in the peaceful, bucolic countryside. The locals held it in superstitious awe, and the peculiar conical mound attracted all sorts of weird and wonderful tales: clocks stopping or running backward in its proximity, animals refusing to graze on its smooth, grassy slopes, dreams disturbed, inexplicable storms, abnormal vapours, people disappearing.

This last one Wilhelmina knew to be true. No mere old wives' tale, it happened. In fact, she was counting on it happening again shortly. She dearly hoped it would happen without complications or company. Ley travel had become difficult enough without interference from Burley Men. In her quest to get to Prague and join Kit and Cass, failure was not an option. She would keep going because she *had* to keep going. The fate of all she held dear depended on it.

These thoughts occupied her until the sun began to sink toward the horizon. From the fields around her she could hear sheep calling and a dog barking. Some farmer was taking in his flock for the night. It was time to be about her business. Pulling on her socks and boots, she set off for the tump.

Moving with all the stealth at her command, Mina started up the steep-angled slope, climbing slowly but steadily. Halfway there she met the little trail that spiralled around from the southerly approach. She crossed it and carried on, stopping only when she came within reach of the summit. Before scrambling up onto the top, she paused and, lying on her stomach, squirmed the rest of the way to peer cautiously over the edge. The flat plateau opened before her. Across the way, lit by the last of the daylight, stood the gnarly knot-bound eminences: the Three Trolls. She gazed at the ancient oaks for a long moment but did not detect any sign of movement around the trunks or among the tangled roots. She even scanned the thick-grown branches, but if any Burley Men were there, they had hidden themselves well.

Perhaps they've gone, she thought. *Good riddance.* But she could not be certain that they, like her, were not merely lurking below the rim of the tump, keeping themselves out of sight. That possibility was confirmed a short time later when, as the first stars appeared in the eastern sky, the first Burley Man emerged. She saw him move out from behind the first Troll on the right and slowly make his way across the hilltop. A moment later Mina felt the familiar prickling on her skin that signalled a live ley line. The portal was open and the Burley Men were ready.

She watched as the thug crossed to the centre of the mound, where he paused a moment, then continued at an angle to her and proceeded to work his way slowly around the outer rim of the plateau. At first she could not make out what he was doing, but as she watched him making a careful circuit of the hilltop, his purpose became clear: he was looking for her!

The Burley Men obviously expected her to appear any moment and were checking the perimeter to see from which direction she might arrive. *Just my luck*, she thought darkly. Still, it would take him a few minutes to make his way around to her. Glancing down the slope behind her, she calculated her position. She would not be able to reach the bottom of the tump before he saw her, but she might reach the trail that spiralled up from the base. If she slid back down the hillside, she might hide in the slight hollow formed by the path as it cut into the side of the mound. In the dim light he might not be able to see her.

It was her only chance. She gave a last look at the Burley Man, and her heart missed a beat. The rogue had stopped, made an about-face, reversed course, and was now headed straight for her.

Think! Think! Think! she told herself. There was no time to slide down the hill, no time to run, no time for anything. She was caught on the exposed side of the hill a scant few feet from the top. He would see her the moment he looked over the edge.

Risking a last furtive glimpse over the edge of the hilltop, Mina marked the Burley Man's stride and distance and then sank back, pressing herself flat against the side of the hill. She held her breath and counted off the paces in her head. Presently, she heard the swish and thump of heavy boots in the long grass. *Thump . . . swish . . . thump . . . swish . . .*

The steps paused. The brute was standing directly above her.

In one swift motion, Mina propelled herself straight up over the edge and grabbed the man's ankle. Already unbalanced, the thug pitched forward. Before he could brace himself, her hand snaked out and snagged his belt. Wilhelmina pulled with all her might. Every last ounce of her strength went into the effort, and the Burley Man was launched into space.

She saw his arms pinwheeling as his body sailed over her and plunged down the side of the hill. His startled yelp was cut short when he hit the ground some distance below and, unable to prevent his descent, began to roll.

Mina did not wait to see what happened next. She scrambled up and over the edge and, without an instant's hesitation, streaked off toward the centre of the mound—marked by a single flat stone—and jumped on it. Standing erect, she raised a fist into the air as if claiming Black Mixen for queen and country. Across the dish-flat plain of the tump she heard a shout. Out from behind the right-most troll appeared the second Burley Man, wielding a dark object in one hand and the end of Baby's chain in the other.

Shouting, he bulled across the distance toward her. "You there!" he cried. "Stop that! Put your hands down!"

Wilhelmina stood her ground.

"Stop that!" he cried, waving the object in his hands. "I'm warning you!"

Mina sensed a thickening in the air and felt static electricity raise the small hairs on her arms and neck. "Come on, come on, come on . . . ," she muttered through clenched teeth.

The Burley Man barrelled closer. "I've got a pistol," he shouted. "I'll shoot you dead."

A hissing sound filled Mina's ears and a cool breeze gusted from nowhere. The rogue sped closer, the cave cat straining on its steel leash. "For the last time, lady—put your hands down . . . now!"

Mina stood with her arm raised high, refusing to budge. A thin, transparent blue shimmer formed in the air above her head. "Come on, come on, come on," she chanted. "Come on, come on, come on . . ."

The wind strengthened, rushing down from unseen heights. The Burley Man raced nearer. "I'll shoot you dead, I will!" he cried.

Statue still, Wilhelmina remained planted on the stone.

"Right!" shouted the rogue. "That's it for you!"

He stopped in his tracks and raised the pistol—an old flintlock contraption with a long barrel and stubby handle. Extending his arm, he lowered the weapon and took aim.

Mina squeezed her eyes shut.

The wild wind shrieked and the air around her sizzled. She heard a metallic click as the Burley Man pulled the trigger, but the powder failed to ignite. He lowered the pistol to cock it again but needed two hands. Baby, straining at the end of the chain, pulled free from his grasp and bounded toward her.

"Hurry up!" Wilhelmina screamed, the wind tearing the words from her mouth. Her limbs grew inexplicably heavy, as if muscles, bones, and sinews had suddenly turned to lead. She struggled to stay upright under the crush.

The Burley Man cocked the pistol and aimed it again. In the same instant, the cave cat gathered its feet and sprang, its lithe, muscular body soaring effortlessly into the air. Mina had a glimpse of fangs and claws sweeping toward her. There was a pop and a fearsome crackle as the pistol charge exploded. She saw smoke and fire spew from the muzzle and heard the crack of thunder.

Everything grew misty and indistinct. The Burley Man appeared to stretch and diminish simultaneously. Light filled her vision, and then everything disappeared in a fizzling pop.

Wilhelmina experienced a sensation of falling; she gulped air, but there was none. For one terrifying instant she thought she would suffocate. Her toes stretched for a foothold in the void. And then the ground came up beneath her feet, and she landed with a jolt that travelled up through her bones from ankles to hips. Both sight and sound returned all at once.

The wind roared, battering her exposed flesh with an icy blast. Her skin was peppered with pellets of ice, and she threw her hands before her face to wait out the incipient storm. But the gale did not cease. It seemed to go on and on, and when Mina peered out from between her fingers, she found herself in a place she had never been before.

All around her the same featureless landscape met her gaze: a blank white wilderness of snow and ice without vegetation or habitation of any kind. The jagged peaks of barren mountains rose in the distance like the blade of a serrated knife. A savage wind sent wandering ropes of snow snaking across a plain of solid ice.

She was freezing cold.

PART TWO

Of Crime and Punishment

CHAPTER 8

In Which Sleep Is Overrated

In Hashimoto, Japan, three school buses containing sixty-seven schoolchildren, their teachers, classroom aides, and bus drivers disappeared on a field trip to Kozuki Park Nature Reserve. The buses, operated by the Wakayam Prefecture Educational Services Co-operative, left the school at 9:30 a.m. on what had become an annual outing. So far as is known, the three vehicles were last seen by several passing motorists on Highway 24 only minutes after leaving the school.

The nine-kilometre trip should have taken no more than twenty minutes. Yet when the school party did not arrive at the designated time, park rangers called the school to enquire whether there had been a change of schedule; they were informed that the children had departed as planned. Fearing an accident, police were called in and a search rapidly mounted. When the first pass failed to locate the three buses, helicopters and additional patrol cars were deployed, along with dog handlers. The entire region was painstakingly combed. The entire Wakayama and Gojo prefectures were put on alert, and the search quickly spread outward into adjoining provinces.

No sign of the buses or their occupants was found, nor was any contact made between those missing and parents or school officials. Their disappearance was troubling—all the more so since, as Principal Kamito Kiyanaka pointed out, "All teachers carried cell phones, and most of the students too. If there had been any difficulty, *someone* would have received a call or text. There would have been multiple calls for help. But we have received no communication at all."

Yet, on a rice farm near Nara-Ken, Japan, three school buses appeared mired up to their wheel-wells in the middle of a rice paddy. The vehicles and their occupants—a number of young children, all dressed in the same peculiar costume, and what appeared to be their adult guardians—were discovered midmorning by field hands arriving for work. The strangers were in a state of extreme confusion and hysteria. Consequently, officials were unable to arrive at a coherent account of what had happened.

No one was able to explain precisely how the large blue vehicles came to be in the paddy field, as the nearest road—an unpaved market track some distance to the north—was unsuitable for motorised vehicles. The mystery was compounded by the fact that, while the strangers appeared to be Japanese, their speech was not readily intelligible to the local, mostly rural population. Linguistic experts posit that the strangers speak an unknown variant of the Shikoku dialect.

Doctors, nurses, and staff administrators beginning their morning shift at the Georgetown Hospital were stunned and alarmed to find that the modern two-story brick-and-glass 450-bed medical facility had been replaced by a single-story clapboard building. Prompt investigation revealed that each of the 150 beds was occupied by a wounded serviceman, most of them either US Air Force or Navy. The patients, many of them officers, maintained that they had received their injuries during ongoing military actions in the Northern Pacific Theatre of Operations. Investigations continue amidst tremendous media attention, but no explanation to date has been offered.

In a somewhat related incident, five TBM Avenger aircraft landed at Up-Park Camp airfield outside Kingston, Jamaica. The planes and their crew were last seen leaving the Naval Air Station at Fort Lauderdale, Florida, for a training mission in low-level bombing. The pilots and their instructor had been in radio contact with the control tower, expressing disorientation and poor visibility, although weather conditions were reported as average for the season. All contact ceased as of 4:00 p.m., and Flight 19 was not heard from again. A thorough and exhaustive search by both surface vessels and aircraft tracing the flight path turned up no wreckage, and no bodies were ever recovered. The official explanation was that the planes were lost due to adverse weather conditions in the Caribbean, although no storms were recorded or reported.

The sudden appearance of the planes and crewmen following a seventy-year absence deepens one of the consuming mysteries of the twenty-first century. Compounding the mystery is the fact that the pilots appear not to have aged a single day and to a man believe the date is still December 5, 1945.

Fifty miles west of Socorro, New Mexico, two visitors were waiting in the small lobby of the Jansky Very Large Array Radio Telescope command centre. One of the men was Gianni Becarria, who, in the estimation of his travelling companion, was exceptional in about twenty different ways. This Tony Clarke had decided after only the second ley jump they had made together. Now, after more than a dozen leaps, Tony was convinced that *exceptional* was too small a word. "Brother Becarria," he said, his tone approaching reverence, "you are a genuine wonder. I cannot imagine what this must be like for you."

Momentarily puzzled, Gianni's brow furrowed. *"Scusami?"*

"Coming here . . . seeing all this . . ." Tony gestured out the observation windows at the radio telescope's array of antennae—twenty-seven enormous, white, track-mounted satellite dishes arranged in a gigantic Y-shaped pattern—spread out across the flat, empty plain of the New Mexico desert. "For you, this is all the future. It must be a continual shock to someone born—what? Over two hundred years ago?"

"But last week I was here," Gianni pointed out.

"Yes—but still. It must take some getting used to."

At last, the Italian priest understood. "We are all of us travellers in time, no?" He smiled. "Some of us travel more rapidly than others, yes, but we all will inhabit the future one day."

"Very true." Tony turned his gaze back to the telescope and the empty desert plain sweltering beneath a crystal-blue cloudless sky. "As to that, you must have an inbuilt future-detector. I would never have believed we could return here less than a week after our first visit." Tony shook his head with admiration. "Pure genius."

"I may have learned a few tricks over the years," the priest cheerfully conceded. Waving a hand at the desktop computer at the receptionist's station, he added, "Though I admit, those machines still perplex me no end."

Tony laughed. On their first visit, Gianni had spent almost an hour chatting with one of the techies who obligingly gave the astronomer priest a crash course in IT 101, explaining computers as one would to a five-year-old. To his credit, the techie did not appear the least perturbed by the priest's questions, nor think it odd that someone like Gianni should demonstrate such ignorance about electronic computational capabilities of the twenty-first century. Come to think about it, Tony concluded, Gianni's clerical collar probably helped; young Kyle was of a generation that did not expect much of priests.

Though he may not have been on the razor edge of computer technology, Gianni's personal computational powers were supremely tuned and extremely accurate. Even including the half-day drive out from Sedona, they had managed to arrive, by Tony's estimation, only six days and seven hours after their last visit, when they had come seeking independent confirmation of what Tony had described as an anomaly in certain calculations that might, if proven, indicate a slowing of cosmic expansion. Now, as they stood at the large picture window in the reception lobby of the Jansky VLA facility waiting for Gianni's guest pass to materialise, Tony had a chance to marvel anew at how fluid time seemed to be when one became a ley traveller.

"They are beautiful," said Tony, watching all twenty-seven of the gargantuan white dishes swivelling in synchronised motion to align themselves to a new trajectory. "It never fails to get the juices flowing."

"Do you think they have had time to conclude the survey we discussed on our previous visit?" wondered Gianni.

"If not, they'll have made a start at least—providing they got the green light from the powers that be." Tony heard voices behind him and turned toward the reception desk. "We'll speak to the OD right away and get a status report."

A young man with a round face fringed in chin whiskers and wearing a green *Gravity Sucks* T-shirt and cargo trousers had just entered the lobby; he hurried over to meet them. "Dr. Clarke?" He held out his hand. "Really sorry to keep you waiting. We just found out you were here. Dr. Segler sent me to bring you up."

"And you are . . . ?"

"Oh, sorry. I'm Jason—third-year graduate assistant. I have to say, this is huge for me—I love your work. Big fan."

"Pleased to meet you, Jason," said Tony, taking the offered hand. "And this is Fra Becarria." The two shook hands and Tony said, "We're anxious to see Dr. Segler, so why don't you lead the way."

"No problem," replied Jason, taking a step backward. At the check-in desk, he paused. "Oh, here. I almost forgot." He handed Gianni a blue nylon lanyard with a plastic tag bearing the word *Visitor* in red letters. Lifting the little aluminium barrier tube at the side of the desk, Jason ushered his charges into the corridor, saying, "I don't know why it always takes so long to get a pass around here. You'd think they had to carve each one out of stone or something."

"Do you still get tourists wandering in over here from Roswell?" wondered Tony.

"Now and then," Jason told him. "Unless there's a convention in town."

"An astronomical convention?" wondered Gianni.

"Nah, a UFO convention. They're up to two or three a year over there these days. You ever been? The place is an absolute riot, man. It's like Mecca for all the LGM hunters who believe aliens routinely visit the planet." He looked to Gianni. "Don't you have UFO freaks over there in Italy?"

"Perhaps," replied Gianni. "Italy has always been a popular tourist destination."

Jason's pleasant face screwed up into a puzzled frown; he could not work out if Gianni was pulling his leg or not. "Cool," he concluded with a shrug. Pushing open a door, he led them up three flights of stairs to the third floor and across a carpeted foyer to a glassed-in office; he knocked once on the door and pushed it open without waiting for a reply. "Here they are," he announced. "Delivered safe and sound."

Jason stepped aside, allowing Tony and Gianni to enter. A man in a crisp white short-sleeved shirt and red bow tie jumped up from behind the desk. "Tony! You're back. Great." He crossed the room with quick strides, holding out his hand to shake. "Good to see you again, Gianni. Welcome."

Before either man could reply, he waved them to seats. "Please, sit down. I'll bring you up to speed. A lot has happened since you were here." To Jason, who was still lingering hopefully by the door, he said, "Thanks, Jaz—get these guys some coffee, please. And one for me."

"Sure thing, chief. I'm on it."

Jason disappeared, and the director of operations turned his attention to his desk, which was heaped with papers and graphs—all of them covered in numbers and diagrams of bewildering incomprehensibility. He pawed through them for a moment, picked up a single page, cleared his throat, and said, "I don't mind telling you, Tony, you've made my cosy little life a nightmare."

"No need to thank me," Tony replied. "That's what friends are for."

"I mean it. I haven't had a decent night's sleep since you let off your bombshell—and I *know* I haven't had a minute's peace. We have every man on board working overtime here, and I've put on extra shifts. This is big stuff. Really big. I hope you're planning on staying around. I could use the extra help."

"Is anything beginning to emerge?"

"Emerge! I'll give you emerge—" He shoved the paper in his hand at Tony. "Just look at this!"

Tony took the page and perused it briefly. "Very interesting," he said, passing it on to Gianni, who studied it intently.

"You *are* kidding, right?" replied Segler. He thrust a finger at the paper in Gianni's hands. "That little bit of *interesting* has the ether vibrating from here to Tokyo. The White House wants to be kept in the loop, and the NSA as well. Ten minutes ago I was informed that we're to expect a delegation from NASA sometime tomorrow, and I don't think they're coming for the fifty-cent tour."

"It might mean a little more to us if you told us what we're looking at," Tony suggested, tapping the page with a finger. "What is this exactly?"

"That, my friend, is the smoking gun."

"Gun?" wondered Gianni aloud.

"Confirmation of the scan completed yesterday—the scan conducted at *your* suggestion, I might add."

"Confirmation," echoed Tony. He glanced at Gianni, who looked over the paper once more and handed it back.

"Correcto-mundo," declared Segler, tossing the page onto the heap once more. "I consider we now have preliminary verification of those initial readings—"

"The anomaly we pointed out," said Tony.

"Yes, verification that the background radiation differential in sector B240-22N altered significantly since close monitoring began."

"So it would not appear to be a system glitch."

Segler was shaking his head. "Not a glitch, not an equipment malfunction, not a mathematical abnormality—nothing like that. Something is definitely happening out there."

"Excuse me, Dr. Segler," said Gianni. "What does your interpretation of the data tell you is happening *out there?*" He lifted his eyebrows toward the ceiling.

"Too early to tell," replied Segler. "What I am saying is that our baseline readings are correct and that the anomaly you brought to our attention has now been confirmed. In the immortal words of Dave downstairs, 'It ain't no freakin' blip.'"

"Then our assumption is essentially correct," concluded Tony. "The technical equipment is not responsible for the data discrepancy."

Segler shook his head. "Nope—not unless three separate telescopes on three separate continents experienced the same technical malfunction simultaneously."

Jason returned with a plastic tray on which were balanced three Styrofoam cups. "I put milk in all of 'em," he said as he handed them around. "I hope that's okay."

"Thanks, Jaz. You can go." The director took a sip of coffee and then shuffled through his papers once more. "Now then—where was I . . . ?"

Jason, hovering by the door and looking hopeful, asked, "Anything else?"

"Yes, find out from Delores when the government guys are due to arrive, and tell Miranda to get guest passes made up now so we don't have them standing around cooling their heels in the lobby half the day."

"No problem, chief. I'm on it." He left, closing the door behind him.

"Okay," said Segler, digging another scrap out of the mass of paper spread before him. "Here's the project schedule for the next forty-eight hours. On the strength of the aforementioned numbers, I've bumped this up to the top of our project list and given it highest priority. Officially, it is project number JA-60922." He handed Tony the schedule. "I've made room for as many sessions as necessary."

Tony glanced at the page. "How long does each pass take?"

"An observation session takes anywhere from two to ten hours—not including calibration," Segler answered. "As you can see, we're in the middle of the ninth session right now. I'm running three shifts to minimise downtime. Weather is not much of a consideration here, so we're able to run flat-out most of the time."

Tony nodded. "I've got to hand it to you, Sam. You seem to have covered all the bases. Who is in charge of data coordination and analysis?"

"We're doing some, of course. The rest is being handled at Cal Tech right now, but I've got calls in to Rudin at Illinois–Urbana and Yeoh at UT–Austin for independent analysis and support. And this morning I put in calls to Puerto Rico, England, and Australia for backup and suggested they might want to mount their own projects. The more heads, the better."

Tony raised his eyebrows. "Is that wise, do you think? Involving so many outsiders at this stage?"

"I'm gunning for nothing short of full corroboration from multiple independent sources," Segler declared flatly. "We're not messing around. Besides, if we're right about all this, we won't be able to keep it under wraps very much longer. There's always the possibility that somebody else will discover it independently. And word is going to spread pretty fast once it gets out." The director took another slug of coffee and stood. "Okay, shall we go see the Desert Rats?"

"I thought you'd never ask," said Tony, getting to his feet.

The three men took the elevator down to a sub-basement level and emerged into a glass booth separating them from a large room crammed floor to ceiling with computer screens of every size—many linked up to form even larger panels. One continuous table formed a sort of ledge that ran around the perimeter of the room with arms poking into the centre; the surface of this ledge was stacked with keyboards and innumerable black boxes with myriad LEDs in blue, red, yellow, and green, all blinking away like Christmas.

A handmade sign taped to the glass door informed visitors that they were entering the domain of the Desert Rats: eight men and six women, the fourteen technical mavens inhabiting the moveable work-stations scattered around the single, large open room.

Segler pushed through the door, and they instantly felt a ten-degree drop in temperature. "Ah, nice and cool. Good for the little grey cells."

Heads swivelled as the newcomers entered, and several of those nearest the door rose to their feet to greet the visitors. Most of those present knew Tony Clarke—by reputation, if not by sight—and several hurried over to shake his hand. "Welcome, Dr. Clarke, it is a pleasure to meet you," said a young man with prematurely grey hair cut short except for a ponytail at the back.

"This is Dr. Leo Dvorak," said Segler. "He is TD for the facility, and he designed the program protocols we're following on the scans. He also acts as floor manager, foreman, and union rep."

"Keeping the rats happy, that's me. I'm sorry I missed you before, but is there anything you'd like me to show you?"

"Gianni cannot seem to get enough of your gear," Tony joked.

Dvorak's eyes lit up. "Then step right this way, Gianni." The technical director took over and proceeded to give his visitors a quick tour of the various stations, introducing the staff, who explained briefly what they were doing. Gianni gazed with unabashed fascination at all the glowing screens with their mesmerising dance of coloured graphs and diagrams, morphing blobs, coloured interference patterns, and blinking spreadsheets; in a state of continual amazement, the priest could only shake his head and murmur, "*Benedicimi*," under his breath.

Tony too was impressed. "What kind of power are you using?" he asked at one point.

"We've got two Cray Zeus-10s linked to a multinode IBM Power8+ server, and that's just for down here," Dvorak told him, sounding pleased as a parent of a prodigy. "You could run the entire Northern Hemisphere from this room. Let's just say we've got all the muscle we need for the job."

"The next session is due to start at eleven," said Dr. Segler. "Are we still on schedule, Leo?"

Dvorak called over to one of his team, who answered with a number expressed as a ratio. The technical director did a quick calculation and looked at his watch. "Yeah, we should make it," he said. "This one runs another six hours. After that we'll recalibrate and start number ten right away. I'm looking forward to that one."

"Why?" wondered Tony. "What is special about scan ten?"

"It's what I call a small bore scan of sector B240-22N," he explained. "We've been getting some interesting numbers from that region, and I'm anxious to see if that represents a trend. If so, that specific region may be our canary in the coal mine." At Gianni's puzzled expression, he explained, "Our early-warning system."

"A moment, please," said Gianni. "Do you suggest that the event we are investigating is not uniformly spread over the cosmic horizon?"

"Doesn't seem to be," replied Leo. "If the preliminary results are anything to go by, it looks pretty lumpy."

"Um, lumpy?"

"As in exhibiting a marked asymmetrical bias—which would be coherent with a category disorder unprecedented since . . ." He paused. "Well, since *ever*. Nothing like this has ever been seen before—"

"Thanks, Leo," said Segler, interrupting. "We'll let you get back to it." He turned and, shepherding his visitors through the glass doors, led them to the elevators and up to his office once more. Gianni thanked him for allowing them to see the data centre and expressed the view that he still found it mind-boggling. Tony, however, wondered why the visit had been curtailed just when it was beginning to get interesting. "I got the feeling we were being hustled out of there," he said. "How come, Sam?"

Segler looked up from below his brows. "Sorry about that, guys. I apologise. It's just that Leo has a tendency to pick up the ball and run—sometimes without waiting to see which direction he should be running."

"But if he's right . . . ," countered Tony.

"If he is right, we'll all know it soon enough. If not, it would be best to refrain from upsetting people unnecessarily, wouldn't you say? Anyway, there's a long way to go before we know for sure what we're dealing with."

"I guess that's what we're here to find out," replied Tony.

"How can we help?" said Gianni. "We put ourselves entirely at your service, Dr. Segler."

"I appreciate that," said the director. "There won't be much happening here until the current session is finished. We have a few hours, so I suggest we go get some dinner and put our feet up for a while. Then we'll come back and hit it fresh later on tonight. Have you got a room yet?"

"Not yet," replied Tony. "I thought we'd just find a motel in Socorro."

"Oh no," said Segler. "You'll do no such thing. You two will stay with me—Linda will be delighted to see you. She's making her *carne asada* tonight and would love some company around the table. But I'm warning you—if I don't get to sleep, then you don't either."

"Sleep is overrated," Tony told him.

"Right." Segler laughed. "Tell me that this time next week."

CHAPTER 9

In Which Contempt Breeds Confrontation

Burleigh heard the now-familiar metallic clank sounding from somewhere down the underground corridor and groaned. *It must be Wednesday*, he thought. Market day: the day when the insufferable German baker brought them food and drink he had purchased in the square. What a fool! His continual meddling made no sense, no sense at all that Burleigh could see—unless, and this was the view Burleigh doggedly maintained, the fat baker nursed an ulterior motive of an extremely subtle and devious kind. That Burleigh lacked evidence for this assertion, and indeed had never been able to discern even the faintest whiff of guile on Stiffelbeam's part, did not matter and was not, ultimately, important. He despised the baker; no other proof was needed.

In a moment, he heard the shuffling slap of shoe leather on the damp stone outside the door, and realising he had been holding his breath in anticipation of the sound, he exhaled and slumped back against the mildewed stonework of the dungeon cell. He closed his eyes and waited for the humiliation to begin anew.

Revenge, reprisal, retaliation—these motives the earl could understand. That the baker would retaliate for the savage beating Burleigh had given him was only natural. It was, after all, exactly what Burleigh would have done in his place. The other theory, sometimes ventured by one or another of the Burley Men, was that Engelbert brought them food for the reason that he said he did: because that was what his Jesus would do. Jesus—who apparently exerted an inordinate influence over His slavish minion—had died preaching love for everyone, including one's enemies. The love of enemies was, to Burleigh's mind, nothing more than an open invitation to be victimised by any and all, not least those self-same enemies. Had not this Jesus been executed precisely for saying such absurdly irrational things? Far better to believe, as Burleigh did, that people only ever behaved in ways that would satisfy some basic desire, whether for power or pleasure or personal gain. Ergo, Engelbert the baker was only seeking to advance some nefarious aim of his own. Bringing food to his tormentors was only a means to an end; Burleigh allowed himself no doubt that the object of the exercise was his complete and utter destruction. That was Burleigh's way. And that was the way of the world.

There were voices outside the cell door, followed in a moment by the click of the lock and a grating whine as the door swung open. As before, as always before, the lumbering oaf stood in the doorway, a little pause before entering. Burleigh raised his eyes to his unwanted visitor. "You again," he intoned in German. "Always you."

"Yes, always me," replied Engelbert, stepping into the cell. The gaoler, who had ceased taking an interest in these visits, closed the door behind him. "I have brought some special things today. The summer sausage is now ready, and many farmers are selling it in the market. I brought one for each of you." He swung the bag off his shoulder, opened it, and proceeded to dig around inside. As he bent to his work, the loathing Burleigh always felt in the baker's presence rose up once more—this time it was so strong and virulent he thought he would vomit. "Your presence sickens me," Burleigh said, his voice thick, almost strangled. "The very sight of you sickens me."

"Perhaps it does," agreed Engelbert affably, "but my absence would soon sicken you much more. I think so, yes."

This produced a snicker from Tav, the only one of his men who had more than a snatch of German. Burleigh whirled on him. "You think that funny? You think that hilarious, do you?"

"No, boss," Tav replied, suddenly solemn. "But why insult him? You want to drive him away?"

"Yeah, boss," agreed Con. "If t'weren't for the baker, we'd ha' starved to death by now. The big lunk's the only reason we're still livin'."

"You call this *living*?" Burleigh shouted.

"Easy, boss," said Con, raising his hands. "Didn't mean nuffin' by it."

Burleigh glared at his two henchmen so hard he thought his eyes might burst. Across the cell, Dex and Mal had risen from their rancid nests; the two said nothing, but it was clear from the looks on their faces that they shared the prevailing sentiment of their mates.

Meanwhile, Etzel pulled the sausages from his bag and began handing them round. "This one for you," he said, passing Con an oblong muslin-wrapped bundle. "And this for you," he said and proceeded to deliver the provisions to each man in turn.

When he got to the earl, Burleigh refused to take the proffered item. After holding it out for a time, the baker simply gave a little shrug and placed the sausage at His Lordship's feet. "You will enjoy this later, I think." He then turned and continued unloading the bag of food. There was bread in dense, dark hemispheres, cheese in pale, flattened globes, a few bunches of carrots and celery, small jugs of beer, knobs of butter, and handfuls of hard biscuits from the Grande Imperial's larder. All this he stacked carefully on the folded sack and then announced, "Summer is good this year. The crops are growing. We will be having apples and pears soon, and blackberries, vegetables, and new cheese. I will bring them as soon as I can."

"No," Burleigh told him, stepping forward. "Do not come here again. I do not want your food . . . your good works. Do you hear? I do not want anything from you!"

At the sound of raised voices, the indolent turnkey shoved open the door and poked his head into the cell. "What is happening here?"

"Get out!" Burleigh screamed. "Get out, do you hear? Get out and never come back."

The gaoler took a step into the cell. "Etzel, is all well?"

"All is well," Engelbert assured him. "I am just leaving."

As he stepped to the door, Tav moved to intercept him. "Pay him no mind, sir. Boss is . . . ah . . ." He fumbled for the German word. "He's sick, see. He don't mean what he says."

"Tav!" shouted Burleigh. "What are you doing? How dare you apologise for me!" Burleigh surged forward. "I am your master, you dog. Shut your fat gob and get away from him!"

"Boss, it ain't his fault. Fella's only trying to help," said Tav, putting up his hands and edging away.

"Ease off, boss." Con moved to interpose himself between Burleigh and Engelbert. "Calm down. He don't mean nuffin' by it."

"Calm down!" roared Burleigh. He balled his fist and swung hard at Con, striking him on the side of the head. Con took the blow and staggered backward. "You presume to tell *me* to calm down?"

Burleigh, blind with fury, bulled past Con, who tried to hold him back. The earl shook him off with another blow and reached for Tav. The gaoler, stepping in, shoved him roughly aside and, pushing Engelbert out of the cell, quickly slammed the door in Burleigh's face. "Never come back!" shouted Burleigh in a voice of strangled rage. "You hear me? Never!"

The footsteps retreated down the corridor, and Burleigh, strength and anger spent, slumped against the door and slid to the floor. Tav bent near to help him to his feet. "Get away from me, traitor!" snarled Burleigh. "Leave me alone. All of you just leave me alone!"

Later that day he got his wish when his men, his very own Burley Men, were removed from the cell and taken to another part of the dungeon. He heard their footsteps recede down the corridor, followed by the creak and slam of a door farther on. He would not see them again.

In the days to follow, Burleigh's unreasoning rage subsided and he had plenty of time in the solitary silence of his cell to think. He told himself that his anger was warranted. It was nothing more than a reaction against the frustration of his present situation—though, in thinking long and hard about it, he could not seem to account for this mysterious sense of unfairness that he felt. Whatever its source, it was this keenly felt sense of injustice that had triggered his outburst. He concluded that his native tolerance had reached its limit and he had lashed out.

This explanation satisfied him and allowed him to sleep at night. However, as explanations go, it proved insufficiently robust. For as the sting of the incident receded, he began to grow hungry and, though he resisted the temptation for as long as he could, need eventually overcame his resolve, and he allowed himself to eat from the allotment of food that Engelbert had provided. While he was gnawing on his bread and sausage, the notion occurred to him that injustice alone was not a sufficient cause for his anger. While his persistent feeling that he was being treated unfairly may have been a contributing factor, the provocation, the root cause of his rage, went far deeper.

Ordinarily, his thoughts were of an angry, retaliatory nature, enflamed by a seething sense of injustice at the callous unconcern exhibited by a bunch of dim-witted, officious lackeys in the service of a legal system that allowed such deplorable treatment of its detainees. This led him into a meandering meditation on the nature of fairness and why he should feel the sting of injustice so acutely in his present circumstances. After all, he was a man who had chosen to live his life outside the bounds of righteousness, beyond the commonly accepted norms of fair play, if not moral rectitude. Yet feel the lash of unfairness he did. And it hurt. Moreover, the prick of injustice produced a slow-simmering anger and a hunger for a benevolence, a pardon, a deliverance he knew in his inmost heart that he did not deserve.

Still, as often as he told himself that he had no right to expect anything but the pitiless indifference of an ultimately heartless universe, the rage and hurt he felt could not be denied. Nor was it lost on him that he, who had so often shown this same pitiless indifference to the plight of his victims, had no reasonable right to rage against it now. He did rage, however; and he did suffer the hurt.

He hurt. There was no denying that. Yet, try as he might, Burleigh could not fathom how he had acquired this gritty, unrelenting insistence that he was owed something better than what the random workings of a coldly impersonal, chance-driven universe had allotted him.

CHAPTER 10

In Which Panic Is Postponed

Blasted by the icy wind and blinded by sleet, Wilhelmina threw her arms around her chest and tried to work out what had gone wrong. The portal had saved her life, probably, but had deposited her on a glacier in the middle of a blizzard in some place known only to God alone, and in a condition for which she was wholly unprepared. The wild gale ripped through her clothes; she had only minutes to figure out a survival plan before the cold began to steal the life from her warm body.

Then she heard a muffled growl. She turned warily. Baby had made the leap with her. Her stomach tightened at the sight of the cave lion crouched in the snow behind her, ready to spring.

Outrunning the creature would be pointless, and fighting it was out of the question: the enormous cat weighed four times as much as she did. What was not muscle was teeth and claws. Mina had no weapons . . . What now? Shivering, she stared at the cave cat, and the cave cat stared back with baleful yellow eyes. However, something about the young lion's posture—its feet under its body and oversized head tucked back against its massive shoulders—gave Wilhelmina a glimmer of hope.

"Oh, Baby," she said, keeping her voice low. "What's the matter, old thing? Are you cold?"

The cat continued to stare.

"I'm cold too." Mina took a slow, deliberate step closer to the crouching cat. "Maybe we can keep each other warm." She took another step and extended an open hand. "What do you think? Shall we keep each other warm?"

The lion's ears flattened to its head and it spat a savage hiss, just like a threatened tabby that knows it has wandered into the wrong garden.

"No need to get stroppy. Everything's going to be all right." The big cat hissed and then spun in place and leapt away. "Then again, maybe not," sighed Wilhelmina.

She watched the frightened animal streak away over the snow-driven ice, its chain trailing along behind, clinking as it went. The creature was soon lost in the snow haze kicked up by the blizzard. Oddly, Mina felt more vulnerable than ever; she definitely felt more alone. The shriek of the wind howling through icy heights mocked the hopelessness of her situation. Tears of cold and desperation welled in her eyes and froze on her cheeks.

"Get a grip, Mina," she muttered, mostly just to hear the sound of her own voice above the howling gale. "You can panic later. Right now you've got work to do."

She cast a quick look around. The mountains in the distance presented an extremely familiar profile; she had the distinct impression that she had seen them before . . . maybe many times before, though, half obscured by blowing snow and freezing fog, she could not say where. There was no time to wonder about this; likely she would freeze to death before solving the mystery. Continuing her survey, she examined the surface of the glacier, looking for any signs of ley activity. She circled the area, spiralling out in an ever-widening radius, keeping her eyes on the wind-scoured ice. The surface of the glacier was glare ice—deep blue with flecks of green and grey. Snow drifted here and there in restless streams, unable to find purchase on the surface of ice and hardpack.

Mina saw a crevice that looked promising, but it was merely a crack, not a ley line, and it petered out after a few dozen paces. Colder now, shaking uncontrollably, she resumed her circling, growing more desperate with every step.

Time was running out. She could not feel her toes or fingers anymore, ice stuck to her hair and eyelashes, and she was shivering so ferociously that standing upright was becoming difficult. Even if there was a ley line nearby, she concluded gloomily, she would not be able to see it.

The thought jolted her. She did not *have* to see it; she might be able to feel it. Returning quickly to where she had started, she stretched out her hands. They were so numb and shaking so violently, she despaired of feeling anything at all, not least the subtle tingle of ley energy.

"Oh, please," she gasped, "don't let me die like this. Please, God."

With that prayer on her lips, she crisscrossed the area where she had landed and saw a small pool of water in a slight, bowl-shaped indentation in the ice. The pool, little more than a large puddle, was quickly scumming over, turning to slush, but that it was there at all was, Mina decided, remarkable given the subzero temperature. *This has got to be it*, she concluded. *Please, God, let this be the spot.*

Extending a frozen hand over the slushy pool, she felt nothing to indicate ley activity. Her slender hope vanished in the scream of the wind. She stared at the dull water and wondered if this would be the last sight she saw. Doubled over in a futile effort to conserve the little warmth she had left, she stared at the pool.

Something was keeping that puddle from freezing . . .

With difficulty, Mina straightened and stepped into the puddle. As cold as she was, the water was even colder—but not as cold as it should have been. She felt like a prize idiot. Was it not enough to be stranded on a glacier freezing to death, now she had to go and jump in a puddle?

The thought brought a smile to her face. She put back her head and laughed, but it was not a happy sound. It was the sound of someone beginning to become muddled and punchy with the cold—a sure sign of hypothermia. She had read that somewhere . . . in a magazine? Or was it a book? It seemed very important to recall the source . . . but . . . *What am I doing?*

Wilhelmina dragged her raddled thoughts together and, standing in ice water up to her shins, she raised a shaking fist into the air. At first nothing happened, but since she had no better plan, she decided she would persist until her last breath—which would not be long in coming.

Quaking with killing cold, her eyelids almost frozen shut, Wilhelmina stood in the icy pool and held herself upright. The grey-white world around her grew muzzy and indistinct. The numbness in her feet had moved steadily up her legs and thighs. Consciousness slipped away, and yet somehow she still stood. The world around her faded, and she sank into the ice water and down.

But she did not stop. She continued sinking—down and down,

through the ice, deeper and deeper still. In her confused state, Wilhelmina imagined that a crevasse had opened up and swallowed her, taking her down to a cave of ice that would be her tomb.

That she did not feel the glacial walls sliding past, bumping her, jostling her, failed to register in her awareness at all. It was not until her stiff and unfeeling feet struck bottom that she felt even the least sensation—though for one brief moment everything went black—and then she thumped down with a shock strong enough to rouse her faltering brain from its stupor.

She landed at the bottom of her descent in a heap and lay where she had fallen. Curiously, it seemed brighter here . . . and warmer. No doubt everyone who froze to death imagined what they craved as their internal organs shut down. Past caring, she simply lay for a time, luxuriating in the light and warmth. Some little time later, it occurred to Mina that the sunlight burning her skin was real and not a hallucination conjured by a dying brain.

Opening her eye, she looked up and saw a long and familiar double row of sphinxes lining an avenue of broken stone: Egypt.

The momentary shock was swiftly swallowed in a rush of relief. She rolled onto her back and gazed up at the bright, empty blue sky and breathed a heartfelt thanks. "I owe You one," she said. "And I won't forget."

Exhausted, she lay until she finally felt strong enough to get up and confront her new environment. She was not out of the woods yet by any means. The Nile was still some distance away, and she had a barren rocky spine of hills to cross. With a smidge of luck, however, she might just reach the little riverside village by dusk. Gathering her strength, she climbed to her feet and, with slightly faltering steps, started down the avenue. As she was passing beneath the vacant stare of the crouching sphinxes on their pedestals, an idea occurred to her: since she was in Egypt, maybe she could find Thomas Young. He had helped her before, and she could definitely do with some help right now.

Just thinking about making contact with the good doctor put Wilhelmina in a better frame of mind—more hopeful than at any time since fleeing Damascus. Her more buoyant mood carried her up and over the arid hills. The climb made her desperately thirsty, but the sight of the green Nile in the distance promised all the water she could want if she just kept putting one foot in front of the other. Finally, just after dusk, she reached the thin, beaten earth trail leading to the village. She had just started down the track when she heard a whistle behind her and, turning around, saw a man in a donkey cart about to overtake her. She smiled and waved, but remained standing in the middle of the track.

"*Sala'am alaykum*," she called, still smiling.

The driver gave her a quick once-over and flicked the donkey with the lash. The donkey picked up its pace and the wagon creaked by without stopping. Wilhelmina sighed and resumed her walk, albeit with a slightly slower pace. It was dark by the time she reached the village; the last light had long since faded in the west and her mouth was so dry she could not spit. She made straight for the well in the wide space that served as the village square, pushed off the wicker cover, and dropped in the leather bucket. She was filling the gourd attached by a cord to the rim of the well when three men and most of the village dogs and a few of its children approached. She called a greeting and, lifting the gourd to her lips, let the cool water pour down her throat. She drank it all and then refilled the gourd. The men watched her, muttering among themselves, and the children, emboldened by their elders' presence, crept near to touch her. Her thirst satisfied, she emptied the bucket back into the well and, replacing the cover, put her hands together, bowed to the men, and said, "*Shukran.*"

Then, accompanied by four or five of the town's scruffy dogs, she made her way down to the river. Hungry and bone-weary, she was happy to plop down on the riverbank. Later, when she had rested, she would stir herself and go in search of food. Stone steps led from the top of the bank to the water's edge. Removing her boots, she sat on a lower step and put her feet in the water. Little by little, twilight spilled across the deep Egyptian sky. Bats appeared, dive-bombing the river to skim up insects. The scent of jasmine wafted on the breeze, along with the smell of fried spices—coriander, cumin, and garlic. A feeling of deep gratitude and contentment stole over her as she sat and watched the water sliding silently away.

Wilhelmina was summoned from her reverie by the sound of music.

Who would be playing the radio? she wondered, then remembered that in this remote place a radio was unlikely. A record player? Equally unlikely; there was no electricity. The music persisted, growing louder. *Where is that coming from?* Mina looked around for the source of the sound. Oddly, there were lights on in some of the houses on the square behind her—and not the dull, flickering glow of oil lamps, candles, and rushlights she was used to seeing in this place.

Determined to get to the bottom of this conundrum, she put on her shoes and stood, and as she turned she saw lights out on the river—big lights and lots of them. What was more, the music seemed to be coming from the river itself. As the lights on the water drifted closer, she realised they belonged to a boat, and a large one; and the music emanated from the boat.

The boat cruised slowly closer until it seemed to fill the river. Wilhelmina stood aghast as a river cruiser the size of a small hotel churned past, dance music blaring. People in dinner dress lined the rails, some with cocktails in their hands; they waved and raised toasts to her as they passed. *Mina, this is not the Egypt you thought it was,* she thought as she read the banner on the side of the boat: *Suntours Nile Cruises.*

Her hopes of finding Thomas Young deflated like a worn-out tyre. *Girl, you've got to go back and start all over again.*

CHAPTER 11

In Which Wilhelmina Closes a Cosmic Loop

Wiping grit from her eyes, Wilhelmina watched as the dust devils raised by the gust that accompanied her arrival swept down the Avenue of Sphinxes. Tired as she was, the prospect of spending the night alone in the desert suited her down to the ground. So long as there were no jackals around, she reckoned she would be all right. With that in mind, she shouldered her simple cloth pack and strode off toward the now-familiar hills. "Once more into the breach," she sighed, and after a swig from the waterskin hanging from a strap on her shoulder, she started for the eastern hills.

Her return to Egypt had necessitated a return to Black Mixen Tump first, and Wilhelmina had taken the opportunity to acquire a few provisions before setting off again. This time, at least, there were no Burley Men on her tail to make life difficult; it had become, she reflected gloomily, plenty difficult enough already.

The sun had set by the time she reached the foot of the trail. Halfway up, she spied a sheltered hollow and decided that was as good a place as any to spend the night. As the fast-fading sunset shaded off into a crystalline desert twilight, Mina picked her way among the ragged boulders and fallen rocks to the place she had spied from below. After kicking over loose stones to check for scorpions and spiders, she pulled off her pack and dug out a little food and water and her blue pashmina to serve as a blanket; a desert night would be chilly, but her stony nook would hold heat for a long time and she would be on the move again at dawn. Thus, curled into her rocky nook, she spread her pashmina and made herself cosy for the night.

For a time she just sat and watched the last light ebb as darkness flowed over the flatlands west of the Nile. The early stars shone with pinpoint brightness and clarity and were soon followed by legions of other, lesser lights, until the entire sky was awash in a spray of pale blue light. The land seemed to sink beneath a soothing balm; harsh desert angles eased, the hard edges softened in the gentle light. After the trauma of the last few days, the quiet of the desert hills calmed Wilhelmina's troubled spirit. Lying back, watching the slow-wheeling motion of the glowing heavens, she felt the ageless peace of the unchanging land seep into her soul. *This is how it has been forever*, she thought and, staring up at the glowing heavens, wondered, *Can it really be ending?*

If Tony and Gianni were right, those heavenly lamps shining so brightly would soon begin to wink out, extinguished in the greatest cataclysm of destruction this world or any other had ever witnessed. Somewhere out there—beyond the edge of vision, or even comprehension—the ever-expanding frontier of the universe was grinding to a halt, and soon the contraction would begin. The end result would be an all-consuming darkness, an insatiable void devouring space and time, destroying all light, energy, and matter, and the annihilation of the entire created order . . . the End of Everything.

Against that, what could she or anyone else do?

Night gathered in around her, and Wilhelmina ate a little from her supplies and drank some water. The bone-weary fatigue she had been fighting overpowered her then, and pulling the pashmina under her chin, she lay back against the powdery stone and gave herself up to a strange sleep of peculiar dreams populated by people from her past, but involving absurd and irrational chores. In one sequence, she was still at work in Giovanni's Rustic Italian Bakery; she had just opened the kitchen and seen a stack of orders for the day. The first order called for cream of onion soup. Thinking someone had made a mistake, she went on to the next, which called for two boxes of mackerel and a crate of lobsters. The next order called for a dozen sympathy wreaths. As she was standing there with the orders in her hand, her boss walked in and demanded why she was not baking. "We have all these orders to fill," he told her. "Get busy!"

"I can't," she complained. "It's impossible!"

Whereupon the dream morphed into a sequence in which she was being chased by a pack of large black dogs over a beach of glass beads beside a raging sea; she was wearing an old-fashioned bathing suit that had a frilly skirt and matching cap, and the wind kept blowing foam from the agitated sea into her face so that she could not see where she was going. She could hear the dogs getting closer and then felt a sharp pain in her feet. Looking down, she saw that the glass beads had become broken shards and her bare feet were being ripped to bloody shreds. But she knew that if she stopped running, the dogs would kill her.

Whereupon the dream changed again; this time she was asleep in bed in her old London apartment and was awakened by voices in the room with her. She could not make out what they were saying, but somehow knew that they were talking about her. The voices belonged to at least three people, and she realised that they were standing over her. She knew she had to get up and run away, but did not dare move a muscle or the people would know she was awake. So she pretended to be asleep and hoped they would go away . . .

But they did not go away. Wilhelmina opened her eyes and, with a shock, saw that she was lying in a hollow in the Egyptian desert and the people were real. Starting up, it took her a moment to understand that the voices were not near at all; the sound was drifting up the hillside from out on the plain below. Looking down, she saw men with camels and donkeys outlined in the pale moonlight. They were, she decided, either farmers heading to market or Bedouin tribesmen travelling by night to avoid the heat of the day. Hunkered down in her hiding place, she did not think they would see her if she remained very still. She watched until they vanished into the night once more, then closed her eyes and slept fitfully until morning.

When she woke again, the sun was just rising, a great disc of muddy red, lighting a hazy eastern sky. She took a swig of water and ate a handful of nuts and dried apricots, then climbed down from her roost and made her way once more over the white hills and into the verdant valley and the tiny riverside village, itching with anxiety over what she would find when she arrived. Would she again be very far off the mark in a village with modern conveniences and a Nile River awash in tour boats? Owing to the increasingly traumatic difficulty of ley navigation, the prospect of seeing a shipload of tourists filled Wilhelmina with horror. *Please let me be right this once,* she prayed.

Happily, that prayer seemed to have been answered. She entered the village and was greeted by the usual gaggle of children and dogs—with nary a tourist or electrical appliance in sight. She stopped for a drink at the well and a refill of her waterskin, and arranged passage across the river with some boys in a tippy fishing boat. Then, as the day was getting on, she proceeded directly to the fold in the hills and the hidden gorge, passing quickly around the tumbled rock at the foot of the hill and into a cool, dim passage now much in shadow. High walls of water-sculpted stone closed in on either hand, looming over her, but the path along the wadi floor remained level and easy underfoot.

Deeper into the gorge, the motionless air was damp with a whiff of minerals and wet sand. The only sound to be heard was the light crunching of her boots in the loose gravel of the wadi floor. The shadows deepened as the sun lost strength and altitude. The shifting light gave greater definition to the all-surrounding stone; the individual colour bands of layered rock glowed in subtle shades of red and orange and bone. Every now and then she heard the single call of an unseen bird high up in the rocks; otherwise she was completely alone.

Or at least she thought she had the place to herself, until she heard the stuttering rattle of a tired, old gas-fired engine pinging along the sinuous corridor of undulating stone. She stopped to listen: whatever was making that sound was coming her way. Unwilling to be seen without knowing whom she might encounter, Mina scanned the wadi round about, searching for someplace to hide. A few dozen yards up ahead she saw what appeared to be a narrow cleft in the smooth rock walls.

She made a run for it, reached the crevice, and wormed her way into it just as a rackety old flatbed truck hove into view. The vehicle drew closer. Wilhelmina pressed herself as deep into the crevice as she could and held her breath, praying she would not be seen. A moment later the truck rumbled past her hiding place. As it passed, she caught sight of the driver and passenger in the front seat. The glimpse was quick, but it was enough. The man sitting in the front passenger seat was Archelaeus Burleigh.

A fleeting glimpse of the rogue was enough to cause her heart to skip a beat. She stifled a gasp and pulled her head back, pressing herself into the rock crevice as far as she could go. She closed her eyes and held perfectly still until she could no longer hear the rattle of the truck. Only then did she dare to risk another look. She poked her head from her hiding place and saw nothing but a fine haze of dust to mark his passing.

Mina breathed a sigh of relief and started down the wadi again. She took but four steps and halted. If Burleigh was in a truck, she reasoned, then clearly she had failed to hit her time target yet again. If not half-stuck in the embrace of stone, she might have collapsed into the gravel and dust and wept at the utter futility of it. As it was, a few frustrated tears welled up and spilled over her lids. *Why is this so hard?*

In the arid desert air, the tears dried on her cheeks almost instantly. Damp-eyed, she turned around and, already aching with exhaustion, started back the way she had come, intending to return to the river village and the Avenue of Sphinxes and start over yet again. Then she had a thought that brought her up short: the vile creep Burleigh was up to something. His presence in the same place she was searching was no coincidence. Mina decided she had to know what he and his goon squad were doing there. Her rendezvous with Kit and Cass would have to wait a little longer.

She started down the winding ravine once more and soon came to the first of a long series of niches carved into the soft stone of the canyon wall. Shrines, she thought; they were too small to be tombs or burial sites. Some were more elaborate than others, featuring plinths and pedestals, lintels decorated with vines or flowers carved into the rock; many had words chiselled on them, but most were too weather-worn to make out, and those she could read were in a language she did not know. All the niches were empty—whether plundered or simply awaiting the next offering, she could not say.

The lesser niches gave way to larger ones and then, dead ahead, she saw a great temple-like façade carved into the ruddy stone of a facing wall. A few dozen paces later, Wilhelmina stepped out into a wide, natural bowl formed by the conjunction of two smaller channels joining the main branch. The place was eerily familiar; and it was not merely Kit's repeated description that made it so. There was an intangible something else, something almost dreamlike. Wilhelmina glanced quickly around, looking both ways up and down the connecting channels. Nothing but rock walls and rubble met her gaze. But in the wider channel there were signs of recent activity: tracks and wheel marks and whatnot in the gravel, a discarded water can, empty tins, scraps of this and that, a bit of frayed rope—the leavings of Burleigh and his crew, no doubt.

"Hello?" she called, and heard her voice pinging off the rocks round about. "Anybody here?"

She crossed to the imposing red stone temple and put her head in through the door. It was dark and cool inside, but empty; the sand that had drifted over the threshold had not been disturbed. She turned around and called again, "Is anybody here? . . . Anybody?"

Silence. The airy, empty hush of the desert was the only reply.

Retreating from the temple entrance, she turned and saw an opening at the base of the curtain wall a little way down the connecting channel. She walked to it and discovered a rectangular hole with steps leading down to an underground chamber. "Well, well, well," she murmured. "What have we here?"

Without a second thought, she started down and reached a small vestibule leading onto a much larger room beyond. These chambers were hollowed out of the living rock of the wadi, and upon stepping through the hand-hewn arch, Mina was overcome with an uncanny sense of déjà vu—more powerful and more vivid than she had ever experienced. The feeling made her almost dizzy, and she reached out to steady herself against the stone lintel. Her hand brushed against something cold: a large steel key hanging on a nail driven into the stone. Without quite knowing why, she took the key and then paused, waiting for the queasiness to pass. As she stood there, it occurred to her that in a way she really had been here before. Kit had told her about it. They had been sitting outside Gianni's observatory taking in the sun and talking about adventures in ley leaping. Kit had described being rescued by her—an act she did not remember having performed. Yet here she was now, key in hand . . .

Mina took a step into the second, larger chamber; it was dark, but enough light slanted down from the steps and glanced off the floor to faintly illuminate the walls, revealing faded murals depicting Egyptian life. The room, so far as she could tell, was empty. She moved to the far end of the chamber toward what she felt certain she would find there: a rusty iron grate covering another, smaller rectangular opening knocked through the back wall of the tomb . . . and there it was.

A few steps from this barred grate, a voice called out, "Burleigh! Let us out. Killing us makes no sense. This is madness! Let us out."

Mina halted. The voice was Kit's, no mistake. But she hesitated.

Was it the same Kit she knew, or another one? Did it matter? *This is doing my head in*, she decided. Anyway, there was nothing for it now but to play out whatever drama was taking place. She fixed a smile firmly to her face and moved closer to the grate.

"Burleigh!" shouted Kit again. "Do you hear me?"

"Kit? Are you in there?"

Silence.

"Kit? You there?"

"Wilhelmina!"

She moved nearer the iron door. "Had enough of Burleigh's hospitality?" she asked.

"Mina, I can't believe it," said Kit, almost breathless with relief. "What are you doing here?"

"Well, I guess I've come to break you out."

She produced the key and put it in the lock. The words came to her without thinking—as if she were rehearsing lines from a play, as if she were going through motions preordained.

"Mina! Mina, listen—I've been trying to find you. I never abandoned you—you've got to believe me. I didn't know where you were, or how to reach you. Cosimo went back for you, but you weren't there, so we asked Sir Henry to help. That's what all this is about—trying to find you."

"And here I am, finding you," she said. Kit's words had the echo of a lost conversation; she knew what he was going to say and what her reply should be. "We'd better hurry. We don't have much time."

"But how—?"

Giles put his head around the corner. "Sir?"

"Oh, Giles, step up here. This is my dear friend, Wilhelmina Klug," he said. "Mina, Giles Standfast."

"Glad to meet you, Giles," said Wilhelmina, uncertain whether she and the sturdy, solemn-faced young man had met before.

"An unexpected pleasure, my lady," replied Giles.

Wilhelmina jostled the key in the lock again, gave it a strong twist, and managed to produce a loud click. She pulled and the heavy iron grate swung open, releasing the two captives. Kit stepped into the vestibule and took Wilhelmina into his arms briefly, then stepped back as if slapped, suddenly awkward. Something had passed between them—she felt it too, but could not tell what it was.

"Thank you, Mina," he said and reached for her hand, gripping it tightly.

"Entirely my pleasure," she said, still trying to fathom what had happened just then. She stepped away. "Well, I think we'd best be on our way."

"I'm sorry," Kit said. "About losing you, getting everyone mixed up in this . . . I'm sorry about everything."

Kit—*this* Kit—seemed to have no idea what they had been through together. "Don't be sorry for a minute," she told him. "Honestly, it was the best thing that ever happened to me." Had she said that before? She started for the stone staircase. Kit hesitated. She turned back. "Anything wrong?"

"Yes. It's Cosimo and Sir Henry—they're dead," Kit replied; he half turned to the room behind him. "We can't just abandon them— walk away as if nothing happened."

"Oh." Mina stood in the dim light of the chamber for a moment, gazing through the open grate and into the darkened tomb beyond. "I know." She moved back, took his hand, and squeezed it. "I'm sorry, Kit—I truly am. But I'm afraid that if we don't leave now we may very well end up joining them." She nodded toward the black void beyond the grate. "I don't see there's anything we can do for them now. We have to go."

Kit regarded her, but still hesitated.

"Look at it this way," she continued. "What better resting place than a royal tomb?"

Giles stepped up next to Kit and put his hand on his shoulder. "Your friend is right, sir. The gentlemen are beyond our help, and it avails us nothing to remain here. 'Let the dead bury the dead'—so it is written, is it not?"

"I suppose," allowed Kit. "But it just doesn't seem right."

"No," Mina replied with some vehemence, "it is *not* right. There is a lot about this we will probably never understand—I know I never will. But if we go now, there may be a chance we can come back and make it right." She paused. Where did that notion come from? Was it even true?

In any case, Kit seemed to accept her reasoning. "Okay, Mina," he conceded. "You lead the way."

I'm doing the best I can, Wilhelmina thought to herself and led them from the tomb. By the time she had climbed the stairs and stepped into the heat and light of the wadi, she knew what she had to do. There was no way she would allow herself to become caught up in the progression of events for whatever alternate time or dimension Kit and Giles inhabited. Who knew where that would lead? She would see them on their way and then, as she seemed destined to ping-pong through Egyptian history, she would continue her self-imposed mission to find Thomas Young.

CHAPTER 12

In Which a Match Is Made

They snaked through the brambles along the riverside to the trail-head and started up the path to the Big Valley Ley, Kit leading the way with Cass at his heels. They had spent a rough night in the rock shelter above the river, had risen early, and were heading back to the ley line to—they hoped—meet up with Wilhelmina. Morning mist clung to the steep cliff face and flowed across portions of the path itself; water dripped from the rock ledges above, splattering on the gravel and oozing into the thick-grown moss. The sky grew lighter as they went, and the air warmer as the sun gained strength and altitude. Upon reaching the neat pile of rocks that marked the spot where the ley terminated, Kit stretched out his hand.

Cass regarded the narrow track with lips pursed in a dubious expression. "Feel anything?"

Kit shook his head. "Not yet. We're on time."

Cass had gathered blackberries from bramble thickets along the river; she carried them in a water lily leaf. She sat down, opened the leaf, and started to eat. "What do we do if Mina doesn't show up?"

Kit sat down beside her and helped himself to a handful of berries. "I've been thinking about that," he said, popping a few of the ripe purple fruit into his mouth. "We could head back to Prague and wait for her there—and we should if she doesn't turn up soon—but I'd rather give it another day at least."

"And if she doesn't turn up this morning?"

Kit rubbed his stubbly jaw. "We'll go on up to the yew tree and see what we can see. To be honest, I think we've got as much as we're going to get out of that tree. I mean, it's beginning to feel like a fool's errand."

They ate from their packs and talked, and the sun rose above the canyon rim. From time to time, Kit checked to see if the ley line was active, and at one point reported that he did feel the tickle of static on his skin. They waited, but Mina did not appear; and when at last the ley activity began to dwindle and eventually cease, Kit climbed to his feet and said, "Well, we did our part. We can try again this evening. Let's head up to the tree."

"I've got a better idea. Take me to that cave."

"That cave?"

"The one with the paintings you told me about. I'd love to see it."

"Okay, sure, why not?" Kit agreed after a moment's thought. "The tree isn't going anywhere. We can check it out later." He started back down the trail. "Have you still got that handkerchief?"

"The one with the smudge? Yeah, I've still got it. Why?"

"You'll find out."

They descended the trail in silence. The sounds of the forest grew loud around them, punctuated by the soft crunch of their feet on the loose gravel of the path. Upon reaching the floor of the gorge, Kit led them downriver, walking easily along the rock-lined bank. Cass picked berries on the way, and Kit forged the trail, keeping a wary watch for jackals, wolves, or bears. His survival skills revived with every step. It was, he decided, like riding the proverbial bike: once learned, never forgotten. All he needed was a little practice and he was back in form.

"Keep your eyes peeled for clamshells along the bank here," he told Cass at one point. "Bears and other beasts eat clams and leave the empties. We'll need a couple of good-sized shells."

"Dare I ask what for?"

"Torches," replied Kit. "The Hall of Extinct Beasts is a fair distance into the cave. We'll need some light to get there."

"And the clamshells will help us how?"

"Tools for gathering pitch."

"Pitch—from pine trees? That should be fairly easy to get—this place is lousy with pine trees."

They continued along the riverbank, pausing now and then to retrieve a clamshell or two from the water's edge; at one place they found a cache of a dozen or more discarded shells. "Otters," said Kit, surveying the detritus. Many of the shells were broken, but some were whole and suitable for the purpose. They rinsed off the sand and mud from the shells and moved on, following the river as it wound around the foot of a towering limestone bluff. Turning the corner, they came upon a small herd of buffalo—seven adults and five young ones—drinking in the shallows formed by the suddenly widening stream.

"*Bison bonasus giganticus!*" Cass exclaimed. "Amazing."

"Well spotted."

"I've seen them before—as bones. They're related to the modern

European bison." She fell into step behind Kit as he started working his way around the herd; the bison had now seen them and were
watching the humans warily. "I think they're more aggressive too."

"Just don't get between a mother and her calf. That's a lesson I
learned the hard way." Giving the creatures a wide berth, they continued slowly around the river bend. "Up there." Kit pointed to a stand of
tall pine trees a few hundred yards ahead. "That looks a likely place."

Upon reaching the pine grove, they made a quick search among
the trees. Kit scanned the slender trunks from the ground to the upper
branches for places where the bark had been damaged—maybe by an
animal or a branch breaking off—some injury to the outer trunk that
caused the sap to leak out. The first few trees were young and unblem-
ished, but several were older, larger, battle-scarred veterans with broken
branches and damaged limbs; one tree had a big gash where some
animal—an elk, most likely—had used it for a scratching post—and
the raw wound was oozing sap; some had coagulated into trails of pale
yellow resin that collected like wax dripping from a candle.

"Just what we're looking for," Kit told her. "We do it like this."
Taking a clamshell, he began using the sharp edge to scoop the sap
off the tree, breaking off the hardened chunks and scraping the rest
into an unbroken half shell.

Meanwhile, Cass busied herself searching among the other trees
in the stand and soon called out, "Hey! I think I found the mother
lode." She pointed up toward the upper boughs. "Up there—a big
glob ripe for the taking."

About two meters up the trunk a large limb had been torn off, and
the raw stump had been bleeding pinesap ever since. The stuff had
formed a sticky lump the size of a large grapefruit. "Good work," Kit
told her. "Now to get it down." He gauged the girth of the tree and

the height of the lowest branch. "I'm not going to be able to reach that," he said, "and the trunk is too big to get my arms around."

"Give me a boost," suggested Cass. She took a clamshell, and Kit cupped his hands, took her foot, and lifted her up the side of the tree. "Perfect," she called down, placing her other foot on his shoulder for balance. "Now just hold steady." She hacked at the agglomeration of dried resin, breaking off chunks into one shell after another, handing them down as she filled them. "You okay down there?" she asked, scraping away at the goopy mass.

"Take your time," said Kit, leaning into the strain. "I could do this all day."

"How very chivalrous."

"That's my middle name."

She laughed and, for the moment, felt the tension of the last days dissipate a little. After a few more passes with the scraper, she announced, "There! Finished."

With Cass back on the ground, Kit lined up the filled shells at the base of the tree and gathered a pile of dry twigs and sticks and larger chunks of pine bark. He then constructed a little platform made of sticks and small stones that he had arranged in a horseshoe shape, and proceeded to kindle a fire using the flint and steel from his pack. He fed pine needles into the mix and coaxed the tiny flame to take hold. Using embers from the fire, he melted lumps of pitch in the clamshells and coated reeds gathered from the riverside to make the torches. Cass took one sniff of the acrid fumes and said, "My, there's a fragrance you don't smell very often."

By the time the pitch had given out, Kit had three rushes with blobs of black sticky gunk on the end. "Well, that's that," he said. "Let's go caving."

He led the way farther downriver until they came in sight of a rock wall rising from the valley floor. "There it is," he said, pointing to an oval-shaped hole a few metres up from the base of the stone curtain. "That's the cave entrance. You go up first. I'll light a torch and hand it up to you."

As with the tree, Kit hefted Cass up the steep side of the cliff wall; she secured a handhold and Kit lifted her higher up the rock face until she could pull herself into the mouth of the cave. He handed two unlit reeds to her, then busied himself for a few minutes kindling the remaining torch from the embers he had brought with them. Once the pitch took flame, he carefully passed the lighted reed to her and, with a last glance at the sun, which had just passed midday, scrambled up into the cave himself. "Okay, no time to dally. We'll have to zip along."

Torch held high, he led them deeper into the cave and into hollows and chambers large and small connected to one another by narrow passages—some so tight they could but scrape along sideways, and others wide enough to have accommodated a double-decker bus. Kit, mindful of the time limit imposed by the torch in his hand, chivvied Cass along at a pace little short of reckless. When they reached a long, roughly rectangular room, he pulled up abruptly and announced, "Behold! I give you the Hall of Extinct Beasts."

Stepping close to the near wall, Kit lifted his torch to reveal a primitive but delightfully evocative rendering of a rhinoceros in red and brown ochre. Beside it a black hump-backed bison protected its mewling calf while, on the wall opposite, two tawny, spindle-legged antelope cavorted before a bear standing at bay, its great arms spread and killing claws extended. The walls on both sides of the passage were filled with animals: fat little horses with spiky manes, a long-horned aurochs being chased by wolves, an imposing elk with a magnificent crown of antlers, more horses, a shaggy red mammoth with a looming head and long, questing trunk, oxen, and even a herd of curly-horned sheep.

"*Un*-believable!" breathed Cass in a reverent whisper.

"Watch this," Kit told her, and holding the torch close, he moved the flickering light slowly along the smooth surface of the cavern wall. The painted creatures appeared to move; the quivering light lent life to the long-frozen animals and they lived again.

"I wonder who did this," she said. "Who painted them?"

"I know exactly who painted them—some of them, at least." Kit pointed to a picture of a bear. "I was here when this one was begun and . . ." His voice faltered at the memory. That was the last time he ever saw his friends.

Cass put her face close to the surface of the painting. "You actually saw them paint this?"

"Most of them were already here," he explained. "The hunters came to paint more animals, I think—or maybe to finish some they had started earlier. But I saw them mixing their paint and making their brushes. I saw them set to work."

"Unbelievable," Cass said again.

"That's not all," said Kit. "This way—just along here . . . somewhere." He moved farther down the gallery and came to a section containing a display not of animals, but of abstract symbols. And there, down low on the adjacent wall, a collection of smaller cyphers—more complex and more precisely drawn, and very, very familiar. "Ever seen these before?"

Cass caught a glimpse in the flickering light and her mouth dropped open. "Incredible." She pressed nearer and crouched down to look at the enigmatic spirals and whorls with their transecting lines and dots. "They're the ones in Gianni's photos."

"The very ones," confirmed Kit. He held the torch a little nearer and looked more closely himself. "Only . . ."

"Only what?"

"I don't remember seeing that many." He passed the burning reed along the wall. "There seem to be more of them now."

"Meaning what?" asked Cass. "Someone has been adding to them since you were here?"

"Maybe." Before Kit could say more, the burning reed started to hiss and sputter. "Quick! Give me another torch." Taking the proffered reed, he held the pitch-covered tip to the dying flame. "Come on . . . come on . . . ," he coaxed. Just as the last flicker died, the new torch sputtered to life.

"That was close," said Cass.

"Too right." He held out his hand. "Let's have that handkerchief."

Cass fished the square of cloth from her pocket and carefully unfolded it before passing it to Kit. He held the cloth against the wall and began moving down the little row of painted symbols until he came to one he recognised. "This is it," he said, handing the torch to Cass. Spreading the cloth, he held it flat to the wall beside the symbol.

"It's a perfect match," said Cass, moving the torch closer.

"Identical twins," remarked Kit.

"Did you know this one was here?"

"Just a hunch. These same symbols are on the Skin Map, and everywhere else." He indicated the small dotted spiral on the wall. "This one probably is too."

"But how did it get here?"

"More to the point," said Kit, "how did that same symbol get on the handkerchief?"

Cass bent her head close to the wall and studied the painted symbol and the faint, dusty image on the square of cloth. Kit watched; he could almost see the gears spinning in her head. Eyes glinting in the firelight, she turned her face to him and asked, "Know anything about quantum entanglement?"

"Let's pretend I don't."

"Well, briefly, any atomic particle that has ever interacted with another atomic particle becomes forever entangled—or connected. Scientists have known about this for years. They've documented it on the quantum level and now they're even able to trace entanglement in larger objects, not just particles and atoms."

"You say the darndest things, Cass."

"Yeah, well, this is Dad's specialty, not mine. But I grew up with this stuff. Anyway, the point is anything that has ever been in contact is connected," Cass continued. "Which, when you think about it, is pretty much everything that has ever existed. If you care to trace it back far enough, back to the Big Bang and everything that followed, all matter in the universe is entangled—connected in some way."

With these words, Kit again sensed the flash of revelation he had been granted in the vision of the smashing teapot. "Everything is connected," he murmured. "Right—so . . . what's that mean, exactly?"

"Well, maybe—and this is just a guess—the rare earth atoms in the Shadow Lamps interacted with the energy of the yew tree—it's pretty fierce, right? So when your lamps burned out, the rare earth particles encoded that particular pattern."

"Assuming all that is true," said Kit, beginning to grasp the chain of events, "how on earth did the symbol get on the cloth in the first place? I don't get it."

Cass returned to her scrutiny of the cloth. "Ever see a bird fly into a plate glass window? One of the labs where I worked had a sliding glass door, and pigeons were forever bashing into it. When that happens, the bird leaves a faint, dusty shadow of itself on the glass. Sometimes you can even trace individual feathers. It's a two-dimensional representation of a bird crash imprinted on the glass."

"So what we see as a symbol on the cloth is a record of the crash."

"Right," she said. "If Dad were here, he'd say that the image on the cloth is a two-dimensional representation of the electromagnetic force field that created it."

"Like an outline of the bird caught in mid-flight. Okay, but the thing is—the rare earth on the cloth came from Gustavus, remember. That powder was never anywhere *near* the yew tree."

"But *you* were," Cass countered. "You were holding the Shadow Lamp when it blew out. Also, don't forget that the ruined lamp was in direct contact with the cloth while I was working on it. That's probably how the connection was made." She traced a symbol on the stone wall with a fingertip. "It doesn't take much, but I'm guessing that any event strong enough to melt your Shadow Lamps was strong enough to entangle everything in the vicinity both then and subsequently. You were there, and that was enough."

"*I'm* entangled?"

Cass smiled at Kit's shocked expression. "We all are, pal. There's no way around it. We're all entangled with everything from cradle to grave—and beyond." She regarded Kit hopefully. "Does that help?"

"I don't know," replied Kit. "Really, I don't know."

"Me neither—but it's something to think about."

At that moment, the second torch began hissing. "New torch, quick," said Kit. He quickly kindled the last torch from the dying flame of the other and said, "We'd better start back while we still have some light."

The words were no sooner out of his mouth than the newly lit torch flared, sputtered, and expired in a fizzling puff of smoke. Kit waved the still-smouldering wand in a vain attempt to rekindle the flame. Cass watched the small red glow waver, shrink, and finally blink out.

"No-o-o," she moaned. A tendril of panic squirmed through her gut as darkness as thick and dense as the stone mountain around them crashed down so fast and heavy it seemed to suck the very air out of her lungs.

"What do we do now?" Her voice jumped a register. "Kit? What are we going to do? We're trapped!"

"Calm down," he soothed. "I got us in here, I'll get us out. Trust me."

"But what if it's happening again? What if—"

"Get a grip, Cass. It's not a reality blip. It's only a torch that's gone out." He stretched a hand toward her voice. "Here, give me your hand." He felt her fingers fumble and grab, then catch as she slid her hand into his. "Take a deep breath. We are not in a hurry," he told her firmly. "We hurry and we get hurt. We go slow and we stay safe. Okay? One foot in front of the other. That's all we have to do."

Slowly, laboriously, like blind Siamese twins, they made their way back through the impenetrable darkness of the cave. Each and every faltering step had to be negotiated; each and every metre gained took on the quality of a minor victory. Kit did what he could to keep the mood upbeat by telling stories of his years with River City Clan. He told how he had been caught in a game trap by Dardok and how the clan took him in; he described being attacked by a bear and how he had been saved by the clansmen coming to his rescue by throwing rocks to drive the animal away; he described meeting En-Ul, and how the Ancient One taught him to communicate using a kind of sixth sense the clansmen possessed; he told about building the Bone House with the young hunters and then being invited inside to attend the Old One while he slept . . .

Kit might have gone on telling his stories, but he glimpsed a faint sheen coating the rock walls up ahead, and a few metres later they were standing in the forechamber of the cave looking out at a late-afternoon sky. After the suffocating darkness of the cave, the pale yellow sky seemed a scintillating display of light.

"Hallelujah!" gasped Cass, relief making her voice tremble. Her jaw ached, and she realised she had been grinding her teeth. She closed her eyes and breathed a silent, *Thank You, God*, then turned to Kit and hugged him tight. "Well done, Kit. You did it."

"We both did it." He puffed out his cheeks and exhaled a long sigh, then inhaled fresh air deep into his lungs. "But that was a little close."

They stepped to the cave opening and looked out at the river and gorge now falling into shadow. "What do we do now?" asked Cass.

"Back to the ley line—and let's hope Wilhelmina is waiting for us."

CHAPTER 13

In Which Persimmons Are the Bitterest Fruit

Emperor Leo stood beneath a sky-blue canopy waiting for the arrival of his guests. Beside him stood his young wife, Empress Zoë—on her head a golden diadem, on her face a scowl that could have curdled milk. Her smooth brows lowered, her eyes squinted into thin, malicious slits; she was the very image of a woman forced to do something very much against her will and determined that the rest of the world should feel her displeasure. Around the royal couple clustered a bevy of court officials, priests, and assorted noblemen; a phalanx of *scholari* spilled across the plaza. These last wore silver-plated armour, highly polished and gleaming in the sun; their weapons, also ceremonial, were nevertheless sharp and functional.

The conquering khan and his entourage entered the narrow street leading to the Bronze Gate. The drummers at the front of the procession quickened their tempo. The booming sound reverberated off the walls all around, the echoes multiplying until it sounded as if an army of ten thousand had conquered the city. The Byzantines lined the street and leaned from the upper windows and balconies of the nearby buildings to see the procession pass. There were no signs of welcome—no rain of rose water and flower petals, no festive garlands, no cheering, no waving. Instead, the dark-eyed citizens of the capital watched with a sullen, cautious wariness.

"They are doubting of the khan," Haven observed to Giles, leaning close to make herself heard over the tumult of the drums.

"They have little reason to love him, I warrant," Giles replied. "Nor do I blame them. No one likes to lose a war."

As the conquerors moved toward the entrance to the palace yard, the jeering began—a few shouts at first, mere noises drowned by the thundering drums. When this failed to stir any response from the invaders, the more aggressive onlookers began throwing horse dung; eggs and rotten fruit followed, sailing over the heads of the crowd to smash into the visiting delegation. Khan Simeon took no notice of the growing commotion; fully regal from crown to foot, he was above such petty disturbances, though his soldiers marked who the troublemakers were and what they were doing.

All might yet have ended well if it had ended there, but it did not.

Upon reaching the Bronze Gate, a gang of young protestors broke from cover and, armed with rotting fruit, proceeded to pelt the khan and his body servants with the stinking, slimy missiles at closer range; many found their mark among those in the forward ranks, but the insult was ignored.

Then Khan Simeon was struck. An overripe persimmon arced through the air, striking the side of his face and exploding in a crimson splash. The king stopped, turned around, glimpsed the perpetrators scuttling away in hasty retreat, and slowly resumed his triumphal march. The regal khan came to stand before the emperor, his face dripping, his fine clothes besmeared with foul-smelling muck.

Emperor Leo, aghast that this should happen and fearful of toppling the delicately balanced peace they had negotiated, flicked a silent command to the captain of the *scholari*, and six soldiers broke rank and raced away. Turning to the khan, he bowed his head and the two exchanged words. The empress, mortified, her face white with embarrassment, fairly quivered with rage. The entire plaza seemed to hold its breath and tremble.

No sooner had they vanished through the open Bronze Gate than the *scholari* returned, dragging two of the dissenters with them. Even from a distance Haven could see that the youths were dressed in paupers' rags. Barefoot, dishevelled, and dirty, they were clearly part of the rabble that had so rudely greeted the conquering khan. The two—brothers by the look of them—were hauled kicking and scratching into the plaza and thrust down at the feet of the emperor, held there by two soldiers.

"They are little more than boys," observed Haven, dread creeping over her.

"Young they may be," agreed Giles, "but unthinking fools all the same."

Leo pointed at the two cowering before him and asked Khan Simeon a question. Simeon nodded in response, then beckoned his lumbering giant of a champion to him. There was a flurry of activity in the ranks of the *scholari*, and after a moment a soldier appeared bearing a battle ax. At the emperor's nod, the soldier presented the weapon to Simeon's bodyguard, who took it, hefted it, swung it a few times, then barked an order to the two guards holding the boys.

The first boy was dragged forward, forced onto his knees, and bent double. One soldier held the boy's hands gripped tightly behind his back and another took a handful of hair and pulled his head forward, stretching out the lad's neck. The youth began writhing and wailing, pleading for his life. The khan's bodyguard took up a position a little to one side and lofted the ax.

"Dear God in Heaven!" gasped Haven. "They mean to kill him before our very eyes!" Seizing Giles by the arm, she urged him forward. "We cannot stand aside and watch this. We must do something."

Haven leapt forward with Giles at her shoulder. Together they pushed through the khan's courtiers; before anyone could reach out to prevent them, Haven threw herself upon the sobbing boy, and Giles placed himself between the boy and his ax-wielding executioner.

"*Desisto! Desisto!*" Haven cried. "Stop! For the love of God, please stop."

The emperor stepped back in surprise, and the khan, frowning mightily, stooped and took her roughly by the arm. "Wait! Wait but a moment, my lord," said Haven.

"What do you mean by this?" demanded Simeon. "Come away from there. Come away before you are hurt."

Two of his bodyguards put hands on Giles to pull him away. Giles resisted, clinging to the boy.

"A moment, my lord. Hear me, I beg you."

Khan Simeon glanced at the emperor, who merely stood looking on, unwilling to intervene. Simeon released Haven and straightened. "Speak."

"Would you tarnish the lustre of this day with the blood of this unfortunate? If you cannot spare this wretch's life, then spare a thought for your majesty and honour, my lord."

Poor though the Latin might have been, the words had an effect on the khan. He turned to the soldiers who had managed to wrest Giles away from the condemned boy. "Release him," he commanded. They did as they were told, and Giles resumed his stand over the boy once more.

"My lord, any low thug may steal a life, but it is only the truly powerful who can restore it," Haven continued, rising slowly to stand before him. "Are you not mightier than this ragged street ruffian? Show yourself greater than those who would belittle you. Let your strength unite with mercy, that your glory may shine the brighter."

Khan Simeon understood the logic of Haven's intercession and hesitated. Silence descended over the crowd; both Byzantines and Bulgars stood with breath abated, waiting to see what the king would decide. Simeon inclined his head in a slight bow of acceptance. He stepped forward and took the boy by the arm and raised him to his feet. "A cloth," he said, holding out his hand. Empress Zoë removed her girdle, a length of peerless brocaded cloth worked in emerald green and azure; she passed it to the king, who handed it to the boy.

Then, kneeling before the quivering miscreant, the Great Khan said simply, "Clean me."

The lad, still shaking and snivelling, began dabbing at the stain on the kneeling monarch's head and shoulder. But the boy was shaking so badly, he could hardly make his hand obey. Patiently, the Great Khan of the Bulgar took the young fellow's hand in his own and wiped away the filth.

When the royal visage and robes had been restored, Simeon rose and, retrieving the brocaded cloth, carefully folded it lengthwise and, stooping, tied it around the lad's waist as a belt to his stained and ratty tunic. Turning to the second boy, the king summoned him to stand beside the other. They stood together, frightened still, but with hope beginning to rise in their grubby young faces. Simeon placed his hands, one on each shoulder, and regarded them with a stern but fatherly look. "Go now—and think on what has happened here today. While you are thinking, remember that your lives were forfeit for your transgression, but this woman"—he indicated Haven standing to one side—"interceded for you and appealed to a higher law. Rejoice that your lives have been saved today, and remember this next time you are tempted to sin."

Releasing the boys, he commanded two of his bodyguards to usher them from the imperial precinct. He then bowed to the emperor and thanked Leo for allowing him to render judgement in this matter.

"That was well done," Leo told him. "Let it be a sign and a touchstone for our two houses—that the path of mercy and compassion is ever before us. We have but to choose it. It would be well to remember this always."

The only person who remained unhappy with the outcome of the incident was Empress Zoë, who had lost a highly prized piece of her wardrobe. But the khan, quick to guess the meaning behind the frosty expression on her elegant face, gallantly removed his golden sash and presented it to her in replacement of her emerald girdle. Considering the value of the sash, she came out of the exchange much the richer.

Relations between the two warring monarchs became much freer and more open, Haven considered. She and Giles fell back to their places, and it seemed as if the incident would be forgotten as the celebration commenced and the royal retinues of both monarchs moved to the palace where the festivities would be held in the *Accubita*, the great Hall of the Nineteen Couches. Some little time later, however, as the guests were sitting down to eat the first of the twenty or so courses they would be served throughout the day and deep into the night, Emperor Leo, feeling friendlier toward his former adversary, leaned close and asked, "That woman of your retinue—the one who spoke with such passion for those street ruffians—whose is she?"

Khan Simeon glanced down among the lower tables where the lesser-ranking members of his party were seated. "Her?" said Simeon, though there was only one person in the entire hall the emperor could have meant. "She is a foreigner—a wayward traveller it would seem— she and her stalwart companion."

"They are not of your people?" wondered Leo, holding up his cup to be filled. The best wine of the empire flowed through the emperor's vats, and he did not stint.

"No, indeed, Lord Emperor, they are not," replied Simeon. The liberal application of sweet, dark Greek wine was making him expansive and generous of spirit. "Lost in the southern plains when we came upon them—no food, water, nothing. Very strange."

"I have never seen anyone like her for spirit," observed Leo. "The man with her seems able too."

"They tell me they are of the Saxon race from the Isle of Prytannia," Simeon explained. "Have you heard of this place?"

"It is known to me." Leo regarded Haven from his couch at the high table. "A very striking creature, to be sure. I wonder if all her kind are possessed of such noble bearing."

Discerning the hint hidden in these words, Simeon pointed out, "We have yet to discuss the arrangements for fosterage and the exchange of chattels and hostages. Allow me to offer a token of goodwill for our pending negotiations." Nodding toward where Haven and Giles were sitting, he said, "Imperial Majesty, please accept the Saxon foreigners as a gift and pledge toward the present peace and future harmony of our kingdoms."

CHAPTER 14

In Which Justice Must Be Seen to Be Served

There was a knock on the door, and the magistrate's secretary put his head into the room. "I am sorry to disturb you, Herr Richter."

"What is it, Pavel?" asked the magistrate without bothering to look up from the papers in his hand.

"It is that man—he is here again."

"Which man, Pavel? More specificity is expected in this office."

"The baker," replied the secretary. "The one from the kaffeehaus on the square."

The chief magistrate felt his heart sink. "Oh, him." He raised his head and glanced at his secretary. "What is it now—six times he has been here? Seven?"

"Nine, Herr Richter. This is the ninth time he has asked to see you."

"Well, send him away." He snapped the papers in his hand with a flick of his fingers. "Can you not see that I am busy? Tell him to go away."

"Of course, Chief Magistrate," replied Pavel. "I will certainly do as you command."

The magistrate returned to his reading, but his clerk remained wedged in the door. The one day of the week when the office was open to public petition was always a nuisance, one inconvenience after another. Today, it appeared, would be no different. "Yes, Pavel?" sighed Richter. "Am I never to get anything done?"

"A thought, merely," replied the secretary. "Far be it from me to tell the chief magistrate how to conduct his affairs—"

"Get on with it, man," demanded Richter. "What is it?"

The clerk stepped farther into the oak-panelled office with its shelves of books and sheaves of papers and scrolls bound in red ribbon. "It simply occurred to me that if, perhaps, you would agree to see him this once, then he might be persuaded to, as you say, go away."

"This has occurred to you?" wondered the magistrate.

"Indeed, Herr Richter. See him—it is all you need do."

The chief magistrate sighed again, more heavily, and tossed the papers onto his enormous black desk. "Oh, very well, Pavel. I will see him. But he must wait his turn. Who is next?"

The secretary frowned. "No one, Herr Richter."

"No one?"

"The baker is the only one to come today."

Richter puffed out his cheeks. "Humph! Well, then let us be done with him for once and all."

"A wise decision, Chief Magistrate. I will send him in directly."

Herr Richter trimmed the wick on his candle and arranged his features in his most forbidding aspect. A moment later the door opened to admit his persistent visitor—a large, well-fed fellow with a shock of pale, unruly hair and the pink, scrubbed face of a much younger man. Clutched in his large hands was a shapeless green hat; he entered with the smell of fresh bread still clinging to his flour-dusted clothes. "Come in, Baker . . . ," Richter searched for a name.

"Stiffelbeam," offered his visitor. "It is true that I am a baker, but my name is Engelbert Stiffelbeam."

The magistrate lowered his brows in displeasure. "If you please, Baker Stiffelbeam, explain to me why you deem it necessary to pester the official organs of the state with your petty concerns. Hmm? What is so important?"

"Forgive me, Chief Magistrate, it is not my intention to irritate the organs of the state."

"I am a busy man, as you can see," grumped Richter. "Declare your business and be on your way."

Engelbert stepped to the desk and placed a small parcel before the magistrate.

"What is this? A bribe?"

"No, Herr Magistrate—it is a pastry. Everyone must eat." He smiled. "I made it myself. For you."

"Oh, well—I see." Herr Richter took the parcel and placed it to one side. "Now then, your business—"

"A baker, as you said—"

"No, no—I mean, why are you here? Why have you come to this office?"

Engelbert nodded and drew a breath, remembering the speech he had prepared. "Good magistrate, I come before you to plead the case of men who are languishing in prison this day. It is my deepest wish that—"

"These men whose case you plead," interrupted the magistrate. "What is the case against them?"

"Assault and battery," answered Engelbert.

"They are friends of yours, these men? Relatives?"

"They are not my friends, Magistrate. Nor are they related to me in any way."

"Then what is your interest here? These men owe you money, perhaps? That is the reason for your concern, eh?" The magistrate wagged his finger at his visitor. "Answer truthfully and be quick about it."

"No, wise magistrate, they owe me nothing."

Chief Magistrate Richter nodded, his eyes narrowing a little further. "The crime they committed—they are innocent, I suppose?"

"Far from it. They committed the crime," replied Engelbert.

"How do you know this?"

"It was me they assaulted—in my own bakery. I was the victim."

"When did this happen?"

"Many weeks ago—twelve weeks, I believe."

"Then why this sudden urgency? Why have you waited until now to speak up?"

"I must beg your pardon, Herr Magistrate, but I did not wait until now. I have been coming here for many weeks. Today is the first time I have been allowed to speak to you."

"Leaving that aside," huffed the magistrate quickly, "you are perhaps thinking that this imprisonment is in some way unjust? You think them wrongly imprisoned, eh?"

"That is not for me to say."

"Who, then? Eh?" Richter gave him a sly smile as if catching a culprit trying to evade his relentless logic.

"Why, *you*, Herr Magistrate. Surely it is for you to hear the case and decide what justice demands."

Richter's stern magisterial frown deepened. He did not care for the way this interview was proceeding. The magistrate wagged his finger again. "I warn you, baker, this flippant attitude of yours will not be tolerated in this office."

Engelbert nodded thoughtfully, then began again. "I beg your pardon, Magistrate. I wish only to see these men released from prison."

Richter studied the benign features of the man before him. "Why?" was all he could think to ask.

"Why?" wondered Engelbert. "Because it is only right and fitting."

"But you have affirmed the charges against them and sworn to their guilt. From your own mouth you condemn them. Why, then, do you seek their release?"

"I am the one who was wronged, and I have forgiven them their sins against me."

"The law is the law," intoned Richter. "Justice must be served and must be seen to be served."

"With respect, Magistrate, I believe these men have suffered enough and that keeping them in prison any longer cannot serve any just or useful purpose." He hesitated, opened his mouth, and then closed it again.

"Yes?" demanded Herr Richter sharply. "What else?"

"I was merely going to point out that they have no one to look after their needs, and they have spent the little money they have on such food and water as they were able to get from the gaoler."

"Humph!" snorted Richter. "They should have thought of that

before they went around assaulting and battering solid, upstanding citizens of Prague such as yourself."

"Of course," agreed the baker. "Yet perhaps the time already spent in prison might be taken into consideration and regarded as fair punishment for the crime. Justice would be served. Then might the men be released?"

Magistrate Richter reached for a little brass bell on the side of his desk. He rang it, and when his clerk appeared, he said, "Assault and battery—there are men being held in gaol. Do we know about this, Pavel?"

"We do, Chief Magistrate. You will recall that this is the case in which the imperial court has taken an interest."

"This is *that* case?"

The clerk nodded solemnly.

The magistrate adopted a grim and forbidding aspect and stood slowly to deliver his verdict. "Your petition is denied. The malefactors will remain in custody until the charges against them can be heard."

"Again I feel I must beg your pardon, sir," said Engelbert. "When will the hearing of these charges take place?"

Richter the magistrate was not used to having his every utterance challenged. He drew himself up in all his magisterial dignity. "The charges will be heard when I decide that it is time to hear them."

Engelbert nodded slowly, then smiled. "I will see you next week."

"You do not understand. The men must be made to answer for their crimes. The charges will be heard in due course. And in any event, the matter is out of my hands. You will kindly go about your business and allow me to go about mine."

"With pleasure, sir. Yet I feel I must explain that the future of these poor men has become my business. I cannot in good conscience let this matter rest until it is resolved."

The magistrate reached for the bell resting at the corner of his desk. "I wish you a good day, Baker Stiffelbeam." He rang the bell and said to his clerk, "This audience is concluded. Please show the baker to the door."

"This way, if you will," said Pavel. "I will see you out."

Engelbert followed the clerk into the outer office. He paused at the door and said, "You said that the emperor had taken an interest in this case, I believe?"

"Indeed, yes," the clerk assured him. "A rare occasion, to be sure. But it happens from time to time. Naturally, we must respect the wishes of His Highness in all things, Baker Stiffelbeam."

"Naturally," agreed Engelbert with a smile. "Thank you for telling me. I will bring *you* the pastry next time."

PART THREE

The Fatal Tree

CHAPTER 15

In Which a Matter of
Life and Death Is Raised

The Copa del Rey final between Real Madrid and Athletic Bilbao for the championship of Spanish football's Primera Division descended into chaos with tragic results when seven bulls charged onto the pitch. Players from both teams raced for the side-lines as the enraged animals thundered in from the players' tunnel during the closing minutes of the first half at Santiago Bernabeu stadium.

Striker Fernando Sola, caught near the Madrid goal, successfully evaded two animals but was trampled and gored by a third in full sight of over eighty thousand screaming fans. The attempt to rescue the wounded player turned into a bloodbath as spectators poured onto the pitch in what one match commentator described as an "impromptu running of the bulls."

Young Spaniards, fuelled by lager and sangria, leaped over the crowd barriers. One witness estimated more than a hundred young men ripped off their shirts and rushed onto the field of play—most to show off their bullfighting prowess and others to help wounded comrades in the inevitable melee. In the carnage to follow, eight people were killed. Five more were crushed by the crowd trying to flee the stadium when rumours of a bomb were broadcast, and three additional victims succumbed to wounds received by the bulls and later died in the hospital.

Police on-site killed four of the animals, and the remaining three were corralled and taken away by livestock handlers drawn from the crowd; these animals would be examined for clues as to their origin. The official story that the bulls were hijacked en route to a bullfight in southern Madrid remains pure speculation.

A statement issued by the Ministerio del Interior indicated that the incident was being treated as an attack by ETA, the Basque separatist movement, in what was labelled an obvious attempt to disrupt Spain's national pastime. Interior Minister Juan Carlos Navarro was quoted as saying the Spanish government would prosecute the perpetrators with the full force of the law and that those responsible would not escape.

However, a spokesman for the Policía Nacional said that although the investigation continued, the police had very little material evidence to pursue. CCTV footage from multiple cameras both inside and outside the stadium showed no suspicious activity of any kind in the hours leading up to the attack. "Where those *toros* came from is a mystery," he said. "It is as if they simply appeared from nowhere."

Both of Spain's largest national newspapers, *El Pais* and *El Mundo*, issued rewards totaling €500,000 for information leading to the arrest of the perpetrators. Despite being inundated with thousands of leads, officials remained stymied.

Wilhelmina gazed around the flattened crown of Black Mixen Tump, deceptively tranquil in the early-evening light. With a last glance around the silent hilltop, she drew a deep, steadying breath and prepared to try yet again. *Sixth time lucky*, she thought, and with that she raised her fist into the air.

Almost instantly, she felt the prickle of electricity on her skin and sensed the surge and swirl of energy around her. The portal was active and strong. A second later the air grew hazy and took on a pale bluish tint, and a wind from nowhere sent waves rippling through the long green grass that covered the top of the ancient hill. She felt the strain in her muscles as a force like gravity enveloped her; her arm quivered as she strove to keep it straight and raised high. The wind shrieked down from frigid heights, and everything around her became blurry and indistinct as if seen through a sandblasted windowpane. Static electricity sizzled around her and Wilhelmina braced herself for the leap. Her last thought was of the object of her search, Thomas Young. His bespectacled face flashed before her eyes. There was a fizzing pop, and everything grew dark.

She blinked and opened her eyes to find herself standing at the end of the Avenue of Sphinxes in a cloud of dust—again. She exhaled sharply and glanced around as dust devils raced down the long double rank of silent statues. A quick look at the sky told her that it was early morning yet, and that was a good thing. She shook her clothes back into place and adjusted her pack, and once again started for the riverside village where she would get a boat to ferry her across the Nile. She had traversed this way so often she could have walked it blindfolded. She tried not to think about that. Better to simply slog on and hope for the best.

She was still hoping for the best when at midday the next day she once more stood at the entrance to the hidden gorge and gazed up at the soaring walls of the wadi yawning before her. From her observation of the village and traffic on the river, she was fairly certain she had achieved a leap to an earlier time than her last attempt. She was where she wanted to be . . . was she also *when?* "Please be there, Thomas," she murmured as she stepped into the wadi. It was marginally cooler in the shaded corridor of the canyon, and she hurried to the T-junction she knew was waiting at the end.

As she walked, she wondered how the other questors were faring in their missions; she thought about the Kit and Giles she had rescued on her last visit to the tomb and wondered what her involvement would mean in whatever reality they inhabited. It wasn't time travel, as she well knew, but perhaps she had closed some kind of cosmic loop for them; or, then again, maybe for herself?

She was playing with the various implications of this when she rounded the last bend and there, in the place where three channels of the wadi met, stood a wing-shaped Arab tent. She ducked out of sight and pressed herself against the ravine wall, took a breath, and inching forward, peeked warily around the corner. A group of swarthy men in blue kaftans laboured among scattered heaps of crates and boxes, some men carrying objects to be packed and others nailing shut the lids.

Very organised for tomb robbers, she thought and continued her chary perusal of the scene. She was debating whether to make herself known when out of the shadowed entrance to the ruined temple emerged a man in a much-battered broad-brimmed hat. It took her a moment to realise that beneath the hat was the man she had come to find. Thinner, and a good deal grubbier than the last time she had seen him—his whiskers were longer and bushier, and his linen coat and trousers were so thoroughly covered in pale powdery dust he looked as if he might have been bathing in the stuff—still, he was the same Dr. Young she had met in London. He was carrying a large jar, which he handed to one of the workmen and then proceeded to a small camp table near the temple doorway.

"Jackpot!" she sighed with knee-weakening relief. Pushing away from the wall, she moved out into the open. A few yards down the right-hand branch she saw large rubble piles and the gaping rectangular hole in the wadi floor leading to the underground Tomb of Anen. Several of the workmen saw her pass; they stopped to stare, but no one called after her or tried to stop her.

At a run, as if afraid the object of her search might vanish before her eyes, she made directly for the man at the table. "Excuse me, Dr. Young?"

The sound of her voice startled him, and he jolted back in his chair. "Great heavens above!"

Glancing up quickly, he looked at her and then beyond her, as if searching for other visitors. Seeing none, he regarded her more closely. "Miss Klug? Is that you?" The renowned Egyptologist stared, his eyes blinking behind his round, steel-rimmed glasses, then rose slowly from his chair as if drawn by the sudden materialisation of an apparition before his very eyes. "Dear girl, is that truly you?"

"Truly me." Wilhelmina laughed, delighted not only that she had found her man at last but that he remembered her. Lifting her face heavenward, she breathed a *Thank You* and put out her hand. "You cannot imagine how good it is to see you, Dr. Young."

He smiled, shaking his head in surprise. "But whatever are you doing here?" he asked, taking her hand and pressing it warmly. "How did you find me?"

Before she could reply, a shout went up from some men who were just then emerging from the excavated hole at the base of the wadi wall. They were carrying a large amphora between them and were followed by a third fellow dressed in white. "Khefri!" shouted Thomas, turning to summon the young man. "Khefri, come here. We have a visitor!"

A moment later Wilhelmina was looking into the deep brown eyes of a slender young Egyptian with a short black fuzz of hair and a deeply puzzled expression on his smooth brown face. He looked a question to Dr. Young, who explained, "Khefri, I would like you to meet Miss Wilhelmina Klug—a very dear colleague of mine."

"Hardly that," protested Wilhelmina. "Hello, Khefri. It is a pleasure to meet you."

"Greetings, *saida*," he said, lowering his head in a slight bow. He glanced quickly around to see if she had been accompanied; seeing no one, he turned back. "You are alone, *saida*? In the desert?"

"I came alone, yes," she told him. "I came to find Dr. Young." She turned back to smile at the still-bemused doctor. "And I am very happy to say that I have succeeded."

"As delighted as I am to see you too, dear, I have to ask again—what on earth are you doing here?"

"I have something very important to discuss with you," she told him, and felt the smile fading from her face even as she spoke. "A matter of life and death. It cannot wait."

"Truly?" wondered Thomas blithely. "A matter of life and death—that sounds very serious, very serious indeed." He blinked at her. "Whose life, may I ask? Whose death?"

Wilhelmina's voice took on a note of utter foreboding as she answered, "Everyone's."

CHAPTER 16

In Which Hate Seeks Its True Source

Without his Burley Men to distract him with their squabbling, arguing, and assorted nasty habits, his lordship the earl at last found a modicum of solitude and quiet. It was not, however, an altogether welcome change. The cell was more peaceful, yes, but the days seemed immeasurably longer. Without his gang around him, filling the fetid air with their idle natter and incessant bickering, Burleigh had long hours of silence to fill and nothing with which to fill them.

For a man more accustomed to a life of unfettered action, this was a novel and uncomfortable condition. Time and again, Burleigh found himself lost in contemplation of thoughts he had never before seriously entertained. Like a dog returning to its vomit, his thoughts turned to his benefactor, the baker.

Why this should be, he could not say. One moment he would

be sitting slumped in a corner of the cell, and the next he would be grinding his teeth over something the good-natured baker had said or done. The sum of all his problems had a name, and that name was Engelbert. Even the word was an affront. Why, it was the name for a clown, a buffoon—not a name for a man. *Engelbert.* What was that in English? Drawing from his meagre store of German, Burleigh was able to cobble together the English approximation as something like "Bright Angel." What parent in their right mind would name their son Bright Angel?

Asinine as that might be, the name was a mere trifle, a trivial curiosity. What was it about the man that brought Burleigh's blood to the boil? The more he thought about it, the more he assured himself that there had to be something substantial beneath the surface. What was it about the well-meaning fellow that rankled, that galled, that raised the bile to Burleigh's mouth the moment he clapped eyes on the merry oaf? Was it his manner? His unfailingly cheerful demeanour, that perpetually pleasant disposition with which he met whatever barbarity life threw at him? Was it the big baker's inane affability or his idiotic do-gooding that provoked hatred? What was the inflammatory thing, the thing that demanded, and received, such a strong response from Burleigh?

Certainly, there was nothing in the man's physiognomy to incite such loathing. The baker was not unattractive in his way, though this quality could not be ascribed to any particular physical attribute; no, his features were regular and unremarkable. It was, Burleigh decided, more that Engelbert radiated a kind of natural warmth and, for lack of a better word, goodness. Engelbert's sweet nature shone through his rather ordinary exterior, transforming it into a far more appealing and pleasing aspect.

Be that as it may, what was there to be so bloody cheerful about? Life was hard and life was deadly. Kill or be killed, eat or be eaten—that was the Law of Nature, the only law the world knew. Burleigh had learned that cruel lesson as a child of the streets, and it had served him faithfully ever since. Anyone who did not recognise that most basic law of life deserved whatever they got—Engelbert Stiffelbeam included.

One day, a week or so after Tav, Con, Mal, and Dex had been taken away, Etzel arrived with his regular food parcel. Burleigh, to avoid giving the insufferable baker whatever satisfaction he derived from performing this good deed, refused to acknowledge his benefactor's presence. Since the Burley Men were no longer around to spoil the effect with their grovelling thanks and unctuous exclamations over Engelbert's unwarranted largess, the earl remained on his mat with his face to the wall, silent—despite the baker's best attempts to rouse him.

Later, after Engelbert had gone, Burleigh rolled over and regarded the little heap of provisions left for him. In the single shaft of natural light that shone down from his grated vent hole he saw the perfect white and brown loaves produced by Etzel's bakery; the plump, greasy sausage purchased in the market; the firm yellow apples; the jug of sweet new wine—all so neatly arranged for him as if in a study for a still life painting, a work of art, an arrangement of beauty. Burleigh realised then that there was something more than simple do-goodism in the act. It had an aim, a purpose . . . but what?

After a time, the earl's hunger got the better of him; he rose and, kneeling over his provisions, began portioning them for the week ahead. Taking one of the loaves, he broke it and pulled off a piece and ate it. Then, still kneeling, he picked up the wine and took a drink. In this way, he broke his fast. The simple meal of bread and wine eased his hunger and satisfied; it was good and wholesome. There was a rightness about it that went beyond the basic elements.

In the act of eating Etzel's food, Burleigh glimpsed something of the attitude behind the offering, and he had an epiphany: Engelbert Stiffelbeam was not the problem—it was his Jesus. *Why should this be?* Burleigh wondered. What difference did it make to Burleigh what the big oaf believed?

The Grand Imperial's chief baker might also believe in pink-spotted green leprechauns for all he knew; people believed a multitude of ridiculous things up to and including the existence of mermaids, unicorns, and fire-breathing dragons. But those deluded beliefs did not inspire in him the same visceral disgust. And just like the imaginary unicorns that haunted the dells and hidden glades of folklore, Jesus was merely an irrelevant nonsense. The brutal indifference of the world proved that much beyond doubt; and Jesus, God's insipid Son, was a phantom, a figment, a myth. In actual fact, the whole of religion everywhere, so far as Burleigh could discern, was a rag-tag bundle of superstition and make-believe: wholesale foolishness concocted by lunatics, peddled by charlatans, and swallowed by the ignorant benighted masses.

Burleigh had always held that organised religion amounted to a kind of madness, a collective insanity embraced by the weak and powerless because it allowed them some small degree of comfort, a grain of solace in the face of the harsh reality that their lives were meaningless, existence had no purpose, and there was no good, wise, all-knowing God looking out for them. The naked truth was that existence had no significance beyond the random shuttling of mindless forces that had produced a blob of sentient matter that was here one day and gone the next. The lives of most human beings had as much meaning as the candle flame that is lit, burns for a time, and is then snuffed out, never to be seen again.

Real men, strong men, rational men of the world did not need such childish fantasies to strengthen a feeble, fragile psyche, or provide a way to avoid staring into the dark abyss of a cold, unforgiving reality. For the greater mass of humanity, however, better a merry fantasy than the bitter, bracing truth: there was no God, no purpose, no meaning in life, and nothing beyond the grave.

Burleigh took another mouthful of bread and was savouring its simple goodness when a thought popped into his head: *"If there is no God, then everything is permitted . . ."*

Where that had come from, he did not know, but Burleigh certainly recognised the sentiment and wholly agreed with it. As an aphorism, it was something he might have said himself once or twice and, if pressed, he could have argued the case most eloquently.

"There is no God," Burleigh declared in his mind—as he would have proclaimed aloud if there had been anyone to hear him. "Thus, every man is free to do what seems right to him."

From the shadowed dampness in the far corner of his cell emerged a dark figure, as indistinct as the shadows it inhabited, its thoughts manifest as a ghostly shade. *"Every man does what is right in his own eyes,"* offered the Voice helpfully.

"Exactly," replied Burleigh, nodding in agreement. "Every man is free to do whatever pleases him for whatever reasons seem best and by whatever means best serve his ambition."

"If there is no God, there cannot be any objective moral standard. No one can say what is right or wrong. Therefore, whatever a man does cannot be either acclaimed or condemned by anyone. It simply is."

"Correct," agreed Burleigh firmly. "If there is no objective standard against which actions may be judged, there can be no right or wrong."

"*By the same token,*" continued the Voice, growing more insistent, "*whatever befalls a man cannot be judged as acceptable or unacceptable. In a universe of no direction or purpose, whatever happens cannot be considered good or bad; it is simply something that happens, an event without significance.*"

Again, Burleigh agreed, though with less certainty than before. He could feel the drift of his thoughts beginning to carry him toward an unseen, possibly unwanted destination.

"*Then why do you rage so against your plight?*" asked the Voice. "*What happens simply is—no meaning, no purpose, just the random collision of events with no significance beyond their immediate interaction.*"

"Ah!" challenged Burleigh. "A man ought to have recourse to justice at least. The accused ought to be able to face his accusers and answer the charge."

"*Ought? Where does this ought come from?*"

"It is only simple fairness," insisted Burleigh, with less enthusiasm than before.

"*Are we going to talk about unfairness and injustice? I thought we had laid that to rest. Why drag all that up again?*"

Burleigh had no reply. He hurt, and the pain was real—maybe that was reason enough to complain.

The Voice was quick to pounce on this. "*You hurt, so you attribute the pain to unfairness, to injustice? Who do you imagine cares to hear your complaint?*"

"It hurts!" Burleigh insisted. "I do not care who hears about it!"

"*Your hurt is a fantasy, a figment, a phantom. There can be no hurt where there is no law. Every man is free to do what he likes. The magistrate likes to keep you locked up. Where is the harm?*"

"But he ought *not* to like it!" snapped Burleigh, losing his patience.

"*Again with the* ought!" chided the Voice, fading back into the shadows and becoming once more merely a damp patch of mildew on the wall. It whispered, "*It seems, brother, that you do not truly believe your own philosophy.*"

"Bugger philosophy!" growled Burleigh. "I bloody well want out of here!"

Another week passed in the dank cell beneath the Rathaus—another week of misery for its once-proud occupant. Truly, Archelaeus Burleigh, Earl of Sutherland, was proud no longer. He was wretched, and knew himself to be so. Indeed, he very much suspected that he was even worse than he knew.

With each passing day, he felt more fragile and unstable—much, he imagined, as an egg—one that had been broken and emptied, and then patched together again with all the cracks showing and some of the pieces missing. He lurched restlessly about his cell trying not to think, for thinking only brought new torrents of misery.

He was in the throes of another bout of painful introspection when the sound of his door swinging open on its rusty hinges startled him. So lost in the maze of his thoughts was he that he had not heard the footsteps in the hall, nor even the key in the lock. He stopped pacing and turned to see the familiar form of the baker framed in the doorway, light streaming in around him. *Bright Angel,* indeed, mused Burleigh. *Come to torment me again.*

The gaoler muttered something, and Engelbert stepped into the cell with his bag of provisions and a great smile on his broad face. "I have news for you," he announced happily, moving to the centre of the cell.

Burleigh said nothing, only stared—half fascinated, half dreading what his good-natured nemesis might say next.

"Your friends are to be released!"

Raising his head, Burleigh glowered as the baker stooped to open his sack. *Friends,* thought the earl. *Where are my friends?* The alchemists and courtiers he had cultivated at the palace . . . where were they now? In the long months of his confinement, none had come to his aid, none had spoken for him, all had deserted him. "I have no friends," Burleigh replied, his voice a low, husky rasp.

"The men who were with you—they were your friends, no?" said Etzel.

"Hirelings," the earl sniffed. "They worked for me. Nothing more."

"I am your friend," declared Etzel cheerfully. He lifted out a fresh brown loaf of rye bread and laid it carefully on the folded cloth that served as the earl's table.

"You!" sneered Burleigh, the old anger stirring once more. "*You* are the reason I am here."

Engelbert shrugged and withdrew a chunk of cheese wrapped in muslin and placed it beside the loaf, then reached in for a clay jug of beer. "You know the reason you are here, I think." He pulled out handfuls of apricots and stacked them neatly on the cloth. "There is a prison cart leaving the city. Your friends are to be taken to Pilzen, where they will be released at the border. But they must promise never again to enter Prague."

Burleigh said nothing for a long moment, then asked, "Will I see them? My men—will I see them again before they leave?"

"I do not think so," allowed Engelbert. "But I will ask."

"Who . . . ah"—Burleigh fumbled for words—"how is this possible? Who made this happen?"

Etzel nodded. "I have been speaking to the magistrate for many weeks. He has grown tired of my begging and has agreed to free the men."

"So," huffed Burleigh. "They can go, but I must stay."

"The magistrate tells me that a crime has been committed and that someone must answer for this. Someone must be responsible." The baker produced something new—a whole roast chicken—from his bag and added it to the other items on the cloth. "I have said to the magistrate that only one man was responsible. Locking up five men for the crime of one made no sense."

"You told him this?" wondered the earl.

"I have told him a great many things. He listens to some of them." Engelbert frowned. "But Herr Richter is an official of the empire. The magistrate listens more to the emperor than to me." The big man cocked his head to one side. "This is the way of things."

"So that is it? I just sit here until I die?"

"May God forbid it!" replied Engelbert quickly. "I have spoken to His Majesty on your behalf. I asked him to release you, but he also tells me that justice must be served. But no matter, I will go to him again and bring a strudel next time."

"You spoke to the emperor for me?" Burleigh shook his head. "Why? Why do you care what happens to me? I hurt you. I *meant* to hurt you. I had no care for you—why do you care for me?"

The baker stood and moved to stand before the earl. "But I have told you this already." Etzel placed his hand on Burleigh's shoulder and gave it a squeeze. "Be of good cheer. The Lord is with you."

Burleigh gazed at him, then shook his head. "I wish I could believe that."

"It makes no matter," Etzel assured him lightly. He turned and stooped to retrieve the empty bag. "I will believe enough for both of us."

With that, he was gone again, leaving only the whiff of a strange fragrance behind—a scent like that of wildflowers, the scent of open spaces and sun-washed air. It lingered long in the cell, causing Burleigh to wonder whether he had indeed been visited by a bright angel.

This notion was so absurd that Burleigh had no argument against it; all he could do was stand and stare at the offering of food so carefully—one could say lovingly—arranged. As he stood there looking, a tear came to his eye. He did not know why; he did not feel sad, only mildly confused. But something deep inside him turned in that moment, and a single tear marked the occasion. Embarrassed, the earl swiped it away, smearing the wetness off his cheek with the heel of his hand. "Big bloody fool," he murmured aloud. "You're losing your mind."

In the empty hours that followed, Burleigh found himself thinking not so much about his own sorry state and the monumental injustice that was keeping him locked in a stinking dungeon cell, but about the *reason* he was rotting in prison. From that moment, his thoughts now centred on the cruelty he had shown in the attack against Engelbert and the regret he now felt. This was a new thing.

Slowly, the circle of his meditations widened outward to include not only Engelbert but others he had wronged throughout his life: Cosimo Livingstone and Sir Henry Fayth; the sweet, trusting Phillipa, his one-time fiancée; Arthur Flinders-Petrie and his grandson, Charles; his Burley Men; Lady Haven Fayth—now, there was a woman after his own heart, someone he could have loved—whatever happened to her? And there were others . . . so many others—and all of them people he had used for his own selfish purposes, only to be ruthlessly cast aside when it suited him. He had earned his condemnation tenfold, a hundredfold, and he deserved the harshest penalty the law and heaven could decree, nothing less.

As he brought his appalling behaviour to mind, he encountered what was for him a strange sensation: a mingled blend of guilt, shame, and sorrow that, on further reflection, he decided must be remorse. This unusual emotion might have been allowed to fade, its potency diminished over time, but for the persistent example of Engelbert, whose virtue threw his own wretchedness into sharp relief. Etzel's simple, uncomplicated goodness burned like a beacon on a distant hill. Burleigh had only to glance up to that shining hilltop to see just how very dark his squalid little valley had become.

Increasingly, Burleigh caught himself looking to that light and wishing he could move closer to it. Strange to say, this feeling did not produce the abhorrence and revulsion it might once have done; rather, in accepting his guilt and owning the blame for his actions, the earl felt more contented—as if something that had long been misaligned was now properly adjusted: the compass needle pointed true north once more.

But that was not all. On those occasions when the earl fixed his mind on the big baker's shining example, he discovered that he was able to find a little respite from the ceaseless churning of his more troublesome thoughts. In contemplating goodness, he found—innocently, unexpectedly, blessedly—peace.

CHAPTER 17

In Which the Peace Exacts a Price

On the third and last day, the feast celebrating the pact between the Bulgars and the Byzantines concluded with a service of prayer and thanksgiving for having come through the travails of war and been granted the peace in which the empire now rejoiced. The sun had just set over the Sea of Marmara when a bell tolled in the plaza tower. The emperor and several high-ranking officials departed the feast, and the entire celebration was moved to the Cathedral of Holy Wisdom located just beyond the imperial palace walls.

To enter the sanctuary of the great church was to cross the threshold into the largest enclosed area the world had ever seen: an enormous, airy expanse uninterrupted by pillars or columns of any kind, a single vast room large enough to swallow two or three normal-sized churches and still have room for a bell tower beneath its heroic domed ceiling. Gleaming mosaics adorned the upper reaches of the walls, and occupying every cornice and cranny of the many-domed ceiling were the colossal figures of saints and angels and winged seraphim with swords of fire. It was an interior to daunt and humble the most prideful worshipper and instil in everyone who entered a sense of the ineffable majesty of the King of kings and Lord of lords before whom mere human creatures—including earthly emperors and potentates—must bow.

The immense space swallowed sound so that only the hush of an eternal, unending tranquillity remained, punctuated now and then by the chime of a bell or the plaintive call of a chant. The floor and outlying columns were multicoloured marble; the high altar was covered in cloth of gold and flanked by twin candles larger than a human being. All that met the eye was smooth stone and gleaming gold. A multitude of scented candles lit the nave, sending up a fragrant silver cloud, the soft lambent light winking and shimmering from every polished surface.

As the imperial entourage arranged itself before the high altar, Haven quickly located Petar, who was standing behind the khan, and manoeuvred herself and Giles into places beside him. He acknowledged their presence with a slight nod. As soon as the royal celebrants were assembled, a score of acolytes dressed all in black entered from the rooms along the sides of the nave; junior clerics dressed in robes of white entered from the central aisle, each bearing a silver cross.

Acolytes and priests formed a ring around the altar, followed by more senior priests in red robes; the first among these held a bell, the second a psalm book. These two took their places on either side of the altar and the rest formed a row behind them. Once they were in place, a bell chimed loudly three times, whereupon the patriarchal procession entered the church. Led by three ranks of clerics in long white robes over which they wore blue chasubles, two bishops came bearing crosses of gold and pearl; directly behind the bishops strode

Emperor Leo in a robe of scarlet silk—the holy *sakkos*—adorned with panels containing thickly embroidered plaques depicting scenes from the life of Christ. On his head the emperor wore a jewelled hat topped by a four-sided cross and on his hands were fine gauntlets decorated with seed pearls, rubies, and amber.

Hobbling in the emperor's wake came an extremely old man. Swathed in rolls of purple silk and wearing a high-crowned, jewel-encrusted, brimless hat, this elderly specimen had a long white beard that might have wafted in the breeze of his passing if it had not been held in place by the enormous pectoral cross hanging on a thick chain of gold around his neck.

"Tell me what is happening," whispered Haven urgently. "Who is that?"

Petar rolled his eyes but grudgingly complied. "That is the Patriarch of Constantinople," he said. "The highest priest of the holy church—second to none but the emperor, of course."

The service began in much the same way as the Latin masses Haven had observed, and not far removed from the Holy Communion Khan Simeon's priests performed in camp. But the trappings—the splendour of gold and silver and jewels, the multitude of candles and clouds of incense, the magnificence of the attendant priests—were unlike any other, and unparalleled in the West. Everything, from the impossibly ornate robes of the priests to the voluminous clouds of fragrant incense, appeared designed to astonish and delight and, ultimately, to awe. If bejewelled robes and purple billows failed to inspire, then the soaring, ethereal chanting of the priests and monks was sure to lift the worshipper to new heights of rapture.

Though Haven strove valiantly to keep pace with the service, she failed; it all washed over her in a tidal surge of sound and light and raw emotion. Before she knew it, the service concluded. The congregation was ushered outside where, in the square before the cathedral entrance, Khan Simeon prepared to take his leave of Emperor Leo and the city of his triumph. The two rulers gripped one another's arms, exchanged the kiss of peace, and made their final farewells; respective attendants began to disperse and go their separate ways. Haven and Giles were drifting along with the rest of Khan Simeon's retinue when they were approached by a thin, long-faced man with a bald head and large, sad eyes.

"By command of the emperor, you are both instructed to come with me," the man informed them in somewhat stilted Latin. Two armed soldiers from the emperor's bodyguard accompanied the servant to lend weight to the summons should any further convincing become necessary.

"I do beg your pardon," replied Haven, and she felt Giles' hand on her back as he moved in close beside her, "but I believe there is some mistake. Khan Simeon is about to leave. We are members of his entourage and must go with him."

"No," the courtier told her curtly. "You are to attend the *basileus*. You will follow me." With that he turned and started away, pausing only long enough to ensure that the two foreigners took their places behind him.

Though Haven begged to be told where they were being taken, no further explanation was forthcoming. The soldiers, gripping the hilts of their short swords, indicated that it was time to move. "I think we must do as he says, Giles."

"I do not see that we have a choice in the matter," Giles replied. Taking Haven's arm, he moved to follow the servant. The two soldiers fell into step behind them. "Perhaps His Majesty merely wishes to speak to us."

Haven cast a worried glance at the two soldiers behind them. "No doubt," she replied, but her tone lacked conviction.

The two were led to the great palace and ushered into an audience chamber, a room well furnished with a number of the low chairs and couches for which the Byzantines showed a marked partiality. There were several tables of various sizes and a number of very ornate jars and containers and candle trees set around the perimeter of the room. A heavy curtain at the single large window was pulled to one side to allow the soft twilight to spill across a floor of polished brown marble.

The courtier made a swift inspection of the room, then turned to the visitors. "You will wait here," he told them.

"Are we allowed to sit?" asked Haven.

Their guide flapped a hand at one of the couches and departed; the soldiers pulled the doors shut behind him and stationed themselves on either side. Haven moved to the nearest couch and sat down; Giles made a quick survey of the room, paused to look out the window, and then took a seat next to Haven. They spoke to one another in English, keeping their voices low; the guards watched them impassively, bored expressions on their faces.

After a time, the door opened and four men entered. One of them was the official who had brought Haven and Giles to the palace; three others, each of them dressed in long grey robes with white sashes over one shoulder, came to stand before the visitors and exchanged a few words amongst themselves while glancing at the visitors from time to time.

"What are they saying?" whispered Giles.

"I cannot understand a word," Haven replied. "Greek."

Then one of the men gestured for the visitors to stand. As Haven and Giles rose, the door opened again and two more men entered—one of them Emperor Leo himself. The courtiers bowed low and the visitors copied them, then rose to find the supreme monarch of the empire standing over them. Gone were the splendid ecclesiastical robes, the chain of gold, and the elaborate headgear; instead, he was dressed in a simple floor-length tunic of cream-coloured satin with a wide black belt and a matching *chlamys* over one shoulder, fastened at the neck by an enormous red brooch of carnelian carved in the shape of a lion.

Leo addressed them in Greek, and when this brought no response, he switched effortlessly to Latin, saying, "Do you know who I am?"

"Yes, Majesty," replied Haven. "You are Leo, *Imperator* of the Romans. May God grant you serenity and long life, sire." This last she added because she had heard Petar sometimes address Khan Simeon that way.

Her reply produced an instantaneous result. The emperor clapped his hands. "Excellent!" He beamed with delight. "You have been well schooled." He turned to Giles. "And you, friend—are you equally schooled in courtly manners?"

Giles understood most of what was said and made his standard reply. "I am as you see me, sire—a servant, nothing more."

"Ha!" laughed Leo, clapping his hands again, and turned to smile upon his attendants. "Most excellent! Would you not agree?"

"Assuredly, sire," replied the long-faced fellow who had first approached the two. "It is, as you say, most excellent. Your wisdom is, as ever, above reproach."

Leo turned to his visitors and raised his hands. "Henceforth you are to be members of the royal house," he declared, his voice taking on a more formal note. "You will be given lodgings within the palace precinct and a stipend, which you may spend at your own discretion.

In exchange for these benefices, you will assume duties according to your abilities."

"I most humbly beg your pardon, Your Majesty, but my command of Latin is limited," said Haven. "Am I to understand that we will be staying here?"

"Your understanding is exceeded only by your beauty, madam," answered Leo. "By what name do you wish to be known?"

"I am called Haven," she answered.

"Perfection!" cried Leo happily. Turning at once to Giles, he said, "And you, my excellent friend? How are you to be known?"

"I am Giles, sire."

The sound of this name provoked an immediate response from the emperor and his attendants, who fell to discussing it among themselves.

"What are they saying about me?" Giles whispered to Haven, who, mystified, could only shake her head.

A conclusion was quickly reached, however, and Leo turned once more to address Giles. "In this house and in my presence, you shall be called Gaius," he declared. "Do you know this name?"

Giles turned to Haven for translation. "I think Giles was too hard for them to understand or pronounce," she explained.

"Pot calling the kettle black, I'd say," sniffed Giles.

"He says you are to be called Gaius instead."

"Gaius?" he wondered, turning to the emperor.

"It is a noble name," Leo told him. "A name worthy of emperors, many of whom have worn it with pride. It is your name henceforth."

Although he did not understand much of what had been said to him just then, Giles knew better than to argue. "Thank you, sire," he said simply. "I am in your debt."

Leo clapped his hands yet once more, this time as a signal that the audience was finished. "You will be taken to your apartment, and tomorrow the skills you possess will be evaluated for your placement within the royal household." He smiled, satisfied with his decision, and then backed away. "I wish you a pleasant night."

Haven opened her mouth to speak, but was warned off with a frown and a stern shake of the head from the sad-eyed courtier. The emperor and his attendants swept from the room as quickly as they had arrived, leaving Haven and Giles alone to contemplate the strange turn fate had thrown them. "Well," suggested Haven, "that was most unexpected."

"We have been taken into the royal household—we are to live here? In the palace?" wondered Giles.

"It certainly seems that way."

"What about the khan? Doesn't he have anything to say about this?"

"Oh, Giles," sighed Haven. "I think we have become part of the peace settlement—a gift to celebrate the treaty. Something of the sort at any rate. The khan has given us to the emperor to do as he sees fit." The reality of their situation broke full upon her then. Her lower lip quivered and her eyes filled with unshed tears. "I begin to fear that we shall never see home again!"

Giles reached out and folded Haven into his arms and held her close and tight—a natural impulse and action that would have been unthinkable a few months before. Haven came willingly, accepting the comfort his strength and warmth offered. She pressed her head against his chest. "What are we going to do?"

Giles considered this for a moment before answering. "I suppose it could be worse. His emperorship might have decided we would make good farmhands or kitchen slaves." He paused, then said, "Though I can readily see you in a field with a spade in your hand and a basket of turnips on your head."

Haven stiffened and pushed away, suddenly defiant, holding him at arm's length to look him in the eye. "Think you this is a cause for jest?"

"*There* is the Haven I know." He smiled.

"You will forgive me if I do not share your sense of low japes," she huffed, though still clinging to him.

"Perhaps not," he allowed and gathered her in once more. "But think you now, we are members of the emperor's royal retinue and will live in the palace. That is better than looking at the back of a horse all day and sleeping in a smelly tent."

Haven was silent for a time, then said, "I can well imagine you, *Gaius*—in the cookhouse, red-faced and up to your elbows in goose fat and feathers."

"Or standing knee-deep in muck in a pigsty."

She gave a little laugh and dabbed at her eyes. "We would make a pretty pair, would we not?"

The door opened just then, and they were summoned by a servant and led through a maze of corridors to a wing of the palace where high-ranking servants and lower court officials and retainers resided. The servant stopped at a door at the end of a long, narrow passage-way. "All has been made ready for you," he said. Pushing open the door, he ushered them into a suite of rooms consisting of two smaller chambers—one of them containing a bed—either side of a larger room containing a simple table, some chairs, and three low couches. There was a small window covered by a wooden lattice that could be opened onto a view of one of the palace's many walled gardens. An interior door led out to the garden so that they might come and go as they pleased.

The servant made a perfunctory sweep of the rooms to see that all was as it should be, then retreated, saying, "This is where you will live. Whatever you lack will be provided by the underchamberlain."

With no more explanation than that, the fellow closed the door on them, leaving the two to their own devices. Haven cast a quick glance around the apartment. The rooms were large enough and pleasant in a spare, uncluttered way; and the bedchamber seemed ample and well supplied with cushions and a padded pallet. "I believe," she said, biting her lower lip, "they must think we are married."

"That would be a useful expedient," suggested Giles.

"Expedient?" She reared back. "You do quite forget yourself, Mr. Standfast. Expedient!"

"Do not gainsay it just yet," said Giles quickly. "Think on it a little. If we were indeed married, it might make things easier for both of us so long as we are here."

"Or make things more difficult," countered Haven. She frowned and shook her head. "No, it is out of the question," she decided firmly. "I will not hear it."

"My lady, I—"

She raised her hand to halt further discussion. "We will not speak of this again."

CHAPTER 18

In Which an Oversight Is Corrected

*I*t was that awkward time of the day: lunch was but a vague memory and dinner yet a distant promise. Even so, Emperor Rudolf, King of Bohemia and Hungary, Archduke of Austria and King of the Romans, while trying to concentrate on the abstruse astrology text before him, found his thoughts bending toward what his kitchen might produce for his evening meal. He was on the point of summoning his chamberlain to send for the Chief Cook and Master of the Imperial Kitchen to discuss the matter when there was a knock on the door of the library, and the Master of Royal Audiences stepped quietly into the emperor's private book-lined sanctum.

"Forgive the intrusion, Highness," said the official, "but Herr Stiffelbeam is requesting an audience with Your Majesty. What is your pleasure?"

"Our pleasure is to be left alone in peace to read for two minutes at a time without interruption," grumped the emperor. He raised his head from the obscure but highly decorated text before him and fixed the courtier with a disgruntled stare. "That is our pleasure."

"To be sure, Highness. I shall send him away."

"Do that—and see that we are not disturbed again." The emperor licked his finger and turned another page, then stopped. "Did you say Stiffelbeam? Engelbert Stiffelbeam the baker?"

"The very man, Highness," confirmed the Master of Audiences.

The emperor twisted around in his chair. "Why did you not tell us this in the beginning, you ninny? Why must we always guess these things for ourselves?"

"I humbly beg your pardon, Majesty. I assumed the man was known to you."

"Do you think us mad? Of course the man is known to us! For a certainty he is known to us! Do not keep him waiting. Send him in at once!"

"Here, Majesty?"

"Where else?"

"One of the royal audience chambers, perhaps?"

"No. Here—in the library. We want to see him at once, and we do not care to go chasing through half the palace to do so. Bring him here, and be quick about it."

The Master of Audiences withdrew, leaving the emperor in blissful solitude for at least ten minutes, after which time he returned with the emperor's guest in tow. He entered the library with a knock, threw open the door, and announced, "Herr Engelbert Stiffelbeam of the Grand Imperial Kaffeehaus."

Rudolf rose and turned to greet his guest who, he was pleased to see, was carrying a small box wrapped in checked cloth and tied with a satin ribbon. Rudolf knew that good things came in such boxes. "Welcome! Welcome, Herr Stiffelbeam," he said, starting forth. "We are heartily glad to see you. Come in. Business is good, we trust? Your health remains robust?"

Engelbert bowed low and greeted His Imperial Highness with good grace, then replied, "I am well and business could not be better. I am truly blessed, Highness."

"Splendid!" The emperor resumed his seat. "Your presence is most fortuitous, Baker Stiffelbeam. Just this very moment we were remembering your inestimable pastries with great fondness—particularly your extraordinary strudel! *Ach*, the strudel."

"Your Highness is very kind," replied Engelbert simply. "Perhaps you will look with favour upon my humble gift." He lifted the gaily wrapped parcel and extended it toward Rudolf. "For you, Majesty."

"Oh! What have we here?" Rudolf relieved the bearer of his package and, placing it on the library table before him, proceeded to unwrap it forthwith. "*Wunderbar!*" he exclaimed as he lifted off the lid and peered inside.

"I made this one especially for you," Engelbert told him. "It is a new recipe, sire, plum with raisin." Lowering his voice, he added, "The plums are soaked in rum." He bowed again. "With my compliments, Your Highness. I hope you enjoy it."

"We must try it at once!" cried the emperor. Turning to the door, he shouted for one of the pages on duty outside. "Plates! Spoons! A knife!" he shouted at the youth who appeared in the doorway. "Bring these utensils at once. Hurry, now! There is strudel to be eaten!"

The page darted away, and the emperor gazed on the perfectly formed golden-crusted delicacy lightly dusted with that sweetest of confections, powdered sugar. "A masterpiece, Baker Stiffelbeam," declared the emperor, lifting the pastry from the box and placing it ceremoniously on the table.

"My customers have been very generous with their praise, Majesty. I am thinking that it should become a celebration strudel—Christmas, maybe, or Easter."

"A worthy thought, to be sure," agreed Rudolf. "All the same, seeing as there are already a great many delicacies commemorating those hallowed and festive seasons, might another holy day be chosen?"

"Of course, Highness. I had not considered that. Perhaps Your Majesty has a special occasion to suggest?"

The emperor's broad face assumed a studious aspect, and after a moment's consideration he replied, "Now that we come to examine the matter closely, it would seem to us that the emperor's name day is singularly lacking in the way of celebratory pastries. This has always seemed a lamentable oversight to us."

"Your Majesty, it would be a very great honour if my strudel could be considered worthy to supply that lack." Engelbert bowed slightly in recognition of this distinction and suggested, "But before making such a judgement, perhaps Your Highness would like to taste the pastry to be certain it will be acceptable."

"An excellent suggestion!" cried Rudolf. "Taste it we shall. We shall!" He turned a stern gaze upon the door. "Just as soon as that blasted page returns with the cutlery, we shall by all means taste it."

Presently, the page and one of the scullion boys returned bearing plates and knifes and spoons for the emperor and his guest. Engelbert sliced the delicate, paper-thin leaves of golden pastry and served Rudolf a healthy slab. Seated at the library table, spoon at the ready, the plate before him, the Emperor of the Romans took an exploratory bite. He rolled the purple sweetness around in his mouth and then sighed, "Ah, it is divine!" He took another bite and declared, "Baker Stiffelbeam, this is without a doubt the best strudel ever to reach the royal mouth. You are to be congratulated. Henceforth, you shall be called a Master Baker."

"You do your servant a very great honour, Your Majesty."

Rudolf took another bite of the celebratory plum strudel and sighed again, this time somewhat wistfully. Engelbert asked, "Is something amiss, Your Highness?"

"If there was anything that could make my pleasure complete, it would be the merest sip of your wonderful kaffee."

Engelbert inclined his head and replied, "Forgive me, Highness, but there is no need to wish for such a thing when it is yours to command. If you will permit me, Your Majesty . . ." He moved to the door and stepped into the corridor, returning a moment later with a young lad carrying a tray, which was covered by a heavy cloth. Placing the tray on the table, the boy removed the cloth to reveal two porcelain cups, a pot of cream, and a tin box containing a copper pitcher nestled in a bed of glowing embers. At a nod from Engelbert, the lad took a fold of the cloth and, wrapping it around the handle of the pitcher, poured coffee into a cup, added a touch of cream, and placed the cup before the emperor.

"Such foresight, such thoughtfulness," extolled the emperor. "We would that all our subjects possessed such presence of mind." He took another big bite and a long drink of coffee and pronounced himself well satisfied with his new name day confection. "Master Baker Stiffelbeam, you have earned the gratitude of Your Imperial Majesty," he said. "If there is anything we can do for you, name it and we shall make it our command."

Engelbert bowed low, accepting his monarch's praise. Then,

rising, he said, "There is one thing that has been on my mind. And it troubles me greatly."

"You have but to speak it out," replied Rudolf around another bite of strudel. "And if it be in our power, that thing shall trouble you no more. What is it? You wish a royal warrant for your bakery? A knighthood? Ask and it is yours."

"I seek nothing for myself, Your Majesty, but for another. There is a man languishing in prison for a crime he committed against me. I have forgiven him completely and ask for his pardon and release."

"We commend you for your humility and compassion, Herr Stiffelbeam." The emperor nodded thoughtfully. "What is the name of this unfortunate?"

"He is a nobleman by the name of Burleigh, Highness. I know him only as Lord Burleigh."

"Burleigh?" The Emperor of the Romans frowned. "Burleigh? Do not speak to me of that rogue."

"I beg your indulgence, sire, but you did ask me to make my request."

The emperor's frown deepened. "The man is a low criminal," he declared. "In addition to crimes against this court, he has committed gross felonies against your good self. I remember clearly now. Perhaps you wish to exact a more fitting punishment, eh? The lash—or even the rope? Hanging would not be too good for him. Is that it, Baker Stiffelbeam?"

"Oh no, sire! On the contrary. I wish to see him released. He has been in prison these many months, Majesty. It is time to grant him pardon and set him free, I think."

The emperor gazed at his petitioner for a long moment, considering the implications of his decision. "We would be better pleased if you had asked anything but that," he concluded. "This earl is nefarious. Not only has he greatly impeded the important work of this court, he has betrayed the royal trust and abused the goodwill of the emperor himself. Justice will not be mocked. Thus, we regret that we cannot grant the remedy you seek." He regarded Engelbert sympathetically. "We hope you understand. Is there another boon you might ask?"

Engelbert thought for a moment, then said, "I beg your pardon, Majesty, but if Lord Burleigh cannot be pardoned, may he at least be tried? Might the magistrate be instructed to hear the case without further delay? That in itself would be a mercy."

Rudolf, King and Emperor, weighed the implications of this request and said, "Your suggestion has merit, Master Stiffelbeam. Moreover, we are inspired by your compassion—misguided though it may be." He tapped his fingers on the table and regarded the delicious plum strudel and made up his mind. He called for his Minister of Domestic Affairs and, while he waited, finished his celebratory strudel and coffee, and was coaxed into indulging in a second piece of the rich plum dessert.

Rudolf was just brushing the last crumbs from his lips when there came a rap on the door, and the minister slipped quietly into the room. "There you are, Knoblauch. Where have you been hiding?"

"Your servant awaits His Majesty's pleasure." He bowed unctuously and low.

"There is a fellow in prison awaiting a hearing," began the emperor. "We are persuaded to allow the case against him to proceed without further delay. See to it."

"Your command will be expedited through the proper channels, sire," replied the minister. "Pray, Highness, how is this man to be identified?"

"Oh, you know the one we mean," answered Rudolf irritably. "It is that earl—that Burleigh fellow. The one who subverted the energies of our court and betrayed our trust and friendship."

"I recall the case, sire. Chief Magistrate Richter will be informed at once."

"There now," said the emperor when the minister had departed. "The case will be called, and we are satisfied that justice shall prevail." He turned the imperial gaze upon the pastry plate. "Yet there is still one oversight that cries out to be corrected."

"What is that, Your Highness?" wondered Engelbert.

"Nothing less than the sad neglect of your wonderful strudel! See here, the remedy must be applied forthwith."

"Allow me to serve you another slice, Majesty," offered Engelbert. "And I believe there is yet a little more kaffee in the jar."

CHAPTER 19

In Which Genesis Is Invoked

The leaps were getting harder. No doubt about that. In Wilhelmina's estimation, the dimensional crossings were not only more unpredictable, they were less comfortable by a clear margin. Though long ago inured to the nausea and disorientation, she now experienced both—with a vengeance. Each leap took a greater toll. She felt sorry for Dr. Young. Having promised him wonders beyond imagining, all he had experienced so far were vomiting, dizziness, and migraine headaches—which was a shame, because in most other ways the Egyptologist was the perfect candidate for the study and practice of ley travel. Blessed with a hardy constitution and an inexhaustible enthusiasm for science, as well as an encyclopaedic knowledge of cultures and languages ancient and modern, Thomas Young was a seasoned explorer—a quality that, as it turned out, he very much needed, because the journey from the wadi of the tomb in Egypt was anything but smooth.

Their first leap nearly ended in disaster when the connecting ley deposited them, not in the hills outside of Prague, but in the middle of a forested hunting run between a fleeing stag and mounted hunters with a pack of hounds in full cry. Fortunately, thanks to some quick thinking by Wilhelmina, they were able to scurry into the underbrush at the side of the run and avoid being trampled by the horses. Two more leaps followed before they reached Prague and the River Ley.

As soon as her eyesight returned to normal, she raised her head and looked around. They seemed to have landed on the path leading down into the gorge she knew as Big Valley. The right place at last—was it also the right time?

But what had become of Dr. Young?

She had held his hand, literally, through the leap, but they had become separated upon landing. She heard a strangled sound and turned to find him on the path behind her, down on all fours, gagging with dry heaves. She hurried to him and put her hand on his back. "Dr. Young, are you all right?"

He raised his head, his steel-rimmed glasses askew on his face. "I daresay I shall survive." He adjusted his glasses and patted his mouth with a folded handkerchief.

"I am so sorry." She held out a hand to help him to his feet. "That was the worst one yet."

Thomas nodded but waved aside the offered hand, preferring to remain on the ground for the moment. Still dressed in his desert digging gear—lightweight coat and trousers of unbleached linen and floppy cricket hat—he looked like a jungle explorer down on his luck. For the first time, she began to doubt the wisdom of inflicting the trauma of ley travel upon the kindly doctor.

"Hey!" called a voice from the trail below.

Mina turned to see Kit and Cass walking out of the early-morning mist to meet them.

"We were just about to give up on you. What took you so long?"

"Don't ask," Mina replied darkly, using a tone that told him she was not to be crossed.

"Well, I'm glad you got here anyway." Kit gave her a quick peck on the cheek, then turned to the stranger. "You brought somebody with you?" He looked again and recognised the newcomer. "Dr. Young?"

He hurried to where the doctor knelt on the path. "It's me, Kit Livingstone. Good to see you again. We didn't know you were coming." Kit stooped and helped him to his feet. "It looks like you've had a rough time of it."

Thomas, swaying slightly, replied, "I once crossed the North Sea during a force eight gale, and it was nothing like this." He wiped his hands on his coat and then shook hands with Kit. "But all is well that ends well."

"Here—there's someone you should meet," Kit told him, then turned to introduce him to Cass. While they talked, Kit pulled Wilhelmina aside. "Why'd you bring him here?"

"Don't start, okay?" she warned. "I had a devil of a time getting here at all. The short version is I got stuck in Egypt and thought maybe we could use a little help."

"I'm not saying you're wrong, but—"

"Leave it out. I'm not in the mood," Mina told him. "Is this dimension stable?"

"So far." He glanced at Thomas, who seemed to be feeling better. "Shall we head up to the tree?"

"Sole purpose of trip," she said. "Lead the way."

They mounted the steep path to the canyon rim and then hiked across the grassy plain to the low, wooded hills, where they paused to drink a little water before entering the forest. A short while later Kit led them into a grove of small beech trees. "Almost there," he called behind him, and pushing through a dense tangle of branches, they entered the ring-shaped clearing of the great yew tree.

From the elephantine roots to the soaring top, the mighty tree surmounted and dominated the other trees round about. The trunk formed a solid barbican wall beneath massive boughs covered in shaggy bark and tufted with branches bearing thin, needlelike leaves. Here and there red berries glowed among the deep emerald spikes. The wide, outflung branches formed a barren circle around the yew, a dead zone covered in spent, rust-coloured needles that assured the singular tree stood proud as any cathedral on a hill.

"Incredible," breathed Thomas at first glance. "It must be a thousand years old."

"If a day," Kit agreed. He gazed up into the entwining branches. "There's some powerful energy in this place. Best not touch anything. We got a nasty jolt just sitting here too long."

"Is it my imagination?" wondered Mina. "Or is this tree even bigger now than last time I saw it?"

"You too? That's just what I said," Kit told her. "Listen."

Wilhelmina and Thomas cocked their heads to one side and listened. A thick, cushioning silence pervaded the clearing.

"Hear that?" said Kit, his voice stark in the unnatural stillness.

"I don't hear anything," Mina said after a moment.

"Exactly. It's like the tree absorbs everything around it—even sound."

Thomas, standing a little apart, lifted a hand to the tree before them and declared, "'Behold! The Lord God brought forth out of the earth each tree fair in sight, and sweet to eat. Also He brought forth the Tree of Life in the midst of paradise, and the Tree of Knowledge of Good and Evil. And of the many trees in the garden these two were the fairest.'"

Glasses glinting as he raised his face to search the upper branches of the great yew, he continued, "'So the Lord God took the man that He had made and put him in His Garden of Delight, to cultivate and tend it. And the Lord God commanded the man, saying, "Of every tree of the garden thou mayest freely eat, but of the Tree of the Knowledge of Good and Evil, thou shalt not eat of it—for in the day that thou eatest thereof thou shalt surely die."'" Thomas gazed up at the branches towering above him. "This reminds me of that first tree—that first, fatal tree."

"Genesis, chapter two," said Cass, then added, "'But of the fruit of the tree which is in the midst of the garden, God hath said, "Ye shall not eat of it, neither shall ye touch it, lest ye die."' That's from Genesis three." At Kit's surprised expression, she shrugged. "I paid attention in Sunday school."

"My friends, we stand in the presence of great mystery," Thomas declared. "This is an ancient story, and like that tree in Eden, its roots go deep into the fertile imagination of the mind. Its meaning is varied, and though wiser heads may disagree, I believe the tale of Adam and the Fatal Tree is intended to convey something of our origins, yes, the genesis of our place in the world as thinking creatures fit to participate with the Creator in the ongoing work of creation.

"See here," the doctor continued, gazing up through the overhanging branches of the massive yew, "the story illustrates the double-edged gift of the self-aware creature—that is, the knowledge or awareness of existence itself. One of the consequences of becoming a self-aware moral creature is to be conscious not only of your own living existence, but its opposite as well—"

"Death," concluded Kit.

"The Fatal Tree," mused Cass, nodding in agreement, "because the fruit of self-awareness brought the knowledge of death."

In the quiet of the clearing, Thomas' measured voice took on a prophetic note. "Poor old Adam ate from the Fatal Tree, and the universe would never be the same."

At these words, the travellers fell silent. The sun passed behind a cloud, casting the clearing into a sudden early dusk, imparting the dim tranquillity of a church sanctuary; but the silence of the clearing was now somehow less than the quiet of a cathedral and more like the funereal hush of the crypt.

After a moment, Wilhelmina said, "So, the thing is, Dr. Young, we have to find a way to get around this tree if we hope to get back to the Spirit Well."

"I do not recall anyone mentioning a Spirit Well." Thomas looked from Wilhelmina to Kit and back. "Have I failed to grasp the object of our mission?"

Kit explained briefly about the Bone House and how he had discovered what Arthur Flinders-Petrie had termed the Well of Souls. "The tree stands on the spot where the Bone House stood," he concluded. "I know how the Bone House works, but I don't have any idea how the tree works. I'm assuming there is a reason why it's here, and if we could figure out what that reason is, then we just might find a way to get past the tree."

They discussed various possibilities of circumventing the yew tree—including chain saws and dynamite—and eventually ran out of ideas. "What do you think, Dr. Young?" Kit glanced around. "Where'd he go?"

"Probably gone on a walkabout," Mina said. "I'll go check round the other side."

She moved off, giving the enormous trunk and spreading boughs a wide berth, and quickly passed from sight. A moment later they heard her call, "Found him! He's over here."

Kit opened his mouth to shout a warning, but before he could even draw breath he heard Wilhelmina cry out, "Wait! Dr. Young . . . don't!"

Kit's feet were moving before the sound was swallowed by the cushioning quiet. Ducking under the lower branches, he dodged around the trunk of the yew tree and caught sight of Wilhelmina moving toward Thomas Young, who was standing with his hands upraised, a strange smile on his face. "You can literally feel the energy!" he announced. "This is extraordinary!"

"Dr. Young, put your hands down!" shouted Kit. Even as he spoke, Kit felt the energy surge convulse the air with a snap and crackle like that of static electricity arcing across a gap. In the same instant a shimmering blue glow enveloped the doctor and Wilhelmina.

"Mina, watch out!" Cass shouted.

She whirled on Kit and Cass. "Stay back!"

The doctor, his face alight with the fascination of discovery, stretched up and took hold of the nearest branch. A searing crack and a blinding blue-white flash lit up the entire clearing. Thomas was struck and hurled backward by the blast. He landed several meters from the tree in a smouldering heap against the hedge wall. Wilhelmina, standing near him, was knocked sideways and blown back by the force of the discharge. She landed awkwardly on her side with her arm bent into an unnatural position beneath her. The air stank of ozone and singed hair.

Kit ran to her and Cass dashed to where the doctor lay.

"Mina!" Kit shouted. "Mina, are you okay?"

Her eyelids fluttered, showing the whites of her eyes, and she moaned. "Don't try to move," he told her. "Here . . . easy now . . ." Kit rolled her onto her back and freed her trapped arm. The movement brought an agonised shriek of pain. "Sorry, sorry, sorry! Let me have a look."

As gently as he could, he examined the injury. Even the slightest touch brought a gasp, and when Kit tried to adjust the arm, Mina screamed in pain and tears welled in her tightly squeezed eyes. "That's over," Kit told her. "It could be broken. We'll have to make you a sling. Just rest easy, okay?"

As the waves of pain subsided, Mina opened her eyes and whispered, "Thomas—where's Thomas . . . ?"

Kit turned to where Cass was kneeling beside the doctor. "Cass—how is Dr. Young?"

Cass raised her head. The colour had drained from her face and her hands were shaking. "Kit?" she said, her voice small and hushed. "I think Dr. Young is dead."

CHAPTER 20

In Which the Cosmic Cliff Is Contemplated

The tenth observation session at the Jansky Very Large Array radio telescope produced profoundly alarming results for two different reasons. A first-pass analysis of the data indicated that the disturbance in sector B240-22N was growing in size. The region where the original discrepancy had first been noticed had mushroomed in the relatively short time since the previous scan. The two other observatories that Dr. Segler had pulled into the project confirmed this result, which brought about the second alarming development: the NASA team that had arrived to look into developments now demanded complete control of the programme.

"They're hijacking Operation Nightfall!" bellowed Dvorak. "They're trying to freeze us out completely. They can't do this—it's *our* programme!" He pounded on the desk for emphasis. "You've got to tell them where they can shove it!"

"Okay, Leo, calm down," Segler said. "Nobody's hijacking anything. I've got a call in to the administrator's office and another to the COCC. We'll get this sorted out. Just be patient." He regarded his technical director with bemusement. "Operation Nightfall, huh? Is that what they're calling it?"

"This wouldn't even be on NASA's radar if it wasn't for us!" Dvorak said, refusing to be diverted. "They can't just take over like this. They don't know how to run the equipment properly, and they're slowing things down. You've got to get them out of here. Send 'em packing."

Dvorak left the office, slamming the door as he went.

"Your concerns are duly noted," Segler sighed, sinking back into his chair once more. "Don't slam the door."

The director raised his eyes to see Tony Clarke watching him from his place at a makeshift desk across the room. "I sympathise, Sam."

Segler gave a mirthless bark of a laugh. "Who with—him or me?"

"With both of you, actually. It isn't right that NASA tries to take over the show. I can't see that being good for anybody. Bad for morale, for one thing, and you're going to need happy campers to advance the operation. I've been project director a few times in my career and, believe me, I know how tricky it can get trying to appease various warring factions and keep the project moving forward."

"That *is* the main thing right now," Segler said, resting his elbows on the table and holding his head in his hands. "Keeping it all together—which we won't be able to do for too much longer anyway. With data being verified and analysed by independent facilities elsewhere, it is only a matter of time before somebody drops a dime to CNN. The whole thing could blow up in our faces any minute."

"You're right, of course. We're not going to be able to keep the lid on this much longer. It is big and it is going to get out. So we've got to keep our eyes on the prize—finding out what is actually going on out there." Tony gestured out the window in the direction of a pale desert sky. "You might disagree, but the main objective at this point, as I see it, is to stay in the game. It is information we want—the best we can get—let's not lose sight of that. We should put our efforts into keeping ourselves in a position to gather and maintain access to information no matter who is running the show."

Sam Segler nodded and gave his old friend a forlorn smile. "Thanks for the pep talk." Seeing Tony's protest forming, he held up a hand quickly. "No, I mean it. I needed to be reminded. This is all about the data. I'll cut a deal with NASA that, if nothing else, will let us keep our place at the table."

"That's the spirit," said Tony. He glanced around the room as if suddenly remembering something he had forgotten. "Where's Gianni got to?"

"I think he must be down in command central. Want me to call him?"

"No thanks," replied Tony, rising from his chair. He stretched his back and neck and started for the door. "I think I'll wander down and see how the troops are getting on. You need me for anything?"

"No, you go ahead," replied Segler, reading off a small desk monitor. "I just got an e-mail saying I'm to expect a conference call from NASA COCC in ten minutes."

"Good luck with that."

Tony closed the door and made his way down to the Desert Rats' den where he found Gianni sitting at a workstation. The technical staff were all huddled around the Italian astronomer, heads down, staring at a monitor. Tony ambled over to the group. "Greetings, Earthlings," he said. "What's up?"

One of the group raised his head. It was Jason, the grad student. "UT–Austin just sent us an updated data sheet," he said, nodding toward the unseen screen. He hesitated.

"And . . . ?" inquired Tony.

"It's definitely whacked."

"Hmmm . . ." Tony nodded. "Maybe I should take a look."

Jason stepped aside, allowing Tony to take his place in the huddle. Leaning over Gianni's shoulder, Tony saw a black LCD screen with a green grid on which was superimposed a jagged line in glowing red tracing a downward trajectory that ended below the green line at the bottom. Tony took in the coordinates on the graph and said, "Is that what I think it is?"

One of the astronomers turned his face to Tony and nodded. "The cosmic cliff, man. That's what it is."

A routine scan of the red-shift values of objects near the cosmic horizon had indicated a disturbance—the initial anomaly that had set the current project in motion. That disturbance had been confirmed by subsequent scans and others from different sectors conducted by participating facilities. Astrophysicists from the Texas facility had applied the data of the last five scans from three separate radio telescopes to a timeline in order to show the predicted course of events. In other words, if trajectories continued as observed, the end result— as portrayed by the graph—would look like the cross-section of a hillside that began as a gently rounded slope and then plummeted like the Grand Canyon.

"What's the time coordinate?" Tony indicated the bottom line of the graph. "Years or months?"

Gianni shook his head gravely. "Weeks," he said, never lifting his eyes from the monitor. "Weeks only."

One of the astronomers put a finger to the screen where the red line met and dropped below the bottom line of the graph. "That is where expansion ends and collapse begins."

"The beginning of the end," whispered another. She raised her head and with moist eyes gazed in shock at her fellow astronomers. "God help us all."

PART FOUR

The Point of
No Return

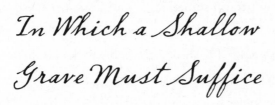

CHAPTER 21

In Which a Shallow Grave Must Suffice

Kit stood over the body of Thomas Young. Tiny tendrils of smoke issued from the collar and cuffs of the doctor's linen coat; Thomas' left foot was bare—the energy surge had knocked off both shoe and sock. The stench of singed cloth, hair, and flesh hung heavily in the air.

"Kit?" Cass, kneeling beside the body, raised her face to him. "What are we going to do?"

Kit knelt down beside the still-warm body and leaned close. There was no breath in the lungs, and the steel frames of the doctor's glasses were skewed, the lenses cracked. He took one of Thomas' hands and laid it gently on the still chest; the other hand was burned almost beyond recognition.

"I'm scared, Kit," Cass murmured. Her voice quivered and her hands were shaking. "I'm really scared."

Kit put his arm around her shoulders and held her close as the first waves of guilt washed over him. He felt as if he should have prevented it somehow. If only he had been more vigilant, more cautious . . . He should have known something like this could happen. He should have been ready. He should . . .

"We've got to do something," said Cass, her voice suddenly strident, almost frantic. "What are we going to do?"

"I don't know." He shrugged off his pack and dug out his leather flask of water. "Here, take this to Mina. Get her to drink some." When Cass did not move, he pushed the flask into her hands. "Go on."

Kit sat back and surveyed the damage. Wilhelmina was badly injured and Dr. Thomas Young—the polymath physician, linguist, Egyptologist, humanitarian, and one of the greatest scientists ever to have lived, Mina's mentor, his friend, the Last Man in the World to Know Everything—was dead. Killed by the Fatal Tree. The name, conferred by Young himself, mocked him now. Staring at the body, Kit felt his stomach roil with grief and remorse. His mouth filled with bile and he swallowed it back down. Putting his head in his hands, he closed his eyes and let stinging tears of sorrow and regret fall. How could he have let this happen?

In a moment, he felt a cool hand on his neck. "It's not your fault," whispered Cass.

"I should have warned him better, made him understand. I should have looked out for him."

"Yes," agreed Cass. "We both should have. But Mina needs us now."

Kit rubbed away the tears and drew a deep breath. He stood. "We have to dig a grave."

"Okay," began Cass, "but maybe first—"

"Right now," Kit insisted. "Mina needs help, and we can't leave

Dr. Young like this." He pushed Cass away. "Take care of Mina. See if you can find something to make a sling for her arm—a scarf or something. I'll start digging a grave." He stood, picked up his pack, and moved toward the doctor's corpse.

Kit fished the small hand ax from his pack and, after scratching a large oval outline in the soft dirt beside the body, began chopping into the outline. When he had scored up a fair section, he scooped out the dirt with his hands, then chopped some more.

Cass joined him a few minutes later, took her place beside him, and started digging. "Mina's pretty foggy, but she thinks she can walk on her own. I gave her some more water and told her what happened."

"How did she take it?"

"How do you think?" Cass snapped, then relented. "Sorry. I didn't mean that. Mina doesn't look good. I think she's in a lot of pain."

Kit nodded and continued to dig. "As soon as we're finished here, we'll head for the Valley Ley. We can rest there until the ley becomes active."

They worked together without speaking and managed to hollow out a shallow grave. When they judged it sufficient, they gently rolled the doctor's body into it. Kit arranged the doctor's limbs and straightened his clothes and glasses, trying to make the man as dignified as possible. Then he sat back on his heels and regarded his handiwork. After a moment, Cass said, "It's got to be done."

Kit nodded and began scooping loose earth onto the body of the great Thomas Young. He would have preferred to cover the mound with stones, but there were none around and he could not spare the time searching for them. The activity reminded him of another burial he had conducted—with Dardok and the River City clansmen when one of the hunters had been attacked and killed by a lion at the entrance to the cave. Wilhelmina joined them as they were finishing and, with her good hand, added a last handful of dirt onto the grave. "It isn't much, is it?" she observed, her voice thick and laboured. "For a man like that there should be more." She gazed at the sorry mound with deep, sad eyes, then dropped her head. "There should be more."

"There should be," Kit agreed, brushing dirt from his hands and knees. "But this will have to do for now."

They all three stood for a time, just looking at the grave, each saying farewell in their own way. Then Kit moved to his pack and slung it over his shoulder. "We should go."

Cass bent down, placed a hand on the mound, and said, "*Vaya con Dios*, Dr. Young."

Kit moved to where Mina stood with her arm in a sling Cass had fashioned out of the blue pashmina. "Can you make it down to the valley?" he asked.

"Don't worry about me," she said. "I'll be fine."

"Okay, we'll go slowly. We stay together and stay alert." With a last good-bye glance at Thomas Young's grave, he pushed through the encircling beech hedge and into the wood beyond. Cass, with an arm around Mina's shoulders, followed, and they slowly, painfully retraced their steps through the thick-grown woodland and out across the grassy plain.

The little herd of gazelles had moved on, and the plain now hosted larger ruminants that Cass identified as *Bos primigenius*, or aurochs— large, lumbering creatures that looked like oversized cows with a high shoulder hump and massive outspread horns. The animals eyed the humans with docile indolence and continued their grazing. Kit called it a good sign and took it to mean that no other predators were around. They reached the trailhead at the canyon rim and paused to allow Wilhelmina to rest a moment, then started down the long slope to the ley point. "We've got plenty of time," Kit told them. "We can rest and eat while we wait."

They made Wilhelmina comfortable and, though no one had much appetite, ate a little from the provisions in their pack, then settled down to nap and wait for the ley to become active. But, though they waited through the long afternoon, they waited in vain. Despite Kit's best efforts and several futile attempts, the travellers failed to detect even the slightest itch or tingle of telluric energy—no prickling on the skin, no tickling of the scalp. The sun had long ago sunk below the western horizon when Kit finally called a halt to their efforts. "Well, this is bad," he said. "This is what happened before."

"Before," echoed Wilhelmina. "You mean—when you got stuck here before?"

"We could be here a long—" began Kit.

"Don't say that," Cass said sharply. "Don't even think it."

"I'm just saying . . ." Kit let it go and glanced to the sky to judge the time. "We'll try again tomorrow. Right now we'd better see about getting some shelter for the night. Come on."

The trail leading down into the gorge was already sunk deep in shadow; here and there the edge sheered away, forcing them to walk single file next to the rock wall lest they stumble and plunge over the side. Upon reaching the valley floor, Kit paused to allow Wilhelmina a chance to rest, but she urged them to move on. "It's best if I keep going," she said through clenched teeth. So they continued on along a path parallel to the river, moving upstream. Kit blazed the trail before them; Cass and Mina followed close behind with grim, robot-like determination.

The river track, forged and used by animals, was bounded on

either side by blackberry brambles, nettles, and stickery dog roses—not a problem in the daytime, but treacherous in the failing light. They kept getting snagged and raked and stung as they pushed through the undergrowth. The air at the bottom of the gorge was heavy and moist, and warmer than on the upper rim. Sweating, swatting gnats and tiny biting flies, the three picked their way carefully along, watching as the last light of day faded in the pale sky above.

Mina, moving with much more difficulty, slowed their progress; the first stars were shining when Kit finally spied the outline of the familiar bluff. He paused, wiped the sweat from his face, and announced to the women a few steps behind, "I see it! Just ahead. We're almost there."

"Thank God," sighed Cass. To Mina she said, "A little farther and then you can rest."

Mina, eyes glassy, jaw clenched, merely nodded.

The way widened somewhat as the path became barren rock leading to the rounded limestone bluff and the cave above. The sky still held a little light, and away to the east a sliver of moon was cresting the canyon rim. Kit stopped. "Here we are," he said, indicating what appeared to be little more than a dark spot in the cliff face. "Listen, Mina, there's a shelf protected by a rock overhang with a small cave behind it. It's a bit of a climb, but we'll get you up. Just sit tight for a second until I get it sorted out, okay?"

Kit disappeared into a gap between two boulders and climbed the old familiar stairway formed by tumbled rocks and rubble. Upon reaching the top, he turned and signalled to Cass. "Okay, ready!"

Wilhelmina raised her eyes to where Kit was waving to them. "I can't do it," she said, looking at the too-narrow gap and the scramble up the rocks protecting the entrance. "My arm is killing me." She glanced around in the failing light. "Maybe I can just stay down here."

"You can make it," Cass said. "Kit will help you from above and I'll support your weight from below. All you have to do is relax and put yourself in our hands. Let us do the work, okay?"

Mina, eyes shut, her mouth pressed tight, gave a nod of resignation.

Cass guided Mina through the gap and up the stony steps. When they were in position, she grasped Wilhelmina around her knees and lifted; Mina used her good hand to steady herself against the rock face and protect her injured arm. Kit, on his stomach, leaning over the ledge, took Mina under her arms and lifted; together, he and Cass slowly manoeuvred her up and over. Mina, biting her lip against the pain, was in tears by the time she collapsed onto the ledge.

"We're there," declared Kit as he eased Mina up onto the platform. "It's over. You made it."

Cass scrambled up into the shelter. "Well done, Mina," she said, wiping sweat from her face. She steered Mina to the nearest wall and eased her down into a sitting position; she put down her pack and joined Kit at the shelter opening, looking out across the lower valley and the curve of the slow-flowing river as it bent around the base of the bluff and out of sight. The water was silky in the soft evening light, and the air was alive with the sounds of cicadas buzzing and birds flocking to roost. She breathed in the soft air and exhaled a heavy sigh. She wanted nothing more than to curl up and forget the last few hours. Instead, she squared her shoulders and asked, "What's next?"

"It might get chilly later on," Kit replied. "I'd better get some firewood up here before it gets completely dark." He stepped to the edge of the shelf and started to climb down onto the path leading to the river. "Look after Mina and I'll be back."

Wilhelmina roused herself sufficiently to say, "Just do what you have to do. I'll be all right for a little while."

"You're sure?" said Cass.

"A hundred percent."

Cass called down to Kit, "Want some help?"

"You could fill the water flasks and cut some fresh bullrushes to add to what we've got. We'll make Mina as comfortable as possible."

Kit and Cass worked until they could no longer see their hands in front of their faces, then retreated to the rock shelter. While Kit hauled up the last of the deadwood he had collected, Cass set about spreading the rushes and arranging them in a neat crosshatch pattern to make a thick pallet for Wilhelmina. Later, after Kit got a fire going, they forced themselves to eat from the last of their provisions. They had light and warmth from the fire, but that was where the comfort ended. They sat and glumly watched the flames and thought about the events of the last few hours as avalanches of regret and guilt crashed down upon them.

Finally, they gave up and decided to get some sleep, but even that proved difficult. One or the other would occasionally drop off, only to be awakened by the howl of an unseen animal or, more often, by Wilhelmina's moaning. Cass eventually achieved something resembling repose, but Kit was not so lucky. He dozed, drifting in and out of consciousness, and each time he surfaced he remembered that Dr. Young was dead. Into his mind flashed the image of the good man's last moments and his crude burial. He saw the makeshift grave and could not help picturing what seemed to him unavoidable: wild dogs or hyenas digging up the corpse for a gruesome nocturnal feast.

Some few hours before dawn he achieved sufficient clarity to resolve that they simply had to get Wilhelmina back to civilization where she could receive proper treatment for her injury. Sunrise, of course, was his next opportunity for ley travel. So when the night sky began to lighten, he woke the two women and said, "Sorry, ladies, but I think we've got to go."

Cass came awake instantly at his touch and then groaned as the grimness of their situation bit hard once more. While Kit went to stoke up the fire, Cass crawled over to where Mina lay and put her palm to Mina's forehead, then gave her shoulder a gentle shake. When this brought no result, she leaned close and whispered into Mina's ear and, after a few moments of gentle coaxing, brought Wilhelmina out of a deep, coma-like sleep. "How are you feeling?"

Mina gave a low moan and said, "I'm thirsty." Her voice was raspy and cracked.

"I'll get you some water," Cass told her. "Where do you hurt?"

"My arm," Mina whispered. "And my side."

Cass brought a flask and raised Mina's head so she could drink. While Mina sipped, she said, "We need to get you home. Do you think you can make it up to the ley line?"

Wilhelmina gave her head a shake and sank back onto her mat. She closed her eyes once more.

"Is she awake?" said Kit, crouching near. "We've got to hurry if we're going to reach the ley while it's still active."

"I don't think she's ready yet. Can we give her a little more time?"

"We don't have a lot of other options here. She needs a doctor. The sooner, the better."

"How are we going to get her out of the cave and up to the ley line?"

"I'll carry her."

"Kit, be reasonable," Cass pleaded. "Think about it."

"I am thinking about it!" he declared hotly. "That's *all* I'm thinking about right now—getting us safely out of here in one piece."

"I know that, Kit," she replied, matching his flare of temper. "And

I thank you for it, but facts are facts. Carrying her is not a real option here. And with her arm the way it is—and who knows what internal injuries she might have—she cannot make the jump. End of story."

Kit stared at her. "What do you suggest?"

"You could go and bring someone back."

"And what if I can't get back to you in time? Or if I get lost, what then?" he challenged. "Things have got very unpredictable lately, if you haven't noticed."

Cass bit her lip. He was right.

Kit pounced on her indecision. "This is the only way. We'll just have to make it work. Once we're on the other side, you can look after Mina while I go for help. But we all go together."

Cass regarded the sleeping Wilhelmina with a doubtful look. "Okay. What if we give her the day to rest and get ready? We can try the ley line this evening."

"I don't know." Kit ran a hand through his hair.

"She can't move, Kit. We can't drag her all the way up there."

"Okay. I hear you," he said, relenting at last. "But we've got to find a way to get her in good enough shape to travel." He followed Cass' gaze to Mina's inert form. "How do you propose we do that?"

"Feed her, keep her warm, give her plenty to drink. And there's another thing we could try—willow bark." At Kit's raised eyebrows, she explained, "It's a natural form of aspirin. The Native Americans used it as an anti-inflammatory and painkiller."

"I can find a willow tree. What do you need?"

"Just some strong young branches to scrape. I can make it up as tea and get her to drink some. It could help."

Kit nodded, glad to be doing something useful. "It's a plan. Sit tight until I get back."

CHAPTER 22

In Which the Wheels
of Justice Grind On

The clickety-tap of the gaoler's heavy hobnail boots in the stone-flagged corridor roused Burleigh from his morose stupor. He heard the iron key in the lock and the creak of the half-rusted door swinging open. The earl, curled up in his corner, did not raise his head when the man called his name and told him to stand. "On your feet," the turnkey called, stepping farther into the cell. "You are wanted upstairs."

At this Burleigh pushed himself up onto an elbow. "*Bitte?*" he said. "Pardon?"

"Get up and wash your face."

"Why? Where are you taking me?"

"You will find out soon enough." The turnkey took his shoulder and gave him a push to get him moving. "*Schnell!* We don't have all day to waste."

On the contrary, Burleigh *did* have all day to waste, but he obeyed—if only for the novelty of the request. He shambled to the water butt and dipped in his hands and splashed tepid water over his face; he smoothed down as best he could his wild, overgrown mass of hair and beard, then allowed himself to be shackled and led from his cell. He was marched along the corridor and up three flights of stairs. The climb left Burleigh breathless and weak-kneed, and slightly disoriented.

"In here," the gaoler said, pushing him through one of the doors at the top of the stairs. The prisoner stumbled over the threshold and into the daylight blazing through the two windows overlooking the square.

Stunned, Burleigh stood blinking, half shielding his eyes with his hands, trying to get used to the brightness. The room was bereft of furniture except for a low wooden bench against the wall opposite a tall, narrow window and, between the two doors on the third wall, a large wooden desk behind which sat a man busily writing something in a great leather-bound ledger. "What is it?" intoned the man absorbed in his work.

"I have brought the prisoner you requested," the gaoler said.

"Over there." The man pointed with his quill at the bench. His nostrils flared with disgust at the stink as Burleigh passed by his desk. "Sit down and wait until you are called."

The gaoler stepped back and took his place to one side of the door to forestall any attempt at escape. They waited. Burleigh, after so many months in the dark recesses of the Rathaus, was happy just to sit and allow the blessed sunlight to wash over him, bathing his light-deprived senses. After a time, the outer door opened and a skinny youth bustled in carrying a roll of paper tied with a red ribbon.

The court clerk held out his hand to receive the document and then motioned the young man away again; he loosed the knot, unrolled the document, and read for a moment. Then, apparently satisfied that all was in order, he pushed back his chair and turned to the door behind him; he gave a single knock and stepped inside, reappearing a moment later. "Come," he said. "The magistrate will see you now."

Burleigh was hauled to his feet, his shackles were removed, and he was pushed toward the inner office. He shuffled into a large book-lined room and was brought to stand before an expansive leather-topped desk occupied by a sharp-featured man in a curly black wig and a stiff-starched white collar tight around his thin neck. The man did not deign to acknowledge his visitor's presence.

"Herr Magistrate," intoned the clerk after a moment. "The prisoner you requested is presented."

"Name," the magistrate said without raising his eyes from the papers spread out before him. When Burleigh did not reply quickly enough, he glanced up. "State your name for the records."

"Burleigh," the earl said, his voice a raspy croak. "Lord Archelaeus Burleigh, Earl of Sutherland." The title sounded ridiculous in the circumstances, even to him. The magistrate glanced up sharply and cast a critical eye over him as if to ascertain the truth of this assertion, then shrugged and, dipping his pen, entered a line on the paper.

Chief Magistrate Richter waved a narrow hand at a corner of the room. "Is this the man who assaulted you?"

Burleigh glanced around to see Engelbert Stiffelbeam standing behind him. He had not noticed anyone else in the room. "This is the man, yes," replied Etzel.

Herr Richter nodded slowly and returned to his papers. After a moment, he said, "And is it your intention to have the charges levied against this prisoner set aside and dismissed?"

"That is my intention," said Etzel evenly. "I wish to have him released."

"You make this declaration under your own volition and of your own free will?"

"I do, yes, Chief Magistrate."

"No one has paid you to do this, or promised you anything of material value, or threatened you in any way in order to persuade you to make this request?"

"No, Herr Magistrate, no one has given me anything. Nor has anyone promised me anything or threatened me. I do this because Jesus has commanded us all to forgive those who have sinned against us."

The magistrate gave a little snort, whether of agreement or annoyance, Burleigh could not tell. Herr Richter, Chief Magistrate of Prague, dipped his pen again and made a note on his paper. Then, replacing the pen, he folded his hands and looked up into the prisoner's face. "These charges are hereby answered. Time served in prison shall be considered just and sufficient punishment for the aforementioned crime. Therefore, it is the decision of this office that the prisoner will be released from captivity pending further charges arising from matters relating to subversion of authority and interference with the lawful work of His Majesty's court."

Burleigh heard the words "released from captivity" and his heart lurched in his chest. But before hope took flight, the stern-faced official continued; pointing at Burleigh with his pen, he said, "You are hereby released on the provision that you remain in the city until all legal proceedings are concluded."

"I am to be released?" said the earl, unable to trust what he had heard. "But where am I to go?"

"That is none of my concern," replied the magistrate sternly.

"So long as you remain within the city walls, you can go where you like."

"My purse, my money—it was taken from me when I was brought here. I will need it."

"Any property you may have possessed is forfeit to the crown until any and all matters arising from any and all cases against you shall be adjudicated," the magistrate intoned curtly. "That is the law." He looked hard at Burleigh. "If you have no money, you can be declared a destitute and charges of vagrancy can be brought against you."

"If my purse is forfeit, how am I to pay my way?"

"That is not the concern of this office."

Burleigh stared at the man. "So then . . . ?"

"You will be returned to gaol to await further legal proceedings. Is that your desire?"

"He can stay with me." Engelbert moved to stand beside the earl. "I am sorry," he told Burleigh, "I meant to say this before." To the magistrate, he said, "If you please, sir, he will stay with me and work in my kaffeehaus to earn his keep. He will not become a vagrant."

"See that he does not," replied Herr Richter. "I agree to release him to your care on the condition that you stand surety for him until judgement is rendered. You are responsible for his upkeep and must see that he fulfils all his obligations. His debts and trespasses become your debts and trespasses—understood?"

Etzel looked at Burleigh as if judging the worth of a sack of flour. "I understand, Chief Magistrate."

Herr Richter reached for the little brass bell at the corner of his great desk and gave it a shake. Pavel, the clerk, appeared momentarily and took his place beside the magistrate, who said, "These men have agreed to the conditions and stipulations of the court; see that they sign the appropriate documents."

Turning once more to the former prisoner, the magistrate gave his head a slight shake—as if he still could not decide what to think about all this—then sighed and, pushing back his throne of a chair, stood up to deliver his provisional verdict.

"Under the conditions just specified and agreed," said the high official, "I hereby authorise the release of the prisoner to the care and custody of Engelbert Stiffelbeam, baker in this city, until such time as the court shall summon Archelaeus Burleigh to receive the judgement of this court regarding all remaining charges against him."

Burleigh, not quite believing what had just happened, looked around at the still-open door behind him. "I am free to go?"

"You are free"—the magistrate thrust a finger at the document now in his clerk's hands—"providing you obey the agreed stipulations and conditions."

"I can go now?"

Nodding, Herr Richter said, "There are papers to sign. The clerk will see you out."

Not twenty minutes later, the earl emerged from the shadow of the Rathaus into the glorious light of a splendid midsummner afternoon. He paused to breathe the clean, fresh, sun-washed air and the warmth of the gentle rays on his pallid skin. It felt like tiny electric fingers dancing all over him, and he closed his eyes to savour the feeling and marvel that he had never felt anything so wonderful in all his life.

CHAPTER 23

In Which the River Is the Only Way

*T*hat first day of freedom and light after so many months in the dim, noisome dungeon cell was intoxicating, and Burleigh wandered the city streets in a daze. Unaware of the effect of his wan and dishevelled appearance on the respectable citizens of Prague, he roamed the busy thoroughfares, lost to the world and lost to himself in the random chaos of his thoughts. The sun had long since set and shadows claimed the streets when he at last turned his feet toward the Old Town Square and the Grand Imperial Kaffeehaus to find Engelbert putting up the shutters for the day. "*Guten Abend*," Etzel called when he saw Burleigh strolling up. "Have you had a good walk?"

Burleigh regarded the baker with an empty, uncomprehending stare, then mumbled, "I shall go out again tomorrow."

Etzel smiled and nodded. "I would do the same. And tomorrow

you must buy some new clothes and get a haircut too, I think." He rubbed his hand over his own round head. "Yes, I think so."

Burleigh looked down at his ragged clothes and rotten shoes and what he saw struck him as indescribably funny. He threw back his head and laughed, his voice pattering across the swiftly emptying square. The few passersby who heard him stole anxious glances in his direction before hurrying on. "You might be right," Burleigh admitted and, still laughing, went inside and up to the room Engelbert had prepared for him.

That night, Burleigh and Engelbert dined together in the kitchen of the Grand Imperial; they were served by some of the younger staff and kitchen helpers who then joined them at table. It was simple, satisfying food of wurst and cabbage, fresh bread and butter and beer; and Burleigh ate, chewing his food with the grim determination of a stoic under torture. After the meal, exhausted by the turns of the day, the earl took a candle from the table and went up to bed. Closing the door behind him, he stood for some time gazing blankly around the room—at the solid oak bed with its clean white linens and down-filled pillow, the little table and basin of fresh water, the chair at the foot of the bed, and the rug on the floor.

"You knew I would be released?" he had asked Etzel when first shown the room. "You never doubted?"

"The magistrate is a reasonable man," Engelbert had told him. "And reasonable men cannot remain unreasonable forever."

With these words echoing in his mind, the earl slowly came to himself once more. He crossed the floor and placed the candle on the table. He then shed his clothes, washed in the basin, and donned the oversized nightshirt Etzel had laid out for him. He slipped between the cool, fresh sheets and immediately fell asleep. The moment he

closed his eyes on that eventful day, perhaps that is when those innocent words began their work; perhaps that is when ferment began.

Though the sleeper passed the first hours of the night in blissful
repose, in the small hours before dawn he grew agitated and restless
and, at last, wakeful. He opened his eyes, and panic descended upon
him like a sodden blanket. One moment he was at rest in peaceful
slumber, and the next he was wide-awake and staring into the darkness as into the abyss. When he could endure that no longer, he threw
back the blankets and rose to pace the boards in the pale, silvery
moonlight seeping through the shutters.

His mind was a confusion of half-formed thoughts and words
and voices and he knew not what—all churning and sliding, emerging and fading . . . only to materialise again before shading into other
yet more outlandish fragments. He could not seem to hold on to
any thought or idea for more than a mere second or two before it
was snatched away and replaced by another equally short-lived scrap
of mental detritus. Perhaps it was the darkness, or being shut up in
a room after so many months in an underground cell, but whatever
the reason, Burleigh could not remain still any longer. Pulling on his
ratty coat and stuffing his bare feet into his shoes, he reached for the
doorknob and, pausing to take a breath, twisted it and threw open
the door—half expecting to be met by the gaoler. There was no one
waiting for him, however. Burleigh stepped out onto the landing and
stopped to listen. The house was quiet; all was at peace and rest.

Stealthy as a shadow, Burleigh crept to the next room and opened
the door. Moonlight from a half-open shutter bathed the form of
Engelbert, asleep in his eiderdown bed, his head cradled in the crook
of his arm. The earl saw the sleeping man and stared as if at an
apparition, or the luminous vision of a saint, an angel made flesh:

innocent, trusting, beyond the vulgar cares of the world. The sight of the virtuous Engelbert produced an instant and violent reaction in Burleigh. Such holy and blameless virtue must not be allowed to live in this world unscathed; it must be punished, eradicated, obliterated, destroyed.

This was not a thought that crossed the earl's rational mind: it was a visceral reaction, a raw emotion untamed by any process of reason. Burleigh saw Engelbert upon the bed, the soft silver moonlight bathing his benign features, and a terrible rage and loathing gushed up inside him, sweeping away any last vestige of coherent thought.

Two silent steps brought him into the room. Three more carried him to the bed where he stood, looming over the tranquil figure—so defenceless, oblivious to all harm, sunk deep in the untroubled slumber of a righteous man, the whisper of a smile on his broad, cheerful face. The urge to smash that face, to crush that skull, to deform and debase those inoffensive, good-natured features seized him, and Burleigh felt a thrill of pleasure ripple up his spine to the top of his head. Here would be recompense for the suffering he had endured; here would be sweet, satisfying revenge.

Burleigh clenched his fists into hate-filled clubs and his lips tightened in a grimace of primal rage. He raised a hand to strike, savouring the moment of release, and . . . the moment passed, and then another, and still he did not strike. He wanted nothing more than to demolish that gentle cherubic face—but wait! He had already done that!

Once before, all those months ago, unrestrained by any will or authority other than his own, he had completely given in to that urge and had struck; he had reduced that benevolent visage to a sodden mass of bruised and bloody tissue, and what happened? What had happened, indeed? Here was the same face—more winsome, more pleasant than ever—while his own handsome features had grown haggard and grey and ravaged by a short eternity in prison. But that was not the worst—far from it!

In a flash of insight, Burleigh glimpsed the barrenness of his own existence; his heart was an immense, hollow cavity that could never be filled. The mere sight of Engelbert threw his lack into painfully sharp relief. In that instant, he understood that the paucity of his own life could not abide the rich fullness enjoyed by a simple, good man like Engelbert. Those two things could not exist in the same world: one of them would have to go. And since he was powerless to do away with Engelbert—he knew that now—it was himself that must be eliminated.

Burleigh saw this clearly, and the sight was marvellous to behold. It was as if he had been walking through life with his eyes swathed in burlap, and now the binding strips had been stripped away. Instantly, he understood how the man born blind felt when the physician removed the surgical bandages and glorious light suddenly flooded into his dark world. He was that man.

"I see it now!" he murmured, his breath catching in his throat. "I see."

Up from the bottomless pit of loathing rushed a flood of disgust and revulsion—disgust for the vicious, venomous wickedness of his life, and revulsion for the depravity of his existence. He had given himself wholly to the unstinting pursuit of ruthless ambition and unrestrained greed, where every kindness had been either shunned or abused, and every good encountered returned with evil. He was a liar, a cheat, and a fake—even his name was a deceit! His entire life was one monumental fraud.

With his new clarity of vision, Burleigh saw himself as a poor, crabbed, miserable creature, with a soul as tiny, black, and hard as a burnt-out cinder. In the blinding flash of revelation, guilt came crashing down on him with the deadweight of all his crimes and transgressions; heavy as a tombstone slammed onto his shoulders, he staggered beneath the crushing burden of his guilt. He could not stand.

Beside the bed of his saving angel whose face shone so brightly and serenely in the moonlight, Burleigh sank to his knees and felt the limitless disgrace of the wretch who knows himself to be lost and doomed, fit only for well-deserved destruction. Dry-eyed—beyond sorrow, beyond remorse—for with sins and iniquities beyond counting, what would a few salty tears avail? Instead, he beat his breast with a fist clenched like a rock and his face burned hot with shame.

The shame! The shame was devastating, more distressing than anything he had endured in prison, greater even than the guilt that bent his back, greater than he could bear. "God!" he moaned. "Please, God, please."

The words escaped his lips before he knew what he said, or even what he expected God to do for him. What did he expect of God?

Instantly, words came back to taunt him. His words, spoken to another blameless soul he meant to destroy, spoken with spite and spleen, and with supreme certainty: *There is no God! There is only chaos, chance, and the immutable laws of nature. In this world—as in all others—there is only the survival of the fittest.*

The arrogance of those words appalled him. The insufferable vanity stole the very breath from his lungs. The wilful, pig-ignorant folly of that proclamation and the ghastly conviction with which it had been declared astounded and unnerved him. How could he have been so stupid, so absurd, so utterly, abysmally, unspeakably mindless? How could he have been so wrong? Prancing around like a bell-hung fool, spouting incoherent nonsense as if it were unassailable truth . . . How could that have happened? How was it possible to be so deluded, and deluded so absolutely?

Burleigh had no answer; he had only the abject humiliation of the realisation that much of what he previously thought and held to be true was a pile of stinking garbage. He realised that now, and knew just how very wrong he had been. Bereft of hope, he knew himself for the vile and wicked creature he was, and the knowledge pierced deep and hard in a stroke that left him desolate, demeaned, and broken. Like an insect first dazzled by the flame, then destroyed by it, Burleigh felt the searing heat of his destruction and, past the point of no return, reeled toward it.

Down the stairs and into the kitchen he went—he did not even remember leaving Etzel's room. Two of the young serving boys were curled up on the floor near the big oven; otherwise the shop was empty. A hollowed-out automaton, an animated shell of a human being, the earl walked out the kaffeehaus door and into the night. He thought—if it could be called a thought, for it was more of a compulsion—that he would end the madness. He would walk to the river and throw himself into the water and rid the world of his empty, meaningless existence.

The Old Town Square was deserted; there was no one about this time of night. Burleigh was alone with his agony as he stole along the moonlit streets, hastening toward the city gates and the river where he would consign himself to the unforgiving water and put an end to the misery. How he would open those barred gates, he did not know. His was not a rational plan; there was no plan, no thought—there was only the bedrock conviction that the world would be a far better place without him in it.

CHAPTER 24

In Which a Pertinent Question Is Posed

Wilhelmina remained quiet through the day, and though Cass' infusion of willow bark water seemed to ease her discomfort somewhat, she was still in no shape to travel that evening. Kit and Cass decided to give her another night to rest; the next morning, however, come what may, they would go.

Kit woke them before sunrise, and together he and Cass eased Mina over the rock ledge in the pale dawn light. As before, it was excruciating for everyone; but after being allowed to catch her breath following the ordeal, Mina seemed to revive somewhat in the cool morning air—she even went so far as to claim that she could walk on her own so long as they did not expect any speed records.

They paused briefly at the riverbank and took care of their necessities, and then set off along the river path. Kit led the way through the bracken and brambles; Cass and Mina followed with Cass at Mina's elbow. No one spoke.

At first they made good progress, but by the time they reached the trailhead and started up the rising track leading out of the gorge, Wilhelmina was flagging. They paused twice to let her catch her breath before resuming the ascent, the early-morning mist clearing the higher they went, until at last Kit announced, "There's the marker. We're here." He looked to Mina; her face was sweaty and the colour of putty. "Well done. We have a few minutes. We can rest a bit."

Mina nodded, and Cass helped ease her down on the path to wait. The sky continued to lighten and took on a pale pinkish glow. After a while, Kit rose and began walking back and forth across the path until at last he said, "It's live. That's a relief. We can go." He moved to Wilhelmina and stooped to help her up. "Ready?"

"Ready as I'll ever be." She winced as she took Kit's hand and rose unsteadily to her feet; Cass supported her on the opposite side, and together they guided her to the place Kit had marked as the start of the ley line.

"Mina, you'll have to walk as quickly as you can. Cass and I will hold on to you, and we'll all do this together, right? Start on three— and we'll make the jump on the seventh step. All together—okay, here we go . . . one . . . two . . . three . . ."

The three started walking and by the fourth stride were perfectly in sync, with Kit counting off the steps. On the seventh step they made the little hop to initiate the leap into the unknown, accompanied by Mina's yelp of pain.

Nothing happened. They returned to the starting point and counted off the steps, made the jump, and remained firmly on the path.

"Blast!" growled Kit.

"Stop it," warned Cass.

"This is what happened last time—"

"No!" Cass snapped. "Do not go there. This isn't like last time. We'll try it again."

Kit craned his neck around to look for the rising sun, then nodded. "Mina, you good for another try?"

Jaw clenched, she nodded. "I have to get home. I don't care what it takes."

"Okay, once more." Tightening his grip on Wilhelmina's hand, he stepped to the mark. "On my count . . ."

As before, Kit counted off the paces, and somewhere between the fifth and sixth step he felt the hair stand up on the back of his neck. His skin prickled to the play of static electricity, and a cool gust of breeze stirred the leaves of the trees. "Ready . . . jump!"

Their feet left the ground and did not connect again right away. The world blurred, as if seen through the frosted window of a high-speed train. The wind shrieked through their clothes, tiny pellets of sleet pelted their exposed faces, and rain drenched them head to foot. Kit closed his eyes against the welcome blast, and when he opened them again he was standing on a narrow path lined with beech trees. The fast-moving sheet of rain swept down the path ahead of them, dissipating as it went. A moment later the sun returned, making dappled shadows on a perfectly straight track. Kit recognised the place as the River Ley outside Prague. It was the right place. *So far so good*, he thought. Was it also the right time? There was one quick way to find out. "Stay here, you two," Kit told them. "I'll be right back."

He jogged off along the track and came to the dirt road that ran alongside the river. Dirt, not tarmac—he took that as a good sign.

Stepping from the shadows of the beechy grove, he moved to the edge of the road where he saw, in the distance, a horse-drawn cart plodding his way—not a motorised vehicle—another good sign. He waited beside the road for the wagon to draw near. From what he could observe of the driver's clothes—the shapeless hat, the rough-spun cloth of short coat and knee-length trousers, the wooden clog on the foot resting on the kickboard—all seemed familiar and pointed to arrival within the desired time frame. When the wagon's occupant came close enough to observe Kit's outfit—the dark wool trousers, voluminous white shirt, and brown waistcoat he was wearing when they bailed out of Damascus—the fellow's friendly expression turned suspicious and wary. Kit, suddenly self-conscious, raised a hand in greeting and then pretended to continue his walk along the road. When the wagon had passed and the farmer no longer seemed inter-ested in the oddly dressed stranger, Kit about-faced and beat it back to the grove where Cass and Mina were waiting.

"Did you forget about us?" demanded Cass. "What took you so long?"

"It's the right time more or less," said Kit. "Fingers crossed—I think we made it." He looked at Mina; her eyes were closed and her lips were pressed into a thin, bloodless line. He took her good arm, draped it around his neck, and said, "Lean on me, old girl. Let's get you home."

Stepping from the shady copse into a bright autumnal morning, the three set off on the river road. The sun dried their rain-rinsed clothes as they went, and after a few hundred metres, two more farmers on their way to market overtook them. The first farmer glanced at them, disliked what he saw, and turned his face away. But the second farmer recognised Wilhelmina as the lady who sometimes bought honey and eggs from his wife; he hailed her and pulled up to offer them a place in his wagon. Mina rallied to exchange a greeting and clamber into the wagon bed, and soon they were bumping along the rutted road to Prague.

They rolled through the city gates a short time later and proceeded to the Old Square, where the weekly market was open for business. The farmer let them off at the far end of the square, and they stood for a moment gazing out across that wide public space lined with shops and filled with kiosks and stalls and handcarts doing a steady trade. Townsfolk thronged the square, drifting among the merchants and vendors, haggling over prices, sampling the wares, and exchanging gossip while children darted here and there in games and races, or clustered around the jugglers and musicians. To the right they saw the soaring spires of the cathedral, and on the left the great, glowering, gothic eminence of the Rathaus; straight ahead, high and remote on its hill, sat the palace of Emperor Rudolf.

It was a scene Wilhelmina had witnessed many times, but in that moment it all seemed exactly as she had seen it that first day when, tired and aching with uncertainty, she had been befriended by a German baker on his way to make his fortune in Prague. Her heart moved within her, and suddenly she wanted nothing more than to see that baker's sweet face once more.

Away on the far side of the busy marketplace she glimpsed the green-and-white awning of the Grand Imperial Kaffeehaus, and her breath caught in her throat. Ignoring the pain in her arm and side, she shrugged off Kit's supporting hand. "Please, I have to do this myself."

"Nonsense," replied Kit. "We got you this far, we'll see you all the way to your door."

But Cass put a restraining hand on Kit's arm and shook her head. "Let her go."

Kit released her, and Mina tottered to the kaffeehaus door. She paused a moment to compose herself, drew her fingers through her hair, then pushed open the door and stepped inside to the warm, steamy interior redolent of coffee and cinnamon, toasted almonds and hot milk. The morning crowd was in full cry, and her green-liveried serving minions were darting here and there with trays stacked with cups and pots and plates of pastries. There was a clutch of customers at the small counter fronting the kitchen. One of the girls saw her and stared, then called an uncertain greeting, but Wilhelmina paid no attention. Heart beating fast with anticipation, she pushed through the good-natured crowd, making her way to the kitchen. Once around the crush at the counter, she moved quickly to the oversized stove where she saw a familiar form bending before the open oven door. "Etzel, I'm home!" she called, hurrying to him. "I've missed you."

The figure started, then straightened and turned. "Why, hello, Miss Klug," he said. "I am sorry, but Engelbert is not here."

Wilhelmina staggered back. "Burleigh!" she gasped, her eyes darting around the kitchen, looking for a weapon—or a way out. Seeing neither, she snapped her attention back to the figure looming before her. "Where is Etzel? What have you done to Etzel?"

A snaky smile came to the dark man's thin lips. "The question is, rather"—he closed the oven door, turned, and took a step nearer—"what has Etzel done to me?"

CHAPTER 25

In Which the Fat Hits the Fan

What are the chances that the data has been corrupted?" asked Carl Bayer. He was the chief astrophysicist of the team assigned to what NASA was calling the Jansky Anomaly. He waved the sheet of paper on which was printed a copy of the graph the team at the JVLA site had produced.

"Not sure, boss," murmured one of his junior associates.

"Speak up, Peters. What are you not sure about—exactly?"

"Well, I mean, it is possible—there *could* be an error somewhere," allowed Peters, lifting his eyes from the copy in his own hands. "But I've combed through the equations and they look good. You want a percentage? Zero to five percent, something like that."

"Right. So . . . ?"

"Well," hedged Peters, "what you have there is only a summary of the data so far collected. There's more to come. Things could change, I suppose."

"Did you check their algorithms? Their calibration records?"

Peters pulled a pained expression. "Of course, yes. Did I go through every last line of code in their programs? No. Could there be a bug in the data feed? Possibly. But I spot-checked various sequence records and cross-referenced them with the scan results from the other communicating facilities."

"And . . . ?"

"Like I say—it all checks out," the younger man replied. "I think we have to accept that what they are telling us is true. We're headed for some kind of apocalypse."

"If what they're telling us is true," Bayer countered, "*apocalypse* is not a big enough word." The NASA chief drew a hand through his thinning hair, then wiped his face with his hand. "Okay, where is Chandra? Mitchell and Rodríguez—where are they?"

"Down in the Rats' Nest, last time I looked."

"Get 'em up here. Second-floor conference room—fifteen minutes."

"What about Dr. Clarke and Director Segler? You want me to bring them in?"

Bayer met the question with a blank expression. "Why?"

"Because it's their show and all. They might have something to contribute."

"They're not part of this," the team leader decided. "We can fill them in later. And get Director Gilroy on the phone—have him patched in to the conference room. I want him to hear this."

"Fifteen minutes? Boss, that's—"

"What are you hanging around for? Go!"

Peters scuttled from the room, and Bayer returned to his desk and leaned on it with both hands. He stared at the printed graph as if it were a recent photo of the Grim Reaper. The neat grid in its rectangular box and tidy rows of numbers and rising red line foretold a disaster that defied comprehension. Here was a harbinger of an event unprecedented in all of human history—what was he to think about that? More importantly, what was he supposed to *do*?

He had no answer to that. Someone with more senior authority and a higher pay grade would have to face that question. His assignment was to pass along his best judgement; he would draw on his abilities and experience and assess all the available information. Like all good gears in a giant machine, he would do his part and let someone down the line worry about the rest.

The conference room on the second floor was empty. He snapped on the lights and closed the door, made his way to the head of the table, and sat down in one of the big uncomfortable leather chairs. In a few minutes, what the six people gathered around this table decided would set the tone for whatever would follow. It was crucial to get it right. Bayer sat down and closed his eyes, composed himself, and waited.

Dr. Chandra, the first of his team to join him, was a dynamo who, despite her grey-streaked hair, bristled with the energy of someone thirty years younger. "You've seen the Doom Chart?" she said as she moved into the room.

Bayer opened his eyes and raised his head. "Is that what they're calling it now?"

"What do you think about it?"

"I think we should wait for the others before getting into that."

The remaining members of his team were not long in coming. Rodríguez was next, together with Mitchell; both were in their thirties with young families, and both wore the foolish expressions of men who were doing their best to mask fear with bravado. "S'up, chief? You miss us?"

"Take a seat, guys. I've got a call in to the director and I'm having it patched in. I'm going to fill him in on what's going on, and I want everyone to hear what is said—it'll save repeating everything later."

They ambled to seats opposite Chandra, who said, "Any chance of some coffee?"

Before Bayer could respond, there was a knock on the door and Peters arrived, leading a shaggy young man with a black plastic UFO-shaped object attached to a telephone cord. "Oh, you're already here. I brought the conference phone." The young IT technician waved the machine in his hand. "You want I should plug it in?"

"Yes, thanks," said the director. "Has the call been made?"

"As we speak," replied the techie. He leaned over the table and poked the cord into a socket hidden by a little flap in the centre of the table. "I'll have it put through as soon as the line goes live."

"Thank you," Bayer told him.

The techie switched on the phone and saw the blue LED light up. "You're good to go. Anything else?"

"That will be all," replied the director, waving him away. "And please shut the door on your way out." To Peters, he said, "Take a seat, Rob."

As soon as the door clicked shut, Bayer pushed the sheet of paper out onto the table before him as if it were the source of a virulent contagion. "Okay, we've seen the data. What do we make of it?"

The team looked at one another for a moment, and finally Mitchell spoke up. "Obviously," he ventured, "we have to run some more scans. Isolate the region of greatest activity and do some rapid mini-scans, and see what's trending."

"We've got the numbers on almost a dozen scans already," Rodríguez pointed out. "How many more do you need before you can see what is staring you right in the face?"

"Look," Mitchell retorted, "we don't know for sure about any of those scans. We weren't here when they were conducted. All I'm saying is they gave us a head start, showed us where to look; now we can zero in and see what's really happening out there."

"And you think that is going to change anything?" challenged Rodríguez. "You think that's going to make a difference? If it is, why stop at twelve scans? Let's do twenty—or thirty. Better still, let's do fifty just to be sure."

"What is wrong with you, man? I only said—"

"Boys! Boys!" scolded Chandra. "Play nice." She turned to Bayer and said, "It is clear that we have had some upsetting news—"

"I'll say," agreed Rodríguez. "The fat has hit the fan big-time."

"And we are struggling here to take it in. But rather than spend our precious time sniping at one another, I suggest we discuss the implications of what the data is showing us."

"*If* it turns out to be right, you mean," said Mitchell.

"It *is* right!" muttered Rodríguez. "Can't you get that through your thick head?"

"Yes, of course," continued Dr. Chandra, overlooking the squabble, "proceeding on the assumption that the data sets are correct."

"That's exactly what I had in mind, Adira. Thank you," said Bayer. "We can generate more numbers, of course. In the meantime, I think we should begin running some scenarios and formulating an interim response."

Glum silence descended over the little group.

"Don't everyone speak at once," said Bayer. "Thoughts?"

His question was answered by a knock on the door—followed directly by JVLA Director Segler, who did not wait to be invited in.

"Hello, everyone. Excuse me, but Duncan said you were having a conference. Not to crash your party, but perhaps we might be of assistance?"

"We?" Bayer frowned. "Who else is with you?"

"Only Dr. Clarke," replied Segler; he pushed open the door and stepped into the room. Tony hovered at his shoulder. "But I can get anyone else we need."

"This is a closed meeting," Rodríguez informed them. "We're on a call."

Segler returned the gaze of the NASA astrophysicist but made no move to leave.

Bayer sighed. "Please come in, gentlemen. Take a seat. Actually, we haven't started yet. We're expecting the call any minute." As the two newcomers took seats at the long table, he said, "I know I don't need to tell you that what is discussed here is to remain strictly confidential and not to be voiced outside this room."

"Understood, Dr. Bayer," replied Segler. "It is not our intention to make matters more difficult. We merely wish to offer our services in whatever capacity you may find useful."

Bayer nodded curtly. "We'll see."

Tony Clarke pulled up his chair. "We are every bit as mindful as you are of the sensitive nature of the problem and just as committed to confidentiality."

"Thank you for that assurance, Dr. Clarke," intoned Bayer. "Now then, unless there are to be any further disruptions, perhaps we might turn to the matter at hand."

"I assume you have the updated Doom Sheet," said Segler.

"This one is from . . . let's see . . ." Bayer pulled the page toward him and read the time stamp. "From 04:00. Is there a newer one?"

"There is," said Clarke. "A little after 05:15 CalTech sent over the data sheets from the Australian scan."

"And . . . ?"

"It conforms to the previous prediction model 26RD measuring blueshift momentum."

"No deviation?"

"Very little," replied Tony. "They're still collating it downstairs, but my initial impression was that the latest scan corroborates everything we've seen so far. Also, I thought it might be a good idea to check the ICRS baseline against the Cepheid variables for the anchor LG galaxies—"

"For an early-warning system?" asked Mitchell.

Tony demurred. "Just to see if there is any anomalous movement in our part of the neighbourhood. It may be too early to detect anything, but we have to start somewhere."

"We'll need to see that data," said Rodríguez, stretching a hand across the table. "Pronto."

Chandra gave her colleague a glance of motherly disapproval and added, "Please, Dr. Clarke, it would be most helpful."

"Don't worry—I'll make sure everyone gets copied in as soon as the report is ready."

"We can go over the fine points later," Bayer said, "but for now we'll take it as read that what we are seeing is a disruption in the expansion of the cosmic horizon—if that is not putting it too strong."

"Too strong?" remarked Rodríguez. "How about this? In plain, simple words—the cosmic horizon is shrinking. The universe is collapsing. It's the Big Crunch." He gazed belligerently around the table. "Am I right?"

"Yeah, you're right," muttered Mitchell. "But what are you going to *do* about it? That's what I'd like to know. What can *anybody* do about it?"

"First things first," Segler told him. "What I'm asking for now is a way to define the situation in nontechnical terms for those whose duty it will be to formulate a defence."

"Given the timeline—and we're talking weeks here—I don't see that we have time to engineer much of a defence—"

"That's assuming we could even *find* a credible defence in the first place," offered Peters. "As it is, the fear is so thick down in the Nest you could cut it with a chain saw. What is going to happen when this goes public? What do you think will happen when Fox News starts running it on their scrolling banner?" His face screwed up and his shoulders began to shake. It took a moment for those around the table to realise he was laughing. "I can see it now! Breaking News: World Ends in Six Days!" He giggled, his voice leaping into a higher register. "A real showstopper! I mean, ad revenues on *that* are going to make the Super Bowl look like Fishing Channel reruns."

"Calm down, son," said Bayer sternly. "No one is suggesting anything like that."

"He's right, though," suggested Mitchell. "Once this gets out . . . can you imagine the chaos?"

"I don't agree," said Chandra. "Look at how the general public responded to the threat of global warming a few years ago. Some grew concerned enough to engage the threat—panic, if you will— but most went about their lives as normal. For most people it was just business as usual."

Mitchell waved her argument aside with a swat of his hand. "This isn't like that at all. This is different. When everyone sees the stars begin to blink out and planets collide, they're going to know something's up. Riots, looting, murder—all hell will break loose. Whole cities will be put to the torch."

"That won't happen," Tony said. "For what it's worth, by the time people see stars blinking out, there simply won't be time to panic. It'll be over in a matter of seconds." He clicked his fingers. "No one will have time to so much as tie their shoes, much less torch anything."

"That's comforting," Rodríguez grumbled.

"People, people," Bayer pleaded. "The goal is to gather verifiable data to help define the situation, not contain it. We can leave it to other authorities to worry about the fallout. Director Gilroy is going to call in a minute, and we've got to have something useful to tell him. What's it going to be?"

Again, a desultory silence descended upon the group. The seconds dragged by slowly. They looked at one another and at the silent conference telephone as if a black hole had suddenly appeared in the middle of the table.

"I'm afraid, Carl," said Director Segler, speaking up at last, "that it amounts to the same thing in the end. I mean, defining the crisis is all well and good, and I agree it is necessary, but communicating that to the outside world inevitably carries the risk that someone some-where is going to run riot with it. Unless we can visualise a potential solution to the problem, it will serve no purpose to alarm people."

"So, because the doctor can't think of a remedy, it is best not to warn the patient that he has a deadly disease. Is that what you're saying?"

"If only it were that simple," countered Segler. "I'd say it was more on the order of a man picnicking at ground zero on an atomic test site and the bomb has already left the plane. There is no way to stop the bomb in midair, and it cannot be called back. What is the best course of action? You can inform the happy picnicker that he has only seconds to live and thereby plunge him into panic, terror, and despair. Or you can allow him to enjoy his few remaining moments in peace and comfort."

Mitchell glared at Segler. "I cannot believe you just said that." He appealed to the others present. "Does anyone else feel that way?" When no one spoke up, he said, "So am I the only one who thinks that is totally nuts?"

"Director Segler has a point," observed Chandra. "If rioting, burning, murder, and chaos in the streets are a logical probability of dispensing this news, then prudence would suggest mitigating the pain and damage."

"Wow," said Mitchell, shaking his head in dismay. "What are you people—robots?"

"I'm speaking as a realist," Segler granted. "There may be other considerations that would argue against such a course. But that, as Dr. Bayer has pointed out, is not our call."

"Whose is it, then?" sniped Mitchell. "People have a right to know that they're about to meet their Maker—how about that for a consideration?"

"Okay!" growled Bayer. "Let's dial it down a notch or two. Deep breath, everybody. Mitchell, remember who you're talking to and try to act like an adult for a change."

"It's all right," said Segler. "We're all a little ragged. None of this is easy."

"That's why they pay us the big bucks," remarked Rodríguez.

"I wish," put in Peters.

Gradually, the tense atmosphere in the room eased and the discussion resumed. At the end of ninety minutes, however, the phone still had not rung and the group had decided on a very tepid description of their findings and projections so far. In frustration, Chief Bayer adjourned the meeting, saying, "We're spinning our wheels here, so we'll wrap this up for now. We'll wait for Dr. Clarke's report and hope that it suggests a way forward." He glanced down at the end of the table. "Tony, send it to me first thing and I'll distribute it."

"Of course," replied Tony.

Bayer nodded and continued, "I will also issue a formal communications lockdown. All information coming into and leaving this facility—as well as all private communications—will be subject to official NSA protection protocol and will require official approval for dissemination." He paused, thought for a moment, then added, "I will draft the notice within the hour and post it to all relevant parties. Any questions?" He did not wait for a reply, but pushed himself away from the table and stood. "Good. Thank you all for your contributions. Back to work."

Dr. Segler joined Chief Bayer for a short conference. Finding himself temporarily on his own, Tony Clarke seized his opportunity—ducking out of the conference room and hurrying down to the Desert Rats. He found Brother Becarria right where he had left him a few hours earlier—hunkered down before a computer monitor surrounded by a mass of papers, many covered with obscure calculations he had made.

"Gianni, thank God you're here," Tony said. "We have to talk."

The priest glanced up into his friend's worried face. "What has happened?"

"Chief Bayer has decided to invoke a communications lockdown—no doubt he is on the phone to the Powers That Be even as we speak. He plans to issue a formal statement—probably within the hour. It will be a complete information and communication lockdown. All contact with the outside world will be monitored and nobody will be allowed to leave. But I think we need to get word back to the others about what's going on and what we've learned so far."

Gianni removed his glasses and rubbed his eyes. "Damascus?"

"No, not Damascus. Cass, Kit, and Wilhelmina—you might be able to catch up with them in Prague. I'd go too, but obviously we can't both just disappear, and in any case I feel I should stay here and do whatever I can to help."

"*Capisco*," said Gianni. "Say no more." He stood. "I will go."

"You'll have to leave at once, I'm afraid—right now, this instant. Once the lockdown is in place, no one will be allowed in or out of this facility. You've got to get out while you can. Do you think you can find your way back alone?"

The priest smiled. "I was making ley journeys before you were born, *mio amico*." He rubbed the lenses of his glasses on his shirt, then replaced the frames on his face. "I am ready. I will go now." He stood and pushed in his chair. "What was decided upstairs?"

"Nothing much," Tony told him. "The meeting went nowhere—no conclusions, no insights . . . They were waiting for a phone call and even that failed to happen."

"No surprises at least," sighed Gianni. He gestured to the pages scattered around him. "None here either."

"In other words, it is as bad as we thought," Tony concluded. "Weeks, not months."

"If that." Gianni raised his eyes toward heaven. "I am not optimistic."

"Me neither," Tony told him. "I'll go ahead with the Cepheid marker report—it might prove useful." He looked at his friend for a moment and could think of nothing more, then added, "I'll see you out."

The two walked casually from the room and rode the elevator up to the main floor. As the elevator doors slid open, Tony said, "I'll have to leave you here. Otherwise the cameras will see us together and I don't want to get involved in a fabricated explanation."

"I understand." Gianni stepped close and embraced his friend quickly. "God be with you, Anthony. Until we meet again."

"Good-bye," Tony said. He reached out and touched Gianni on the arm. "One more thing. Please tell Cassandra that I love her and that my last thoughts . . ." His voice caught and he struggled to continue. "Tell her my last thoughts will be of her."

Gianni inclined his head in acknowledgement of the request and stepped from the elevator. He approached the reception barrier, waved his plastic ID card at the young lady behind the desk, and then swiped it against the electronic pad. The little gate opened, and Gianni walked across the room and out the entrance. No one save the receptionist saw him leave. Fifteen minutes later the official order was issued to lock down the facility to all traffic and to reroute all communications through the director's office. The front gate was locked and the security guards placed on high alert.

But by then Gianni was in a car miles away and speeding west across the New Mexico desert toward Sedona.

CHAPTER 26

In Which the Past Continues to Haunt

Burleigh!" shouted Kit. He charged into the kitchen. "Get your hands off of her, you bastard!"

He bowled around the corner of the counter and drove headlong into the man bending over Wilhelmina, who lay at his feet on the kitchen floor.

Leading with his shoulder, Kit launched a flying tackle, striking Burleigh in the stomach with a blow that doubled him over. Burleigh crashed against the oven and collapsed onto the stone tiles. Kit fell on him and began pummelling him with his fists, punching again and again, battering the earl about the face and head amidst a ferocious wailing.

Kit only ceased when he realised that Burleigh was not resisting and he was the one making all the noise. The next thing he knew, strong hands were pulling him up and away from his victim, and

Engelbert's big friendly face was gazing at him with an expression of shock and alarm. Wilhelmina, on her knees beside him, called, "Kit! Enough! Stop it!"

He looked around—as much stunned by his own actions as by finding Burleigh standing over Wilhelmina's body. "Mina? Are you okay? Did he hurt you?" He tried to struggle out of Etzel's grip, but the baker held him fast.

"I'm fine, Kit. It's not what you think. Burleigh didn't attack me. I got a little light-headed is all," Mina said. "I'm all right, really."

Kit turned his attention once more to the earl, who was still lying on the floor hard up against the oven. Burleigh's eyes were closed and he was not moving. "What's he doing here?" Kit thrust out an accusing finger and turned to Etzel.

Engelbert turned to Mina, and the two exchanged a few brief words. Mina replied, "He says that Burleigh has been in prison—"

"Good!" sneered Kit.

"And that he still has charges against him that must be answered in the magistrate's court—"

"Serves him right. What else?"

"Kit, please, if you'd shut up for a minute and let me finish—"

"Okay, fine," huffed Kit, glaring murderously at his enemy. "Go on."

"Etzel says that until the earl has his day in court, he is living here and helping in the kitchen."

"He's *what?*" Kit shrugged off Engelbert's hands and turned on him. "Are you crazy?" To Mina he said, "Ask Etzel if he is crazy, taking in that murderer!"

"No, Kit." Mina put out a hand to prevent him from attacking Burleigh again. "You don't understand. Just calm down."

"Calm down! That scumbag killed Cosimo and Sir Henry. He

shot Giles and he tried to kill me," Kit shouted. "And you tell *me* to calm down?"

Cass, who had been looking on from the doorway, came to Kit's side. "Come here, Kit. Come with me." Taking him by the arm, she pulled him forcefully aside. "They are trying to tell you something, but you're going to have to cool off a little so you can hear what they have to say." She held his eyes with her own. "No, don't look at him. Look at me. Did you hear what I said?"

Under Cass' coaxing, Kit finally relented and allowed himself to be gentled into a more reasonable frame of mind. She had one of the serving girls bring him a cup of sweet coffee and made him sit down and drink some. His rage ebbed away slowly as he sipped his coffee; he gave Cass a nod to show he would try to control himself. "Okay," she said, "now let's just sit here and find out what this is all about. Can we do that?"

Kit nodded again and then glared across at Burleigh, who was just then levering himself up onto an elbow. Engelbert hovered over him with a wet cloth to sponge away the blood from his split lip and the cut above his eye.

Leaving Kit to one side, Cass pulled a chair from the corner of the room and quickly carried it to Mina and sat her down. "*Sie braucht einen Arzt,*" she told Engelbert in clipped German. "Can you get a doctor for her?"

"*Sind Sie krank?*" he asked, stooping beside Mina's chair.

Wilhelmina shook her head. "*Nein, ich bin verletzt.*" She pointed to the makeshift sling. "*Mein Arm.*"

Engelbert turned on his heel, dashed to the counter, and summoned one of the servers. He spoke a brief command that sent the girl running from the shop. "*Danke, mein Schatz,*" Mina told him, then asked him to tell her how Burleigh came to be staying at the Grand Imperial.

Etzel nodded and replied, "He had nowhere else to go, you see—and no one else to speak for him. It is our Christian duty to help those in need."

"Speak for him? I'm a little lost," she said in German. "I think we must start at the beginning." She reached for Etzel's hand. "Slowly. You tell me, and I will tell the others."

While Kit and Cass looked on, Engelbert began to tell how Burleigh had come to be in his care. Mina translated as he went, and the story that unfolded was remarkable, to say the least. Burleigh, still pressing the damp cloth to his face, sat sprawled on the floor and listened impassively to the account, never objecting or contradicting anything Engelbert said about him. Kit, on the other hand, interrupted several times to question the account, but he was waved off by Wilhelmina, who was asking questions of her own.

"*Vielen Dank, Etzel,*" said Burleigh, speaking up for the first time. "*Es ist in Ordnung.*" To the others, he said, "You must remember, I spent months in prison with no hope of release. I had great violence in my heart—violence stored up to avenge the hurt and injustice I imagined I had been made to suffer. I meant to make someone pay!" Burleigh pushed himself up into a sitting position, but made no move to stand. "I fully intended harm to Etzel, but when it came to the crux, I realised the person who must be made to pay was myself."

"What did you do?" asked Wilhelmina, struggling to maintain her composure in the presence of the man so roundly despised and distrusted.

"What did I do?" echoed the earl. "I hardly know. I remember going into Engelbert's room while he slept. Burning with hatred, intent only on destruction, I stood beside the bed of my good and faithful friend, and in the light of his virtue I saw myself for what I was—a vessel worthy only of destruction." He glanced around at his listeners, willing them to understand, then looked to Engelbert beside him. "I saw that gentle face in the moonlight and understood that he was beyond touch of any earthly power, while I was a slave to all manner of worldly evils. There was but one solution," concluded Burleigh, "and that was for me to drown myself forthwith, to kill the evil thing that I had become and rid the world of my own vile presence. I went out—right then and there. I made the decision and acted on it at once lest I change my mind."

"Really?" Kit could not believe what he was hearing. The man who had caused such great and terrible pain to so many on the quest was confessing his crimes—confessing fully and freely, his voice drenched in remorse. Still, he was determined not to be taken in. "You were going to kill yourself?"

Burleigh repeated his intention and continued, "I went out, as I said, but I do not remember leaving the kaffeehaus, crossing the square, or anything else. You see, I was utterly consumed by the solitary thought that I must die. That alone compelled me. I was a mindless automaton—seeing nothing, hearing nothing, feeling nothing—seeking only the release of death."

"You managed to avoid it, I see," sniffed Kit derisively—and earned a reproachful glance from Engelbert.

Burleigh only nodded. "I came to myself at the city gate. It was closed. It was the darkest hour of the night and the gate was locked. The night watch was nowhere to be seen. I must have stood there for some time, gazing at the iron bolt and the heavy beam that barred the door. How was I to open it?

"That door was all that stood between me and the river—between me and my destruction—and I could not open it." Burleigh raised his face. A single tear trickled down his grizzled cheek. "That was it, you see—the final revelation. I was nothing, possessed nothing, could change nothing. I lacked even the power to do away with myself!

"I stood helpless before that gate, and whatever solidity was left of me simply melted. I collapsed upon the cobblestones and wept for the futility and littleness of my pitiable, crabbed life and the hateful thing I had become. I was a lost and destitute soul—beyond hope, beyond redemption. There were no words to describe the desolation I felt at that moment. Lying in the street like a heap of refuse, like filth cast off to be trodden underfoot . . ." Burleigh fell silent, contemplating again that moment—only days removed, but already a lifetime ago.

When he did not speak again, Cass asked, "Is that where Etzel found you?"

The earl glanced up, smiled sadly, and shook his head. "No—it was in the church."

"The church?" wondered Mina. "Our church?"

"I don't know how long I lay in the street. The only thing I remember is that I cried out, and the next thing I heard was the tolling of the church bell. I didn't even know they did that at night."

"It rings only twice during the night," Mina confirmed, "the last just before dawn."

Burleigh nodded. "In any event, I heard that bell and I stood up and took myself to the church. I do not know why—unless, perhaps, I fancied that I might hide there. I stood at the door and I remembered something I'd heard somewhere: 'Knock.' I gazed at the door and I remembered more: 'Knock and the door will open.' Where those words came from, I cannot say. But I raised my hand

and knocked, and the door simply opened and I went in—that door, at least, was not barred to me.

"The church was dark. There were only a few candles burning on the stand before the icon, and I fell into a seat in the back. There I sat, knowing neither what I expected, nor what might happen next." Burleigh closed his eyes, reliving the memory. "I was still sitting there when who should come in but Engelbert?"

"He does that," Wilhelmina offered, looking across to Etzel, who was still hovering over his charge. "He sometimes goes to early mass before opening the shop for business. What did he say when he found you there?"

"Nothing." Burleigh allowed himself a wan, wistful smile. "He said nothing. He simply slid into the seat next to me and waited for the service to begin." He raised grateful eyes to his benefactor. "The thought that I might be there for any reason other than to attend mass would not have occurred to him."

"Go on," said Kit. "Then what happened?"

Before Burleigh could answer, two things happened almost simultaneously: first, the physician appeared to examine Wilhelmina, who was forced to adjourn the story. The doctor had just begun his examination when another face appeared over the counter and a voice was heard to say, "You're all here! Thank God I am not too late."

Kit turned. "Gianni!"

The priest stumbled around the counter and entered the now-crowded kitchen. He seemed to stagger and catch himself as he lunged toward the table. Kit took one look at Gianni's filthy clothes and the dull grey pallor of his face and darted to his side. "Here, let me help you," said Kit and motioned for Cass to bring another chair. "Etzel—get him some water. Quick! He's dead on his feet."

Mina translated the request, and Gianni sank heavily into the offered chair. The physician attending Wilhelmina glanced up from his examination of Wilhelmina's arm and called a command to Engelbert, who disappeared into the larder at the back of the room. "The doctor has ordered schnapps for him," Mina said.

"Ah, *mio cuore*, a thousand thanks." Gianni closed his eyes and leaned back in his chair.

"You look like you've been dragged through a rat hole," remarked Kit. The Italian's elegant black suit was not only travel-stained, it was torn in several places and one sleeve was all but ripped off. "What happened to you?"

Engelbert appeared with a bulbous bottle of crystal-clear liquid; he pulled the stopper and dashed some into a cup. *"Trinken—das ist gut für Sie."* He put the cup into Gianni's hand. The priest took a sip of spirit and grimaced, then took another and coughed.

"In all my experience, never have I endured such difficulty. I was forced to resort to lines I had forgotten years ago." Gianni took another swig of schnapps. "The worst of it is, I fear our troubles are only beginning."

Kit, Cass, and Wilhelmina exchanged a worried look. "Like Damascus?" asked Cass.

Gianni finished the schnapps with another grimace and placed the cup on the table. He stared at it a moment before he spoke again. *"Signorina,* is this not what I have come to tell you?" Raising his eyes, he glanced around the room at the anxious faces looking back at him. *"Mio amici,* we have to talk."

CHAPTER 27

In Which the Gaolbird Sings

"So far, Prague seems to be stable. We haven't noticed any cosmic weirdness here," Wilhelmina said. "But we've had a pretty rough time of it in other respects."

Gianni had bathed and changed into clean clothes—if old-fashioned and oversized—and they had all eaten a somewhat subdued supper of beans, ham hocks, and onions. As soon as the dishes were cleared away, the talk began. Burleigh, having disappeared shortly after Gianni's arrival, was nowhere to be seen; and Engelbert, who had to rise early to start the baking, went up to bed, leaving the questors to their discussion. They now sat around the kitchen table by candlelight, reviewing what they had learned so far.

Gianni turned his eyes to Kit and said, "It is to be expected. Some dimensions will remain more stable than others. Some are farther away from the event horizon, so to speak. Like an onion—" At the puzzled looks, he explained, "When an onion begins to spoil, the rot affects some layers more than others, no?"

"But it spreads through all the layers eventually," said Cass, finishing the thought. "The onion deteriorates completely in the end."

"Just so," said Gianni.

"How soon?" said Kit.

The priest shook his head. "Predictions are imprecise—perhaps meaningless."

"How soon?" Kit asked again.

"A few weeks. Maybe more. Maybe less."

"Then it's worse than we thought," concluded Wilhelmina gloomily.

"You were able to get back to the yew tree," said Gianni after a moment. "What did you learn?"

"Nothing, really—at least, nothing we didn't already know," Kit replied. "The tree is dangerous and unpredictable. It channels a vast amount of energy . . ." He paused and choked back a surge of grief and regret before continuing. "Which Dr. Young found out, to his cost."

At Gianni's questioning glance, Wilhelmina said, "Dr. Young was killed when he came in contact with the tree." She indicated her bandaged arm. "I was standing next to him at the time."

"Ah, *mio cara*, I am so sorry," said Gianni softly and made the sign of the cross with his thumb and forefinger. He was silent for a moment and then said, "May God have mercy on his soul."

Silence settled over the group, so thick they could hear the hissing of the candles burning in their holders in the centre of the table. Kit glanced at the grim faces around the table; illumined in the candle-light, they seemed to float disembodied above the board. He saw hopelessness writ large on every face, and Tess' fighting words came back to him.

In the last moments, just before the Zetetics fled Damascus, the canny old lady had sent them off with a rallying cry, a last call to arms. He could still see her birdlike form as she stood framed in the doorway of the courtyard. Her voice had quavered slightly, but her words were strong. "For this purpose we were formed, and to this place our steps have been directed. This is the battle to which we have been called, and we must trust in Him who has led us here to lead us on."

In the quiet of the empty room, Kit heard the echo of that challenge and said, "We all knew this was coming. You remember what Tess said—it is why we're here." He looked around the table. "So what are we going to do about it?"

"If we could only find a way to get around the tree," said Cass. "Or use it somehow."

"Then we could get back to the Spirit Well," said Wilhelmina. She looked around the table at the others. "But what would we do once we got there?"

"I don't know, but we have to find a way to get there first," Kit pointed out. "Which we obviously cannot do as long as that blasted tree stands there blocking the way."

"What about cutting it down?" Cass suggested. "Or blowing it up somehow? That would get rid of it."

"Perhaps," granted Gianni thoughtfully, "but at the risk of making matters worse. Unless we knew precisely the results of such an action, I would advise using such a violent solution only as a last resort."

"Well, then what about going back to a time before the Fatal Tree was there?" wondered Cass.

"Don't you think I've thought of that?" Kit said. "If I knew how to do that, we wouldn't be having this discussion."

"Stay focused," Mina said. "What about trying to find another way to get to the Spirit Well? I mean, we know that ley lines often branch out to more than one destination. Maybe there's another way to get there."

"A way no one else has ever discovered?" said Kit. "Unlikely."

"But not impossible," said Cass.

"No," allowed Kit. "Not impossible—but if another ley line existed, I don't know how we'd find it in the time we have left."

"We could if we had Shadow Lamps," said Mina.

"Which we don't," said Kit.

"No, *we* don't," agreed Mina. "But I know a man who does."

All three looked to Kit to gauge his reaction. "Oh no," he growled, instantly angry. "We are *not* getting Burleigh involved. He has no part in this whatsoever. If I had my way, he'd still be in prison. Better still, it would be him in that tomb in Egypt, not Cosimo."

In the silence that followed this outburst, a voice spoke from the doorway at the back of the room.

"I do not blame you for feeling the way you do—"

"Burleigh!" shouted Kit. He jumped to his feet so fast it sent his chair crashing to the floor behind him. "Get out of here! Or so help me—"

"I can only express my deepest regret. The sins of the past will haunt me the rest of my life." He moved close to the table, stepping into the circle of light, his expression solemn and contrite. "I have wronged you and many others. I beg for a chance to atone."

"Liar!" shouted Kit, darting around the table. "Get the hell out!"

Gianni reached out a hand and grabbed Kit's arm as he passed. "Peace. We will hear him out." Kit, bristling with rage, shook off his hand. To Burleigh the priest said, "Please, we are listening. Speak."

"I know nothing of the catastrophe you are discussing," he began. "But I—"

242

"How long have you been spying on us?" demanded Kit. To the others he demanded, "Why are we listening to him?"

"Because," replied Burleigh simply, "I can help."

"My name is not Archelaeus Burleigh. Needless to say, I am not an earl, nor in any other way ennobled. I was born Archie Burley—that's B-u-r-l-e-y—in the slums of London's East End to an unwed mother. My father was a wealthy man in the north of England, but he refused to acknowledge me or marry my mother. She died destitute." He fell silent at the memory of his stark, joyless beginnings.

Against Kit's strident protests, the earl had been granted a chair at the candlelit table, and now all except Kit were listening intently to the man they knew as Burleigh talk about his life and the devious paths he had taken to reach this place and time. Kit stared swords and daggers at his enemy sitting across from him.

"Was your father a lord?" asked Wilhelmina after a moment.

Burleigh shook his head. "No. Maybe. I remember nothing of him. Granville Gower, the Earl of Sutherland, was my benefactor, and I was his protégé, his ward. I took his title when he died. It was through Lord Gower that I learned the trade that brought me into contact with Charles Flinders-Petrie—though by that time, I was already deeply engrossed in the study and application of ley travel."

"Excuse me," interrupted Gianni. "We know nothing of Arthur's relations. Am I to assume that Charles was Arthur's son?"

"Grandson," corrected Burleigh. "Arthur had one son, a boy called Benedict. I never met him, but Benedict begat Charles. Whether Charles had any offspring, I never learned."

"Speaking of Charles," said Cass. Kit gave her a glare; he disliked her even talking to the man he considered a monster. Cass ignored the look. "Was it Charles who told you about the Skin Map?"

"Not in so many words," Burleigh replied with a rueful smile. "But I can be very persuasive when I choose to be, and Charles, as a young man, was very easily persuaded."

"Manipulated, you mean," corrected Mina.

"Manipulated . . . extorted . . . blackmailed . . . To my shame, the list goes on," Burleigh conceded, lifting a guilty hand. "In any event, once I got wind of the map, I moved heaven and earth to find it. I have spent several lifetimes chasing it in one way or another—first through study, and then through adventuring." He raised his eyes to Mina. "Have you seen it?"

"Only a part of it," replied Wilhelmina. For all his demonstration of honest and heartfelt repentance, she was still more than wary of trusting the man completely. There was that about his lean and haunted aspect that did not suggest honesty.

"What about you?" asked Gianni. "Have you ever seen the map?"

"Only once," Burleigh sighed. "On the beast, so to speak. The Man Who Is Map—I met him."

"You met Arthur Flinders-Petrie?" said Wilhelmina. "In Egypt?"

"In China." Burleigh nodded to himself as he recalled that fateful meeting. "When the day finally came to leave the books and take to the road, I was an exceedingly wealthy man. I obtained and outfitted a ship and hired a crew for the expedition. I had spent years tracking down my quarry—mostly through clues his grandson Charles had inadvertently supplied.

"Combining ley travel with traditional methods, I was—at great expense and difficulty—finally able to catch up with Arthur in Macau.

That is where he got all his tattoos—did you know? In any event, it was my plan to invite the great adventurer to join me in a partnership—a glorious enterprise with the aim of furthering our explorations. I thought that if we became partners, then I would eventually learn all his secrets." Burleigh spread his hands. "But that was not to be. Arthur was jealous of his confidences and took against me right from the beginning. Very likely I was not subtle enough. Desire made me impetuous and impatient. It was ever my undoing. When I saw there would be no persuading him, I decided to take the map by force."

"Cut it off him, you mean!" muttered Kit, through clenched teeth.

Burleigh merely lifted his shoulders. "Shocking, I know. In truth, I was not above such heavy-handed tactics. In any event, I knew I might never get another chance. At the time, it seemed much the simplest solution."

"But you did not succeed," surmised Gianni.

"Oh, I did try, but the attempt failed and Arthur escaped with his much-decorated skin intact." He gave a rueful smile. "The irony is that the map was cut off him in the end, but by then I had lost all track of him—or it. I never saw him again."

Wilhelmina weighed what he was saying and decided that his story possessed the ring of truth. "Still, you never stopped trying to find the map," she said.

"Having come so close only drove me to greater boldness, greater impudence, and, in the end, greater lawlessness. To say I redoubled my efforts is to spin it too finely. Getting my hands on that map became my great obsession, driving me to commit ever more reprehensible acts.

"I burned with the need to own that scrap of parchment, and the flames took everything." Burleigh gazed across the table to Kit.

"Again, I can but express my sincerest regret and own the fault that caused me to behave as I did—toward you, and Cosimo, Sir Henry, and everyone else I have ever met."

Burleigh's frank admission was met with silence. Finally Gianni spoke up. "You offered to help us. Can you tell us what you have in mind?"

"Indeed," replied the earl. "I believe I overheard your mention of something called a Shadow Lamp—curious name." He looked to Wilhelmina. "Would this be the same instrument I call a ley locator?"

"I assume so," Mina confessed. "I convinced Gustavus to make copies of yours."

"How very enterprising of you," Burleigh said. "I knew you to be a worthy adversary."

"A dubious distinction at best," remarked Mina.

"What led you to the rare earth substance that powers the device?" asked Cass.

"Rare earth?" questioned Burleigh, arching his thick black eyebrows. "Why, there is nothing rare about it at all. The material is what I call activated earth, and it is merely common garden-variety soil that has been transmuted by exposure to the considerable energy of a ley portal over time and then refined by the alchemists into a more potent form."

"A portal like Black Mixen Tump?" suggested Wilhelmina.

"Black Mixen is one such portal, yes," affirmed Burleigh. "But there are any number of others—such as Sant'antimo in Italy, Silbury Hill in Wiltshire, Montículo del Diablo in Spain."

"Sedona in Arizona," volunteered Cass, earning her another sour look from Kit. "There they call them vortexes."

"There is one near the Abbey at Montserrat," added Gianni.

"And," concluded Burleigh, "I know of at least one currently underwater off the coast of the island of Bermuda in the Sargasso Sea. As I say, there are many others—"

"Fascinating," grumbled Kit. "But all this talk is getting us nowhere."

Wilhelmina gave him a disapproving frown, and Cass nudged him with an elbow.

"What?" demanded Kit. Then, in frustration, he flung out a hand at Burleigh. "He said he could help us! Well, I'm still waiting to hear anything remotely helpful. Look, people, the clock is ticking down. We can't waste time with all this . . . this blather. Yet here we are waffling on like a meeting of the Women's Institute and we've got all the time in the world."

Wilhelmina's frown deepened and turned icy. "Are you quite finished?"

Kit crossed his arms over his chest and jerked his chin down. "For now. I may have more to say later."

She turned back to Burleigh, who simply gazed impassively at Kit, his face blank. "Sorry for my hotheaded friend here."

"Do *not* apologise for me!" snarled Kit. "Do not apol—"

"Please," Burleigh interrupted. "Mr. Livingstone is right to feel the way he does. I am the one who should be sorry—and I assure you I am most deeply sorry. And it is true that there are weighty matters before us. Confession may be good for the soul, but it is getting us no closer to a solution to the problem." He placed his hands on the table in a gesture of capitulation. "I am your servant."

"Any help you can give us would be appreciated. You have no idea of the magnitude of the problem we are facing."

"Don't tell him anything," said Kit. "He offered help. Let's see it."

"Very well. You say you need ley locators. I can get them," said Burleigh, adopting a businesslike tone. "I may be persona non grata at court, but as we know, Bazalgette has few scruples. With a little greasing of the wheels I can get you your Shadow Lamps—as many as you need. However," he continued, "I am thinking there is more at stake here than merely finding the Skin Map, is there not?"

"You really don't know what we're up against?" asked Cass. "You didn't hear that part?"

Burleigh gave a slight shake of his head. "If I am to be of better service to your enterprise, I suggest you tell me everything."

"Don't do it," said Kit. "I mean it. We need Shadow Lamps, and he's offered to get them for us. Let that be the end of it, I say."

"Shut up, Kit," said Mina. "Will you just give it a rest?" She turned to Burleigh and said, "We can discuss the details later, but for now suffice to say that the threat we face is the complete and utter destruction of the universe and everyone and everything in it. Forever."

Burleigh's face registered neither alarm nor amazement, but merely modest interest. He glanced at Gianni, who confirmed Mina's assertion. "It is true. The End of Everything is the problem we are attempting to solve."

"In that case," suggested Burleigh, "you are going to need a bigger Shadow Lamp."

PART FIVE

Bright Empires

CHAPTER 28

In Which Our Questors Debate the Efficacy of Conversion

I'm being unreasonable?" Kit shouted. He could hear himself getting shrill but did not know how to stop it. "This . . . this *psychopath*
comes over all smooth and contrite. He's ever so sorry, now he's seen
the light and he's on the side of the angels—and that's supposed to
make everything all right?"

"Nobody is saying any such thing," Wilhelmina countered. She
cradled her injured arm with the other and eased the sling's weight
on her neck.

"The man is a cold-blooded killer. He has killed at least once
and he will kill again. If I had my way, he would be stood up before
a firing squad. In fact, that's actually a very good—"

"Keep your voice down," snapped Wilhelmina. "Others are trying to sleep."

"Sleep! How any one of us can even stomach being under the

same roof with that murderer is beyond me. Do you really think he'd hesitate to slaughter us all in our beds if it suited him?"

Wilhelmina shook her head wearily. Her arm hurt, and the non-stop cavalcade of events of this day had pushed her past exhaustion. They were standing in the half-darkened kitchen. It was late, and everyone else had gone to bed. Over Kit's loud protests, they had agreed in principle to accept Burleigh's help. Wilhelmina had stayed behind to see if she could help assuage Kit's anger and frustration, but they had been having this argument so long it was beginning to repeat itself.

"Well, go ahead. You all cosy up to him if you want to, but keep him out of my way." Kit kicked the chair he had been sitting in. "Bloody hell, Mina. Have you lost your mind?"

"I'm not saying you have to like it," she said, trying a different tack. "But Burleigh has something we desperately need, and like it or not, he has agreed to help us get it. In case you haven't noticed, there is a bit more at stake here than your grievances."

"My *grievances*?" Kit stared at her and then threw his hands in the air. "Boy, that's rich. I'm supposed to just forgive and forget, is that it?"

"It would be a start."

"It's crap."

"Look," said Mina, softening her tone, "I'm not thrilled with the idea of partnering with Burleigh any more than you are." Kit opened his mouth to protest, but she cut him off. "Despite what you may think, I'm not joining his fan club. Burleigh is a low-down snake and worse. We all know that. And he may one day be called to answer for his crimes. I hope he is. Honestly."

She fixed Kit with a stern, uncompromising stare before continuing. "But none of that is going to happen if the world ends tomorrow—is it? You can cling to your abused sense of justice if you want to, and insist on the rightness of your cause—and, yes, you are in the right as we all know and you never tire of telling us—but do you really want to be the one who ruins what may be our only chance of figuring out how to save the universe?" She stared at him defiantly. "Do you want to be that guy?"

She let the words sink in a moment, then added, "If the world ends next week and all life in this or any other world is extinguished because of your pigheaded refusal to accept help, I hope it will be some comfort in your last moments to know that, well, the universe and everything in it may have been destroyed, but at least Kit Livingstone held fast to his principles."

Kit glared at her and looked away. As he did so, he saw Cass standing in the doorway to the kitchen.

"Mina's right, Kit." Cass moved to Kit's side of the table. "We don't have to like it, but it's our only hope. There is the greater good to consider."

"*Et tu?*" he sneered. "How long have you been standing there?"

"Long enough," she said. "As if anyone could sleep with all the shouting going on down here. Listen to Mina. We have to rise above the hurt and injustice. We have to think of the big picture."

"So Burleigh gets off scot-free or I'm the big bad guy, is that it?"

Cass shook her head. "There is such a thing as repentance, Kit." She moved closer to him. "Burleigh will one day have to answer to a higher authority for what he has done. He will have to stand before God—as will we all. But right now is not the time, and we are not the ones to judge."

Kit stared at her dully, unable to think of a suitable reply. Mina saw his hesitation as a sign that she had gained some small advantage;

she pressed it. "You know very well Burleigh has more knowledge of ley travel than anyone else. His experience is invaluable. If there is even the slightest chance he can help, we have to take it," said Mina. "You must see that."

A sneer curled Kit's lip before she had finished speaking. "If you believe he has some new unheard-of method of interacting with ley lines, then you are a bloody fool, Mina."

"And you are a blind, stupid idiot, Kit. Just because we didn't know about ley manipulation until tonight does not mean that it doesn't exist. We didn't know about Shadow Lamps either—until I accidentally discovered what Burleigh was up to with the alchemists." When she saw this line of reasoning was not working, she switched to another track. "Look, I don't see we have anything to lose in at least letting him demonstrate the power he is talking about. If it is all fake and bluster, then we'll know soon enough. But if it really works . . . well, that's a game changer."

The possibility of ley manipulation had surprised them all. The term had been dropped into the conversation casually enough, but it had caused an immediate sensation. Burleigh's offer of help had included making new Shadow Lamps for everyone, and also instruction on how to use them. "The name ley locator is a bit of an understatement," he had told them right after suggesting that they were going to need a more powerful device. "The instrument can do far more than simply locate ley lines. For example, the newest model can find not only the lines but very often the people who use them."

"So I discovered," Wilhelmina had told him. "It saved me weeks, maybe months, of trial and error."

"That alone would be most helpful to us now," Gianni agreed, "when we have so very little time to waste."

"What else can Shadow Lamps do?" asked Cass. Of the questors, she was the least affected by the earl's criminal past; whatever he had been or done did not seem to bother her in the least—which infuriated Kit all the more.

Burleigh had turned to her, his dark eyes glinting with a strange, devious light. "When used in linked conjunction with one another, they can manipulate the ley lines themselves."

As ripe with promise as that simple declaration seemed, precise details were not forthcoming. The assertion, it turned out, had not been tested to any great extent; it remained more of an observational phenomenon only. "You mean you don't really know," Kit had charged, and then accused Burleigh of lying.

The earl had absorbed the allegation equably enough, but then refused to expand on his claim, saying only, "You said you needed help. This is what I have to offer. You can believe me or not, that is your choice." He rose from the table. "I will leave you to think about it."

He turned and walked to the door. Wilhelmina rolled her eyes in exasperation at Kit. "Why did you have to do that?" she said under her breath. To Burleigh she called, "But you *will* help us get more Shadow Lamps?"

"I said I would, and I will." He did not pause or look back. "Good night."

The discussion had broken down completely after that. Gianni had suggested that it had been a long and taxing day, and that a good night's sleep would do everyone good. They would resume their discussions in the morning. That had been over an hour ago.

Kit shook his head wearily, then rubbed both hands over his face as if trying to wash away a stain. He was outgunned and he knew it. At best, he could only negotiate an unpalatable peace. "You're right—both of you," he conceded, his voice cracking over the words. "But, by God, it stinks. It stinks to high heaven."

"Then why don't we let God deal with it?" said Cass. "Let's leave it in His hands."

CHAPTER 29

In Which Wilhelmina Calls in a Debt

Obtaining a batch of new Shadow Lamps proved more challenging than anyone expected. The alchemists of Rudolf's Magick Court were disinclined to provide their services—owing, no doubt, to the trouble over helping Lord Burleigh the first time. "The earl is no longer welcome at court," Gustavus told her when Wilhelmina approached him about making more of the devices. "Besides, Bazalgette has imposed a ban on all such practices."

"Such practices as working on projects for court outsiders," she said. "Is that what you mean?"

"It is because of your friend the earl. When the emperor found out, he blamed the Lord High Alchemist, and Bazalgette blamed me."

"I guess Arthur wasn't the only one to poison a well," sighed Mina.

"Excuse me?"

"Only thinking out loud," replied Wilhelmina. "Does this mean you cannot help us?"

The young alchemist lifted the shoulders of his too-big green velvet robe in an elaborate shrug. "There is nothing I can do."

"Not even after all the help I've given you in the past? All the bitter earth I've supplied for your experiments—not to mention all the free coffee and pastries?"

"We are in your debt," acknowledged Gustavus.

"I am calling in that debt." She held his gaze with hers until the young man looked away.

"Please, Fraulein Wilhelmina," he said, embarrassed now. "The emperor was very angry with us. It is his decision. To be seen working for you without permission would mean prison for me. And Bazalgette, as things stand now, would never give me permission."

Mina was not about to allow the matter to fall at this first hurdle. "But you have free time, don't you?"

Gustavus nodded warily.

"Well then, you could make them in your spare time."

"You do not understand," the alchemist complained. "Making so many instruments . . ." He shook his head. "I would be seen. Even if I was working on my own time, as you say, I would still be using court equipment and materials. Someone would quickly find out what I was doing. The palace is a beehive. There is no way to hide it."

"Then do not make them at the palace," Wilhelmina countered smoothly. "You could make the devices down here at the Grand Imperial." She waved a hand at the dining room filled with patrons. "People see you come here all the time. No one would think anything of you coming and going."

Gustavus frowned.

"We can make a little workshop in one of the bedrooms upstairs."

Gustavus bit his lip. "I would need special tools and materials."

258

"Just give me a list of everything you need and I will get it for you—a worktable, tools, metal—anything. Just write it down and I will get it."

The young alchemist shook his head. "Bazalgette would find out. I would lose my position—they might even put me in the Rathaus."

"No," Mina told him. "I won't let that happen." She gripped his arm with her good hand. "What do you say, Gustavus?"

Still he hesitated. Wilhelmina could see him teetering on the brink of the decision. She needed something to tip him her way. "I cannot begin to tell you how important it is that we have those instruments. But believe me when I tell you that it is a matter of life and death." She tightened her grip on his arm. "Please, Gustavus, you're the only one who can help us. We need you."

He sighed. "I will do it. On one condition." He raised a finger in the air.

"Anything," agreed Mina. "Name it."

"You must promise to teach me the secret of astral translocation."

"Astral trans—" She stared at him, then smiled. "Ley leaping, you mean? Very well. If that is what you want, I will teach you the secret—*after* we have tested the ley lamps."

The young alchemist removed his floppy fur hat and bowed low. "I would expect no less."

"I will also give you free pastries while you work. Now, you sit down and finish your coffee. I will go get something to write on, and we will make your list."

"*Jah*," agreed Gustavus, "we begin at once. This is good."

Even with everyone working on the list, it had taken the better part of two days to acquire all the items the young alchemist required. Burleigh's sole responsibility was to collect enough of the active earth to make six lamps—one each for the questors and Burleigh, plus an extra in case any malfunctioned. As Kit said, "The last ones we had melted down to cinders."

With Cass' help, Mina turned the room Burleigh was using into a workshop; she had Kit and Gianni move the bed and chest to one corner, then brought in a sturdy table and bench and assembled the necessary tools, equipment, and materials. As for heat—that would be supplied by the kitchen ovens. Burleigh, meanwhile, collected a quantity of activated earth from a stash he had hidden in the city; he supplied a bag containing several pounds of the raw material, which looked more or less like what it was: fine brown dust. All was ready for Gustavus to begin.

With Burleigh to help and oversee the process, work progressed at a reasonable pace. Kit and Gianni assisted with some of the less technical aspects of manufacture, such as fabricating the cases. Because time was precious, they used ready-made hip flasks—the round pewter pocket containers hunters used to carry schnapps and *Jägertee* while in the field. They cut the flasks in half and drilled small holes for the coloured glass that would form the lights. They affixed the tiny supports for the internal structures Gustavus would fashion. It was exacting work, made tedious because of the repetition required to fabricate six devices; but at least it kept Kit's mind off the vile necessity of having to tolerate Burleigh.

When, six days later, the first of the new gizmos were ready for testing, the questors took them to the ley line Wilhelmina knew about in the countryside a few miles north of the city. Burleigh, flouting the terms of his probation, accompanied them to the line, marked by a shallow ditch carved along the brow of a hill. "This is where I practiced with my first Shadow Lamp," Mina told them as the hired carriage rolled to a stop. "I haven't used it lately, but it always seemed fairly reliable."

Whoever had dug the ditch had long ago passed from the pages of history, joining the builders of dolmens and cromlechs and other Neolithic architects. Trees had grown up around it, so now the line passed through a thin wood. Gianni handed out the three finished Shadow Lamps—one each to Kit, Burleigh, and Wilhelmina. He and Cass would serve as objective observers for the experiment. Then the earl offered his explanation of how to manipulate the ley line. Burleigh, holding one of the new-model devices, told the group to gather around and he would explain what was involved and how to do it.

As the explanation unfolded, Kit decided that manipulation was something of an overstatement—*interacting* would be a better description. The phenomenon could be broken down into two basic components: the physical and the mental. The physical side consisted of two parts—the Shadow Lamp and the ley line; the mental side, so far as Kit understood it, was whatever the ley traveller brought to the game.

"I knew it!" exclaimed Wilhelmina when she heard the explanation. "I always suspected there was something more to this."

Kit gave her a dubious look. Though he secretly agreed with her, he was not about to let Burleigh see it.

"Things always seemed to go smoother when I was in the zone and concentrating very hard on where I wanted to go and who I wanted to see."

Gianni confirmed her experience, saying, "The human will—intention—combined with purpose is well known to influence and even alter atomic interactions. I suspected something of the sort was at work, but never had a way to quantify it."

"Until now," Burleigh told him.

"Show us," said Kit.

He lifted the device on the palm of his right hand. Bigger than the original version, and a little ungainly in appearance, it nevertheless seemed a very reasonable effort under the circumstances. They watched and waited, and just as Kit was beginning to think their work had come to naught, the little row of lights around the outer edge of the one-time flask began to glow—a shade of turquoise as it happened, because they had not been able to find blue glass and had to use green that they got from a broken bottle.

"It works!" said Mina to murmured approval all around. "Great! Now what?"

"Listen very carefully," Burleigh told them. "We will each of us step onto the ley line together. It would be best to maintain a little distance between us—two or three yards. But once in position, do not move. Remain in place and I will tell you what to do next."

Burleigh stepped into the centre of the ditch, and Kit and Mina followed his example. Burleigh turned to face them and held out his Shadow Lamp. The little lights were glowing brighter now that they were actually standing in the ley line. "Hold out your device where you can see it." He waited until they had complied. "What is the destination of this ley—where does it lead?"

"Nowhere nice," Wilhelmina told him. "It is a storm-ridden place—all rain and ferocious wind, so filthy you can hardly see your hand in front of your face. I never stayed long enough to find out where it was exactly. I just used it as a shortcut to and from London."

"Be that as it may, it will serve for our demonstration. Now then, in a moment I will ask you to concentrate very hard on reaching that destination."

"That's it?" scoffed Kit. "That's all there is to it?"

Burleigh's eyes grew hard. He held his temper, but the effort clearly taxed him. "We must learn to walk before we run, Mr. Livingstone," he intoned icily. "For now, all I want you and Wilhelmina to do is concentrate on that destination. Simply hold it as an image in your mind."

"And that will do what, exactly?" said Kit.

"You shall see," Burleigh told him.

"Behave, Kit," Mina said. "Just do as he says."

"Remember, once the effect begins, stand still as statues. Do not move."

"Understood," said Mina. "Kit?" she asked pointedly.

"Yeah, still as statues. Got it."

Satisfied with this assurance, Burleigh raised his lamp a little higher. "Ready? I will count to three."

The earl counted, and Kit lowered his eyes to the ley lamp in his hand. He tried to picture the destination—a grey world, wind-scoured and wet. Seconds passed. Nothing happened. He became aware of the breeze rustling in the trees, and that Cass and Gianni were watching them. He grew a little self-conscious and felt ridiculous for going along with what was obviously a load of old tosh. He glanced up.

Burleigh saw the movement and said, "Stop . . . You are not concentrating, Mr. Livingstone."

"Kit!" said Wilhelmina. "Would it kill you to just cooperate for thirty seconds? Do you think you could do that?"

"We will try it again," Burleigh said. "It may help you to remember the place as you last saw it, perhaps. Hold that image in your mind."

Once again, Burleigh counted to three, and Kit concentrated his attention on the ley lamp in his hand. He closed his eyes and cast his mind back to the time he had made the leap with Mina to what he thought of as the hurricane world. He remembered the rain slashing at him, driving freezing water through his clothes. He remembered the unholy howl of a wind that never ceased. He heard Wilhelmina say, "Oh . . . my . . . gosh!"

Kit was so deep in the memory that it took him a second to realise he had not imagined it—Mina had actually spoken. He opened his eyes and saw a blaze of opalescent colour ripple along the ditch marking the ley line.

"Did you see that?" she gushed. "Amazing!"

"I missed it," Kit said. "All I saw was a flash."

"That was impressive," Cass said. She and Gianni were grinning. "Do it again."

Kit, mildly disappointed to have missed the display, asked, "What was it?"

"I don't know," Cass told him. "It looked sort of like a tunnel of light running down the entire length of the ley line. But it seemed to have a surface of some kind with all these colours moving over it—like an oil slick in the rain when the light hits it."

"A very good description," Gianni said. "It vanished when you looked up."

"That," Burleigh informed them, "was the visual manifestation of the ley energy at work here. It appeared because for that brief moment our three minds were concentrated on a single intentional thought— in this case, the destination."

"Then why did it go away so fast?"

"It vanished because both of you became distracted," Burleigh explained. "That is to be expected. It was your first time. With practice, we will be able to sustain our unified concentration for more extended periods."

"Let's try it again," Mina said. "And this time, Kit, keep your eyes open so you can see it."

Kit did keep his eyes open for the next try. It occurred to Kit that what he was being asked to do was very like the method he had learned to communicate with En-Ul and River City Clan: clearing his head of extraneous or intrusive details, concentrating on a simple object, action, or desire, and holding that in his mind as a pictorial image. He used the same technique on this attempt, and this time the magic—the phenomenon Burleigh called the visual manifestation of the ley line—appeared more rapidly, and they were able to sustain it long enough for Kit to get a good look. And it looked like nothing Kit had ever seen before.

CHAPTER 30

In Which a Few Things Begin to Make Sense

C ass had called the phenomenon a tunnel of light, and Kit could see why she described it that way: it was long and hollow, with a curved, overarching aspect. There the similarities ended. Observed from the inside, where Kit stood now, the effect seemed more like an endless series of truncated halos—each one superimposed upon another, each blending into the next, rank on rank, receding into infinity. The shifting colours Cass described were present, but to Kit they appeared as random patterns of transparent shimmering evanescence continuously flowing and changing—glittering red and gold, green and blue, forming an animated rainbow of prismatically refracted light. Viewed from where he stood, the effect was mildly disconcerting, possessing a sort of telescoping motion, as though he or it or both were moving and yet stationary at the same time.

The old ley leap motion sickness squirmed through his gut.

Bile rose into his throat and he gagged and swallowed it back down. That reflex was enough to break his connection with the ley, and the light channel disappeared.

"Wow," breathed Kit, dragging his sleeve across his mouth. "That was intense."

"I want to try," said Cass, moving quickly to join Kit. "Come on, Gianni, let's you and me give it a go."

"Be my guest." Kit handed her his Shadow Lamp and warned, "You might get a little travel sick. It sneaks up on you."

Mina gave her ley lamp to Gianni, and the experiment was repeated with fresh participants. From the sidelines, Kit and Mina watched the three motionless figures attempt to conjure the living rainbow into existence. After two false starts, they managed not only to produce the desired result but to hold it for almost a minute—after which Cass felt dizzy and faint with nausea and had to sit down.

"How did you discover this . . . this singularity?" asked Gianni.

"Quite by accident," Burleigh replied, "as is usually the case with explorers of any sort. My men and I were preparing to make a routine leap, and we happened to be walking single file along the line. We each had a ley locator in hand and"—he lifted a hand to the space where the multicoloured archways had been visible only moments before— "you saw what happened."

"Impressive," said Mina.

"Not at all," demurred Burleigh. "You are seeing the end result of countless frustrating trials over many months merely to repeat the effect, and then it would be several years before I could achieve even the most rudimentary understanding of it. My earliest attempts at manipulation met with failure and frustration. Yet the amount of time and effort saved since then has been more than worth the investment."

"Okay, you paid your dues," said Kit dismissively. "But you keep using the word *manipulate*. What does that mean?"

"Yes." Burleigh turned to him. "Now that you have seen, you will be more fully prepared to understand what I am about to say."

"Just get on with it already," said Kit, and received a warning look from Wilhelmina.

Burleigh overlooked his insolence and disregarded Kit entirely. Turning to the others, he said, "Ley lines are sympathetic to time, as you must surely know."

"When you show up in the other dimension depends on your jumping-off point—is that what you mean?" said Cass.

"Correct." The earl nodded. "No doubt you have discovered this through trial and error, yes?"

"A lot of trial and a lot of error," Wilhelmina agreed. "Go on."

"As it happens, the interplay between the more powerful ley loca-tor and the ley line makes those time-sensitive places visible. You will have noticed that the tunnel of light, as you call it, possessed a ribbed quality—"

"It looked like a series of arches," suggested Cass.

"Or halos," added Kit.

"Each of those halos, or archways"—Burleigh acknowledged Kit and Cass in turn—"corresponds to a specific temporal bifurcation."

"Temporal *what?*" said Mina.

"A time split, you might say," suggested Gianni. "*Bellisimo!* I under-stand. The various ribs or archways correspond to places in time where bifurcations, or splits, in reality have occurred. They are markers."

"The moment when one reality has split off from the main line?" said Kit, trying to get his head around it. He dimly recalled seeing a diagram of a ley line that Cosimo had drawn when Wilhelmina had been lost during that fateful first jump. Cosimo and Kit, together with Sir Henry Fayth, were setting out to find her, and the two elder questors had drawn a map of sorts that looked like a tree on its side with all sorts of limbs branching out from a slender trunk. At last, Kit thought, what he had seen that day began to make sense.

"*Essato.*" Gianni rubbed his chin a moment and said, "Another way to think of it is passing trains. The trains run on different lines parallel to one another, yes? You happen to occupy a particular coach, or time, on the train. But if you were bold enough, you might jump from your coach into a coach of the passing train."

"I've seen it done," mused Kit.

"Really?" wondered Cass. "You saw somebody leap from one moving train to another?"

"In the movies," replied Kit. To Gianni he said, "So by counting the train cars as they pass, so to speak, I could jump onto the other train as a specific car passed the coach I occupied."

Gianni looked to Burleigh for an answer. The earl allowed that it was a fair analogy. "The difficulty, as always, is in knowing which carriage to jump into as it passes. That," he added, "is where the second important feature of the ley locator comes into play." Indicating the silver device balanced on his palm, he said, "When properly activated, the lamp will allow you to select the temporal reality you seek."

Kit stared at the earl with something approaching admiration. He still loathed the man, but he could at least appreciate his indefatigable dedication to the science of ley travel. What is more, he could sense a glimmer of possibility in what Burleigh was showing them. That gleam was elusive, however; he could glimpse its subtle shimmer but could not quite bring it into clearer focus.

"How?" he asked. "How do you select the reality you're looking for?"

By way of an answer, Burleigh extended the Shadow Lamp on his palm. "The lights on the device act as time and directional indicators," he replied. "For example, if you were searching for someone particular, the lights would glow more brightly the closer you came to the dimensional reality that person inhabited."

"That explains it!" said Mina. "I *knew* something like that was happening."

"Again," continued Burleigh, "you must train yourself to create the image of that person in your mind steadily and clearly. It takes a good deal of practice."

"That is how you always seemed to know where we were," said Kit. "You were able to find us whenever you wanted."

"Not always," answered Burleigh, suppressing a sly smile. "But it does make tracking people easier."

"Extraordinary." Gianni shook his head in admiration. "Harnessing your mental energy and uniting it with the telluric energy of the ley line. It is ingenious."

"That is the reason I called the device a locator," Burleigh told him. "At first that is all I imagined it could do, and that is still its prime function."

"So," said Mina, "people, places, time periods—given enough information, the Shadow Lamp can locate them for you."

"Let us rather say," amended the earl, "the device can make the search a good deal less onerous. Of course, success depends very much on what the operator is able to contribute."

"By way of mental energy?" asked Cass.

"Through mental energy, yes, but desire and will play a large part too—the strength of your intent. Willpower, if you please. That is why I suggested three of us acting in unison."

"That increases willpower and makes success more likely," concluded Kit. The more he heard, the more Burleigh's explanation made sense of things he had always wondered about.

"Okay, let's try it!" suggested Wilhelmina. "Show us what to do."

They spent the next hour or so attempting to put the things they were learning into practice until the window of ley activity closed for the day. "I guess that's it," said Kit. "Too bad we have to quit just when we were getting the hang of it."

"We can practice again this evening, can't we?" said Cass as they headed back to the carriage.

"I think we should," agreed Mina, "and with any luck Gustavus will have enough activated earth refined to make another Shadow Lamp or two. Then we can all have one. I can't wait to try an actual leap while inside the light."

They discussed this on the way back to the city. Burleigh held his own counsel, however, saying little and only replying when one of the others asked him a direct question. They returned the horse and carriage to the hostler at the lower end of the square nearest the gate, then made their way along the shop fronts toward the Grand Imperial Kaffeehaus.

"Kit, you coming?" called Cass as Kit stood watching the wagon trundle away.

"I don't trust that snake," he said darkly. "He's scheming up something. I can tell."

"He seemed okay to me. A little quiet on the way back, maybe." She put her arm through Kit's and drew him away. "Come on. Let's get something to eat. We didn't have breakfast, and I'm starving."

They hurried on across the square, passing beneath the shadow of the towering Rathaus. Burleigh, walking some paces behind them, lowered his head and averted his eyes, taking on the aspect of a hunted man. Upon emerging from the shadow, Wilhelmina halted, bringing the group to a stop.

"What?" asked Kit, following her gaze across the square. He saw only the ordinary midmorning traffic and commerce of a city going about its mundane business. "What is it?"

"It's the wrong colour," breathed Mina. She turned to the others. "Don't you see it?"

"Everything looks all right to me," replied Kit. "What about you, Gianni?"

Before the priest could answer, Wilhelmina shrieked, "It's *yellow!*"

Kit stared at her. "*What's* yellow? Mina, you're not making sense . . ."

Cass pushed him aside. "Mina, tell us what is wrong."

"The kaffeehaus—the colour." She pointed across the square. "It's green and *yellow.*"

"Yes," agreed Cass. "I see that. What is wrong with that?"

"It was *never* green and yellow," Mina said, her face stricken. "We decided against that. We painted it green and white instead. It has *always* been green and white."

Cass bit her lip and glanced at Kit. "Don't ask me," he said. "I never really noticed."

"That is not all," Burleigh said, stepping up behind them. "The guards at the gate were in blue uniforms just now, and there were no banners on the walls."

"How is that significant?" said Kit.

"The soldier's uniforms have always been red and black," the earl replied. "And there were banners on the wall when we left this morning."

"It's happening," Cass concluded. "Damascus all over again." At

Burleigh's puzzled look, she added, "This present reality is becoming unstable."

"We don't know that," said Kit. His tone lacked all conviction, and he turned his gaze to the kaffeehaus once more. "Let's go check it out."

They continued across the square and to the door of the Grand Imperial. "I'll go in first if you want," said Kit.

Wilhelmina shook her head. "I'll go first." She put her hand to the door, steeled herself for what she might find, and entered. Inside, all seemed normal enough. The aroma of fresh baking met them in a rush. The tables were full of businessmen drinking their coffee; serving girls in green-and-yellow aprons were ferrying trays back and forth to the kitchen; and Engelbert could be glimpsed behind the kitchen counter, placing iced buns on a plate.

"Not too bad," observed Kit. "Maybe the—"

He was stopped by Wilhelmina seizing his arm and digging her nails into his flesh.

"Oh my God," breathed Cass.

A moan escaped Mina's lips. "No-o-o . . ."

Then Kit saw it too: out from the kitchen stepped a duplicate Wilhelmina in a green-and-yellow apron and matching bonnet. She was carrying plates of strudel in one hand and a small tray with coffeepot and cups in the other. "*Einen Moment, bitte,*" she called cheerily and continued on into the dining room with barely a glance at the newcomers.

"I think I'm going to be sick," groaned Mina, her face ashen.

"Keep it together, girl," Cass told her.

"Cass is right. It is Damascus again." Kit glanced around, and in his peripheral vision saw that the Old Town Square had vanished and was now a meadow with cattle grazing on it. He blinked, and when he looked again, the expanse had changed back into a market square. "It is *definitely* happening."

"What is this?" asked Burleigh, his brow furrowed in concern as he watched Wilhelmina's doppelgänger disappear into the dining room. "What is happening here?"

Cass was composed enough to give a coherent answer. "The dimensional reality we currently inhabit is breaking down. It is no longer stable."

"*Alterazioni*," added Gianni. "The errors, they grow and multiply until the entire reality becomes, ah—unsustainable."

"What happens then?" asked Burleigh.

"We don't know," Kit replied. "We think the whole dimension might just collapse. If that happens, then—"

"The dimension is extinguished," Burleigh concluded. "And everything and everyone along with it."

"Exactly," said Kit. "We can't stay here. We've got to move." He touched Mina on the arm; it felt cold and rigid as carved marble. "I'm sorry, Mina."

"Where can we go?" asked Cass.

"I've got an idea," said Kit. "Gianni, get Wilhelmina out of sight. Go to the cathedral. Cass and I will buy some food and meet you there. I'll explain everything when we get there."

"What about me?" said Burleigh.

"I don't really care what you do," Kit told him. To Gianni, he said, "Go now—before somebody sees them both together."

They all backed out of the kaffeehaus. Gianni, with an unresisting Wilhelmina in tow, moved off toward the cathedral on the far side of the square; Burleigh went along behind them, staying close but out of the way. Kit and Cass quickly gathered a few provisions from the shops and vendors around the square and then hastened to rejoin the others.

"So what's the plan?" asked Cass as they hurried to the church. "Where are we going?"

"There's really only one place to go," Kit told her.

"The Fatal Tree," concluded Cass. "What makes you think it will be any different this time?"

"This time we have new Shadow Lamps and know how to use them."

"We've only got three lamps," Cass pointed out. "Maybe we should wait for Gustavus to finish making the rest."

Kit was already shaking his head. "Wait," he said, "and watch everything get weird around us and eventually collapse. Besides, the way things are changing here, there's no guarantee Gus is working on getting us more lamps, or even if he's still here."

"But only three of us will have lamps," Cass pointed out again.

"Then three will have to be enough."

After a hurried consultation in the cathedral porch, the questors left the city and made their way to the River Ley. They arrived at the beech grove in plenty of time and settled in the sun-dappled shade at the foot of the path to eat and rest and wait for the ley to become active. They spent the afternoon brainstorming various options for dealing with the Fatal Tree. During a lull in the conversation, Burleigh, who had said little since leaving the city, spoke up. "I think you should tell me what is going on," he said.

"You know what's going on," Kit replied. "We told you—the

universe is imploding and we're trying to find a way to keep it from destroying itself and everything in it."

"You have told me some, perhaps, but there is much you are holding back," the earl said. "I think it is time you told me *all* your secrets."

"There *is* no secret," Wilhelmina insisted. "Honestly. What Kit said—that is the truth."

"I don't believe you." Burleigh's voice took on a tone of menace.

"Maybe because you've spent your whole life in deceit and betrayal, you can't recognise the truth when you hear it," Kit snarled.

Burleigh's brow darkened and lowered dangerously. Gianni was quick to intervene. "We are keeping no secrets. I will tell you anything you wish to know." Kit appeared about to protest, but Gianni cut him off. "My friend," intoned the priest softly, "he has a right to ask. His fate is bound to ours, and ours to his—like it or not. No?" To Burleigh, he said, "Please, what would you like to know?"

"We can start with whatever it is you call the Fatal Tree. I have heard you mention it several times. Tell me about that."

Gianni explained with admirable brevity about the yew tree and how it guarded a portal unlike any they had ever encountered. Wilhelmina picked up the account, saying, "The tree has become embedded in, or entangled with, the portal."

"It's channelling such enormous power that any physical contact is dangerous in the extreme," added Cass. "Even the slightest touch can kill."

"A very dear friend touched a branch and died instantly," Mina said. As if to prove the truth of her assertion, she indicated her arm in the sling. "That's how I was injured."

Burleigh absorbed this thoughtfully, then said, "And this portal with the tree is the one you hope to manipulate?" Cass and Mina nodded; Kit remained unresponsive. "Why?" asked Burleigh. "What is so important about that portal in particular?"

Gianni answered, "It is our belief that this portal leads to the Spirit Well—the place Arthur Flinders-Petrie discovered and held as a jealously guarded secret for the rest of his life."

"The Spirit Well," mused Burleigh, then shook his head. "The name means nothing to me."

"Arthur apparently believed that he had discovered the legendary Well of Souls," offered Mina. "We think he may have considered it a sort of fountain of immortality—something like that."

"Ah . . ." Burleigh's sigh of resignation and relief spoke volumes. "It is no less than I suspected." His eyes flicked back to Wilhelmina. "How did you acquire this information?"

It was Kit who answered. "I saw him there," he said. "I saw Arthur Flinders-Petrie at the Spirit Well, and I saw what he did."

"You met him? You met Arthur?"

"No," Kit replied. "I didn't say that. He didn't see me, but I saw him and I saw what he did."

"And am I right in thinking that what he did that day," began Burleigh, piecing the story together, "has something to do with the impending cataclysm—this so-called End of Everything?" He glanced around the group in the fading afternoon light. "I see that I am correct in my assumptions. So tell me—what did Arthur do?"

After a moment's hesitation, Kit replied, "I saw him bring a dead woman back to life."

"The Well of Souls," mused Burleigh. "I see it now. That was his great secret. It all makes sense to me now."

"You knew about this?"

"I have long suspected . . ." Burleigh shook his head. "But no. Suspicions only, that is all."

"Do you know who the woman was?" asked Cass.

"I believe the woman was Xian-Li, Arthur's wife. She was the daughter of Wu Chen Hu, the artist who made the tattoos for Arthur. And no—before you ask—I did not kill her. Indeed, I know nothing of how she died, but I long since guessed that she must have at least suffered some trauma that Arthur had redressed somehow. Although, in a way, I was the one who made their union possible."

"How so?" wondered Mina.

"I told you that I tried to take the map by force," Burleigh explained, "but that Arthur escaped. It was Xian-Li who came to his aid that day."

"This is your fault," grumbled Kit. "Why am I not surprised?" Disregarding Wilhelmina's warning glance, he continued, "If you had not attacked Arthur that day, they would never have met, and having never met, they would never have married, and Arthur would never have had cause to save her." Kit's hand described a series of loops as if to indicate the continuing roll of events springing from that one act.

"And you feel this makes him responsible?" asked Gianni. "The chain of causation is long indeed—who can say what might or might not have happened if one thing or another had been slightly different?"

"You are kind to try to defend me," acknowledged Burleigh. "But he is right. I am responsible for bringing them together. Whatever flowed from that meeting is to my account too—at least in part. I own the fault and I will do my best to put it right. Whatever it takes, even to the giving of my life, I will do it."

"A bit late for that," growled Kit, and earned himself a smack on the arm.

"The Zetetics have a saying," said Gianni, breaking in. "There is no such thing as coincidence. Your actions that day may have set in motion a train of events that put Arthur on the path to destroy all creation. Yet here you are, putting in our hands the means to save it."

"That's why we're here," said Cass. She raised her Shadow Lamp and showed the others that the little green lights were glowing. She rose and brushed off the leaf mould from her trousers. "Well? Let's go see if we can, you know, save the universe."

CHAPTER 31

In Which the Past Is Prelude

*E*verybody okay?" Kit dashed water from his eyes and glanced around for the others. Cass was on all fours in the middle of the narrow cliffside path, and Mina lay sprawled on the ground beside her, moaning gently. Gianni and Burleigh knelt together a few paces behind. The leap had been rough and the attending storm fiercer than any they had experienced so far, with biting wind and lashing rain. The travellers were shaken and soggy, but at least all were present.

"Oh-h-h, man," said Cass. "I hope I never—"

Before she could finish the thought, she cupped a hand to her mouth and promptly threw up. That set off a chain reaction. Wilhelmina and Kit vomited in turn, and Burleigh, grim faced, succumbed to a bout of dry heaves. Only Gianni evaded the worst symptoms of ley sickness, but he looked none too spry. Wet hair plastered to his head, his skin paled to a wan pastiness, he looked like a shipwreck victim washed up onshore. "I do think that was the worst crossing yet," he observed, dabbing his face with a soggy handkerchief.

"They are getting tougher," agreed Kit, wiping his mouth on a damp sleeve. He moved to Wilhelmina's side and helped her to her feet. "How's the arm?"

"I'll live," she said, her eyes dull with pain.

"We can rest a minute if you want," Kit told her. "It's a bit of a trek from here to the tree, you know."

Mina pushed wet hair away from her face. "Let's just get on with it."

"Are you sure?" said Cass, fanning the fabric of her clingy wet shirt.

Mina swayed slightly, steadied herself, and uncorking a small bottle of reddish-brown liquid, took a tiny sip, grimacing at the bitter taste of the laudanum. She jammed the cork back in and stuffed the bottle into her pocket, then gave a curt nod. "Ready."

"Right," said Kit. "Let's get cracking."

The climb up the canyon trail to the rim of the gorge was made more arduous and slightly harrowing by the fact that the trail had deteriorated since their last visit. The surface was badly eroded, and in places the edge had sheared off close to the cliff face, forcing the travellers to hug the wall. Once they reached the top, Kit paused to allow everyone to catch their breath while he repeated his warning about keeping an eye out for carnivorous predators that roamed the prairies and forests.

They set off across the plain, but aside from a herd of graceful gazelle-like creatures that bounded away through the long grass and a flock of startled partridges, they saw no other animals. The walk in the fresh air and warm sunshine restored them, and they reached the edge of the wood in better spirits than when they had begun. After another short break, a stint of stealthy hiking brought them to the wall of saplings surrounding the Fatal Tree.

"Here we are," Kit said. He turned to the others as they gathered around behind him. "Remember to keep your hands down at your side and do *not* touch the tree—even the smallest part. It's lethal."

"As if *that* needed saying," muttered Cass.

"I mean it," insisted Kit. "We don't want a repeat of last time." He looked to Burleigh. "You are here to advise us, nothing more. Got that? I don't want you interfering in any way."

"I am yours to command," replied Burleigh graciously.

"Okay, then. Everybody ready?" Kit looked into the eyes of each of the others in turn and, satisfied that all were in agreement, said, "Let's do this." He turned and forced his way through the close-grown ring saplings that formed a shielding wall and stepped into the presence of the mighty yew.

The quiet within the circle was almost deafening; the air was dead. The questors gazed up at the heavy green boughs towering above them, dwarfing them, and felt a cold dread spreading up through the ground into their bones and blood. A few paces away on the edge of the perimeter lay the grave mound of Thomas Young—undisturbed, still fresh as the moment they left it.

Gianni saw the grave, went to it, and stood for a moment; then, folding his hands, he bowed his head and offered a prayer in Latin: "*Domine Iesu, dimitte nobis debita nostra, salva nos ab igne inferiori, perduc in caelum omnes animas, praesertim eas, quae misericordiae tuae maxime indigent.*"

The others stood in reverent silence, listening to the cadence, if not understanding the words. He ended, saying, "*In nomine Patris, et Filii, et Spiritus Sancti. Amen.*"

Kit added his own "Amen," and then, forcing himself back to the task at hand, turned to Burleigh. "What do we need to know about manipulating portals? Tell us what to do—keeping in mind that our Shadow Lamps burned out the last time we tried to use them in this place."

Burleigh gazed up into the top branches of the giant tree, lowered his eyes, and said, "This is unlike any portal I have seen. I cannot say what will happen, but I can tell you what has worked in other places."

"Weasel words noted," said Kit. "Get on with it."

"Of course," replied Burleigh evenly. He took a few paces farther along the clear zone, examining the girth of the tree, and then turned and came back, saying, "I think the first thing to attempt is aligning the locators. No doubt the devices burned out last time because you lacked fundamental symmetry."

"Ah, yes," said Gianni. "How do we align the devices?"

"With a portal," began Burleigh, "since there is no straight path as in a linear ley, we must position ourselves equidistant around the perimeter. In view of your past experience, I would suggest screening the devices with your bodies until you are ready."

"Fine," said Kit. "Just tell us where to stand."

They watched as Burleigh paced off the circumference, then marked positions on the perimeter for each holder of a lamp. Kit, Cass, and Mina each moved to a designated spot. "Okay, now what?" Mina asked when they had taken their positions, forming an equilateral triangle around the base of the enormous tree, each in full sight of the others.

"As with the ley line," replied Burleigh, raising his voice to be heard in the stultifying atmosphere of the clearing, "you will attempt to harmonise your thoughts by visualising the intended destination. Once your minds are properly entrained, we will discover what opportunities for manipulation exist."

"Okay, you heard him," called Kit. "Ready? On the count of

three, we take out our lamps." He counted off and brought his out of his pocket. The little turquoise lights were ablaze, and the pewter shell grew instantly warm in his palm. He braced himself for the quick sputter of flame and the stench of scorched metal. When it did not happen, Kit called out, "Okay, it seems to be working. I'll count to three, and we concentrate our thoughts on the Spirit Well."

Again, he gave the count and, holding the lamp on his palm, turned his thoughts to the Spirit Well, filling his mind with the image of that strange pool of golden liquid light. When, after a minute or two, nothing had happened, he halted the experiment. "Take a break!" he called. "But don't move, we'll go again in a second."

They did try again—two more times, with the same result; aside from a few bursts and sputters of sparky light, very little seemed to be happening. During the fourth attempt, however, the feeble flicking light not only took hold, it strengthened and grew, filling the clearing with a bloom of radiance.

"That's it!" Kit called. "Keep—" A flash of brilliance to his right drew his attention. Glancing away from the tree, he saw Burleigh standing a few paces away with a Shadow Lamp in his hand. "Burleigh!" he shouted. "What are you doing?"

"I thought you could use a little extra muscle," he replied.

"Where did you get that lamp?"

"Oh, it was safely tucked away." The device was similar to the old lamps, but slightly larger, and from what Kit could see, it had an additional row of light-emitting windows, and three knobs or dials on the top. "A more advanced model than the shabby imitations you concocted," Burleigh told him. "Do you like it?"

"You used us!" exclaimed Kit, anger searing through him.

"Well, you did not genuinely expect I would miss my chance to see the Spirit Well, did you? After all I've been through?" A wicked grin spread across Burleigh's face. "Are you *really* that naïve?"

"Traitor! I knew it! We were fools to trust you."

Burleigh gazed back mildly. "Do as I say, and we will all get where we want to go." Turning his attention back to the Fatal Tree, he raised his ley lamp and touched one of the dials. Lines of bright turquoise light streamed from the holes around the rim of the device like a fan of laser beams.

"Kit?" called Mina. "What's going on?"

"Burleigh's got a Shadow Lamp. He's been holding out on us."

"Quiet! All of you!" shouted Burleigh. "This is the most delicate phase of the operation. Total attention is required." He touched another of the dials on his Shadow Lamp and a bolt of living light arced from the device, linking it with the other three around the tree, joining each to the other. "Concentrate!"

Kit felt the Shadow Lamp vibrate in his hand and heard a faint hum—low pitched and muted—as if seeping up through the earth. The hum grew louder, gaining both pitch and resonance, picking up additional notes, wringing odd harmonics from the air. The hair on his arms and scalp pricked up on end. The keening sound combined with the crackle of static electricity, climbing into the upper registers, morphing into the howl of an untuned radio.

"Almost there," shouted Burleigh, trying to make himself heard above the wild shriek. "Any moment . . . hold steady . . ."

The lamp in Kit's hand grew warmer still—not uncomfortable yet, but getting close. The vibration increased, and he could detect a metallic whiff in the air.

The light bloom expanded to encase the entire tree in an envelope of radiance. Each limb and branch took on a lustrous, ethereal quality—as if dipped in glow-in-the-dark shellac—and the green, needlelike leaves became tiny luminous spikes, bristling with energy. The ever-rising pitch of the radio squeal finally passed beyond the range of human ears, trailing off into a shrill whine that faded into silence—an attenuation accompanied by a parallel increase in the brightness of the radiance enveloping the tree. Suddenly there was a flash; Kit threw his hand over his eyes and looked away.

"Behold!" cried Burleigh. "The portal is open!"

Kit opened his eyes and saw that the great yew tree had been replaced by a towering pillar of brilliant blue pulsating light—so bright that it was like looking into the flame of a welding torch. The column spun slowly around an invisible axis, giving off glints and shimmers as motes of light like fireflies streamed outward into the atmosphere.

Startled by the change, Kit almost dropped his lamp; and when he looked again, he saw that the Fatal Tree was, in fact, still there, but it seemed to be composed entirely of a sort of transparent plasma that hummed and pulsed with the pure blue radiance of unbounded energy. Tiny filaments streamed from the branches of the translucent tree—telluric energy leaking into the air—forming networks of living light. His skin tingled all over. The firefly sparks formed and leaked from the ends of his hair and the tips of his fingers and ears.

He felt at once buoyant and heavier than concrete, as if he were being stretched between two opposing forces . . . and yet he felt neither pain nor discomfort. Instead, the world around him faded, growing paler and thinner. Around the base of the yew tree the ground was bleached white as snow; Kit could see both Cass and Wilhelmina at their stations, eyes wide, their lamps extended like flashlights, beams streaming with turquoise sunrays from the tiny holes in their lamps. The image wavered and danced; it was like looking through hand-blown milk glass as it slowly revolved.

"*Formidabile!*" Gianni breathed, his face bathed in the unearthly glow.

"Kit! Gianni!" called Cass. "Are you seeing this?"

"We are!" Kit answered, but his reply was swallowed in the roar that accompanied the flare of energy that blinded him—a flash so bright it shone through his eyelids with a pure white light. His Shadow Lamp fizzed and sparked and grew too hot to hold. He dropped it, and in the same instant a shock wave slammed through him, knocking him off his feet and onto his back.

Oddly, there was no heat—just the sound, light, and pressure wave . . . and the feathery touch of snow on his skin and eyelashes. Kit rolled onto his side and looked up to see, not the Fatal Tree, but the Bone House.

In place of the encircling hedge of beech saplings stood a wall of slender pines, their boughs bending beneath a heavy layer of snow and, in the centre, that curious construction made up of the most fantastical assortment of skeletal fragments: pelvises, spines, leg bones, vertebrae, femurs, ribs, and more. The bones of a score of different creatures, including the enormous curving tusks of a mammoth, the heavy horned skull of a rhinoceros, and the splayed palmate antlers of a giant elk—all of them long extinct.

Head throbbing, ears buzzing, aching in every limb and joint, Kit pushed himself up on his hands and knees and looked across the clearing. Cass and Mina, their faces distorted, were shouting at him. Kit could see their mouths moving, but their voices reached him as incoherent babble, like voices heard underwater, drowned by the deep-rooted hum and thrum of the energy pulse that had blasted them into another dimension—or maybe it had peeled away a layer or two to reveal the one beneath.

He shouted for the others, his voice sounding muted and distant. "Stay put, everybody. I'll come to you." He staggered up onto his feet and started around the Bone House. Gianni lay on his back a few feet away. Kit shuffled over to him. Covered in snow, he appeared stunned, almost comically so, as one of the lenses of his glasses was cracked in a starburst pattern. Other than that, the priest seemed to be uninjured. Kit helped him to his feet, and the two moved to where Wilhelmina and Cass were now standing, brushing snow from one another. Two Shadow Lamps lay in the snow nearby; one was scorched and discoloured by heat and smoke, but the other appeared undamaged, though it glowed and hummed with aberrant vigour.

"Everybody okay?" asked Kit, his voice loud so he could hear himself above the buzz in his ears.

"You know this place?" said Mina. "It's the Bone House, right?"

She had to repeat the question before Kit answered, "That's right—and it's just as I remember it."

"Incredible . . . ," murmured Gianni, peering sideways through his ruined glasses. "Never have I seen anything like it."

Lost in thought, Kit gazed at the Bone House as the memory of what had taken place there replayed in his mind.

"We're going to freeze to death out here," Cass said. She pointed at the igloo-shaped hut. "Can we go inside?"

Kit turned his attention to the snow-covered clearing and scanned it quickly. "Where's Burleigh?"

"He was standing right there before the blast," said Wilhelmina. A swift search of the perimeter and surrounding wood, calling his name and shouting to rouse him, failed to turn up any trace.

"He must have ended up somewhere else," Cass concluded.

"Suits me," said Kit. "We can't waste time looking for him now."

"We're freezing out here," Cass said again. "We've got to do something."

Kit glanced around the clearing one last time, then picked up the intact Shadow Lamp and started around the side of the Bone House. "I've got an idea," he said. "Follow me."

CHAPTER 32

In Which the Bone House Yields a Secret

Getting everyone into the Bone House was a tight squeeze; the structure was never meant to hold so many. Washed-out sunlight filtered down through the chinks and cracks in the bony roof, casting the interior in a dim half-light that was neither day nor night. The floor of the hut was packed snow spread with pine branches and the skins of deer and buffalo. Immediately upon entering, Wilhelmina and Cass pulled up one of the pelts and draped it over themselves; Gianni did the same. Once everyone was settled, Kit said, "I don't know how much any of you know about this place, but this is where I sat with En-Ul while he was—" He hesitated, trying to decide how to describe what it was the old clan chief was doing. "Well, I know it as Dreaming Time . . ."

"You have mentioned this before," said Gianni. "Can you tell us more about it?"

"I can try," said Kit. "But the thing is—River City Clan had fairly primitive language skills. They communicated mainly through what I thought of as a kind of mental radio—once you were able to tune in, they spoke to you through mental images of whatever it was they were trying to tell you."

"I remember you saying"—Mina pulled the cork from her laudanum bottle, took a sip, and swallowed hard—"images, impressions—that sort of thing, right?"

"What do you think he meant by *dreaming time?*" asked Gianni.

"Well, he didn't use exactly those words," Kit explained. "The clansmen didn't have many words, remember. But that is the sense I made of what he was trying to tell me. I guess I supplied the words. Oh," added Kit, recalling the urgency and gravity of what had been communicated to him. "And also that what he was doing was incredibly important—life-and-death important, as if survival of the clan depended on it."

"In what way?" asked Cass.

"I honestly do not know. The precise meaning was fairly vague, but that was the sense I got of what he was telling me. Anyway, the impression I got from En-Ul was that here, in the Bone House, he was able to interact with time."

"Creating time? Changing it?" asked Gianni.

"More like he was seeing what time would bring and somehow interacting with what he saw." Kit shook his head. "I can't say."

Cass, who had been studying the interior of the Bone House with professional interest, exclaimed, "I get it now!" All eyes turned to where she sat huddled under the heavy pelt. "It's symbolic—don't you see?"

"What's symbolic?" asked Mina, sitting next to her.

"This place—the Bone House—it's a symbol. Get it?" When

the others continued to stare, she hurried to explain. "Stay with me here, okay? My mother was an anthropologist, and she told me once that old Scandinavian poets used a device called a *kenning*. It was a way of expressing a thing obliquely by referencing something else—like saying 'battle sweat' to mean *blood* or saying 'swan road' to mean *sea*—a metaphorical way of speaking, and heavily symbolic. So, using that model, Bone House would be . . ." She paused to consider.

"Maybe it's your body," said Mina. "The place where your spirit lives?"

"Could be," Cass allowed, her brows lowered in thought.

"Your skull," declared Gianni suddenly. He appeared as surprised as anyone else by his utterance. "It is obvious. The skull is the dome of bone that houses your mind. Your consciousness *lives*, so to speak, inside your skull—"

"Inside a house of bone," added Kit, finishing the thought.

"That fits," said Cass. "Kit, I think your friend En-Ul was telling you more than you know! All this is symbolic—only instead of trying to explain it to you, he acted it out. He was *showing* you how things worked. Don't you see?" Cass rocked back and forth in her excitement. "By sleeping in the Bone House, he was demonstrating his fundamental understanding of the world and his place in it."

"Do you think he was visiting the Spirit Well to do whatever he was doing?" asked Mina.

"Possibly," granted Kit. "It is surely no coincidence that the Bone House sits on the portal that connects directly with the Spirit Well."

Gianni cleared his throat. "Before we were so thoroughly diverted," he said, "you said you had an idea."

"We're directly on top of the portal," Kit replied. "We can use it to get to the Spirit Well, and I think I know how to turn it on."

Kit went on to explain how he had spent hours watching over En-Ul while the Old One slept, and how, after three years of inactivity, his Shadow Lamp had inexplicably sparked to life. "In my excitement, I stood up and fell through the floor—"

"Like at Black Mixen Tump," suggested Wilhelmina.

"Just like Black Mixen Tump," replied Kit. "Only instead of connecting to Egypt, this leap took me to the Spirit Well. I think that whatever En-Ul was doing opened the portal and allowed me to go through."

Gianni, nodding thoughtfully, said, "You seem to be suggesting that the conscious mental activity of the Bone House occupant initiated the portal." He peered around at the group through the shattered lens of his glasses and concluded, "That would support Cass' hypothesis—and it would be easy enough to test."

"By doing what En-Ul did," said Cass. "Is that what you mean?"

"Right," said Kit. "Whatever En-Ul did, he did it while asleep—or at least very relaxed. Eyes closed, meditating. That sort of thing."

"Then let us try that," said Gianni. To Mina he said, "Your Shadow Lamp will show us if we succeed in activating the portal."

"What shall we meditate about?" asked Mina.

"Think about the future," offered Gianni.

"Like En-Ul," said Kit. "Imagine yourself in the future and what you want to have happen there."

After a little more discussion, the travellers settled back to contemplate various possibilities of life for themselves in time to come. They closed their eyes and turned their sight inward. After the fraught events of the last few hours, they slowly succumbed to the calm and quiet of the place, and one by one drifted off.

The first thing that came into Wilhelmina's mind was the

kaffeehaus. She saw herself in the kitchen of the Grand Imperial working with Engelbert, happy, prospering; she saw the two of them together and realised just how much they complemented one another—Etzel with his quiet strength and peerless character, and herself with her creativity and business savvy. The image changed abruptly then, and she saw a white stucco house with a red tile roof in a pleasant corner of Old Prague with a tiny orchard garden filled with flowers and vegetables. Two little towheaded girls fluttered around like butterflies while Etzel picked apples and she, with a ledger in her lap, did the weekly accounting. Thinking of herself and Etzel together seemed right and good, and filled her with a warm glow of pleasure.

Perhaps it was the setting—the Neolithic structure of the Bone House guiding the direction of her thoughts—but Cass saw the nearby gorge and river where she and Kit had spent those days while waiting for Wilhelmina to join them. Only this time, she saw it without the overlay of anxiety and fear. Instead, she saw the placid river reflecting the white cliffs all around; she heard the lazy hum of insects and the pure-throated calls of the blackbirds in the rushes along the bank. She saw herself writing and making sketches in a notebook for research, observing long-extinct animals in their natural habitats, exploring the caves with members of River City Clan as guides. She saw herself and Kit together and imagined they were building a house—an old-fashioned dwelling of wattle and daub. Kit was up a makeshift ladder, thatching the roof with reeds gathered from the riverside; she was there, holding up a bundle for him to use . . . She imagined them in their cosy dwelling together, and he was holding a skewer threaded with sliced onions and cubes of meat over the fire on their round stone hearth . . . She saw them swimming in the river by the light of a rising moon . . . She saw them holding hands and sharing a kiss as they sat on a stone ledge and watched the stars come out . . . She imagined this and felt how fine it would be if they could enjoy a life together—a life of adventure and discovery, every day new.

Upon closing his eyes, Gianni's first thought was of the JVLA and the marvellous work they were doing there. He saw the man who had, in a very short time, become a dear friend; he saw Tony Clarke working with the other scientists there, working to understand the coming cataclysm . . . And then he saw himself and Tony in his old observatory at Montserrat and they were very excited about some-thing they had seen—followed by a picture of himself and Tony on a stage in a great hall with lights all around, and they were sharing a prize for one of their breakthrough discoveries; they were dressed in black tie and tails, standing at a podium in a gleaming golden hall, beaming as they received the applause of an august audience for their singular achievement. Was it the Nobel Prize? The feeling of accomplishment suffused him with pride, which both surprised and embarrassed him.

For Kit, the exercise took a little time to bear fruit, but when it did, it came in abundance. His mind filled with the faces of people he had met, and some he had lost, along the way. He did not try to impose an order on them, but simply allowed the images to come as they would. He saw Brandon and Mrs. Peelstick and the rest of the Zetetics—happily continuing their work, maintaining the genizah, reaching out to travellers, expanding their knowledge of the ways of God in creation. He saw Tess and pictured the white-haired octoge-narian laying a wreath on a newly erected memorial. The writing on the simple slab of granite said:

Cosimo Christopher Livingstone, the Elder
Traveller, Explorer, Adventurer
Good & Faithful Friend

No dates were given, but that did not matter. Cosimo was remembered, his passing marked and respected, and that seemed to be enough. Next to that grave was a second inscribed in similar fashion for Sir Henry Fayth. That the two friends should rest together in this way seemed right and proper to Kit. *Bless you, Tess,* he thought, and then reminded himself that he had only imagined it. Yet somehow that did not make what he saw seem any less real.

Other faces came before him: Haven and Giles . . . what had happened to them? He imagined them together—in a great city, perhaps, where Haven's beauty and spirit would shine, for she would need refinement and sophistication to be truly happy. As for loyal, stouthearted Giles, Kit imagined him thriving and attaining a rank he deserved—as a respected retainer in a noble household, perhaps, in a position where his devotion and trustworthiness could be both appreciated and rewarded. This seemed right to Kit: Haven finding a measure of contentment with a man like Giles whose steady hand could temper her mercurial nature. He imagined that would be a good thing.

He saw a campfire, the lambent glow flickering on the stone walls of River City Clan's rock shelter . . . En-Ul was there, and Dardok, and the rest of the clan. He imagined them in their summer dwellings at River City, protected by high rock walls near the river's slow-flowing water; he saw young ones dabbling in a brook, their mothers nearby, keeping watch while picking blackberries. He saw En-Ul sitting under a tree, thinking deep thoughts, guiding his people with wisdom and care . . . and Dardok with an infant son. Kit saw the clan surviving—more, he saw them safe and flourishing, carving a niche for themselves in an often harsh and unforgiving age and going from strength to strength. He saw himself introducing the clan to Cass, and them accepting her as they had accepted him.

And then, just as he glimpsed himself and Cass sitting on a rock by the river, watching the moon rise, the image blanked out—not into darkness, but into a bright and all-pervading light. Kit had a sensation of movement.

In that instant the four separate minds with their individual thoughts and images fused into a single combined consciousness; they were one and they were falling, plunging blind into a blazing, colour-less void.

Their downward plummet accelerated, turning gradually into flight; they felt the unnerving, giddy sensation of flying, of travelling at immense, mind-bending speed over distances beyond reckoning at a velocity that exceeded the speed of light; it seemed to them that they were covering impossible distances with the swift felicity of thought itself. Encased in an incandescent shell, they detected no possibility of the journey ever coming to an end. An age passed between one breath and another, an eternity in the blink of an eye, and still they sped on.

When it began to seem as if they would remain forever frozen in flight—a mere speck of dust in a cosmic glacier of time—they saw a faint shape emerge in the distance. At first little more than a shadow, it slowly took on form and substance; patterns of light and dark solidified and spread across the light horizon, growing steadily, filling the void with the distant hope of a destination.

But the light gradually faded, evaporating into the darkness of deep space spangled with a spray of starlight and the perfect blue orb of a world far away. The planet rushed toward them at such speed that they had no time to brace themselves: they were dropping through the cloudless heavens, and the collective consciousness separated into its constituent parts once more.

One moment Kit was free-falling through the atmosphere, and the next he was lying facedown on a beach of flawless white sand, his clothes soaking wet as if he had just been for a swim. He did not remember plunging into the water, but he was wet and the sea waves soughed gently behind him. He raised his head and took in his surroundings, inhaling the sweet air and savouring the warmth of the sun as the recollection of his first visit came rushing back in a surge of vivid memory. Behind him, the sparkling turquoise sea spread to the far horizon. Before him rose a verdant wall of green, almost radiant vegetation, exactly as he remembered it. Beyond that lush green wall, in a secluded jungle glade, lay the Spirit Well.

CHAPTER 33

In Which There Is No Going Back

*I*s *everything in this world more alive?* Kit wondered. Perhaps the gravity of this planet was subtly different and that made things seem more vibrant; from the jewel-like colours to the impossibly blue sky and flawless white clouds—everything seemed fresher, newer, more intensely present. The assault on the senses was powerful. Within seconds of stepping from the warm sea wash, the sheer beauty of the place overwhelmed him anew. Nothing in his memory matched the brilliance, the splendour, the unutterable magnificence of the reality before him.

He moved up the beach toward the jungle, and his feet had just touched the grassy verge when he heard a splash behind him. Glancing back, he saw Cass standing knee-deep in the surf. He called out to her and waved as he turned and started back to meet her; he was halfway to the water's edge when Wilhelmina materialised. Like a ghost taking on flesh, she just simply appeared—kneeling, up to her hips in the waves. Seconds later, Gianni arrived. Like Mina, he appeared first as a vague and hazy outline that rapidly filled in, becoming flesh before his eyes.

Kit hurried to greet the dazed, disoriented newcomers. "You made it!" he called. "I was beginning to think I was the only one to make the leap." He ran to help Mina up out of the water. "You okay?" She gave him a groggy nod as he took her good arm and raised her to her feet. "Here, let's get you onto dry land."

"Where are we?" asked Cass, wading over to help. "Is this the Spirit Well?"

"No," Kit replied. "I don't know what this place is called, but the Spirit Well is through that bit of jungle over there. It's just a short walk from here." He turned to where Gianni stood gazing around with an odd expression on his face. "You okay over there, Gianni?"

The priest gave a start and came to himself. "*È così bella*," he sighed. "So very beautiful."

"You haven't seen anything yet," Kit told him. "I'll show you."

They crossed the beach and were soon on the path leading into the jungle paradise. All around them grew strange, exotic shrubs and trees: plants with foliage that resembled lacework fans or billowy clouds of tiny green stars or long, tapering feathers of spun gold. Flowers and fruit grew in profligate abundance—in bunches and clusters, clutches and clumps, in banks and drifts like clouds: flamingo pink, violet, saffron, ultramarine, citrine, and others that no earthly tongue had ever named. Everywhere they looked, some new and arresting form met the eye—in shapes that beggared description, and all of it fresh and unspoiled as if rejoicing in its first hour of existence. From the graceful elegance of the trees and shrubs to the contours and patterns of their leaves and the pristine elegance of the flowers—it was all so arresting the travellers found it difficult to avoid continual distraction.

As they moved through the wildly exuberant foliage, they sensed the strange resonance of a sound just beyond hearing; it permeated the atmosphere with the reverberation of a symphony when the final triumphant chord has faded, yet still lingers in the air. "Listen," whispered Gianni, pausing in midstep. "It is the music of perfection—the sound of creation in harmony."

Farther into the jungle, they struck a wide grassy path. "We're close now," Kit told them, and a few paces later the travellers emerged from the sun-dappled path into a wide, shallow, bowl-shaped clearing. In the centre of the clearing lay a crystalline lake of translucent, shimmering liquid. The calm, mirror-like surface reflected the sky and overarching branches of the surrounding trees and hinted at unfathomable depths below.

Gianni crept to the edge and knelt down to examine the pool more closely.

"Is this it?" wondered Wilhelmina, frowning slightly. "Is this the Spirit Well?"

"This is it," replied Kit, noting her expression. "Disappointed?"

Mina held her head to one side. "I thought it would be different. This looks like a pond in a park. Nice but, you know . . ."

"Nice?" Kit shook his head. "Anyway, it's not so much what it looks like, it's what it does."

"Now that we're here, what are *we* going to do?" she asked.

"I was hoping—" began Kit, and was interrupted by a nudge to the ribs.

"We've got company," said Cass, indicating the opposite bank where a man had just emerged from the surrounding foliage.

"Bloody hell!" growled Kit. "Burleigh, you rat!" he shouted. "How did you get here?"

"Good to see you too," Burleigh replied. He waved the Shadow Lamp in his hand. "Superior tools, dear fellow. Even so, I doubt I could have found my way here without you. Well done." He stuffed the ley lamp into his coat pocket and turned his attention to the pool. "Now, if you will excuse me. I believe I have a rendezvous with destiny."

"He's going into the water," said Mina.

"We can't let him do that," Kit told her. "We've got to stop him. Come on!" He dashed off around the perimeter of the pool.

Burleigh, poised on the edge of the pool, raised a hand in warning as Kit scrambled nearer. "Stay back!" he snarled. "Do not come any closer."

"Listen to me," Kit pleaded. "You don't know what you're doing!"

"I know exactly where I am and what I'm doing," countered Burleigh. He turned his eyes back to the Spirit Well. "This has been my life's sole ambition. It is what I have lived for. This is Arthur's treasure, his legacy. I am about to undo all the wrongs I've ever done and all that have been done to me. From the moment I first learned about it, this is all I ever wanted—the chance to make it right." His voice softened. "The chance to make everything right."

"No!" cried Kit, horrified. "You don't understand! Arthur was wrong. You can't undo what has been done. You can't re-create the past."

"Oh, but you can. You said so yourself. Arthur did it, and so can I."

"Kit is telling you the truth," said Cass, joining Kit where he stood on the bank a few paces from Burleigh. "Arthur made a serious mistake bringing Xian-Li back to life. What you're about to do will only make things worse."

Burleigh was shaking his head. "You're wrong. I can make things better. Don't you see? In one single act of will, I can change it all— make things the way they were supposed to be. I do not have to be the bastard son of a mother who died in gin-soaked poverty and . . ."

His voice caught in his throat, and it was a moment before he was able to speak again. When he continued, his tone had softened further. "I do not have to be the street ruffian who grew up ragged and hungry, without schooling, without friends, without dignity, or even the grudging compassion of my fellow men. Do you know what it is like to grow up that way? Do you know what that does to a young heart?

"But here"—he waved a hand at the pool—"here is where all that can change. I do not have to be the unloved son, I do not have to be the man who spurned the love of a good woman." He closed his eyes and drew a shaky breath, then said, "I can be the man my Philippa loved and would have gladly married."

Burleigh paused and swallowed. There were tears in his eyes as he stood at the edge of the pool. "In the waters of this well, I can be made new. Don't you see? I can be a better man."

Gianni joined Kit and Cass on the bank. "My son, I understand why you feel the way you do," he said, adopting a priestly tone. "What happened to you should not have happened to anyone. But it did happen. Sadly, it did happen.

"We all have regrets and sorrows in life, *mio amico*. We all have our trials, and these must be borne with courage and fortitude. It is for us to shoulder our burdens and go forward in hope and trust into the future God has ordained." He put out a hand toward the pool at Burleigh's feet. "But this place, this Well of Souls—it is not about remaking the past. It is about the future. Whatever you take from the pool, you steal from the future. This is a theft that creation cannot endure."

"The apocalypse we talked about," said Wilhelmina, stepping forward, "is the death of all creation. It began a long time ago, and was caused by Arthur stealing from the future to remake the past for his own purposes. He was wrong to do that, and what he did poisoned the well."

"You cannot know that," Burleigh said, his voice slurred. He turned his attention back to the pool and took a slow, deliberate step into the liquid.

"No!" shouted Kit, dashing to the place on the bank where Burleigh entered the pool. "Stop!"

"There is no going back now," Burleigh told him. "I will do what I have come to do."

"For the love of God, Burleigh," shouted Wilhelmina. "Please stop!"

Burleigh took another step, deeper into the pool. Wind gusted through the treetops round about; it swirled around the pool, shaking the branches with sudden violence. Leaves began falling from the trees, and the forest fruit shrivelled on the stem, dropping to the ground. The grass lining the banks of the well began to wither and die; before their very eyes it dried and blew away.

"We've got to get him out of there," said Mina. "Kit, we've got to do something."

"Burleigh!" Kit called. "Look around. See what's happening! Listen to me, you've got to come out of there. You're making things unstable."

Burleigh took another step; slow ripples of light scattered across the pool. He was now up to his knees in the Spirit Well. Leaves and petals spun to earth, falling like snow, some of them striking the pool, sending tiny pulses of light racing across the surface wherever they touched. The wind, which had been gusting fitfully, dropped away to nothing, and an eerie silence settled over the glade.

Cass, standing close to Kit, let out a cry halfway between a gasp and a stifled scream. "I do not believe it," she said, her voice quivering. "Kit, look." She pointed to the forest behind them. "What's happening?"

Kit looked where she was pointing and saw a second Cass step out of the jungle. Wearing the outfit she had been wearing when Kit first met her—the odd combination of long peasant skirt, billowy blouse, blue-checked shawl, and high-topped shoes—she looked around with an expression of puzzled apprehension, saw the others, but made no move to join them.

"That's me," Cass said. "That's what I was wearing when I first met Haven and Giles."

"Stay calm," Mina told her, shuddering at the memory of meeting her own twin in Prague. "She is probably more freaked out by this than you are. Just turn around and don't look at her."

Kit turned to Burleigh, who was wading deeper into the pool. "Do you see that?" he shouted. "You caused that! You've got to come out of there."

Burleigh regarded the duplicate Cassandra, who was just then joined at the Spirit Well by another doppelgänger. "Oh no," gasped Wilhelmina as a second Gianni appeared. This one was dressed in the robes of a priest. "It's Brother Lazarus."

Gianni regarded his twin: long black cassock, short tonsure, and the owlish round-rimmed glasses—it was himself as he had been when in residence at the Montserrat observatory. Like the others, this new-comer appeared disoriented and confused, but then he saw Gianni and instantly recognised him. After a moment's hesitation, he lifted a hand in a tentative wave. Gianni waved back and called a warning for the doubles not to come any closer. To Kit he said, "We *must* get Burleigh out of the pool—now! Before something else happens."

"I'm going to have to go in and pull him out."

"That's not safe," Mina said. "It could make things worse."

"I don't see we have any choice."

Kit stepped to the edge of the pool, but before he could enter, Cass cried, "Kit, wait!" She stabbed a finger at the screen of foliage behind him.

Kit spun around as another man stumbled from the jungle bearing his dead wife in his arms: Arthur Flinders-Petrie as Kit had seen him on that first, fateful visit to the Spirit Well. Haggard, careworn, and desperately tired, Arthur gaped in startled amazement at the strangers on the opposite bank. It was a moment before he found his voice, and when he did, all that came out was a hoarse croak. "Who are you?"

"Stay where you are!" Kit, standing between Burleigh in the pool and Arthur out of it, raised both hands to prevent Arthur coming any closer. "I'm warning you. Stay back!"

Arthur looked beyond Kit and saw Burleigh in the pool. "You!" he snarled and staggered back a step. Looking around furiously, he said, "All you people—what are you doing here? What is going on?"

Burleigh seemed not to hear; he had turned his attention to the pocket where the lights of the Shadow Lamp were glowing through the fabric of his coat. He pulled it out to reveal an instrument glowing with a bright, pulsating, greenish light. Sparks leaked from the little holes around the outer rim, and the device gave off a distinct, waspish hum. Burleigh stared at the Shadow Lamp, seemingly transfixed by what he saw.

"This is getting way too weird," Mina said.

"It just got weirder," Cass told her, unable to suppress a shiver as another Wilhelmina joined the doppelgängers at the pool's edge. This Wilhelmina had a wan, dull appearance; her hair hung in limp ropes and there were dark circles under her eyes. She was dressed in skinny black slacks and a black turtleneck, and had a much abused hand-knitted purple scarf around her neck and sheepskin boots on her feet. Behind her came yet another Wilhelmina—this one dressed in her desert assault gear with the blue pashmina. Cass leaned close to Mina. "Is that really you?"

Mina shook her head in disbelief. "It used to be," she admitted. To Kit she said, "Kit, it's getting bad. We've got—"

Whatever she was about to say would remain forever unsaid. For at that moment, yet another figure appeared out of the foliage. This man was old. The few strands of hair on his bare head were as wispy as spider silk, and his wrinkled skin was blasted brown by the sun and wind. He looked leathery and tough and as withered as a mummy, but the eyes, sunk deep in his skull, glinted hard and bright with quick, dark intelligence. He was dressed simply in loose-fitting trousers and what had once been a white shirt. The trousers were ragged and travel-stained; the shirt hung off him in tattered scraps, allowing those on the bank to see clearly and distinctly that the skin of his chest was decorated with dozens of curious glyphs: lines, half circles, dots, spirals, triangles, and odd half-geometrical, half-organic pictograms.

Kit glimpsed the familiar collection of symbols and knew the stranger's identity. They had met before. Only where once the man had been vigorous and in the prime of life, he was now a wizened old man; and where once the tattoos splashed across his torso had been bold and bright indigo, now they were faded, grey, and sagging with the skin on which they were inscribed.

"It's *him!*" gasped Cass. "It's Arthur Flinders-Petrie . . . again! And he's ancient."

The old Arthur gazed with rheumy eyes at all the strangers standing around the pool. "You should not be here," he said, his voice a wheeze in his chest. "This place is not for you."

"That's what Friday told me," murmured Cass. "His exact words."

The wind gusted sharp and chill, rending the last leaves from the trees. Threatening clouds loomed overhead.

"It's Damascus again," moaned Wilhelmina.

The young Arthur, furious, tightened his grip on the body of his dead wife and started forward. "Stand aside, sir. I will not be detained any longer."

Kit refused to be moved. "What you mean to do is wrong. I can't let you do it."

"Try to stop me." Arthur made to barge ahead, but Kit put his hands on Arthur's chest and held him back. "Gianni! Help me!"

The elderly Arthur answered Kit's call for help. Stepping quickly behind his younger self, he opened his mouth and, with unexpected vigour, shouted, "You there! Turn around and look at me!"

The young Arthur ceased struggling to get past Kit and glanced over his shoulder. His features drained of whatever colour was left. "Stay away from me," he cried. "Whoever you may be, stay away."

"I will not," replied the old Arthur. "It has taken me a lifetime to find you. I will not walk away now. I mean to stop you from making the worst mistake of your life."

"It is a trick," complained the young Arthur. "I don't know you, sir."

"You know me, Arthur, as I know you." The old man moved closer to his younger self. Kit and the others watched, spellbound. "And I know that what you came to do must not be done." He pointed to the body in young Arthur's arms. "Xian-Li is dead, and so she must remain. You have no idea of the hardship that will flow from this wicked selfishness."

Arthur closed his eyes and shook his head. "No . . . no . . . no," he murmured. "It is lies—all lies. Get out of my way."

The old Arthur moved closer to his younger self. "Hear me! Your damned stubbornness will be the death of many. You may snatch a few years of happiness, but it will bring untold suffering on scores yet unborn. That is reason enough to stop you. And, by God, you will be stopped." The young Arthur glanced away, as if appealing to the others to intervene.

"Look at me!" The elder Arthur held out his arms as if he would take the dead Xian-Li from his younger self. "She is dead, Arthur. Her death is already woven into the fabric of the universe. It is meant to be. Are you wise enough to know who should live and who should die? Are you the Lord God Almighty now, that you can grant life or take it away?"

With Kit and the others distracted by the clash between the two Arthurs, Burleigh saw his chance. He stepped yet deeper into the Spirit Well. The wind swirled and whined through the newly bare upper branches, and thunder rolled in the distance. Gianni noticed the movement and rushed to Kit's side. "Burleigh is making his move! Hurry!"

Kit whirled around. "Keep Arthur back," he shouted and plunged into the pool. He reached Burleigh in three running strides, seized him by the collar of his coat, and yanked him bodily backward. Burleigh twisted and made a wild swipe with his fist. The blow struck Kit on the side of the head, but Kit held on. The next swing missed and Kit edged back a step, hauling Burleigh with him.

Burleigh twisted in his grasp, but Kit clung on, gaining another step. The Shadow Lamp, spitting sparks and throwing beams of light across the pool, sizzled and popped. Burleigh, unable to connect a solid punch, tried to squirm out of his coat. He succeeded in getting one shoulder free, but Kit forced him back another step. Gianni and Cass rushed to the edge of the bank, ready to help when Kit gained another step or two.

"Give it up," Kit shouted. "It's over."

"Never!" shouted Burleigh. He freed the other shoulder and pulled one arm from the sleeve.

Kit felt the coat slip off and made a desperate lunge as Burleigh attempted to transfer the Shadow Lamp to his free hand. The action knocked it from Burleigh's grasp and sent it tumbling through the air to land in the pool a few feet away. Still sparking and fizzling, it rested briefly on the surface and then slowly sank into the depths of the Spirit Well. Burleigh spun around and struck Kit a blow to the head. Kit staggered back but held on, pulling Burleigh with him. Gianni seized the struggling Burleigh and Cass took hold of Kit; together they dragged both men onto the bank.

"Get back, everybody!" shouted Mina. "Something's happening!"

Out in the pool where the Shadow Lamp had sunk, the liquid was glowing with a lurid light and the surface was quaking as if agitated from below by something large and angry. The turgid liquid did not so much bubble as heave and roil.

Even as they watched, the glow spread into fingers—a blush of ruddy-gold tendrils snaking through the translucent fluid. Miniature bolts of lightning streaked away, losing themselves in the unfathomed deeps. The glistering luminescence spawned a host of unusual shapes: rings and spirals and half-moon crescents with lines and whorls and zigzag slashes . . . shapes they all knew by heart; they had seen them inscribed on the Skin Map and painted on the walls of a tomb in Egypt and a Stone Age cave. But these glittering glyphs were not the two-dimensional representations, nor were they static: they moved and morphed, merging and melding, each becoming part of another, joining and combining in new and more elaborate formations before dividing and fragmenting, only to reunite with other fragments in different configurations to create new three-dimensional objects—like miniature figurines made of diaphanous strands and filaments of light.

The objects proliferated, each spawning new ones, and those splintering off to form still more. The surface of the pool quivered and bulged; the bulge expanded, glowing with an ominous purple light.

"That can't be good," said Cass.

"We should leave," said Wilhelmina. "Now!"

"Run!" shouted Kit. Snatching Cass by the hand, he pulled her away.

Gianni and Wilhelmina spun around and started for the jungle. They managed only three or four flying steps before they were overtaken by the shock wave of a horrendous explosion. The sound, like that of a runaway jet engine or a volcano igniting, shook the ground beneath their feet, and the world blanked out in a blaze of brilliant, all-consuming fire.

CHAPTER 34

In Which the Numbers Do Not Lie

irector Segler slumped in an overstuffed chair on the second-floor lobby of the JVLA headquarters. It had been a long, exasperating night—the third in a row—and he had slept only minutes snatched among meetings, phone calls, and virtual conferences with colleagues from Illinois to Australia. Eyes closed, he could hear the electronic hum of distant machines churning over the latest data gathered by his massive radio telescope and the shush of air-conditioning forever recycling the same flat air. He also heard soft footsteps padding toward him across the carpet.

"What is it?" he yawned.

"Sorry to wake you, chief," said Leonard Dvorak in a hushed voice.

"I'm not asleep—just resting my eyes." He tilted his head to see his technical director standing over him with an odd, almost apologetic look on his face. "Whatcha got?"

"I can't—I mean, I don't really know . . ." He glanced down at a paper in his hand. "But I thought you should see this."

Segler rubbed a hand over his face and sat up. At this rate, it was very likely that he would never enjoy a full night's sleep again, he thought. On second thought, with time itself ending in a few days, that was one less thing he would have to worry about. He reached out and took the offered paper.

"What is this?" he asked, scanning the page. It was a string of equations and values. There were no words that he could see. "Lay it out for me."

"I noticed a slight differential in the current scan and just started playing with the numbers. I plugged them into our prediction formula and this is what came out." The technical director gave his boss a fishy look. "I thought you should see it."

"Okay." Segler yawned again. "I've seen it. So?"

"Don't you think it's . . . well, strange?"

The director sighed. "Strange, Leo? My office has been invaded by NASA and I am a prisoner in my own facility. I haven't slept horizontal in I don't know how long, and the last meal I had came from a vending machine that takes only quarters. I haven't seen my wife in a week, and as things are going I will probably never see her or speak to her again. Fox News and CNN and NBC and the BBC and the *New York Times* and everyone else with a camera and microphone are all sniffing around like jackals on the scent of a kill, and we are only hours away from this story going viral and inciting a global panic that will demolish whatever society we have left. And if all that was not enough, the president of the United States calls me every hour to find out what I'm doing to save the planet." He thrust out his chin in defiance of his besetting woes. "So forgive me if I seem a little too preoccupied to guess the meaning of your numerical riddles."

"Sorry, chief."

"Forget it. Just tell me, okay? Can you do that, Leo?"

Dvorak stared at his boss, then swallowed and said, "It's just that the numbers indicate that our anomaly has changed."

"Define changed."

"The rate of blueshift appears to be slowing. Not only that, it looks"—Dvorak paused to find the right word—"lumpy."

"Lumpy?"

"Yeah, you know . . . like it could be breaking up somehow."

Segler jerked to attention. He leaned forward and examined the equations more closely. "Breaking up—are you sure?"

"Not a hundred percent," the technical director confessed. "But pretty sure. The numbers don't lie, chief." He tapped the page in his boss' hand. "Blueshift is slowing and returning to the red. It's happening pretty fast."

"How fast is pretty fast?"

Leo frowned. "Well, I can't tell. The scan isn't complete, obviously—but if the trend holds true, we won't be able to keep up with it."

Segler jumped to his feet, all thoughts of exhaustion forgotten. "Who else has seen this? Who knows about it?"

"Nobody. Like I said, I was just fooling around with the equations. But when the scan finishes, others are sure to notice. We're all looking at the same thing, you know."

"How long before the scan finishes?"

"It's got another four hours to run."

Segler nodded. "Okay. Here's what we're going to do. First off, keep this under your hat. Don't breathe a word to anybody. I'm going to terminate the current scan and start another right away. Set it up. Narrow focus, zero in on the region where you picked up the greatest—um, lumpiness. Get the TA coordinates and be ready to push the button when I say the word."

"What about the NASA boys? They'll know something is up if you terminate the scan and start recalibrating the array."

"Don't worry about that. I'll handle them." Segler started for one of the unoccupied offices. "You hurry downstairs and clear the decks—get Patrick to help you run the new numbers as they come in. I want a second set of eyes on this. If it checks out, I'll get Hernandez at Aricebo to drop everything and run corroboration for us."

"And then?" wondered Dvorak.

"We'll cross that bridge when we come to it. In a few hours we should have a better idea what's going on out there. Until then, we keep it low key." Segler sent his technical director away, then called to him as he headed for the stairs. "By the way, have you seen Dr. Clarke around? Is he down in the den?"

"He was last time I saw him—that was an hour ago."

"If he's still down there, tell him I need to see him up here right away."

"You could page him . . ."

"I want to keep this to ourselves for now, okay?" Segler said. "No sense getting people all worked up if it turns out to be a false alarm." The elevator arrived and the door slid open. "Go!"

The director returned to his office and slid into his chair; he grimaced at the phone, hoping no one would call him until he had a chance to either verify or disprove Dvorak's observation. He did not doubt his technical director, but the stakes were ultra-high, and before he went on record with any mind-blowing revelations, he wanted to be absolutely convinced. He was still planning his next moves when there was a knock at the door and Tony Clarke poked his head into the room. "You rang, Sam?"

"That was quick."

"I was already on my way up to see you when I ran into Dr. Dvorak. What's up?" He stepped into the room and closed the door.

"You were coming up to see me?" asked the director.

"To ask you if I could go home," Tony explained simply. "There's nothing more I can do here. I'd like to see my daughter before . . ." He paused, then let the thought go. "You know."

"If it were up to me we'd all be home in our beds right now, Tony. I hope you know that." He shook his head in sympathy. The last few days had aged his friend years; he was looking gaunt and haggard, as if hollowed out by some wasting disease. Before Tony could object or reply, he hurried on. "But listen, we may be on to something that could get us all home very soon."

"I'm listening." Tony moved to the desk and folded himself into one of the visitors' chairs. "What sort of something?"

"A game changer," said Segler. "Leo was just up here, and he may have found evidence that the universe is no longer contracting. He's got new blueshift figures that seem to indicate the rate of contraction is slowing. He thinks redshift has restarted."

"The last scan is still running, and so far—"

"I know. He told me." The director shoved the piece of paper across the desktop to his friend. "Have a look—this is what he came up with."

Tony pulled the page to him and read through it quickly. Halfway down he stopped, went back to the top, and started again, and then read it all once more just to be sure he hadn't missed anything. "I assume Dr. Dvorak didn't pull these numbers from thin air?" said Tony, running his finger along a relevant line of figures.

"The equations are Leonard's," Segler confirmed. "The numbers he plugged in came from the current scan. He pulled them on the fly—I guess he noticed discrepancies he thought didn't make sense."

"What this shows is that the contraction in sector B240-22N has slowed significantly," Tony observed.

"Leo thinks there's more to it than that. He thinks the anomaly may be breaking up."

"But that's impossible." Tony lifted his gaze from the page now clutched tightly in his hand. "Contractions in the fabric of the universe do not simply disperse like so much fog on the wind."

"Tell me about it." Segler held out his hand for the paper. "That's why we're keeping quiet about this until we've got an idea of what is actually going on out there"—he gestured vaguely at the ceiling—"in the great beyond."

"Good call," agreed Tony, handing back the paper. "What's the next step?"

Director Segler outlined his plan and Tony listened, nodding from time to time in agreement. Segler concluded, saying, "It would be a massive help if you could work directly with Leo on this. I told him to have Patrick help with the donkey work, but it would be good to have a steady hand on the wheel to, you know . . ." He shrugged. "Keep things from drifting off course."

"I hear you—and I agree. We want this nailed down tight before we take it to Bayer and his crew."

"Let's just say I don't want to be the kid who cried 'False alarm!' while Rome burned."

"Only this time, if Rome goes up in flames, nobody is going to care—or even remember."

Segler pulled a sour face and Tony stood. "I'll head downstairs—unless you have any other bombshells to throw at me."

"No, that's it. You go. I'll stay up here and keep NASA busy. Remember, don't let on about the redshift—at least until we get outside confirmation. And pray this nightmare is really over."

Tony crossed to the door, his step markedly lighter, his posture straighter than when he first entered the room. He paused with his hand on the doorknob and glanced back. "We do seem to forget that we're not in this alone."

Segler gave him a rueful nod. "Too true."

Tony made his way down to the Rats' Nest where he found Leonard Dvorak and Keith Patrick in a far corner hunkered down over a bank of monitors. "The reversal pattern is holding," Dvorak announced as Tony joined them.

Tony glanced at the monitor and then looked at the clock; it was a little after four thirty. Oddly, he did not feel tired anymore. "I think we're all going to wake up tomorrow and wonder what all the fuss was about."

CHAPTER 35

In Which Footsteps Are Traced

The blazing fire in Kit's eyes was matched only by the howling squeal in his ears. Whether he was dead or alive he could not say; the former appeared by far the more likely because he seemed to float suspended in a timeless nowhere. Eternity? There was no physical discomfort, only the raging whine in his ears and the formless white that obscured all vision—the after-effects of the explosion that had killed him.

The explosion! Yes, there had been a blast of some kind. He remembered that now. As more of his shattered consciousness returned, he sensed also that the light that washed out all sight was beginning to fade. Slowly, slowly, the all-pervading brightness gathered itself into a sphere that shrank and shrank until it eventually blinked out, leaving him in darkness soft and close. But just before the light went out, Kit felt a change in his state of buoyant equilibrium: a slow-revolving fall combined with the odd weightless sensation he generally experienced when making a ley leap. There was movement and direction, and suddenly it seemed that he was speeding through a void, a black zone, a region without form or feature.

As he sped along, the velvet envelope of darkness that enclosed him began to thin and wear away. He perceived tiny flecks of light glinting through its fabric like fireflies flickering in the night. These first scattered specks were gradually joined by more and more until Kit was flying headlong through a spray of luminous effervescence, massed arrays of glowing particles coursing through the void in onrushing waves. Photons flashed around him and through him, blending into streaming rays that carried a sound like that of surf washing a distant shore. On and on he sped, the particle streams thickening into currents, blending, braiding, joining one another to become many-branched rivers. These shimmering plaits coagulated, steadily congealing into what looked like islands of light amidst an ocean of endless night.

Attracted by an invisible force, these isolated beacons drifted together, slowly merging and melding into one another, knitting together to form whole continents. As Kit raced on and ever on, one of the nearer landforms of light contracted, compacting into a dense glowing mass that erupted in a blinding flash. When Kit could see again, he saw a band of silver radiance seeded with the swirling spiral disc of a newborn galaxy.

All across the limitless void, Kit witnessed the same pattern: islands of light coalesced, contracted, and flared into life, illuminating the darkest reaches of never-ending night. Soon, even the emptiest regions of space were alight and shining with the brightness of ten thousand suns, each glittering island a separate galaxy spinning with graceful, measured elegance—each and every one a bright empire containing realms and worlds beyond number.

Kit gazed upon the spangled deep and glimpsed part of the answer: each and every world was a subtle variation on the original, created as a way for the universe to work out the myriad possibilities of the decisions made by the innumerable souls inhabiting those realms. These bright empires would continue to bloom into being until every variable, every permutation, every possibility of existence had been explored, every expression articulated, every potential achieved. Then, and only then, would the Omega Point arrive—that great and glorious celebration of eternal existence—to transform the universe into the paradise promised and purposed from the beginning of time.

Dazed by the gleaming array spreading before him, Kit plunged dizzily through it, drinking in the sight, revelling in it, breathing deeply of the prodigious creative energy suffusing all he saw. And still it came, expanding in ever-widening rings with no end in sight. Engulfed, immersed, Kit perceived all of creation spread out before him and knew that he was intimately connected to it, forever entangled. As he gazed upon this firmament of infinite space, he sensed the restless vitality that permeated the Omniverse. More than mere energy, more than a force, this creative dynamism of the cosmos was in all and through all, but also beyond all—not only sustaining and supporting everything it touched, but also nourishing and gently guiding it toward its endowed potential.

Strangest of all, however, Kit felt that this vast, formless power *knew* him, accepted him, and cherished him. It also possessed an individual character, and that character expressed itself as a will with desires and rational faculties not unlike his own, but of a magnitude far beyond his abilities of comprehension, ceaselessly working to bring about its purposes and designs.

Streaking like a comet through this living presence, Kit was stunned into inarticulate awe; the magnificence overpowered comprehension. He could not take it all in, much less understand or make sense of more than the merest fraction of the whole. His only thought was that he was being allowed a fleeting look into the heart of a mystery greater than life itself.

Bewildered, numb with wonder, Kit reached the point of exhaustion. Unable to take in any more, he closed his eyes on the dazzling spectacle, seeking refuge in the darkness behind his eyes. But escape was denied him; even with his eyes closed, he could still see the vision of creation burned into his brain. Sometime later—a day, a year, a few seconds only?—Kit sensed that his flight was slowing. The end came with the suddenness of a drop from a high ladder. He fell to earth.

Head throbbing, ears plugged, aching in every limb and joint, he lay on his side and assessed his state. Aside from the shock, he seemed to be uninjured. He opened his eyes; he was lying on the ground. Thin, watery light filtered down upon him through cracks in a roof fashioned from the skeletal remnants of many animals. His first coherent thought was: *Bone House.*

Raising his head, he looked around. He was alone. Where were the others? Had they survived?

He rolled over, pushed himself up on hands and knees, and crawled to the entrance of the structure. The day outside was sunny and cold. Fresh snow lay undisturbed all around, glistening beneath a sky so brilliant it stung his eyes. He drew a deep breath and tasted the cold tang of the air, like electricity on the tongue. He rose and was just getting his feet under him when he heard voices. The first one said something he could not make out, but a second voice answered, "I'll check inside . . ."

Kit started around the side of the Bone House; he managed two steps before his legs went slack and he fell with a grunt face-first into the snow. A moment later a shadow passed over him. He wiped snow from his face and looked up to see Wilhelmina peering down at him. "Kit, you okay?"

She called to someone he could not see. "Found him! He's back!"

He pulled himself upright, stood, and turned—coming face-to-face with Cass. She threw her arms around him and squeezed him until it hurt. "What a relief! We didn't know where you were."

"We? Who else is here?"

"Everybody. I mean, Gianni, Burleigh, Mina, me. We all made it back."

"Any doppelgängers?"

She shook her head. "Just us."

Kit regarded her closely, trying to discern whether her return matched his own experience. He hoped it did, because he knew he would never be able to describe, much less explain, all that he had witnessed.

"Are you okay?" she asked.

Kit smiled. "Never better. We can talk about it later." He scanned the area. "So where are they?"

"Just over here." She looped an arm through his and led him around to the other side of the Bone House, where Wilhelmina was standing over Gianni, who was crouching beside Burleigh, who was sitting on the ground. "He's a bit distraught," confided Cass.

". . . according to His will," Gianni was saying as they came up. "I can only think that this has been His purpose all along, *capito*?" He glanced up as Kit and Cass joined them. "Kit!" he exclaimed. "Thank God you have returned safely."

Burleigh raised his eyes, nodded glumly, and then lowered his head once more. "You do not understand," he muttered sadly. "It was my one hope of redemption. Can you not see that? I could have been a better man."

"But you *are* a better man," countered Gianni.

"No . . . no, I'm not."

"Yes, you are," Gianni assured him. "Not as good as you will be, perhaps, but better than you were."

As Kit looked on, he found himself unexpectedly moved by this tender display. Burleigh did appear to be genuinely distressed by his failure to effect a change for himself at the Spirit Well. Perhaps he had been telling the truth about wanting redemption.

"It is so hard," moaned Burleigh, putting his head in his hands. His shoulders began to shake. His next words came out as a sob. "It is so very, very *hard.*"

Gianni sighed. "It has ever been thus. The way is hard and narrow, it is true. But it is a path beaten smooth by the countless others who have gone before us. And good news! We do not have to walk it alone. God Himself is with us and has blessed us with friends for the journey."

"Friends!" Burleigh's head jerked up, a sneer on his face. "*You* have friends, maybe. I have none."

"We can work on that," said Gianni, placing a hand on his shoulder. "We can work on that together, you and I."

Burleigh sniffed and brushed the tears away with the heels of his hands. "Blubbing like a baby," he murmured. "What has happened to me?"

"Maybe you *are* changing," Kit said. Burleigh glanced up at him and then, embarrassed, looked away.

Leaving the two of them to talk, Kit led Cass and Mina aside. "It isn't just Burleigh that's changed," he told them.

"What do you mean?" asked Wilhelmina.

"What do I mean?" said Kit. His smile grew wide and he burst out laughing. "We did it! That's what I mean. Think about it—we kept Arthur out of the pool. We prevented him from using the Spirit Well to change things for himself and destroying all creation in the process."

"I guess so," Cass agreed. "And you stopped that one"—she gave a nod toward Burleigh—"from doing the same."

Mina squinted her eyes and cocked her head to one side. "Disaster averted? Everything back to normal?"

"Well," Kit replied, "I see only one of you—I take that as a good sign. Although I'd love to talk to Tony and Brendan and see what they have to say."

Wilhelmina shivered and rubbed her injured arm. "Why don't we move this reunion somewhere warmer? If we stand around here much longer we're going to freeze."

"We should be going," agreed Kit. "With any luck we can get down to the Big Valley Ley before it wakes up."

"Too bad," said Cass. "I'd like to come back, maybe see if we can find your River City friends and stay awhile."

"It could be arranged," replied Kit. "You'd enjoy that?"

"Like you need to ask," she replied. "You know I would."

"Well, I just want to get home," said Wilhelmina, "and see what Etzel is cooking." She turned and hurried away. "I'll fetch Gianni and Burleigh. You two get going. We'll catch up."

The travellers threaded their way through the forest to what, in other seasons, was a wide, grassy plain. The snow was a little deeper here, so the going was slower and more taxing, but they were warmed by the exertion as they went. They walked easily in one another's company, content with their own thoughts and the knowledge that whatever the future brought, it would include the love and companionship of what Gianni had called friends for the journey.

The sun was fading into a white haze in the west as they reached the rim of the Big Valley gorge and started down the cliffside track. The path was only lightly dusted with snow, and it squelched under their feet. Their breath hung in misty clouds. Blue shadows deepened in the valley. A few paces from the start of the ley, Kit put his hand in his pocket and pulled out the sole remaining Shadow Lamp. The little turquoise lights were all aglow.

"It looks like we're just in time," observed Cass, tapping the pewter carapace.

"You know there's no such thing as coincidence," Kit replied lightly. "Right?"

"Yeah, right," said Cass. "Let's go home."

Epilogue

*I*f anyone had told Lady Fayth that she would find fulfilment in playing governess to two young princesses, she assuredly would have chided that person for being a witless bletherskite and laughed in his face. Much to her surprise, then, as the days slipped by, slowly passing into weeks to be succeeded by months, she awoke one morning to the realisation that, in fact, she was very happy with her role in the royal household. Her chores were neither onerous nor overly taxing, and her responsibilities matched her innate sense of status; to be accounted a member of the imperial household, she discovered, was no small thing. As if anything more was required to make the position perfect, the two little girls were a constant delight.

Princess Anna and Princess Eudokia considered their mistress a beautiful, exotic creature who in their young eyes could do no earthly wrong. After their initial shyness had passed, the two girls pestered Haven for stories of her travels and life in other places, and insisted on her being included in every family outing and royal event that they themselves were expected to attend—anywhere the family was accustomed to appear, whether in public or private. Under Haven's watchful eye, the imperial palace precinct became the children's playground, and there was not a corner or courtyard that did not at one time or another chime with their laughter or clatter with the musical instruments Haven improvised for their mock processions.

Against all odds and every expectation, Haven found her true calling, and for the first time anywhere—or *anywhen*—discovered herself contented. The emperor too was more than satisfied with his decision to employ her as child minder to his daughters. Indeed, he was so impressed with his latest addition to his staff that he conferred on her the title of Procuratrix. Thus, the presence of the pale foreigner soon came to be taken for granted and, as part of the royal household, she was no longer to be remarked upon.

As for Giles, when Emperor Leo learned that the young man was accustomed to the care and feeding of horses, he put his newly acquired servant to work in the royal stables. A lowly job, but Giles not only showed a flair for grooming the beasts, he demonstrated a ready knowledge of breeding practices unknown to the Byzantines. He also showed he knew a thing or two about training horses, and displayed such skill in their handling that he was promoted to looking after the emperor's personal riding stock. In his new position as assistant chief stable master, Giles was offered the opportunity to teach young Prince Constantine to ride—a circumstance that brought him into regular contact with not only the upper echelon of the emperor's staff but also the emperor himself. In Leo he found a man of keen intelligence, refinement, and integrity—a man worthy of his service.

Emperor Leo possessed an outsized sense of occasion—a minor fault, expressing itself in the propensity to imbue even the most trivial happenstances of life with an import far exceeding any useful consideration. He took everything far too seriously. To all appearances, Leo lacked a sense of humour. Thus, upon the rare occasions when

328

something Giles said or did made the emperor smile, Giles was reminded of the heavy weight of nobility and went away feeling as if he had done a good day's work. The day Giles invited Leo into the riding ring to hold the halter rope and call the commands himself, the look of rapture on the emperor's face as he put a young stallion through its paces gave Giles to know that he had secured a patron for life.

As pleasant as their positions in the royal household might have been, it did not prevent the ley travellers from wondering what Providence had in store for them a little farther down the road. On the one hand, they enjoyed a very sheltered, even privileged, position from which to contemplate their next steps. On the other hand, they had no idea what those next steps might be, much less how to take them or where they might lead.

"Are we ever going to get away, go home?" asked Haven one night when, as was their custom, they withdrew to their private apartment after their official duties were finished for the day.

"Are we ever going to get away from here?" echoed Giles. It was not the first time she had asked that question; indeed, in various forms it regularly surfaced as an item of conversation when they were alone. But this night was different somehow; it struck Giles that he already knew the answer—in fact, had known it for some time. "I fear not," he said gently. "I think we must face the fact that we are not going to leave Constantinople."

Haven glanced up sharply. His bluntness took her aback. She had merely been thinking aloud and not really expecting an answer. "You are harsh tonight, Mr. Standfast. I scarce know what has come over you to speak so."

"I do not speak from harshness—only from conviction. I believe I see clearly tonight the folly of clinging to false hope."

"Our hope is anything but false, sir. You ought to know that as well as anyone. We have Sir Henry's green book to use as a guide. We have but to—" She stopped, halted by the slow, steady shake of Giles' head. "Why do you wag your head so?"

"Haven, think. We have the green book, yes—but if it contained any information or instruction useful to us in our present situation, would we not have made use of it long ago? We have had ample opportunity to employ that book, but the truth is that there resides within its pages neither implement nor information to lead us from here to any better place." He moved a few steps nearer. "We have come to the end of the road. For us, the quest for the Skin Map is over."

Haven stiffened her back as if to resist the remorseless tide flow of his logic, all the while knowing in her heart that he was right. To flee, to escape, to leave would present problems so difficult as to be insoluble—not the least of which was the fact that they did not have the slightest idea where they might find a nearby ley line, nor, having found it, could they guess where it might lead. In all the time they had been in Constantinople, they had never felt so much as a quiver of ley energy anywhere inside the city or out. Yet, supposing that they did somehow discover a ley line to take them away . . . what then? Wherever they landed, they would still be quite as lost as they were now, but without any of the benefits Providence had so graciously provided them in this time and place.

"Are we ever going home?" Giles continued, taking up the question anew. He moved to stand directly before her. "My lady, I am thinking we are already home."

Haven searched his clear dark eyes and saw the light of conviction. "I do not say you are wrong," she replied a little hesitantly.

"Only, it would be some consolation to let our friends and relations know what has become of us."

"Yes, there would be comfort in that," allowed Giles. "Though if it meant leaving all this behind, I would count it but cold comfort. In truth, dear lady, I feel as if we are meant to be here. Might we find a better place? Perhaps. Yet there is a rightness in our position here that I feel to the soles of my feet when I walk the streets or stand in the training ring. In this place, I am more than groom and footman. And you—I have seen the way you shine when you have come from a day spent schooling those little girls. Begging your pardon, I mean no offence by it, but I believe it is in the way of making you a better person than the one I knew before."

Haven dropped her head. "I take no offence. It is true. I do so love my situation—such that I cannot now imagine parting without also imagining the pain and guilt leaving my little ones would bring in train. I do believe it would make of me a most wretched creature."

"Then let us speak no more of leaving a world and life that has become dear to us, and that I truly believe has been provided for our benefit," Giles said firmly. He placed his hands on her shoulders as if to steady her. "Think you now—is there anything back there that we do not have here?" He paused a moment to allow her to consider. "I say not. Let us henceforth declare that the past is indeed past, and our only future is here and what we make of it."

Haven remained silent for a moment, then nodded. "Very well," she agreed at last, her voice falling. "I do believe you are right—my heart tells me you speak the truth. But it is a bitter truth and goes down right hard." She sniffed, holding back the tears that started to her eyes.

Giles felt a shudder pass through her slender frame. He pulled her

closer. "Perhaps," he suggested lightly, "I may offer a bit of sweetness?" He put a finger to her chin and raised her face to his. "My lady,
will you do me the honour of becoming my wife?" Before she could
reply, he added, "Marry me, Haven Fayth, and let us make a life here
together come what may."

She smiled sadly. "Are you very certain, Mr. Standfast, that you
want a wife at all? I have seen the way the ladies of the household and
court gaze upon your manly form when they think no one is looking.
You could have your pick of any one of them."

"Dearest Haven, I made my choice long ago. I chose you, and it is
you I come home to every night. It chafes me sore to live with you as
a brother or cousin, when it is a husband I would be." He held her in
his steady gaze. "I ask you again, will you marry me?"

"I will, Giles," she answered, and felt an unexpected relief well
up inside her; it took the form of a sudden, irrepressible giddiness.
"Yes! I will marry you, my darling man. You are and have ever been
my heart's true friend. And I shall be yours—you will see. I shall be
the wife you deserve."

Giles kissed her then, quickly, lest she change her mind. When
she made no resistance, he kissed her again, longer this time, and
more sweetly, then gathered her into his embrace.

They stood holding one another for a time, and then Haven
suddenly reared back in his arms. "But, oh! How can this be?" she
said. "The emperor and his court think we are married already. To go
before them now with this would be an embarrassment to them and,
worse, would likely bring condemnation down on our heads for the
regrettable lie we have been living. I fear the punishment would be
most severe and long regretted."

"To be sure," agreed Giles. "Still, I would not have urged this course if I did not also consider the consequence. Yet there is hope. I think I have a way to proceed so that no one at court need ever know." He took her hand and led her to the low divan beside the table where they dined. "We will go to one of the little churches outside the palace district and have the proper ceremony performed there in secret. There is one such church a short distance from the Forum of Theodosius, and it is named for Saint George. It is small and much neglected. The priest there is old and half blind, but he is a kindly soul and most understanding."

"He will marry us? You have spoken to him?"

Giles nodded. "He will—and for a small donation to help fix the roof of his church, he will not only conduct the ceremony, he will provide the wedding feast."

Haven gripped his hands and squeezed. "Then let us do it soon, my love, and end this gross deception with a grand flourish of honesty, propriety, and loyalty." She kissed him again. "Let us be married as soon as possible."

A week or so later, the opportunity arose when the royal family sailed to their summer lodge at Prínkēpos, an island in the Marmara just off the southern coast of the city. Giles was not needed, and Haven was to follow six days later with a few other courtiers. Thus, they had time to themselves, and wasted not a moment. Giles dashed ahead to alert the priest and then hurried back to meet Haven on the way.

The day was warm and bright, and Haven dressed in a white silk gown the empress had recently given her, complaining that it did not fit her as well as she had hoped. She had braided her hair with tiny wild daisies and myrtle, and looked every inch the bride Giles had hoped one day to wed. He met her at the entrance to the forum and led her along the maze of narrow streets to the church—a simple stone edifice surrounded by a walled garden planted with olive trees—where the priest and his wife were waiting at the gate. The plump little woman held a lace veil that she insisted Haven wear, and the priest gave Giles the use of his best robe and red sash.

Then, satisfied that the celebrants were properly attired, the white-bearded priest led them to the outer door of the church where the first part of the ceremony was performed. Although Giles' facility with Greek had grown by leaps since entering the emperor's employ, there was much in the ancient rite he could not follow; Haven filled in the gaps for him and told him when to respond and what to say. Then they were led into the tiny church where they lit a candle and knelt before the altar; the priest looped a satin stole over their joined hands to tie them together, said a long prayer for their health and prosperity, and then it was over.

The priest's wife clapped her hands with joy and kissed them both on both cheeks, and then the priest ushered them to his house and to the tiny courtyard where the wedding feast would be held. To honour the occasion, he had invited some of his parishioners and the poorer folk of the neighbourhood. "What is a wedding without a celebration?" he said. "And some of these good folk do not have a single thing to celebrate one Easter to the next."

"Bring them all," Haven told him, placing her hand on his arm. "They are welcome at our wedding feast."

"You are most gracious, lady," replied the priest with a bow. He sat them down in wicker chairs beneath a blue canopy and declared, "We will drink wine and eat bread in memory of our Saviour, and we will roast a lamb to make this day a day to remember always."

The little priest and his wife beetled off to finish the preparations and summon the guests, leaving Giles and Haven alone for a moment. Giles, glowing with pride at his new bride, saw her eyes tear up and became concerned. "Why sad, my love?"

"I am not sad, husband," replied Haven, dabbing her eyes with a corner of her sleeve. "It is just the thought that we shall never see our families again."

"My dear sweet wife," replied Giles, "since that is not to be, we shall simply have to make a family of our own." He raised her hand to his lips and drank in the sight of her. "And what a fine and handsome family it will be."

On What Happens Next

AN ESSAY BY STEPHEN R. LAWHEAD

The telling of any story must, inevitably, come to an end—although the story itself goes on. This tale is no different.

However, readers, for one reason or another, will have formed attachments to various characters and will no doubt have questions regarding those characters. The impulse to know What Happened Next can be very strong—an itch that, unless scratched, can become an affliction. After all, if the characters have lived within the pages of the book, then those lives continue and our involvement may seem arbitrarily, almost cruelly, cut off when the pages run out.

Whilst I cannot prolong this particular story, I am nevertheless in a position to relate a few details of which I am aware, and which might be of interest to the reader:

The Zetetics continue to operate, primarily out of Damascus, where in happier times it was this author's privilege to walk down The Street Called Straight—following in the footsteps of one who heard the audible voice of God—and to visit the faithful few who keep the

336

archives of the Society. Should you or anyone else care to call in at 22 Hanania Street, you will find a welcome in a place where travellers may meet and discuss adventures, or browse the rare volumes in the genizah, or ruminate about the grounds of reality and our place in the universe. The quest now is for understanding, and most of all for wisdom. Through oppression, conflict, wars and the atrocities of war, still the Zetetic Society stands firm—owing in large part, no doubt, to the formidable and unshakeable Mrs. Peelstick, who seems never to age, and to her colleague and ally, Brendan Hanno, whose steady hand on the tiller steers the society through the roughest waters. Of course, endless cups of strong mint tea continue to be served to all and sundry who find, however unexpectedly, that they have landed on the step outside that shiny black-lacquered door.

You will recall that the Burley Men—Tav, Con, Dex, and Mal—were exiled for their crimes and forbidden to return to Prague; and, after Burleigh's conversion, they could expect no further employment there in any case. Happily, the long, dreary weeks spent in the Rathaus gaol and Engelbert's kindly ministrations were not lost on any of them, and although the gang broke up, each was not only chastened by his imprisonment but was inspired by Etzel's generosity, compassion, and gentle, forgiving spirit. You may not believe it if I tell you that Marcus Taverner became a devout follower of Luther and eventually a pastor in a Nonconformist church in a remote corner of the Duchy of Pomerania in what is now northeastern Germany. Malcolm Dawes settled down in the cosy Pinzgau Valley in Austria where, after a stint as a labouring farmhand, he was able to obtain a little land on the shady side of the valley and thus became a farmer himself—not a very good farmer, it must be said, but he managed to eke out an honest living by distilling the local *Vogelbeeren* into the regionally famous medicinal schnapps—and, with the help of the strict Austrian social mores and a robust farmwife to guide him, his criminal past slowly receded into distant memory. Dexter Parrot and Connie Wilkes became itinerant tinkers travelling the villages of Bavaria; owing to their expertise with knives and simple tools, they went on to build a modest trade as blacksmiths in Rosenheim. Of course, we know by now that there is no such thing as coincidence, but it is interesting to note that their little forge was only a stone's throw from the Stiffelbeam Bakery owned by Engelbert's family, where they became regular customers, often receiving news of their former benefactor in Prague.

Douglas Flinders-Petrie's end has been narrated in full within these pages. But no one knows what became of Snipe, that feral youth whose misfortune it was to be taken under the wing of the last and least of the Flinders-Petrie line. Douglas only used the boy, imparting to him no useful skills nor any worthwhile education during the time that they travelled the cosmos together. It is presumed—and evidence would seem to support the conclusion—that poor Snipe became one of those bandit outcasts who roamed the wild Italian hill country, living off the land and robbing travellers passing through the lonelier stretches of the countryside. These bandits, or *briganti*, much feared throughout history, are celebrated in folklore and song in cultures the world over. Thus, Snipe may well have gained a smattering of status as a cultural curiosity.

Gianni spent the next few years contemplating what actually happened at the Spirit Well when the questors plunged through the Bone House portal. His experience of that deeply mysterious event led him to research the role of conscious intention in a multiverse environment, for which he devised experiments to test the effect of human free will on natural phenomena—a hot topic in quantum physics circles. He later persuaded Tony Clarke to work with him on what became known as Coincidence Theory—which states, to put it in layman's terms, that there is no such thing.

As theorists, the two garnered many supporters in addition to the usual detractors; the former were by far the more numerous, however, and Gianni, as befitting the last in a long line of scientist-priests, was eventually awarded the Nobel Prize for physics, which he shared with his long-time colleague and collaborator J. Anthony Clarke III. The two friends made memorable speeches that were glowingly reported in all the major news media. Unfortunately, about six months after receiving the prize, Gianni disappeared, and his whereabouts remain a mystery to be solved: whatever became of Gianni Becarria? All was not lost, however, for his research was taken up by a brilliant scientist in São Paulo by the name of João Cristo, who rose to sudden prominence from nowhere and whose intuitive understanding of Becarria's foundational work led him to further discoveries that sparked research into space-time shifts, possibility and probability theory, and the development of models for alternate and converging realities.

Speaking of time and space, neither allows us to relate what happened to so many others who came into contact with the individuals whose stories have been recounted in this series. No doubt some were extinguished in one reality only to survive in another; although that is speculation, and even Gianni's paradigm-shifting work does not fully account for this—at least, so far.

All that remains to be said is that as this manuscript was in revision, a major financial group broke ground for its international headquarters in the City of London on the site of an old guesthouse.

As required by law, archaeologists were brought in to identify and recover any items of importance before permanent foundations were laid. The archaeologists did their survey and cleared the site for construction, but missed one interesting and noteworthy piece: a silver spoon with a large teardrop-shaped bowl and a figure of the apostle Peter. This item was discovered by a construction worker, who slipped it into his pocket just moments before eight metric tons of concrete were poured into a trench. When the popular television program *Antiques Roadshow* came to south London a few months ago, that construction worker decided to see if his find had any value. He stood for hours in a slow-moving queue at Dulwich College before receiving the good news that the spoon dated from the mid-1660s and was typically carried by the professional classes when dining in one of the many chophouses and dinner clubs that were popping up in the city at the time. Deemed "unique of its kind" and "of considerable interest to collectors and museum curators," it was given a provisional value of £13,000–£17,500, and thus became one of those *Roadshow* items that, as the saying goes, "came in a bus, but went home in a taxi." The lucky workman put the artefact up for auction at Sotheby's in London and donated the greater share of the proceeds to the Coram Trust, a charitable body providing a range of support services for orphaned and abandoned children. Burleigh, that inveterate trader in collectible artefacts, would no doubt have approved.

Stephen R. Lawhead
Oxford, 2014

Acknowledgments

I am grateful to the many experts, editors, friends, and advisors with whom I have traveled and consulted during the research and writing of the Bright Empires series. Each has provided much-needed inspiration, guidance, and correction, and they all have my sincere appreciation:

Wael El-Aidy
Allen Arnold
Clare Backhouse
Daniele Basile
Sabine Biskup
Amanda Bostic
Hailey Johnson Burgess
Bettina Heynes
Andrew Hodder-Williams
Danuta Kluz
Matthew Knell
Drake Lawhead
Ross Lawhead

Scott and Kelli Lawhead
Suzannah Lipscomb
Nabile Mallah
LB Norton
Michael and Martina Potts
Richard Rodriguez
Sam Segler
Jessica Tinker
Adrian Woodford

AN EXCERPT FROM

Hood

Prologue

The pig was young and wary, a yearling boar timidly testing the wind for strange scents as it ventured out into the honey-coloured light of a fast-fading day. Bran ap Brychan, Prince of Elfael, had spent the entire day stalking the greenwood for a suitable prize, and he meant to have this one.

Eight years old and the king's sole heir, he knew well enough that he would never be allowed to go out into the forest alone. So rather than seek permission, he had simply taken his bow and four arrows early that morning and stolen from the caer unnoticed. This hunt, like the young boar, was dedicated to his mother, the queen.

She loved the hunt and gloried in the wild beauty and visceral excitement of the chase. Even when she did not ride herself, she would ready a welcome for the hunters with a saddle cup and music, leading the women in song. "Don't be afraid," she told Bran when, as a toddling boy, he had been dazzled and a little frightened by the noise and revelry. "We belong to the land. Look, Bran!" She lifted a slender hand toward the hills and the forest rising like a living rampart beyond. "All that you see is the work of our Lord's hand. We rejoice in his provision."

Stricken with a wasting fever, Queen Rhian had been sick most of the summer, and in his childish imaginings, Bran had determined that if he could present her with a stag or a boar that he had brought down all by himself, she would laugh and sing as she always did, and she would feel better. She would be well again.

All it would take was a little more patience and . . .

Still as stone, he waited in the deepening shadow. The young boar stepped nearer, its small pointed ears erect and proud. It took another step and stopped to sample the tender shoots of a mallow plant. Bran, an arrow already nocked to the string, pressed the bow forward, feeling the tension in his shoulder and back just the way Iwan said he should. "Do not aim the arrow," the older youth had instructed him. "Just think it to the mark. Send it on your thought, and if your thought is true, so, too, will fly the arrow."

Pressing the bow to the limit of his strength, he took a steadying breath and released the string, feeling the sharp tingle on his fingertips. The arrow blazed across the distance, striking the young pig low in the chest behind the front legs. Startled, it flicked its tail rigid, and turned to bolt into the wood . . . but two steps later its legs tangled; it stumbled and went down. The stricken creature squealed once and tried to rise, then subsided, dead where it fell.

Bran loosed a wild whoop of triumph. The prize was his!

He ran to the pig and put his hand on the animal's sleek, slightly speckled haunch, feeling the warmth there. "I am sorry, my friend, and I thank you," he murmured as Iwan had taught him. "I need your life to live."

It was only when he tried to shoulder his kill that Bran realised his great mistake. The dead weight of the animal was more than he could lift by himself. With a sinking heart, he stood gazing at his glorious prize as tears came to his eyes. It was all for nothing if he could not carry the trophy home in triumph.

Sinking down on the ground beside the warm carcass, Bran put his head in his hands. He could not carry it, and he would not leave it. What was he going to do?

As he sat contemplating his predicament, the sounds of the forest grew loud in his ears: the chatter of a squirrel in a treetop, the busy click and hum of insects, the rustle of leaves, the hushed flutter of wings above him, and then . . .

"Bran!"

Bran started at the voice. He glanced around hopefully.

"Here!" he called. "Here! I need help!"

"Go back!" The voice seemed to come from above. He raised his eyes to see a huge black bird watching him from a branch directly over his head.

It was only an old raven. "Shoo!"

"Go back!" said the bird. "Go back!"

"I won't," shouted Bran. He reached for a stick on the path, picked it up, drew back, and threw it at the bothersome bird. "Shut up!"

The stick struck the raven's perch, and the bird flew off with a cry that sounded to Bran like laughter. "Ha, ha, haw! Ha, ha, haw!"

"Stupid bird," he muttered. Turning again to the young pig beside him, he remembered what he had seen other hunters do with small game. Releasing the string on his bow, he gathered the creature's short legs and tied the hooves together with the cord. Then, passing the stave through the bound hooves and gripping the stout length of oak in either hand, he tried to lift it. The carcass was still too heavy for him, so he began to drag his prize through the forest, using the bow.

It was slow going, even on the well-worn path, with frequent stops to rub the sweat from his eyes and catch his breath. All the while, the day dwindled around him.

No matter. He would not give up. Clutching the bow stave in his hands, he struggled on, step by step, tugging the young boar along the trail, reaching the edge of the forest as the last gleam of twilight faded across the valley to the west.

"Bran!"

The shout made him jump. It was not a raven this time, but a voice he knew. He turned and looked down the slope toward the valley to see Iwan coming toward him, long legs paring the distance with swift strides.

"Here!" Bran called, waving his aching arms overhead. "Here I am!"

"In the name of all the saints and angels," the young man said when he came near enough to speak, "what do you think you are doing out here?"

"Hunting," replied Bran. Indicating his kill with a hunter's pride, he said, "It strayed in front of my arrow, see?"

"I see," replied Iwan. Giving the pig a cursory glance, he turned and started away again. "We have to go. It's late, and everyone is look-ing for you."

Bran made no move to follow.

Looking back, Iwan said, "Leave it, Bran! They are searching for you. We must hurry."

"No," Bran said. "Not without the boar." He stooped once more to the carcass, seized the bow stave, and started tugging again.

Iwan returned, took him roughly by the arm, and pulled him away. "Leave the stupid thing!"

"It is for my mother!" the boy shouted, the tears starting hot and quick. As the tears began to fall, he bent his head and repeated more softly, "Please, it is for my mother."

"Weeping Judas!" Iwan relented with an exasperated sigh. "Come then. We will carry it together."

Iwan took one end of the bow stave, Bran took the other, and between them they lifted the carcass off the ground. The wood bent but did not break, and they started away again—Bran stumbling ever and again in a forlorn effort to keep pace with his long-legged friend.

Night was upon them, the caer but a brooding black eminence on its mound in the centre of the valley, when a party of mounted searchers appeared. "He was hunting," Iwan informed them. "A hunter does not leave his prize."

The riders accepted this, and the young boar was quickly secured behind the saddle of one of the horses; Bran and Iwan were taken up behind other riders, and the party rode for the caer. The moment they arrived, Bran slid from the horse and ran to his mother's chamber behind the hall. "Hurry," he called. "Bring the boar!"

Queen Rhian's chamber was lit with candles, and two women stood over her bed when Bran burst in. He ran to her bedside and knelt down. "Mam! See what I brought you!"

She opened her eyes, and recognition came to her. "There you are, my dearling. They said they could not find you."

"I went hunting," he announced. "For you."

"For me," she whispered. "A fine thing, that. What did you find?"

"Look!" he said proudly as Iwan strode into the room with the pig slung over his shoulders.

"Oh, Bran," she said, the ghost of a smile touching her dry lips. "Kiss me, my brave hunter."

He bent his face to hers and felt the heat of her dry lips on his.

"Go now. I will sleep a little," she told him, "and I will dream of your triumph."

She closed her eyes then, and Bran was led from the room. But she had smiled, and that was worth all the world to him.

Queen Rhian did not waken in the morning. By the next evening she was dead, and Bran never saw his mother smile again. And although he continued to hone his skill with the bow, he lost all interest in the hunt.

PART ONE

Day of the Wolf

CHAPTER 1

"*B*ran!" The shout rattled through the stone-flagged yard. "Bran! Get your sorry tail out here! We're leaving!"

Red-faced with exasperation, King Brychan ap Tewdwr climbed stiffly into the saddle, narrowed eyes scanning the ranks of mounted men awaiting his command. His feckless son was not amongst them. Turning to the warrior on the horse beside him, he demanded, "Iwan, where is that boy?"

"I have not seen him, lord," replied the king's champion. "Neither this morning nor at the table last night."

"Curse his impudence!" growled the king, snatching the reins from the hand of his groom. "The one time I need him beside me and he flits off to bed that slut of his. I will not suffer this insolence, and I will not wait."

"If it please you, lord, I will send one of the men to fetch him."

"No! It does not bloody please me!" roared Brychan. "He can stay behind, and the devil take him!"

Turning in the saddle, he called for the gate to be opened. The heavy timber doors of the fortress groaned and swung wide. Raising his hand, he gave the signal.

"Ride out!" Iwan cried, his voice loud in the early morning calm.

King Brychan, Lord of Elfael, departed with the thirty-five Cymry of his mounted warband at his back. The warriors, riding in twos and threes, descended the rounded slope of the hill and fanned out across the shallow, cup-shaped valley, fording the stream that cut across the meadow and following the cattle trail as it rose to meet the dark, bristling rampart of the forest known to the folk of the valley as Coed Cadw, the Guarding Wood.

At the edge of the forest, Brychan and his escort joined the road. Ancient, deep-rutted, overgrown, and sunken low between its high earthen banks, the bare dirt track bent its way south and east over the rough hills and through the broad expanse of dense primeval forest until descending into the broad Wye Vale, where it ran along the wide, green waters of the easy-flowing river. Farther on, the road passed through the two principal towns of the region: Hereford, an English market town, and Caer Gloiu, the ancient Roman settlement in the wide, marshy lowland estuary of Mor Hafren. In four days, this same road would bring them to Lundein, where the Lord of Elfael would face the most difficult trial of his long and arduous reign.

"There was a time," Brychan observed bitterly, "when the last warrior to reach the meeting place was put to death by his comrades as punishment for his lack of zeal. It was deemed the first fatality of the battle."

"Allow me to fetch the prince for you," Iwan offered. "He could catch up before the day is out."

"I will not hear it." Brychan dismissed the suggestion with a sharp chop of his hand. "We've wasted too much breath on that worthless whelp. I will deal with him when we return," he said, adding under his breath, "and he will wish to heaven he had never been born."

With an effort, the aging king pushed all thoughts of his profligate son aside and settled into a sullen silence that lasted well into the day. Upon reaching the Vale of Wye, the travellers descended the broad slope into the valley and proceeded along the river. The road was good here, and the water wide, slow flowing, and shallow. Around midday, they stopped on the moss-grown banks to water the horses and take some food for themselves before moving on.

Iwan had given the signal to remount, and they were just pulling the heads of the horses away from the water when a jingling clop was heard on the road. A moment later four riders appeared, coming into view around the base of a high-sided bluff.

One look at the long, pallid faces beneath their burnished war-caps, and the king's stomach tightened. "Ffreinc!" grumbled Brychan, putting his hand to his sword. They were Norman marchogi, and the British king and his subjects despised them utterly.

"To arms, men," called Iwan. "Be on your guard."

Upon seeing the British warband, the Norman riders halted in the road. They wore conical helmets and, despite the heat of the day, heavy mail shirts over padded leather jerkins that reached down below their knees. Their shins were covered with polished steel greaves, and leather gauntlets protected their hands, wrists, and forearms. Each carried a sword on his hip and a short spear tucked into a saddle pouch. A narrow shield shaped like an elongated raindrop, painted blue, was slung upon each of their backs.

"Mount up!" Iwan commanded, swinging into the saddle.

Brychan, at the head of his troops, called a greeting in his own tongue, twisting his lips into an unaccustomed smile of welcome. When his greeting was not returned, he tried English—the hated but necessary language used when dealing with the backward folk of the southlands. One of the riders seemed to understand. He made a curt reply in French and then turned and spurred his horse back the way he had come; his three companions remained in place, regarding the British warriors with wary contempt.

Seeing his grudging attempt at welcome rebuffed, Lord Brychan raised his reins and urged his mount forward. "Ride on, men," he ordered, "and keep your eyes on the filthy devils."

At the British approach, the three knights closed ranks, blocking the road. Unwilling to suffer an insult, however slight, Brychan commanded them to move aside. The Norman knights made no reply but remained planted firmly in the centre of the road.

Brychan was on the point of ordering his warband to draw their swords and ride over the arrogant fools when Iwan spoke up, saying, "My lord, our business in Lundein will put an end to this unseemly harassment. Let us endure this last slight with good grace and heap shame on the heads of these cowardly swine."

"You would surrender the road to them?"

"I would, my lord," replied the champion evenly. "We do not want the report of a fight to mar our petition in Lundein."

Brychan stared dark thunder at the Ffreinc soldiers.

"My lord?" said Iwan. "I think it is best."

"Oh, very well," huffed the king at last. Turning to the warriors behind him, he called, "To keep the peace, we will go around."

As the Britons prepared to yield the road, the first Norman rider returned, and with him another man on a pale grey mount with a high leather saddle. This one wore a blue cloak fastened at the throat with a large silver brooch. "You there!" he called in English. "What are you doing?"

Brychan halted and turned in the saddle. "Do you speak to me?"

"I do speak to you," the man insisted. "Who are you, and where are you going?"

"The man you address is Rhi Brychan, Lord and King of Elfael," replied Iwan, speaking up quickly. "We are about business of our own which takes us to Lundein. We seek no quarrel and would pass by in peace."

"Elfael?" wondered the man in the blue cloak. Unlike the others, he carried no weapons, and his gauntlets were white leather. "You are British."

"That we are," replied Iwan.

"What is your business in Lundein?"

"It is our affair alone," replied Brychan irritably. "We ask only to journey on without dispute."

"Stay where you are," replied the blue-cloaked man. "I will summon my lord and seek his disposition in the matter."

The man put spurs to his mount and disappeared around the bend in the road. The Britons waited, growing irritated and uneasy in the hot sun.

The blue-cloaked man reappeared some moments later, and with him was another, also wearing blue, but with a spotless white linen shirt and trousers of fine velvet. Younger than the others, he wore his fair hair long to his shoulders, like a woman's; with his sparse, pale beard curling along the soft line of his jaw, he appeared little more than a youngster preening in his father's clothes. Like the others with him, he carried a shield on his shoulder and a long sword on his hip. His horse was black, and it was larger than any plough horse Brychan had ever seen.

"You claim to be Rhi Brychan, Lord of Elfael?" the newcomer asked in a voice so thickly accented the Britons could barely make out what he said.

"I make no claim, sir," replied Brychan with terse courtesy, the English thick on his tongue. "It is a very fact."

"Why do you ride to Lundein with your warband?" inquired the pasty-faced youth. "Can it be that you intend to make war on King William?"

"On no account, sir," replied Iwan, answering to spare his lord the indignity of this rude interrogation. "We go to swear fealty to the king of the Ffreinc."

At this, the two blue-cloaked figures leaned near and put their heads together in consultation. "It is too late. William will not see you."

"Who are you to speak for the king?" demanded Iwan.

"I say again, this affair does not concern you," added Brychan.

"You are wrong. It has become my concern," replied the young man in blue. "I am Count Falkes de Braose, and I have been given the commot of Elfael." He thrust his hand into his shirt and brought out a square of parchment. "This I have received in grant from the hand of King William himself."

"Liar!" roared Brychan, drawing his sword. All thirty-five of his warband likewise unsheathed their blades.

"You have a choice," the Norman lord informed them imperiously. "Give over your weapons and swear fealty to me . . ."

"Or?" sneered Brychan, glaring contempt at the five Ffreinc warriors before him.

"Or die like the very dogs you are," replied the young man simply.

"Hie! Up!" shouted the British king, slapping the rump of his horse with the flat of his sword. The horse bolted forward. "Take them!"

Iwan lofted his sword and circled it twice around his head to signal the warriors, and the entire warband spurred their horses to attack. The Normans held their ground for two or three heartbeats and then turned as one and fled back along the road, disappearing around the bend at the base of the bluff.

King Brychan was first to reach the place. He rounded the bend at a gallop, flying headlong into an armed warhost of more than three hundred Norman marchogi, both footmen and knights, waiting with weapons at the ready.

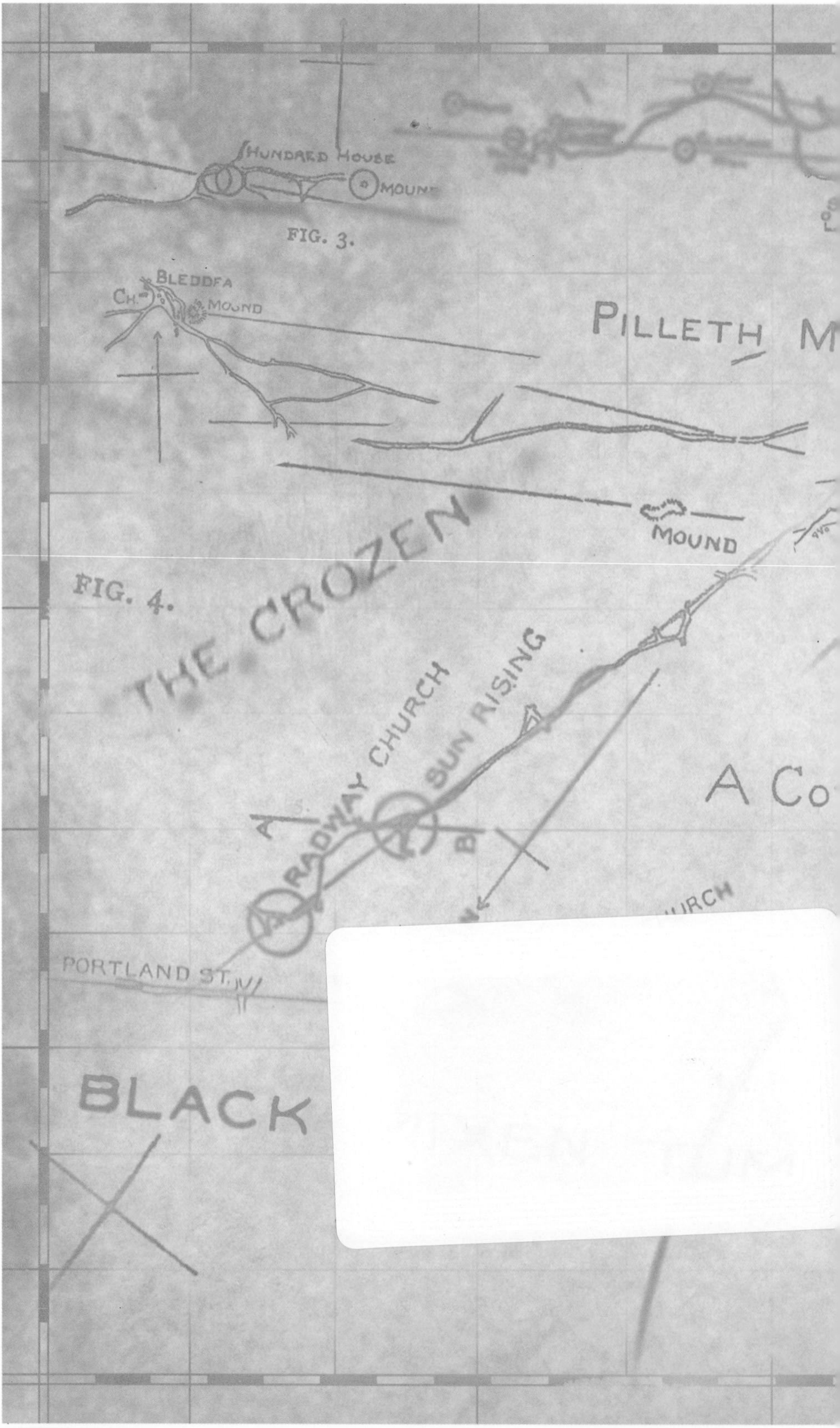

HUNDRED HOUSE

MOUND

FIG. 3.

BLEDDFA

Ch.

MOUND

PILLETH M

MOUND

FIG. 4.

THE CROZEN

RADWAY CHURCH

SUN RISING

A Co

URCH

PORTLAND ST.

BLACK